IMPOSSIBLE

Sasha is a traditionalist – now widowed, she knows she was married to the most wonderful man in the world. Liam is an artist, half-in and half-out of a marriage that his own impossibly impulsive behaviour has helped tear apart. While Sasha has been methodically building her father's Parisian art gallery into an international success, Liam has been growing into one of the most original and striking young painters of his time, and the miracle of art brings them together. Then a family tragedy suddenly alters Liam's life, forcing a choice and a sacrifice neither one of them could have expected.

IMPOSSIBLE

IMPOSSIBLE

by

Danielle Steel

Magna Large Print Books
Long Preston, North Yorkshire,
BD23 4ND, England.

British Library Cataloguing in Publication Data.

Steel, Danielle
    Impossible.

    A catalogue record of this book is
    available from the British Library

    ISBN   978-0-7505-3295-2

First published in Great Britain 2005 by Bantam Press
an imprint of Transworld Publishers

Copyright © Danielle Steel 2005

Cover illustration © David Ridley by arrangement with
Arcangel Images

The right of Danielle Steel to be identified as the author of this
work has been asserted in accordance with sections 77 and 78 of
the Copyright, Designs and Patents Act, 1988

Published in Large Print 2010 by arrangement with
Transworld Publishers

Magna Large Print is an imprint of Library Magna Books Ltd.

Printed and bound in Great Britain by
T.J. (International) Ltd., Cornwall, PL28 8RW

To my exceptionally wonderful, loving children, Beatrix, Trevor, Todd, Nick, Samantha, Victoria, Vanessa, Maxx & Zara, who not only make my life possible, but joyful, happy, and loving in every way. How blessed and fortunate I am to have you, with all your laughter, love and tender moments that we share so abundantly. I celebrate you, I thank you, I appreciate you more than I can ever say. May you be as blessed as I am, with children like you one day.

With all my love,
Mom

What does that mean – 'tame'?
It is an act too often neglected...
It means to establish ties.
To me, you are still nothing more than a little
boy who is just like a hundred thousand other
little boys. And I have no need of you. And you
on your part have no need of me...
But if you tame me, then we shall need each
other. To me, you will be unique in all the world.
To you, I shall be unique in all the world...
If you tame me, it will be as if the sun came to
shine on my life. I shall know the sound of a step
that will be different from all the others. Other
steps send me hurrying back underneath the
ground. Yours will call me, like music, out of my
burrow... Think how wonderful that will be
when you have tamed me!...
Please – tame me!
One only understands the things that one tames
... there is no shop anywhere where one can buy
friendship... If you want a friend, tame me...
What must I do to tame you?
You must be very patient ... first you will sit
down at a little distance from me – like that –in
the grass. I shall look at you out of the corner of
my eye, and you will say nothing. Words are the

source of misunderstandings. But you will sit a little closer to me every day...

As yet you are nothing. No one has tamed you, and you have tamed no one... But I have made him my friend, and now he is unique in all the world.

Antoine de Saint-Exupéry, *The Little Prince*

if you tame me
    and i tame you,
        you will not lose
        your wild
            and wonderful,
    your freedom
        or the air
            you breathe,
    not lost
    but found,

once tamed
    and joined
        together
            silently,
    you will
            find me,
and i will
    at last have
        found
        you.

d.s.

Chapter 1

The Suvery Gallery in Paris was housed in an impressive building, an elegant eighteenth-century *hôtel particulier* on the Faubourg St. Honoré. Collectors came there by appointment, through the enormous bronze doors into the courtyard. Straight ahead was the main gallery, to the left the offices of Simon de Suvery, the owner. And to the right was his daughter's addition to the gallery, the contemporary wing. Behind the house was a large elegant garden filled with sculptures, mainly Rodins. Simon de Suvery had been there for more than forty years. His father, Antoine, had been one of the most important collectors in Europe, and Simon had been a scholar of Renaissance paintings and Dutch masters before opening the gallery. Now he was consulted by museums all over Europe, held in awe by private collectors, and admired although often feared by all who knew him.

Simon de Suvery was a daunting figure, tall, powerfully built, with stern features and dark eyes that pierced through you right to your soul. Simon had been in no hurry to get married. In his youth, he was too busy establishing his business to waste time on romance. At forty he had married the daughter of an important American collector. It had been a successful and happy union. Marjorie de Suvery had never involved herself directly in the gallery, which was well established before Simon married her. She was fascinated by it, and admired the work he showed. She loved him profoundly and had taken a passionate interest in everything he did. Marjorie had been an artist but never felt comfortable showing her work. She did genteel landscapes and portraits, and often gave them as gifts to friends. In truth, Simon had been affected but never impressed by her work. He was ruthless in his choices, merciless in his decisions for the gallery. He had a will of iron, a mind as sharp as a diamond, a keen business sense, and buried far, far beneath the surface, well concealed at all times, was a kind heart. Or so Marjorie said. Though not everyone believed her. He was fair to his employees, honest with his clients, and relentless in his pursuit of whatever he felt the gallery should have. Sometimes it took him years to acquire a particular painting or sculpture, but he never rested until it was his. He had pursued his wife, before their marriage, in much the same way. And once he had her, he kept her as a treasure – mostly to himself. He only socialised when he felt he had to, entertaining clients in one wing of the house.

They decided to have children late in their marriage. In fact it was Simon's decision, and they waited ten years to have a child. Knowing how Marjorie longed for children, Simon had finally acceded to her wishes, and was only mildly disappointed when Marjorie gave birth to a daughter and not a son. Simon was fifty when Sasha was born, and Marjorie thirty-nine. Sasha instantly became the love of her mother's life. They were constantly together. Marjorie spent hours with her, chortling and cooing, playing with her in the garden. She nearly went into mourning when Sasha began school, and they had to be apart. She was a beautiful and loving child. Sasha was an interesting blend of her parents. She had her father's dark looks and her mother's ethereal softness. Marjorie was an angelic-looking blonde with blue eyes, and looked like a madonna in an Italian painting. Sasha had delicate features like her mother, dark hair and eyes like her father, but unlike both her parents, Sasha was fragile and small. Her father used to tease her benevolently and say that she looked like a miniature of a child. But there was nothing small about Sasha's soul. She had the strength and iron will of her father, the warmth and gentle kindness of her mother, and the directness she learned early on from her father. She was four or five

19

before he took serious notice of her, and once he did, all he spoke to her about was art. In his spare time, he would wander through the gallery with her, identifying paintings and masters, showing her their work in art books, and he expected her to repeat their names and even spell them, once she was old enough to write. Rather than rebelling, she drank it all in, and retained every shred of information her father imparted. He was very proud of her. And ever more in love with his wife, who became ill three years after Sasha was born.

Marjorie's illness was a mystery at first, and had all their doctors stumped. Simon secretly believed it was psychosomatic. He had no patience with illness or weakness, and thought that anything physical could be mastered and overcome. But rather than overcome it, Marjorie became weaker with time. It was a full year before they got a diagnosis in London, and a confirmation in New York. She had a rare degenerative disease that was attacking her nerves and muscles, and ultimately would cripple her lungs and heart. Simon chose not to accept the prognosis, and Marjorie was valiant about it, complaining little, doing whatever she could for as long as she was able, spending as much time as she had the strength for with her husband and daughter, and resting as much as possible in between. The disease never snuffed out her spirit, but eventually, as predicted, her body succumbed. She was bedridden by the time Sasha was seven, and died shortly after she turned nine. Despite all the doctors had told him, Simon was stunned. And so was Sasha. Neither of her parents had prepared Sasha for her mother's death. Sasha and Simon had both grown accustomed to Marjorie being interested in all they did, and participating in their lives, even while in bed. The sudden realization that she had disappeared from their world hit them both like a bomb, and fused Sasha and her father closer together than they had ever been. Other than the gallery, Sasha then became the focus of Simon's life.

Sasha grew up eating, drinking, sleeping, loving art. It was all she knew, all she did, and all she loved, other than her father. She was as devoted to him as he was to her. Even as a child, she knew as much about the gallery, and its complicated and intriguing workings, as any of his employees. And sometimes he thought, even as a young girl, she was smarter about it, and far more creative than anyone he employed. The only thing that annoyed him, and he made no bones about it, was her ever increasing passion for modern and contemporary art. Contemporary work irritated him particularly, and he never hesitated to call it junk, privately or otherwise. He loved and respected the Great

21

Masters, and nothing else.

As her father had before her, Sasha attended the Sorbonne, and got a 'license,' a master's degree, in the history of art. And as she had promised her mother she would, she earned her PhD at Columbia in New York. Then she spent two years working as an intern at the Metropolitan Museum of Art, which rounded out her education. During that time, she returned frequently to Paris, sometimes just for a weekend, and Simon visited her as often as possible in New York. It gave him an excuse to visit his clients, as well as museums and collectors in the States. All he really wanted to do was see Sasha, and he used any excuse to do so. What he wanted more than anything else was for Sasha to come home. He was irritable and impatient during her years in New York.

The one thing Simon had never expected was the appearance of Arthur Boardman in Sasha's life. She met him the first week of her doctoral studies at Columbia. She was twenty-two at the time, and married him, despite her father's grumbling protests, within six months. At first, Simon was horrified at her marrying so young, and the only thing that mollified him, and made him consent to the marriage, was that Arthur assured his father-in-law that when Sasha was finished her studies and apprenticeship in New York, he would move to Paris with her and live there. Simon nearly made him sign it in blood. But even he couldn't resist seeing Sasha as happy as she was. Simon finally conceded that Arthur Boardman was a good man, and the right one for her.

Arthur was thirty-two, ten years older than Sasha. He had gone to Princeton, and had an MBA from Harvard. He had a respectable position in a Wall Street investment bank, which conveniently had a Paris office. Early on in their marriage, he began lobbying to run it. Within a year, their son Xavier was born. Two years later, Tatianna arrived. In spite of that, Sasha never missed a beat with her studies. Miraculously, both her babies managed to arrive in the summer, right after she finished her classes. She hired a nanny to help her with them while she was in school and working at the museum. She had learned how to keep many balls in the air, while watching her father run the gallery when she was a child. She loved her busy life, and adored Arthur and her two children. And although Simon was a somewhat hesitant grandfather at first, he warmed to it quickly. They were enchanting children.

Sasha spent every spare moment with them she could, singing the same songs and playing the same nursery games her mother had played with her. In fact, Tatianna looked so much like her maternal grandmother that it unnerved Simon at first, but as Tatianna grew older, he loved just sitting and watching her, and thinking of his late wife. It was like seeing her reborn as a little girl.

True to his word, Arthur moved the entire family to Paris when Sasha finished her two-year internship at the Met in New York. The investment bank was literally giving him the Paris office to run, at thirty-six, and had full confidence in him, as did Sasha. She was going to be even busier there than she had been in New York, where she'd been working only part time at the museum, and spent the rest of her time caring for her children. In Paris, she was going to work at the gallery with her father. She was ready for it now. He had agreed to let her leave by three o'clock every day, so she could be with her children. And she knew she would have a lot of entertaining to do for her husband. She returned to Paris, victorious, educated, excited, and undaunted, and thrilled to be home again. And so was Simon to have her home, and working with him at last. He had waited twenty-six years for that moment, and it had finally come, much to their mutual delight.

He still appeared as stern as he had when she was a child, but even Arthur noticed, once they moved to Paris, that Simon was softening almost imperceptibly with age. He even chatted with his grandchildren from time to time, although most of the time, when he visited, he preferred to just sit and observe them. He had never felt at ease with young children, not even Sasha when she was small. By the time they moved back to Paris, he was seventy-six years old. And Sasha's life began in earnest from that moment.

Their first decision was where to live, and Simon stunned them by solving their dilemma for them. Sasha had been planning to look for an apartment on the Left Bank. Their small family was already too large for the apartment the bank owned in the sixteenth arrondissement. Simon volunteered to move out of his wing of the house, the elegant three-floor domain he had occupied for his entire marriage, and the years before and after. He insisted it was far too big for him, and claimed the stairs were hard on his knees, although Sasha didn't quite believe him. Her father still walked for miles. He volunteered to move to the other side of the courtyard, on the top floor of the wing they used for additional offices and storage. He quickly set to work remodeling it with charming *oeil de boeuf* windows under a mansard roof, and put in a funny little motorized seat, which sped up and down the stairs, and delighted his grandchildren, when he let them ride it. He walked up the stairs beside them while they squealed with excitement. Sasha helped him with the decorating and remodeling, which instantly gave her an idea. Not one he liked at first. It was a plan she'd had for years, and had dreamed of all her life. She wanted to expand the gallery to include contemporary artists. The wing that had previously been used for storage was perfect for her plan. It was across the courtyard from their offices and her father's new home. Admittedly, opening the ground floor would cramp their storage space, but she had already consulted an architect to build highly efficient storage racks upstairs. At her first mention of selling contemporary work, Simon went through the roof. He was not going to corrupt the gallery, and its venerable name, selling the garbage that Sasha liked, by unknown artists he insisted had no talent. It took her almost a year of bitter arguments to convince him.

It was only when she threatened to leave the gallery and set up shop on her own that Simon finally relented – albeit with considerable rancor and a ferocious amount of grumbling. Although gentler in style, Sasha was as tough as he was, and had held her ground. Once the plan was agreed to, she didn't even dare meet her new artists in their main offices because her father was so rude to them. But Sasha was as stubborn as he was. A year after they moved back to Paris, she opened the contemporary arm of the gallery with style and fanfare. And much to her father's astonishment, to unfailingly great reviews, not just because she was

Sasha de Suvery but because she had an eye for good, solid contemporary work, just as her father did in what he knew best.

Remarkably, Sasha kept a foot in both worlds. She was knowledgeable about what he sold so competently and brilliant about newer work. By the time she was thirty, three years after she had opened Suvery Contemporary on his premises, it was the most important contemporary gallery in Paris, and perhaps in Europe. And she'd never had so much fun in her life. Nor had Arthur. He loved what she did, and supported her in every move, every decision, every investment, even more than her father, who remained reluctant though ultimately respectful of what she'd accomplished with contemporary work. In fact, she had brought his gallery into the present with a bang.

Arthur loved the contrast between her business life and his own. He loved the playfulness of the art she showed, and the zaniness of her artists, in contrast to the bankers he dealt with. He traveled with her frequently to other cities when she went to see new artists, and loved going to art fairs with her. They had transformed their three-floor wing of the house into nearly a museum of contemporary art by emerging artists. And the work she sold at Suvery Contemporary was far more financially accessible than the Impressionists and Old Masters sold by her

27

father. Their business thrived on both.

Sasha had been running her arm of the business for eight years when they faced their first real crisis. The bank Arthur had become a partner of years before insisted that he come back to Wall Street to run it. Two of the partners had died in a private plane crash, and everyone insisted Arthur was the obvious choice to run the bank at home. In fact he was the only choice. There was no way for Arthur to refuse to do it, in good conscience. His career was important to him too, and the bank was not letting him off the hook. They needed him in New York.

Sasha cried copiously when she explained the situation to her father, and there had been tears in his eyes as well. For all the thirteen years of their marriage, Arthur had fully supported her and every aspect of her career, and now she knew she had to do the same for him, and move back to New York. It was too much to ask of him to expect him to leave his career for hers, so she could stay at the gallery with her father, although, undeniably, he was growing old. Sasha was thirty-five by then, and although he didn't look or act it, Simon was eighty-five years old. And they'd been fortunate that Arthur had been able to stay in Paris for as long as he had, without damaging his career. But now it was time for him to go home, and for Sasha to leave with him.

In typical Sasha fashion, it took her exactly six weeks to come up with an idea. They were moving back to New York within a month. She took her father's breath away and horrified him at first. He was totally opposed to it, just as he had been when she suggested selling contemporary art. But this time she didn't threaten him, she begged him. What Sasha wanted was to open a branch of their gallery in New York, for both traditional and contemporary work. Her father thought the idea was insane. Suvery Gallery was the most respected gallery in Paris. Americans contacted them daily for important purchases, as well as museums around the world. They had absolutely no need to open a branch in New York, except now Sasha would be there, and she wanted to work for her father, and the gallery she loved, as she had for nine years.

It was a turning point for them. Arthur thought it was brilliant, and gave the idea his full support. In the end, he convinced her father for her, although even when they left, Simon insisted it was a mad idea. Sasha offered to put her own money into the project, and Arthur volunteered as well. But in the end, her father came through for her as he always did. As soon as she got to New York, she found an apartment on Park Avenue for them, and a brown-stone on Sixty-fourth Street, between Madison and

Fifth avenues, for Suvery New York. And as always, when Sasha put her mind to something, and backed it with an incredible amount of energy and work, it turned out to be a brilliant idea. Her father came to visit several times, and grudgingly admitted that the space was perfect for them, on a small scale of course. And by the time he came to the opening of the New York gallery nine months later, he was wreathed in smiles. Sasha was the toast of the art world in New York. At thirty-five, she was becoming one of the most important dealers in the world, as her father had been and still was, and she had just joined the boards of both the Metropolitan and Modern Art museums, an unheard of honor for her, to be on both.

Xavier and Tatianna were twelve and ten by then. Xavier loved to draw, and Tatianna would grab any camera she could lay her hands on and take incredibly funny pictures of startled adults. Tatianna looked like a small blond elf, and Xavier looked like his father, only with his mother and grandfather's nearly jet-black hair. They were beautiful and loving children, and both were bilingual. Sasha and Arthur agreed to put them in the Lycée in New York, and Tatianna talked constantly about wanting to go back to Paris. She missed her friends. Xavier decided almost instantly that he preferred New York.

For the next two years, Sasha enjoyed running her gallery in New York. She traveled frequently to Paris, usually twice a month. Sometimes she took the Concorde for important meetings with her father, and returned the same night to Arthur and her children in New York. And in summer, she always took the children back to France. She spent time with her father in the house he had rented for years in St. Jean Cap Ferrat, but she stayed at the Eden Roc with the children. Although Simon loved them, the children made him nervous if he spent too much time with them. And although Sasha didn't like admitting it, her father was getting old. He was eighty-seven, and little by little, he was slowing down.

With great regret, they had talked about what she would do when she would be alone running the business. She couldn't imagine it, but he could. He had led a long life, and had no fears about moving on. And he had trained his people well. In time, she would be able to live in New York or Paris, and have competent people to work for her in either place. She would have to spend time in both galleries, of course, and commute regularly, but the choice of where to live was hers, thanks to her father's competence and foresight. They had excellent managers in both places. But Paris still felt like home to her, although she enjoyed living and working in

31

New York. There was no question that Arthur was too entrenched at the bank by then to live anywhere but New York. She knew she was stuck there until he retired. And since he was only forty-seven years old, he was nowhere near retirement. She was just lucky that her father was still running his end of the business at eighty-seven years of age. He was remarkable, although he had slowed down almost imperceptibly. But despite that, or perhaps because of it, Sasha was stunned when he died suddenly at eighty-nine. She had expected him to live forever. Simon died exactly as he would have wanted to. He had a massive stroke at his desk. The doctors said he didn't suffer. He was gone in an instant, having just concluded an enormous deal with a collector from Holland.

Sasha flew to Paris in a state of shock that night, and moved around the gallery aimlessly, unable to believe that he was gone. The funeral was dignified and important. The president of the French Republic attended, as well as the minister of culture. Every person of importance in the art world came to pay their respects, his friends, clients, Arthur and the children. It was a cold November day, and pouring rain, when they buried him at Père Lachaise cemetery, in the twentieth arrondissement, on the eastern edge of Paris. He was surrounded by the likes of Victor Hugo, Proust, Balzac, and

Chopin, a fitting resting place for him.

After the funeral, Sasha spent the next four weeks in Paris, working with the lawyers, organizing things, putting away her father's papers and personal effects. She stayed longer than she had to, but she couldn't bear leaving this time. For the first time since she had left Paris, she wanted to stay home, and be near where her father had lived and worked. She felt like an orphan a month later, when she finally flew home to New York. The stores and streets decorated for Christmas seemed like an affront after the loss she had just sustained. It was a long hard year for her. But in spite of that, both branches of the gallery flourished. The ensuing years were peaceful, happy, and productive. She missed her father, but slowly put down roots in New York, as her children grew up. And she still returned to Paris twice a month, to continue to oversee the gallery there.

Eight years after her father's death, both galleries were strong and equally successful. Arthur was talking about retiring at fifty-seven. His career had been respectable and productive, but he privately admitted to Sasha he was bored. Xavier was twenty-four, living and painting in London, and showing at a small gallery in Soho. And although Sasha loved his paintings, he was not ready for her to show. Her love for him did not blind her to the progress he still needed to make. He was talented, but as an artist not yet fully mature. But he was passionate about his work. He loved everything about the art world he was part of in London, and Sasha was proud of him. She thought he would be a great artist one day. And in time, she hoped to show his work.

Tatianna had graduated from Brown four months before, with a degree in fine arts and photography, and had just started a job as the third assistant to a well-known photographer in New York, which meant she got to change film for him occasionally, bring him coffee and sweep the floors. Her mother assured her that that was the way it worked at first. Neither of her children had any interest in working at the gallery with her. They thought what she did was wonderful, but they wanted to pursue their own lives and work. Sasha realized how rare it had been to learn all she had from her father, the opportunity he had given her, and the priceless education she'd had of growing into the business with him. She was sorry she couldn't do the same with her children.

Sasha wondered if one day Xavier would want to work at the gallery with her, but it seemed less than likely for the time being. Now that Arthur was talking about retiring, she felt as though she was drifting toward her roots in Paris again. As much as she loved the excitement of New York, life always seemed gentler to her when she went home. Paris was still home to her, despite dual nationality, thanks to her mother, and sixteen of her forty-seven years, a third of her life, spent in New York. At her core she was still French. Arthur wasn't opposed to the idea of living in Paris again once he retired, and they had been talking about it more seriously that fall.

It was October and the very last of the hot weather, on a sunny Friday afternoon, as Sasha made a brief inspection tour of some paintings they were planning to sell to a museum in Boston. They kept their Old Masters and more traditional work on the brownstone's two upper floors. Sasha's office was tucked away in a back corner on the main floor.

After her tour of the upper floors, she put some papers in her briefcase, and looked out at the sculpture garden behind her office. Like most of their contemporary work, it was a reflection of Sasha's taste. She loved looking out at the pieces in the garden, especially when it snowed. But snow was still two months away, as she picked up her bulging briefcase. She was going to be out of the gallery the following week. She was leaving on Sunday morning for Paris, to check on things there. She still made a routine visit every two weeks, as she had since her father's death eight years before. She was a hands-on dealer, in both cities, and was used to the commute by now. It seemed easy to her. She managed to have a life, and friends, as well as clients, in both cities. Sasha was as much at ease in Paris as New York.

She was thinking about the weekend ahead, as the phone rang, just as she was about to leave her office. It was Xavier calling her from London, as she glanced at her watch and realized it was nearly midnight there. She smiled the moment she heard his voice. Both her children were precious to her, but in some ways she was closer to Xavier. He had always been easier for her. Tatianna was closer to her father, and also like Sasha's father in some ways. There had always been something hard and judgmental about her, and she was less inclined to bend and compromise than her older brother. Xavier and his mother were soul mates in many ways, equally gentle, equally kind, always willing to forgive a loved one or a friend. Tatianna had a harder line about people and life.

'I was afraid you'd already left,' Xavier said with a smile and a yawn. As she closed her eyes, thinking of him, she could see his face. He had always been a beautiful child, and was now a handsome young man.

'I was about to leave. You just caught me. What are you doing home on a Friday night?' Xavier had an active social life in the London artists' scene, and a weakness for pretty

36

women. Lots of them. It always amused his mother, and she teased him frequently about it.

'I just got in,' he explained, defending his reputation.

'Alone? How disappointing,' she teased. 'Did you have fun?'

'I went to a gallery opening with a friend, and then we had dinner. Everyone got drunk, and things started to get a little wild, so I thought I'd get home before we all got arrested.'

'That sounds interesting.' Sasha sat down at her desk again, and looked out at the garden, thinking of how much she missed him. 'What were they doing to get arrested?' Despite his fondness for women, most of Xavier's pursuits were harmless and fairly tame. He was just a young man who liked to have fun and still acted like a boy at times, full of mischief. His sister liked to claim she was far more respectable than he was, and thought the women he went out with were disgusting. She never failed to say so, not only to her mother but to her brother, who hotly defended them, no matter who they were, or how racy.

'I went to the opening with an artist I know. He's a bit of a madman, but a hell of a good artist. I want you to meet him sometime. Liam Allison. He does fantastic abstracts. It was a pretty good show tonight, although he didn't think so. He got bored at the opening, and got drunk. Then he got drunker when we had dinner at the pub.' Xavier loved calling her and telling her about his friends. He had few secrets from her. And his tales of his exploits always amused her. She had missed him ever since he left home.

'That's charming, his getting drunk I mean.' She assumed his friend was about his own age. Two boys misbehaving, all in good fun.

'Actually, it was. He's very funny. He took his pants off while we sat at the bar. The funny thing was that absolutely no one noticed, until he asked some girl to dance. I think he'd forgotten it himself by then, until he got out on the dance floor in his jockey shorts, and some old woman hit him with her purse. So he asked her to dance and swung her around a few times. It was the funniest damn thing I've ever seen. She was about four feet tall, and she kept hitting him with her purse. It looked like a scene from Monty Python. He's a terrific dancer.' Sasha was laughing as she listened, imagining the scene of the artist in jockey shorts, dancing with some old woman while she hit him. 'He was very polite to her, and everyone was laughing their heads off, but then the barkeep said he'd call the police, so I took him home to his wife.'

'He's married?' Sasha sounded startled by

38

that piece of information. 'At your age?'

'He's not my age, Mom. He's thirty-eight years old, and he has three kids. They're cute kids. Nice wife too.'

'Where was she then?' Disapproval crept into her voice.

'She hates going out with him,' Xavier said matter-of-factly. Liam Allison had become one of his closest friends in London. He was a serious artist, with a light touch about life, an outrageous sense of humor, and a fondness for practical jokes, mischief, and pranks.

'I can see why his wife hates going out with him,' Sasha commented about her son's friend. 'I'm not sure I'd enjoy going out with a husband who takes his trousers off in public and asks old ladies to dance.'

'That was pretty much what she said when I got him home. He passed out on the couch before I left, so I had a glass of wine with her, and then I left. She's a good woman.'

'She'd have to be, to put up with that. Is he an alcoholic?' Sasha sounded serious for a moment, wondering what sort of people he was hanging out with. Xavier's friend didn't sound like an ideal companion, or not a good influence in any case.

'No, he isn't an alcoholic.' Xavier laughed. 'He was just bored, and he made a bet with me that no one would notice for an hour if he took his pants off in the pub. He won. No one noticed till he started dancing.'

Well, I hope you kept yours on,' she said, sounding like a mother, as Xavier laughed at her. He adored her.

'Actually, I did. Liam thought that was pretty cowardly of me. He said he'd pay double or nothing if I took mine off, too. I didn't.'

'Thank you, darling. I'm relieved to hear it.' She glanced at her watch then. She had promised to meet Arthur at six, and it was already ten after. She loved talking to her son. 'I hate to do this, but I promised to meet your father at home ten minutes ago. We're driving out to the Hamptons after dinner.'

'I figured you would. I just wanted to check in.'

'I'm glad you did. Anything special planned for this weekend?' She liked knowing what he did, and Tatianna as well, although she checked in less often. She was trying to spread her wings. And she was more likely to call Arthur these days than her mother. Sasha hadn't spoken to her all week.

'I'm not doing anything. The weather has been disgusting. I thought I'd paint.'

'Good. I'm flying to Paris on Sunday. I'll call you when I get in. Do you have time to come over and see me this week?'

'Maybe. I'll talk to you Sunday night. Have a nice weekend. Give Dad my love.'

'I will. I love you ... and tell your friend to keep his pants on next time. You're lucky you

40

didn't both wind up in jail. Causing a riot, or indecent exposure, or having too much fun. Or something.' Xavier always had a good time wherever he was, and apparently so did his friend Liam. Xavier had mentioned him before, and always said he wanted his mother to see his work. One of these days she would, although there was never enough time. She was always rushing, and when she went to London she had artists to visit whom she already represented, and wanted to see Xavier. She had told him to tell Liam to send her slides of his work, but he never had, which suggested to her that he was either not serious about it, or didn't feel ready to show it to her. Either way, he sounded like a somewhat outrageous character. She already represented several of those, and wasn't sure she wanted one more, no matter how entertaining Xavier thought he was. It was a lot easier dealing with artists who were serious about their careers, and behaved like grown-ups. Badly behaved nearly forty-year-old men who took their clothes off in public were a headache, and she didn't need one more of those. 'I'll talk to you Sunday.'

'I'll call you in Paris. 'Bye, Mom,' Xavier said cheerily, and then hung up, and Sasha smiled as she rushed out of her office. She didn't want to keep Arthur waiting, and she still had to make dinner for them. But it had been wonderful talking to her son.

41

She waved at everyone as she left the office in a hurry, and hailed a cab for the short ride to the apartment, still thinking of Xavier. She knew Arthur would be waiting for her and anxious to leave town. The traffic was always awful on Fridays, though slightly better if they waited until after dinner. The weather had been gorgeous. Even though it was October, it was warm and sunny. She sat back in the cab for a minute, and closed her eyes. It had been a long week, and she was tired.

The apartment she was going home to was the only thing in their life she felt she had outgrown. They had lived there for twelve years, since they had moved back from Paris, and now that the children were gone, it seemed much too large for them. She kept trying to get Arthur to sell it, and move to a smaller co-op on Fifth Avenue, with a view of the park. But if they were going to move back to Paris when he retired, they had agreed to wait until they firmed up their plans. If they moved to Paris, all they needed was a tiny pied-à-terre in New York. It was one of those rare times in their lives when she felt their life in flux. It had seemed that way to her since Tatianna graduated and moved to her own place. Sasha's life felt empty at times now with the children gone. Arthur teased her about it whenever she said it, and reminded her that she was one of the busiest women in New York, or anywhere else. But she missed the children anyway. They had been an integral and vital part of her life, and she felt sad at times, diminished and less useful now that they were gone. She was grateful that she and Arthur enjoyed traveling and spending time together. If possible, they were even closer now than they had ever been, and even more in love. Twenty-five years had not diminished their love and passion for each other. If anything, familiarity and time had added a bond to them that attached them more and more to each other with age.

Arthur was waiting for her at the apartment when he got home, and smiled the moment he saw her. He was still wearing the white shirt he had worn to the office, with his sleeves rolled up. His jacket was casually tossed over the back of a chair. He had already put a few things into a bag for the weekend at their house in Southampton. She was planning to toss a salad and put some cold chicken on a plate. They liked leaving after the traffic; it was murder on summer and fall weekends.

'How was your day?' he asked, planting a kiss somewhere on the top of her head. She wore her dark hair pulled back in a knot, as she had for her entire lifetime. In the Hamptons on the weekends, she wore it down her back in a long braid. She loved wearing old clothes, jeans, tattered sweaters, or faded T-shirts. It was a relief not to have to be dressed as she was in the gallery every day. Arthur loved to play golf and walk on the beach. He had been an avid sailor in his youth, as their children were, and he loved playing tennis with her. Most of the time, on the weekends, she did some gardening, or curled up with a book. She tried not to work on weekends, although she brought papers with her sometimes.

Like the city apartment, the house in the Hamptons was too large for them now, but it bothered her less there. She could easily imagine grandchildren there one day, and the children often came to stay and brought their friends. The house in the Hamptons always seemed alive to her, perhaps because of their view of the ocean. The apartment in the city seemed lonely and dead to her now.

'Sorry I'm late,' she apologised, as she hurried into the kitchen, after kissing him. After all these years, they still loved each other and had fun together. 'Xavier called just as I was leaving.'

'How was he?'

'A little drunk, I think. He'd been out with some very badly behaved friend.'

'A woman?' Arthur asked with interest.

'No. An artist. He took his pants off at the pub.'

'Xavier took his pants off?' Arthur looked

44

stunned, as Sasha tossed the salad.

'No, his friend did. Another crazy artist.' She shook her head as she put the chicken on a platter.

Arthur stood and chatted with her, as she organised dinner for them, and set it on the kitchen table, with linen placemats and napkins, on pretty plates. She enjoyed doing things like that for him, and he always noticed it, and complimented her.

'That's a mighty full briefcase you brought home, Sasha,' he said, eyeing it as he served himself some salad, looking relaxed and happy. He loved their weekends at the beach. They were sacred to both of them. They never allowed anything to interfere with their weekends, except major illness, or some sort of unavoidable event. Otherwise, every Friday, rain or shine, winter or summer, they were on the road to Southampton by seven P.M.

'I'm leaving for Paris on Sunday,' she reminded him as they ate their salad, and she served him a piece of the chicken the housekeeper had left for them.

'I forgot. How long are you staying?'

'Four days. Maybe five. I'll be home by the weekend.'

They exchanged the classic patter of people who have been married forever, and were used to each other. Nothing important was said, it was just good to be there together. He told her about someone retiring, a minor business deal that hadn't gone according to plan. She told him about a new artist they'd signed, a very talented young painter from Brazil. And she mentioned that Xavier had said he'd try to come to Paris to see her the following week. He was good about doing that, and made his own schedule, unlike Tatianna, who was at the mercy of the photographer she worked for. Her employer worked long hours, and she liked spending the rest of her time with her friends. But then again, she was two years younger than her brother, and still fighting for her independence.

'Who's the girl of the week?' Arthur asked with a look of amusement. He knew his son well, as did Sasha. And as she looked over at Arthur with a smile, she noticed, as she often did, how handsome he still was. Tall, lean, fit, with chiseled features and a strong chin. She had been in love with him since the moment he walked into her life. More so now than ever, in fact. She knew how lucky she was. Many of her friends in New York were divorced, one or two were widowed, and none of them ever seemed to be able to find a man. They never failed to tell her how lucky she was. She knew it anyway. Arthur had been the love of her life since the day they met.

'The last time I asked it was some artist's

model he met in drawing class.' Sasha grinned. Xavier was famous among his friends and in the family for having a constantly changing chorus line of adoring women at his feet. He was extremely handsome, and a nice person on top of it, and women always found him irresistible. He was equally unable to resist them. I don't even ask their names anymore,' Sasha said, clearing the table, as her husband smiled admiringly at her. She put their dishes in the dishwasher. They had a low-maintenance life these days, although when the children were still at home, they had had serious dinners together every night. Now he and Sasha ate a light, easy meal at night in the kitchen, which was simpler.

'I haven't asked Xavier the names of his girlfriends in years.' Arthur laughed at her comment. 'Every time I called one of them by name, it turned out he'd had five since then. I know better now.' He went to change into khaki pants, and a comfortable old sweater, and Sasha did the same.

Twenty minutes later they were ready to leave, and took off in Sasha's station wagon. She still kept it after the kids left, because it was useful to pick up work from young artists. She had some groceries in the back, and a small overnight bag for each of them. They kept their beach clothes in Southampton, so they didn't have to bring much

47

with them. She also had her suitcase for Paris, and the bulging briefcase he had mentioned. She was planning to go to the airport from Southampton on Sunday morning, and would be leaving nearly at dawn, in order to get to Paris at a decent hour in the evening. When she had to, she took the red-eye, but there was nothing pressing, and it made more sense for her to take the day flight, although she hated to miss Sunday with Arthur.

They were in Southampton at ten o'clock, and Sasha was surprised to realize she was tired. As always, Arthur had done the driving, and she had dozed off on the trip out, and was happy to climb into bed with him before midnight. They sat on the deck before that, and looked at the ocean in the moonlight. The weather was warm and balmy, the night crystal clear. And once in bed, they fell asleep the moment their heads hit the pillow.

As they so often did at the beach, they made love when they woke up in the morning. Afterward, they lay together and cuddled. Their loving had not suffered from boredom over the years, if anything it had gotten better from familiarity and deep affection. He followed her into the bathroom afterward, and she bathed while he showered. She loved their lazy Southampton mornings. Afterward, they went down to the kitchen together, she made breakfast, and they took a long walk on the beach. It was a glorious day, hot and sunny, with barely even a breeze. It was the last week in October, and fall would put a chill in the air soon, but not just yet. Summer still seemed to be here.

Arthur took Sasha out to dinner on Saturday at a small Italian restaurant they both loved. They sat on the deck at the house afterward, drinking wine and talking. Life seemed easy and peaceful. They went to bed early that night, as Sasha had to get up early the next morning to go to the airport and catch the flight to Paris. She hated to leave him, but it was an ordinary occurrence in their lives. Leaving him for four or five days was nothing. She snuggled up to him in bed that night, and kept her arms around him, her body pressed close to his as they fell asleep. She had to get up at four, and leave at five, to be at the airport by seven, for a nine A.M. flight. It would land her in Paris at nine P.M. Paris time, and she'd be at their house by eleven at night, local time, and get a decent night's sleep before working the next day.

When the alarm went off at four she heard it and turned it off quickly, held Arthur for a long moment, and then got up regretfully. She tiptoed to the bathroom in the dark and dressed in blue jeans and a black sweater. She wore a comfortable pair of old Hermes loafers that had seen better days. But she had long since stopped dressing fashionably for

long flights. Comfort seemed more important. She usually slept on planes. She stood
for a long moment and looked at Arthur
before she left, and then she bent to kiss him
gently on the top of his head, so as not to
wake him. He stirred anyway, he always did,
and smiled in his sleep. A moment later, he
squinted at her through half-closed eyes and
his smile grew broader, as he held out a hand
and pulled her close to him.

'I love you, Sash,' he whispered sleepily.
'Come home soon. I'll miss you.' He always
said things like that, and she loved him all
the more for it. She kissed him on the cheek
after he said it, and then tucked him in just
as she used to do for their children.

'I love you, too,' she whispered. 'Go back
to sleep. I'll call you when I get to Paris.' She
always did. She knew she'd catch him before
he drove back to the city, and wished she
could stay there with him.

It would be nice when he retired and
could travel everywhere with her. She liked
the idea of that more than ever, as she softly
closed the bedroom door behind her, and
then walked out of the house. She had
called for a cab the night before. The driver
was waiting just outside, and hadn't rung
the bell, as she'd requested. She told him
what airline and which airport, and looked
out the window as they drove, smiling to
herself. She was well aware of her blessings.

She was a lucky woman with a lucky life, a husband she loved who loved her, two children who were terrific, and two galleries that had given her endless joy and a good living all her life. There was nothing more she wanted, or could have. Sasha de Suvery Boardman knew she had it all.

Chapter 2

The flight to Paris was uneventful. Sasha had lunch, watched a movie, slept for three hours, and woke up as they landed at Charles de Gaulle airport. She knew most of the attendants on the flight, and the chief purser, and knowing her habits, they left her alone. She was an easy passenger and pleasant person, who drank nothing but water on the flight. She was well versed in what to do to avoid jet lag. She ate lightly, slept, drank water, and went to bed as soon as she got home, and she knew in the morning she'd be fine, and adjusted to the time change. She had been commuting between Paris and New York for twelve years.

The weather in Paris was cool and rainy. Although it was Indian summer in New York, it was winter here. She had brought a cashmere shawl to put over her jacket when she landed, and as always, a car and driver were waiting for her. They chatted about the weather and the flight on the drive in to Paris, and the house was quiet when she got home. The cleaning woman who came daily during the week had left food in the refrigerator, as she always did. And as soon as Sasha walked in the door, she picked up the phone and called Arthur. It was five in the afternoon for him and he sounded delighted to hear her. He was just closing up the house in Southampton and about to head home.

'I miss you,' he said, after she reported on the weather in Paris. Sometimes she forgot how depressing the winters were there. 'Maybe you should open a gallery in Miami,' he said, teasing. He knew that despite the bad weather, in her heart of hearts she wanted to move back to Paris, and he was willing to do that with her in the coming year, when he retired. He had enjoyed living there too in the early days of their marriage. He liked both cities. All he cared about was being with her, and he enjoyed sharing life with her.

'I'm going to Brussels for the day on Tuesday, to see a new artist, and check on one of our old ones,' Sasha mentioned.

'Just be home for the weekend.' They had plans to go to a birthday party for one of her best friends. The honoree had been widowed the previous year, and was going out with a new man no one seemed to like. She had dated several people in the last year, none of whom was a hit with her friends. Everyone was very fond of her, and hoped the latest new man would vanish soon. Her late husband had been one of Arthur's closest friends, and had died a long, slow death from cancer. He had died at fifty-two, and his widow was the same age. She made bad jokes about how depressing it was to be back on the market after twenty-nine years of marriage. Arthur and Sasha both felt sorry for her, so they put up with her grim dates. Sasha knew better than anyone, from their conversations, how lonely she was.

'I'll try to come home Thursday, otherwise Friday. I want to see Xavier and it depends when he can come.' Sasha filled him in on her plans.

'Give him my love,' Arthur said, and they chatted for a few more minutes. She made herself a salad after they hung up, went through some papers the gallery manager had left for her to look at, and opened her Paris mail. There were invitations to several parties, a flood of announcements of art openings, and a letter from a friend. She rarely went to dinner parties in Paris, except when given by important clients, where she felt she had to go. She didn't like going out without Arthur, and enjoyed the quiet life they led, except for art events, or dinners with close friends.

53

She called Xavier, as promised, and he was out. She left a message on his machine. She was in bed by midnight, asleep shortly after, and in the morning awoke at eight to the sound of her alarm. It was raining and misty, and looked like the heart of winter. She put on her raincoat to run across the courtyard to the gallery at nine-thirty, and met with her manager at ten o'clock. The gallery was closed on Mondays, which gave them all a peaceful day to work. She and Bernard, the manager, were planning shows and ad schedules for the following year.

She ate at her desk, and the afternoon sped by. It was nearly six o'clock when her secretary told her that her daughter was on the line from New York. Xavier called her far more often than Tatianna, and she had spoken to him twice that day. He was coming to have dinner with her on Wednesday, so she could get back to Arthur on Thursday. Sasha picked up the phone with a smile, anticipating more complaints about the photographer Tatianna worked for. She just hoped Tatianna hadn't quit. She was headstrong at times, and didn't like being subservient to other people, or treated unfairly, and Sasha knew she thought her new boss wasn't treating her well. With a fine arts degree from Brown, she had expected to do more than pour him coffee and sweep the studio after he left.

'*Bonjour, chérie,*' Sasha said in French unconsciously, and was surprised to hear silence on the other end. She assumed they had been cut off, and Tatianna would call again. She was about to hang up when she heard a guttural sound that sounded more animal than human. 'Tati? *C'est toi?* Is that you? Darling, what's wrong?' She could tell now that her daughter was crying, sobbing into the phone. It was a long time before she spoke.

'Mommy ... come home...' For all her brand-new sophistication, she suddenly sounded five years old.

'What happened? Did you get fired?' It was the only thing Sasha could think of that would put her in such a state. Tatianna had no boyfriend at the moment, so it couldn't be a romantic disaster.

'Daddy...' she said, and broke into sobs again, as Sasha's heart gave a lurch and nearly leaped out of her chest. What in God's name could have happened to him?

'Tatianna, tell me what happened. Quickly. You're scaring me.'

'He ... they called me from his office a few minutes ago...' It was nearly noon in New York. Sasha knew that if he had had an accident on the way into the city, someone would have called her the night before. He carried all her numbers on him, as she did his.

55

'Is he all right?' Sasha could feel a vise squeezing her chest as she asked the question, and Tatianna continued crying uncontrollably.

'He had a heart attack ... in his office ... they called the paramedics...'

'Oh my God...' Sasha squeezed her eyes shut as she listened, waiting for the rest as her hand shook as it gripped the phone.

'Mommy ... he's dead.' The entire world stopped for Sasha as Tatianna said it. The room turned upside down. Without realizing it, she held the phone with one hand, and with the other she clutched what had once been her father's desk, as though to steady herself. She felt as though she were falling into an abyss.

'He's not. It's a mistake,' Sasha said, as though she could deny it or will it not to happen. 'That's not true!' she shouted, as tears sprang to her eyes. She felt as though every fiber of her being had received a nearly fatal electric shock. She was fighting for air.

'It is true,' Tatianna wailed miserably. 'Mrs Jenkins called me. They took him to the hospital, but he was dead. Mommy ... come home...'

'I'm coming,' she said, and stood up with a look of panic, glancing around the room, as though she expected someone to materialize to help her and tell her it wasn't true. But no one came. She was alone in the

56

room. 'Where are you?'

'I'm at work.'

'Go home ... no, don't go home. Go to the gallery. I don't want you to be alone. Tell them what happened. They'll understand.' All Tatianna did was cry as she listened. Sasha knew there was a flight to New York at nine o'clock, and she'd be in New York seven hours later. And it was six hours earlier in New York. She'd be in the city by eleven o'clock that night, New York time, five A. M. in Paris. She knew her faithful assistant would take Tatianna to her parents' apartment. 'Stay where you are, Tati. I'll have Marcie pick you up.' Marcie had worked for Sasha since she'd opened the gallery. She was a kind woman in her early forties, never married, with no children, and she loved Sasha's as her own. And then as an afterthought in the midst of lightning and chaos, 'I love you, Tati. I'll be home as soon as I can.' Sasha was shaking from head to foot as soon as she put down the phone. And in a moment of total madness, she dialed Arthur's cell phone. His secretary, Mrs Jenkins, picked it up. She had been just about to call Sasha. Tatianna had gotten to her first. For an insane instant, Sasha wanted to believe Arthur would answer his phone. His secretary did instead.

'I'm so sorry, Mrs Boardman ... I'm so sorry ... it was so sudden. I didn't know ...

he never called me... I saw him five minutes before. I went in to have him sign some papers, and he was slumped over his desk. He was already gone. They tried ... but they couldn't do anything.' She spared Sasha the scene of horror that she'd seen when they tried to revive him and failed. She was crying, too. 'I'll do everything I can. Is there someone I should call? The hospital? The funeral home? I'm so sorry...'

'I'll do it all when I get home.' Or Marcie would. She didn't want anyone else making decisions about her husband. She didn't even want to be making them herself. And first, she had to call their son.

Sasha quickly told Eugénie, her secretary in Paris, what had happened, asked her to get her on a flight, and to go next door to pick up her things. Her secretary was stunned. She didn't want to believe it at first, but when she saw the look on Sasha's face, she knew it was true. Sasha was sheet white and looked like she was in shock. Eugénie watched Sasha's hands shake like leaves when she picked up the phone to call Xavier.

Eugénie left the room then, and came back a moment later with a cup of tea, and then disappeared to make her flight arrangements. By then, Sasha was crying on the phone to Xavier, who was as distraught as she was. He offered to fly to Paris to meet her, and fly home with her. But if his flight was delayed, she knew they might miss each other. She told him to go straight to New York, that night if he could. Not that it would make a difference to his father now, but it would to her and Tatianna. Xavier was crying softly when he hung up. The rest of the night was a blur.

Eugénie had packed Sasha's bag as she'd asked her to do, and canceled her plans for the week. Her trip to Brussels would have to wait. Her whole life had just been destroyed in a single moment. Sasha couldn't even get her mind around it, and didn't want to try. Her secretary and her gallery manager drove her to the airport, and after hovering over her like worried parents, they put her on the plane. They discreetly explained to the agent at the gate what had happened, after she boarded. They were both afraid of how she would be on the plane. Bernard, her manager, had offered to fly with her, but Sasha had bravely declined, and regretted it the moment the plane took off. She was overwhelmed by a wave of panic so powerful, she was afraid she would have a heart attack herself. One of the flight attendants told another that Sasha had literally turned green and broken out in a sweat. They covered her in blankets, asked the passenger next to her to move to another seat, and the purser had sat next to her for a short time. They asked her if she had tranquilizers with her and she

59

said she didn't, and never took them. But she had never before lost her husband, either. She hadn't even felt this way when her father died, which was bad enough. But he had been eighty nine years old, and he himself had warned her frequently that it would happen one day, and she knew it would. She had been prepared for it, more or less. But not for this. Not Arthur. He had told her he loved her only the day before. She had left him asleep in bed in Southampton, and now he was gone. It wasn't possible. It wasn't happening. Except it was. The only time she remembered feeling this way, totally out of control and frightened, was when her mother had died when she was nine. Now she felt like a child again. An orphan. She cried all the way to New York. And after a call from Bernard in Paris, Marcie had come to the airport, and was waiting for Sasha as she came through customs. She had left Tatianna with a friend at the apartment.

Marcie didn't ask her how she was. She didn't need to. Sasha could hardly talk. She was the most capable woman Marcie had ever known, and she looked utterly destroyed. Marcie quietly put her arms around her, hugged her close, and led her from the airport, as Sasha cried and strangers watched. She got her into the car a moment later, and the driver sped off toward New York. Sasha was too distraught to talk, and then halfway into town she began babbling, asking questions, to which none of the answers mattered now. No matter who or how or where or when, Arthur was gone. Without a warning. Without a sound. Without saying good-bye to his children or wife. Gone. The reunion between Sasha and Tatianna half an hour later at the apartment was painful to watch. Marcie just stood silently and cried. Feeling helpless, she made sandwiches for them, which no one ate. She poured water and coffee, which no one drank. She tried to talk Sasha into having a drink, which she didn't want either. And at two in the morning Xavier arrived from London. He had called a friend to pick him up. One of his young artist friends was right behind him as he came through the door and went straight to his mother. He put his arms around her and Tatianna, and the three of them just stood there hugging and crying. It nearly killed Marcie to watch them. They sat up and talked through most of the night. The only one who ate the food Marcie made was Xavier's friend. The others ate and drank nothing.

And in the morning, reality set in. Sasha went to the hospital, and insisted on seeing her husband. She wanted to be alone with him, and when she came out of the room, she looked like a ghost, but she wasn't crying. She looked shell-shocked. She had said good-bye to him. After that they went to the funeral home and made arrangements. The minister came to see her at the apartment, and Marcie was with her the entire time. Xavier had gone to Tatianna's apartment with her. After the minister left, she turned and looked at Marcie. 'Is this really happening? I can't believe it. I keep waiting for someone to tell me it's all a terrible joke. But it isn't, is it?' Marcie shook her head.

They got through the day, with Sasha looking and feeling like a zombie, and trying to comfort her children. They finally ate pizza that night, and nothing else. Tatianna went to sleep in her old bedroom, Xavier went out with friends and came home drunk. Sasha sat in the living room staring into space. She couldn't stand going back to their bedroom, all she wanted was him. And when she finally went to bed that night, too exhausted to sleep, she could smell his aftershave on his pillow, and burrowed her face in it and sobbed. Marcie stayed and slept on the couch, faithful friend that she was. She spent hours that night calling their friends and telling them about the funeral. She called the gallery in Paris. Everyone there was coming.

Marcie ordered the flowers, Sasha picked the music. Friends began to drop by and offered to help. Ushers were chosen from among Arthur's partners and best friends. Sasha felt as though she would die when she had to pick his clothes. And somehow they all got to the funeral dressed, and on time. People came to the house afterward. And long after, Sasha admitted that she remembered absolutely nothing. Not the music or the flowers, or the people who were there. She had no recollection of who had come to the apartment. She had appeared normal and sane, and as composed as was possible. But essentially, she was in shock. And so were her children. They clung to each other like people off a ship that sank, and were drowning. And Sasha was. The hardest part came the day after. Real life, without Arthur. The day-to-day horror of living without him. The pain of it was beyond belief. Like surgery without anesthesia, Sasha could not believe what it was like waking up every day, knowing she would not see him and never would again. Everything that had once been dear and wonderful and easy was now agonizing and excruciatingly hard. There were no rewards to getting through the days without him, no point getting up in the morning, nothing to look forward to, no reason to stay alive, except for her children.

Xavier went back to London after two weeks. He called his mother often. Tatianna had gone back to work after a week. Sasha called her every day, and most of the time,

Tatianna just cried whenever she heard her mother's voice. The only comfort Sasha got, other than the discreet sympathy of her employees and the staunch support of Marcie, was when she talked to friends who had gone through the same thing. She hated talking to them, and most of the time it depressed her, but at least they told her honestly what to expect. And none of it sounded good.

Alana Applebaum, whose husband had been Arthur's friend, and whose birthday Sasha had missed because Arthur's funeral had been the day before, told her the first year had been torture from beginning to end. And sometimes it still was. But after the anniversary marking the first year, she had made a concerted effort to go out with other men. She said that most of them were jerks, and she hadn't met a decent one yet, but at least she wasn't at home, crying and alone. Her theory was that no matter how bad a man she went out with was, it was better than being alone.

One of Sasha's closest friends in Paris, who had lost her husband three years before in a skiing accident in Val d'Isère, saw it differently. She said she'd rather be alone than with a jerk. She was forty-five years old, had been widowed at forty-two, and said there just were no decent men available, all the good ones were married. The others were idiots, or worse. She insisted she was happier alone. But Sasha was acutely aware that in the past year or two, she had started drinking too much. And often when she called Sasha to comfort her, having miscalculated the time difference, she had been drunk. She wasn't managing so well, either.

Sasha commented on their calls to Marcie, 'Maybe the only way to survive this is to become a drunk.' It was depressing listening to all of them. And the divorcées Sasha knew were no better. They didn't have intolerable grief to live with, and they could hide behind their hatred of their ex-husbands, particularly if they'd been left for other, younger women. It was frightening listening to all of them. As a result, Sasha avoided them, isolated herself, and tried to get lost in her work. Sometimes it helped. Most of the time, it didn't.

The first Christmas without Arthur came and went in a series of large and small agonies. Xavier and Tatianna spent the night with her on Christmas Eve, and by midnight they were all sitting in the living room, sobbing. None of them wanted to open their presents, least of all Sasha. Tatianna had given her a heavy cashmere stole to wear, since Sasha seemed to be cold all the time, probably because she rarely ate or slept. And Xavier gave her a series of art books he knew she wanted. But it wasn't Christmas without Arthur.

The next day both her children went skiing with friends. She took a sleeping pill at eight o'clock on New Year's Eve, and woke up at two o'clock the next afternoon, grateful that she had missed it. She and Arthur had never done anything spectacular on New Year's Eve, but at least he had been there with her.

It was May before she felt even halfway human again. By then, it was seven months since Arthur's death. All she had done since then was travel to Paris once a month, where she sat huddled and freezing in the house at night, finished her work as quickly as possible, and flew back to New York. She delegated as much as possible to both her gallery managers during those months, and she was grateful for their help. Without them, she would have been utterly and totally lost, and nearly was. Sundays were the worst days of all for her, in either city, because she couldn't go to work. She hadn't been to the house in the Hamptons since he died. She didn't want to go back without him, nor did she want to sell it. She just let it sit there, and told her children to use it whenever they wanted. She wasn't going to. She had absolutely no idea what to do with the rest of her life. Other than work, which was now completely devoid of joy for her, but it was the only saving grace she had. The rest looked like a wasteland of despair. She had never felt

66

as lost or without hope in her entire life.

Both of her gallery managers, and even Marcie, were urging her to see friends. She hadn't returned any calls, except for those from the gallery, in months. And even those calls she handed off to others whenever she could. She hadn't wanted to talk to anyone since Arthur died.

In May, she finally felt a little better. Much to her own amazement, she accepted a dinner invitation from Alana in June, and regretted it as soon as she did. She regretted it even more when the night arrived. The last thing she wanted was to put on clothes and go out. Marcie had told her that Arthur would want her to go out. He would have been devastated if he could see the state she was in. She had lost nearly twenty pounds. People who didn't know her well said she looked fabulous, and had no idea why. To them, being emaciated from grief looked fashionable and trim. So, on a fateful night in June, she went out for the first time. She wore a black silk pantsuit and high heels, and her hair straight back in a bun. The diamond earrings she wore had been a gift from Arthur the Christmas before he died. She cried when she put them on. And her clothes hung on her. She was rail thin, and everything she owned was suddenly too big.

The dinner party she went to started out more pleasantly than she had expected it to, and most of the faces were familiar. Alana had yet another new beau by then, and this one seemed unexpectedly decent. He chatted with Sasha for a little while, and she discovered that he was a collector of contemporary art, and had been a client of her gallery once or twice. The agony for Sasha came when she discovered that Alana had asked him to bring a friend, who launched himself at Sasha during dinner. He was intelligent and might have been interesting, except that he proceeded to interview Sasha, as though she had signed up for computer dating, which she hadn't, and had no intention of doing, now or ever. She knew that Alana had met men on Internet dating services more than once. The thought of it horrified Sasha. She didn't want to date anyone, not this one or any other. She intended to mourn Arthur forever.

'So how many children do you have at home?' he asked her bluntly before they sat down to dinner, while Sasha was wondering if she could claim a sudden migraine and vanish. But she knew Alana would be insulted. She knew her hostess meant well, but this was not what Sasha wanted. All she wanted was to be left alone. Her wounds were still wide open. And she had no desire to replace Arthur. Ever.

'I have two grown children,' Sasha said bleakly.

'That's good,' he said with a look of relief. She knew he was a stockbroker, and he had volunteered that he had been divorced for the past fourteen years. He looked to be around fifty, two years older than Sasha.

'Actually, it's not good,' she said honestly, smiling sadly at him. 'They're gone. I miss them terribly. I wish they were younger and still at home.' He looked more than a little uncomfortable with her answer.

'You're not planning to have more, are you?' She had the feeling that he had a checklist and was working his way down the questions.

'I'd love to, but I'm a widow.' For her, that answered the question. For him, it didn't.

'You'll probably end up remarried.' Poof, with one fell swoop, he had erased Arthur, and moved on to the next one. Sasha hadn't.

'I will not remarry,' Sasha said, looking stubborn, as they moved into dinner, and she discovered with dismay that he was seated next to her. Alana clearly had a plan.

'How long were you married?' he asked with renewed interest. Women who were shopping for husbands were not what he wanted. In that case, do not pass go, do not collect two hundred dollars.

'Twenty-five years,' she said primly, as they sat down. He didn't miss a beat or his questions for a minute.

'Well, then I can see why you don't want to remarry. Gets boring, doesn't it, after all those years? I was married for eleven, that did it for me.' Sasha looked at him with horror, and didn't answer for a long moment.

'I was not bored in my marriage,' she said firmly. 'I was very much in love with my husband.'

'That's too bad,' he said, digging into the first course. It was the only breather from him Sasha had gotten. 'You probably remember it better than it was. Most widowed people suffer from that kind of delusion. They all think they were married to saints, after they're gone. While they were here, they weren't that crazy about them.'

'I assure you,' Sasha said, looking haughtily at him, wanting to throw something at him, 'I was crazy about my husband. That is a fact, not a delusion.' Her tone was glacial.

'All right, fine,' he said, looking nonplussed, 'I'll take your word for it. So how many men have you been out with since he died?' Alana happened to look over then, saw the look on her face, and realized it was not going well. Sasha was white with outrage.

'I have not been out with anyone, nor do I intend to go out with anyone. Ever. My husband died eight months ago, and this is the first social invitation I've accepted.' Her dinner partner stared at her in amazement.

'Oh my God, you're a virgin.' He seemed

70

to first view it as an oddity, and then as he looked at her with interest, as a challenge. But he had met his match in Sasha.

'No, I'm not a virgin, as you put it. Nor do I intend to be deflowered. I am a forty-eight-year-old widow, who was very much in love with her husband.' And with that, she turned her back on him, and spoke to her dinner partner on her other side, who was a man she and Arthur had known well. He was married, and she and Arthur had been fond of him and his wife.

'Are you all right?' Her old friend looked at her with concern as she turned to him with her eyes blazing. He spoke in an undertone, and her eyes were filled with tears as she nodded. The man on her left had been not only insulting but depressing. This was what she had to look forward to now as a widow. She was beginning to wonder if in future she should just tell people she met that she was married. She had no desire to be someone's 'virgin.' It robbed her of all the dignity and respect she'd taken for granted while married to Arthur. Not only had she lost the man she loved, but she realized now that overnight she had become embarrassingly vulnerable, and had lost the social protection of a loving husband, and the safe, comfortable shield of marriage.

'I'm fine,' she said softly to her seatmate.

'I'm so sorry, Sasha,' he said sympathetically, patting her hand, which made the tears in her eyes spill onto her cheeks, and she had to dig in her evening bag for her hankie. She could no longer afford to be without one. And as she blew her nose into it, she felt pathetic and embarrassed.

For the rest of the meal, she picked at what was on her plate, and disappeared with as much aplomb as she could muster while the others were moving into the living room for coffee. She didn't even have the strength to tell Alana, and promised herself she'd call her the next morning.

She didn't have to. Alana called her at the office. It was a Saturday, but as usual now, Sasha was at the gallery, working. No more weekend trips to the Hamptons, which she'd loved with Arthur and couldn't face alone.

'What happened?' Alana sounded plaintive. 'He's a really nice guy when you get to know him. And he liked you. He thought you were terrific!' Sasha found that piece of news even more depressing.

'That's nice of him. I didn't want a date, Alana. I just wanted to come to dinner.'

'You can't stay alone forever. Sasha, sooner or later, you have to get out there. You're a young woman. And look, realistically, there just aren't that many decent guys around. This one's a good one.' Or at least Alana thought so. But she had proven over the past year that her judgment had been colored by desperation.

'I don't want a good one,' Sasha said sadly. She liked her friend, or always had, but hated what she was becoming. Her good taste, good judgment, and dignity seemed to have gone out the window the moment she became a widow. Sasha was sure that not all widows were like her. Alana also had severe money problems, and was desperate to find a husband to solve them. And as Arthur had said before he died, men could smell it. Eau de Panic, as Arthur had called it. It was not a perfume men liked.

'You want Arthur,' Alana said, rubbing salt in her wounds. 'Well, if you want to know the truth, I want Toby. But they're gone, Sash. They're not coming back, and we're stuck here without them. We have to make the best of a bad situation, any way we can.'

'I'm not ready to do that,' Sasha said kindly. She didn't tell her friend how foolish she looked, or how embarrassing she was becoming. 'Maybe staying alone is the right answer. I can't even imagine dating.' Nor did she want to.

'Sasha, you're forty-eight years old, I'm fifty-three. We're too young to be alone forever.' Sasha had felt young when she was married to Arthur. Since he had died, she felt ancient.

'I don't know, Alana. I don't know what the answer is. I just know that right now I'd

73

rather be dead than dating.' As always, she was painfully honest.

'Be patient with yourself. Give these guys a chance, sooner or later you'll find one you want.' Judging by the men Alana had been dating for the past year, with the exception of the current one, none of them were men most sane women would have wanted, except maybe for their money. Alana had a whole different agenda than Sasha. All Sasha was trying to do was survive Arthur's loss. 'In a few months, you'll feel different. Wait till after the first year. Then you'll be ready.'

'I hope not. I have my children, my galleries, and my artists.' Although without Arthur, nothing but the children meant anything to her. She could hardly concentrate on her work now. All it did was get her out of the apartment in New York, or her house in Paris. But nothing in her life brought her joy.

'That's not enough, and you know it,' Alana chided.

'Maybe it is for me.'

'Well, it isn't for me,' Alana said firmly. 'I want to find a nice guy and get married.' Or if not a nice one, a rich one. Sasha had no interest in either. 'Give yourself another six months, and you'll be out there looking too.'

'God, I hope not,' Sasha said grimly. Just thinking about it depressed her more.

'We'll see,' Alana said, as though she knew

better. But one thing was for sure, it wasn't easy for anyone, divorced or widowed, to find men these days. Alana said she'd been hearing that from all her friends. So had Sasha, not that she cared.

She went back to Paris the following week, and stayed for two weeks this time. For the first time in months, she visited her artists, in several cities in Europe – Brussels, Amsterdam, and Munich. And she stopped in London on the way home to visit her son. He was in much better spirits, and producing some very interesting new work. She was impressed when she saw it. She gave him the name of a gallery she thought he should talk to, and he was pleased. He didn't want to show at Suvery. It reeked of nepotism to him, and he was determined to make it on his own.

Xavier had mentioned his friend Liam Allison to her again several times in recent months. He insisted that Liam was one of the most talented artists he had ever known, and he wanted her to see his work.

'I'd be happy to, but I want him to send me slides first.' She didn't want to waste her time, and seeing his slides was a screening process for her. But no matter how many times she told Xavier that, his friend never sent them to her. Xavier claimed he was shy, which wasn't unusual for a young artist, or even an older one, but he sounded anything but shy from the tales Xavier always regaled her with. Every time Xavier got out of control or misbehaved, went to a wild party, or did something outrageous or irresponsible, miraculously Liam seemed to be there. Most recently, they had gone to lunch together on a lazy Sunday afternoon, drank too much wine, took a cab to the airport afterward, and went to Marrakech for four days. Xavier said he had never had so much fun in his life. He called his mother when he got back. She'd been worried after he hadn't returned her calls for nearly a week.

'Let me guess,' she said when he finally surfaced again, and told her where he'd been. 'That Liam character was part of it.' She could almost predict it now. Every time Xavier did something unexpected or slightly insane, the next thing he said to her was that Liam had been with him. 'He must be completely mad. His wife must be a saint.'

'She's a good sport,' Xavier conceded easily, 'although she gets a little fed up with it sometimes. She works, and she expects him to keep an eye on the kids.'

'She's probably supporting him, and the kids,' Sasha said knowingly. She knew other artists like him, though none quite so exuberant or as indifferent to accepted standards of behavior, from what Xavier said at least. 'If I were in her shoes, I'd kill him.'

'I think she threatened to a few times. I

76

don't think the trip to Morocco was a high point in their marriage.'

'No small wonder. He sounds like one of those children I wouldn't let you play with when you were little, because they always got you in trouble. One of these days he will, or get himself into some mess that will be awkward to get out of.'

'He's not mean-spirited, and he never does anything dangerous. He just likes to have a good time, and he hates being told how to behave. I think he grew up with a lot of rules or something. He's allergic to doing what's expected of him. He likes to have free rein.'

'Apparently. I can hardly wait to meet him,' Sasha said ruefully. In fact, she was hoping, if he ever sent her slides, that she would hate his work. He sounded like a headache she just didn't need. Although sometimes people with his energy and personality had enormous talent. What artists like Liam needed, according to Sasha, was to be harnessed, scolded severely, and whipped into shape, or they forgot to get to work. Although Xavier claimed Liam was diligent and conscientious about his painting. He was just irresponsible about everything else. And Xavier was still determined to introduce them. He was convinced that Suvery was the perfect gallery for his friend. But so far, Xavier had never been able to get them together, much to Sasha's relief.

Sasha spent the month of July in New York, but never went near the house in the Hamptons. She just couldn't, and told Tatianna to use it. Sasha didn't even want to see it. And in August, she went to St. Tropez for two weeks to visit friends. She felt oddly detached these days and rootless. She spent the rest of the month in the house in Paris, feeling like a marble in a shoebox. The whole world felt too big for her now without Arthur. Her life was like a pair of shoes that no longer fit. She had never felt so small in her entire life. Even when her father died, she had Arthur around constantly to buffer it for her. Now she had no one, except memories of him, and occasional visits with her kids.

She went back to New York at the end of August, and was finally brave enough to go to Southampton over the Labor Day weekend. It was the first time she had been back in nearly a year, and in some ways it was a relief. It was like finding a piece of him again, a piece she had sorely missed. The closet was still full of his things, and when she looked at their bed, she remembered the last time she had seen him. He had whispered that he loved her the morning she left, she had kissed him, and he went back to sleep.

The memories were overpowering here, and she spent hours thinking of him and

78

walking on the beach. But here, finally, she felt the healing begin.

She went back to the gallery looking better after the Labor Day weekend. For nearly a month now, she had been toying with an idea. She hadn't made a decision yet. It was something she had planned with Arthur. And now it made even more sense to her than before. She wanted to go home. Being in New York without him was too hard for her.

September sped by with an opening for a new artist, which she curated, and another solo show. She curated all their shows, choosing which work to hang, and where to hang it, seeking contrasts and combinations that would set each painting off to its best advantage. She had an instinctive knack for it and always loved it. She also met with several old, familiar clients, sat on her museum boards, and was planning a memorial service for Arthur, to mark the first year since his death. Xavier had promised to fly in for it. The service was, predictably, a somber moment for all of them. All of his partners were there, her children, and their close friends. Their friends were saddened to see how serious and unhappy she looked. As they left the church, it was hard to believe it had been a year.

Tatianna told her that night, after the memorial, that she had quit her job, and was going to travel in India for several months with friends. She wanted to take photographs, and when she got back, she was going to look for a job on a magazine. She promised to be back by Christmas. She was twenty-three years old, and said she needed to spread her wings, which worried Sasha a little, but Sasha knew she had no choice but to set her free. And then she shared her own plans with them. She had decided to move back to Paris, run the gallery there, and reverse the commute she had been doing for thirteen years. Ever since Arthur's death, all she wanted was to go back to her roots. And with Tatianna gone, at least in Paris she would be closer to Xavier. Tatianna was startled by her decision, but Xavier was pleased.

'I think that will be good for you,' he said kindly. He had worried about her all year. In the past, she had always seemed happier to him in Paris, and maybe now she would be. She had been so utterly miserable for the past year.

'Are you selling the apartment?' Tatianna asked, looking worried. She rarely stayed there anymore, but she liked knowing it was there. She didn't know of her father's plans to retire, and their conversations about selling the apartment and buying a pied-à-terre.

'Not yet. I'll use it when I'm here.' Tatianna looked relieved. In fact, moving to Paris would change little for Sasha. She would be in Paris for three weeks a month now, instead of one or two, and in New York for a week, or more if she needed to. She had her feet firmly planted in both cities, and had already lived that way for thirteen years. Her managers in both places were perfectly trained to do what she wanted, and were in constant communication with her, whenever she was away. It was going to be an easy adjustment for her.

Sasha waited till November to move to Paris. October was always a busy month in the art world in New York. She had board meetings to go to, shows to organize, and before she shifted the bulk of her time to Paris, she wanted to see some friends in New York. She hadn't seen most of them for nearly a year. She gave a small dinner party for Alana, who had just become engaged and looked enormously relieved. She was marrying the man she had introduced to Sasha the previous June, and they both seemed pleased. And as usual, Alana couldn't resist asking her if she was ready to date. She asked Sasha that every time they spoke. It was a mantra Sasha had come to hate.

'Not yet.' Sasha smiled pleasantly, and drifted away. Not ever, she told herself. She spent a last weekend in the Hamptons before she left, and celebrated Thanksgiving with friends. Xavier was back in London, and Tatianna was in India, traveling with her friends. It was easier for Sasha to be at someone else's house for Thanksgiving. It seemed more impersonal, and less painful that way. At her own home, the year before, Arthur's absence had been too fresh and too acute for all of them. This year was better. And she was surprised to run into an old friend at the dinner she went to, and discover that, after thirty-four years of marriage, he had just gotten divorced. He was Arthur's age, and they hadn't seen him in years. He told Sasha discreetly over dinner that his wife had become an alcoholic, and had had severe mental problems for the last twenty years of their marriage. He was sad, but relieved, to be out of it, and sorry to hear that Sasha was moving away. They had a nice time talking over dinner, and Sasha saw their hostess watching them hopefully. She had hoped that something might come of it when she invited both of them. They were the only single people there. And Sasha was startled to hear from him the next day. He called as she was packing her things for Paris. She was leaving the following day.

'I was wondering if you'd like to have dinner with me,' he said, sounding hesitant, and somewhat awkward. He had always liked her and Arthur, and like Sasha, he hadn't dated anyone in years. He sounded nervous and unsure.

'I'd have loved it,' she said easily. She knew she was leaving, so it was not an issue for

82

her, and wouldn't have been anyway. As far as she was concerned, they were nothing more than old friends, nor would they be. 'I'm leaving for Paris tomorrow. I'm moving back,' she said with relief. She knew she had made the right decision for her. Even her children agreed.

'I'm sorry to hear it. I was hoping I could get you to a movie sometime, or dinner.' He had been pleased to run into her again. And even Sasha would have had to admit, there was nothing wrong with him. He was a nice man. He just wasn't Arthur, and she had no interest in being involved with anyone else.

'I'll be back for a few days every month. You'll have to come to one of our openings sometime,' she said vaguely, and he promised he would.

'I'll call you if I come to Paris. I have business there once in a while.' But he was looking for someone more geographically and emotionally accessible, and she knew she'd never hear from him. She didn't really care. He wished her luck, and the next morning, she took a cab to the airport. By nine o'clock she was in the air, and half an hour later, she was sound asleep. It had been a crisp sunny day in New York when she left, and when she arrived in Paris, it was bitter cold and pouring rain. Sometimes she forgot how depressing Paris winters could be. But she was glad to be there anyway. She went to sleep that night, in her bed in Paris, to the sound of the pouring rain.

When she awoke on Sunday morning, the fog was so low it was nearly sitting on the rooftops. It was cold and gray and the house was damp. And when she slipped into her bed that night, even her sheets felt uncomfortable, and she was chilled to the bone. Just for a moment, she missed the warm, cozy apartment in New York. What she realized as she tried to sleep was that wherever she went now, her miseries came with her. It didn't matter what city she lived in, or in which bed she slept. Wherever she was, in whatever country, or city, her bed was always empty, and she was alone.

Chapter 3

Sasha's life was busy in Paris in December. The gallery was doing a booming business. She met with many of their most important clients, who seemed to want to make important purchases, or sell part of their collections, before the end of the year. And she spoke to Xavier in London nearly every day. She had arranged a skiing trip for herself and both her children. They were leaving the day after Christmas for St. Moritz. She also had several important clients there.

Her social life in Paris was far more formal than it normally was in New York. Her clients in New York were successful but often more informal, and many of them had become friends over the years. The people she liked there were interesting and varied in their origins and lines of work. In Paris, there were certain social lines drawn that were more typical of Europe. Her major clients came from aristocratic, often titled, backgrounds, or fortunes that had been established for generations, like the Rothschilds, and others who entertained lavishly, many of whom had been her father's friends as well. The parties she was invited to were infinitely dressier and more elaborate than those she went to in New York, or did when Arthur was alive. And here the invitations were harder to turn down, since many of the people who invited her had bought important pieces of work from her. She felt obliged to go. She complained about it to Xavier, and he insisted it would do her good. But even at her age, she was often by far the youngest person in the room, and more often than not, she was bored. For business reasons, if no other, she went anyway. And was always happy to go home.

In mid-December, working in her office on yet another gray foggy day, her secretary told her that a client had come to see her.

She had met him at a dinner party the night before. He was interested in buying an important piece of Flemish work, and she was pleased that he had followed up on their conversation. She left her office to see him, and showed him several paintings that he seemed to like.

It was obvious to everyone except Sasha, in the course of his two-and-a-half-hour visit, that he liked the gallery owner as well. He invited her to dinner at Alain Ducasse the next day to discuss his eventual purchase with her. It was one of the finest restaurants in Paris, and she knew it would be a three- or four-hour meal, which she found boring and tedious. But she saw it as an opportunity to close a million-dollar sale. All she thought about now was work, except when she called Tatianna or Xavier.

'Maybe he's interested in more than just the painting, Mom,' Xavier teased her when she told him about the dinner she had accepted for the next day.

'Don't be silly, my father went to dinners like that with clients all the time. And believe me, no one was pursuing him.' Although she knew a few women had after her mother died. But she never saw her father show romantic interest in anyone. Like her, he had been faithful to his wife's memory till the end. Or at least, it was the impression he had given her. She had never discussed it with him. If there were women in his life over the years, he had been extremely discreet, but she doubted that there were.

'You never know,' Xavier said hopefully. Neither he nor his sister wanted her to wind up alone. 'You're a beautiful woman, and you're still young.'

'No, I'm not. I'm forty-eight years old.'

'Sounds young to me. One of my friends is going out with a woman older than you.'

'That's disgusting. That's child molestation,' she said, laughing at him. The idea of a younger man seemed ridiculous to her.

'You wouldn't say that if it were a man your age going out with a young woman.'

'That's different,' she said emphatically, and this time Xavier laughed at her.

'No, it's not. You're just used to seeing that. It makes just as much sense if the woman is older, going out with a younger man.'

'Are you telling me that your latest paramour is twice your age? If you are, I don't want to know about it.' And at least, Sasha knew if that was the case, the woman would be gone within a week. With Xavier they always were, whatever their age. Where women were concerned, he had the attention span of a flea.

'No, I haven't tried that yet, but I would if I met an older woman I liked and wanted to go out with. Don't be so stuffy, Mom.' She wasn't usually, in fact he loved how open-minded she always was about him. She was very French about those things, and never got upset about his active love life. She had been far more liberal than other people's mothers when he had gone to school in New York and had American friends. She had made a habit of buying condoms for him and all his friends, and leaving them in a giant mason jar in his room. She asked no questions, but kept the jar filled regularly. She preferred to be realistic about such things. In that sense, she was very French.

'I warn you, if you marry a woman twice your age, I'm not coming to the wedding, particularly if it's to one of my friends.'

'You never know. I just think you should keep an open mind for yourself.' He knew she hadn't dated yet. They were so open with each other that he knew she would tell him if she had.

'Maybe I should start hanging out at the local preschool, or hand out my phone number at the Lycée. I can adopt one of them, if I don't find a date.' She was laughing at him, and the utterly absurd and somewhat disgusting visual of herself with a young boy, or even a much younger man. She was used to being with someone older than she.

'When you want to find a date, Mom, you will,' Xavier said calmly.

'I don't want to,' she said firmly, the laughter fading from her voice. It was a subject she didn't want to explore with him, or anyone else.

'I know. But hopefully one of these days, you will.' His father had been gone for fourteen months, and he knew better than anyone how lonely she was. She called him night after night from home, and he could hear the sadness in her voice, whenever she wasn't at work. He hated to think of her that way. Tatianna was off in India and much less in touch with their mother than he. And he had the feeling that his mother spoke more openly to him. They had that special bond that sometimes exists between mothers and sons, as confidants and friends.

She told him she was going to New York for a board meeting the following week, and she was flying back the day before Christmas Eve.

He and Tatianna were due to arrive in Paris the afternoon of Christmas Eve. And the day after Christmas, they were off to St. Moritz. They were all looking forward to it. Her new prospective client had a house there, too. She hoped to have made the sale by then.

The following day her client came to pick her up for dinner, and took her to Alain Ducasse at the Plaza Athénée. She would far rather have had a simple but elegant dinner at Le Voltaire, but this was business, and she had to go where the client wanted.

It was easy to figure out that he was trying to impress her, but she had never been particularly fascinated by complicated, rich food, however many stars the chef had. Alain Ducasse had three.

Predictably, it was an astounding meal. The conversation had been interesting, and the sale seemed imminent as Gonzague de St. Mallory drove her home. He was charming, well educated, extremely rich, a count, and an enormous snob. Le Comte de St. Mallory. He had been married twice, had five children he spoke about and acknowledged, and three she knew he didn't. In matters of that nature, France was a small country, and Paris a small city. His affairs were legendary, his mistresses well taken care of, and his illegitimate children the talk of the town.

'I was thinking that I might like to try the painting in the house in St. Moritz, before I make a decision,' the count said pensively, as he drove her home in his Ferrari. A car like his was a rare sight in Paris, where large cars were inconvenient. Sasha drove a tiny Renault, which was easier to park and maneuver. She felt no need to show off with an expensive car in Paris, or anywhere else. 'Perhaps you could come and see it and tell me what you think,' he said as they pulled up in front of the *hôtel particulier* that housed the gallery, and her home.

'I could do that easily,' she said pleasantly.

'We can ship it to you in St. Moritz, and I'll be there with my children in two weeks.' He looked annoyed the moment she said it.

'I was thinking you could stay with me. Perhaps you'd like to take them there some other time.' Her children were easily dispensed with, as far as he was concerned. She didn't agree.

'I'm afraid that's not possible,' Sasha said clearly, looking him straight in the eye. 'We've planned this trip for a long time. And even if not, I'm looking forward to a holiday with my children.' She was trying to give him the message that he was barking up the wrong tree, regardless of her children. She had no intention of mixing business and pleasure, particularly not with him. He had an extremely racy reputation. He was fifty-four years old, and well known for carousing with young women.

'I assume you want to sell the painting,' Gonzague said just as clearly. 'I think you understand, Mademoiselle de Suvery.'

'I do, Monsieur le Comte. The painting is for sale. I'm not. Even for a million dollars. I'll be happy to come and look at it while I'm there,' she said, a little more gently. But by then, his eyes were blazing. They had both made themselves clear. And he didn't like what he was hearing. Women never said no to him, particularly not women Sasha's age. As far as he was concerned, he'd have been doing her a favor to sleep with her. She looked like a sad, lonely woman to him. But apparently not as lonely as he thought. And not desperate for a sale.

'There's no need to come and see it,' he said coldly. 'I've decided not to buy the painting after all. In fact, I have some serious concerns that it might be a fake.' As he said it, he got out of the car, and came around to open her door politely. She was already standing on the sidewalk, looking at him with fury, as he reached her side of the car.

'Thank you for a lovely dinner,' she said coolly. 'I had no idea, from your reputation, that you purchase women, and at such high prices. I would think that a man with your charm and intelligence would be able to get them for free. Thank you for a delightful evening.' And before he could say another word, she walked to the bronze door, let herself in with the code, and disappeared. Seconds later, she heard him race away. She was shaking with outrage as she let herself into her house. The bastard had tried to buy her along with the painting, and thought she was so hungry for the sale that she would sleep with him. It was beyond insulting. No one would ever have dared treat her that way when Arthur was alive. She was still shaking when she called Xavier and told him the story moments later. He positively crowed with glee when she told him what she had said to him at the end.

'You're fantastic, Mother. You're lucky he didn't run you down with the Ferrari when he left.'

'I'm sure he would have liked to. What a total rotter he is,' she said, and he laughed again.

'Yeah, I'd say. But you should be flattered. I hear he goes out with girls younger than Tatianna. He spends a lot of time at Annabel's over here.'

'I'm not surprised.' It was a private nightclub in London, frequented by all the most elegant people, as well as a lot of old men and much younger women. She and Arthur had been there many times. They were members of the club, as well as Harry's Bar, both of which were owned by the same man. 'How do men get away with behaving that way?'

'Some women love it. Most gallery owners would probably have slept with him to sell the painting.'

'Yes, and when they did, the next day the painting would come back anyway.' Her father had warned her about men like that when she came into the business. Gonzague de St. Mallory was anything but unique, and certainly ill mannered, as far as Sasha was concerned.

She was still fuming about it when she lay in bed that night. And the next morning she told her gallery manager that they would not be selling the painting to the count.

'Oh? I thought you were having dinner with him last night,' Bernard commented.

'I did. The count behaved very badly, and is lucky he didn't get slapped. Apparently, he was expecting to buy my services along with the painting. He thought I should stay with him in St. Moritz, and cancel my holiday with the children.'

'And you didn't accept?' Bernard pretended to be shocked. 'What bad salesmanship on your part, Sasha. My God, think of it, a million dollars. Have you no sense of responsibility to your father's business?' He loved to tease her. After fifteen years at the gallery, they were friends.

'Oh shut up, Bernard,' she said with a half smile, marched into her office, and went back to work. As far as Sasha was concerned, it was the most insulting offer she'd ever had. And the following week she told her manager about it in New York, who was genuinely shocked.

'Americans don't behave that way,' Karen said, staunchly defending her fellow countrymen.

'Some of them probably behave worse. I'm beginning to think it's about men, not nationalities, although admittedly the French might be a little bolder about things like that. But I'm sure it happens here as

94

well. Hasn't anyone ever implied that you should sleep with them in order to sell a painting?' Sasha sat back in her desk chair with a chuckle. It was finally beginning to seem funny. Karen, her New York gallery manager, thought about it for a minute, and then shook her head.

'I don't think so. Maybe I missed the point.'

'And what would you have done?' Sasha was playing with her now.

'I would have slept with him, and paid him the million dollars,' Marcie, her assistant, piped up. 'I saw him in a magazine. He's gorgeous, Sash.'

'Yes, he was,' Sasha admitted, looking unimpressed. She thought her late husband was far more handsome. She didn't like the overpolished, sleazy looks of the count. She preferred Arthur's far more clean-cut Gary Cooper appearance. Men like Gonzague de St. Mallory were a dime a dozen, with or without a Ferrari. She knew the type.

The three days Sasha spent in New York were busy and went quickly. She had a number of artists to see, big clients she had promised to have meetings with, and the board meeting that had brought her over. The first two nights she spent in her apartment, going through some of Arthur's things. She had promised herself she would put at least some of them away. It had taken her fourteen months, and her closets looked empty and sad when she had done it. But it was time.

On her last night she went to a Christmas party given by friends. There was something very bittersweet for her about being in New York before Christmas. It reminded her of when her children were small and she took them skating at Rockefeller Center, and of when Arthur was alive, two Christmases before. It was hard for her being there. She was glad to see her friends, but tired of explaining to them that there was no man in her life. It seemed to be the only question anyone asked her anymore. As though she didn't exist unless she was attached to a man. It made her feel like a failure, in an odd way, that her husband had died, and she was now alone. Watching all her married friends leave with each other made her feel like the only single species on Noah's ark. She was relieved to go back to Paris the next day, and excited that her children would be there the day after.

She had someone come in and cook Christmas goose for them on Christmas Eve, and she had decorated a tree, and put decorations around the house. She was thrilled to see Tatianna, whom she hadn't seen in two months. She looked well and happy and had had a wonderful time. She could hardly wait to show her mother the photographs. They were sorting through them, as Xavier told her about Gonzague.

'Mom nearly canceled our trip to St. Moritz' was his opening volley. Tatianna looked surprised. 'She was going to go without us, to a sell a million-dollar painting to a French count.'

'No, I wasn't, you rotten kid.' She told Tatianna the story then, who looked shocked that a Parisian playboy had tried to bed her mother, with the lure of his purchasing a million-dollar painting.

'That's disgusting, Mom,' Tatianna said with feeling, and sympathy for her mother. She could easily imagine how humiliating it must have been for her.

'No, it wasn't. I think she should be flattered,' Xavier added.

'You're a disgusting chauvinist,' Tatianna said, glaring at her brother. 'That's horrible for Mom.'

'All right, all right. You both win. I'll go and punch him out. Where does he live?' He turned to his mother and she laughed.

'I never should have told you. You'll never let me live it down.'

'Yes, I will. And by the way, I keep forgetting to tell you. Liam is finally sending you slides. He showed them to me. They're good,' he said proudly on behalf of his friend.

'I'm looking forward to seeing them.' She knew that sometimes Xavier had a good eye, and sometimes he tried to help his friends, at her expense. She was never sure which to expect, but it was worth a look. She had been hearing about the young American artist in London for ages. Far more about his adventures and escapades than his art.

'I think you'll be impressed by his work,' Xavier reassured her. Sasha nodded and didn't comment. She still hoped she wouldn't. He sounded like a handful to her.

'What's his last name again?' she asked vaguely.

'Liam Allison. He's from Vermont. But he's been living in London since he got out of college.'

'I'll remember the name. If I like the slides, I'll try to see him next time I come.' Once in a while, Xavier did some good scouting for her, and this might just be one of those times. She was always willing to look. It was why she had the reputation she did. Sasha had an adventuresome spirit, and an unfailing eye. But she also knew in advance that Liam was a loose cannon. It was an unavoidable conclusion after all the mischief Xavier had gotten into with him.

They went to midnight mass that night, and spent a cozy day together the next day. Tatianna had brought her mother a beautiful sari from India, and some lovely gold sandals to go with it. And Xavier had bought her a gold bracelet from an antique shop in London. It was the sort of thing his father would have given her and it warmed his heart to see her face light up when she put it on.

She looked at both of them when they went to bed on Christmas night, and smiled lovingly at both her children. 'I'm the luckiest woman in the world,' she said, and meant every word of it. For the first time in a long time, she knew she was.

Chapter 4

Sasha and her children had a wonderful time in St. Moritz, although they teased her mercilessly about Gonzague. They stayed at the Palace Hotel in opulent accommodations. She enjoyed spoiling them once in a while, particularly on vacations. She and Arthur always had. They felt fortunate to be able to, and the trips they had taken were memories they all cherished. St. Moritz that year was one of them.

She skied with the children some of the time, and the rest of the time on her own. Xavier was an outstanding skier, and Tatianna was as skilled as he, just a trifle more sensible and less daring. Both of them met people they went out with at night. And more often than not, Sasha ate dinner in her room alone. She didn't mind. She had brought several books with her, and she didn't want to be part of the nightlife. She was rested, happy, and relaxed, when they went back to Paris. Tatianna only stayed a few days, she wanted to get back to New York to find a job, and Xavier lingered a day or two after she left, and then went back to his studio in London. Before he left, his friend Liam Allison's slides arrived. And much to her surprise and chagrin, they were even better than Xavier had promised. Sasha was impressed, although in order to make a decision about representing him, she needed to see his paintings in the flesh.

'I'll try to come over next week, or maybe the week after,' she told Xavier, and meant it. But it was the last week in January when she finally went to London, to see three of her artists, and meet Liam. She fitted him into her schedule on her last afternoon in London, with some trepidation. The adventures and bad behavior Xavier had described to her did not make her anxious to represent him, but his talent was impossible to ignore. She felt she had to see him. And once in his studio, she was glad she'd come.

Liam let her into the studio himself with a look of anxiety, and a nervous smile. Xavier had accompanied her, and patted his friend on the shoulder to give him courage. He knew how anxious Liam was. Sasha seemed cool and businesslike when she walked in, and almost stern. She had worn black jeans and a black sweater, black boots, her hair looked almost as black as the sweater, and as she often did, she had pulled it tightly back and wound it into a bun. And even as small as she was, Liam thought she looked terrifying when he shook her hand. He knew that whatever she said, or thought, about his work would have an impact on his life forever. If she dismissed it as inadequate, or decided it wasn't worthy of being represented by her gallery, he would feel it almost like a physical blow. As he watched her cross the studio, he felt vulnerable and afraid. She thanked him politely for inviting her to come. He had no way of knowing, despite everything Xavier had said, that what appeared to be coolness to him was in fact that she herself was shy. What interested her was the art, even more than the person. But undeniably, Liam himself was hard to ignore. She had heard too many stories about him from her son. She knew what an outrageous, often badly behaved, person he was. The only mitigating factor, she hoped, was his wife and three children. She thought that he couldn't be totally irresponsible and without merit, if he had a wife and family. Xavier had never suggested that he was promiscuous, only that he was 'irrepressible' and a prankster of the first order, and he didn't like being told how to behave. He resisted any effort to modify his behavior, or expectation of his acting like a grown-up, as a form of 'control.' According to Xavier, he leaned heavily on the fact that he was an artist, and felt it gave him license not to live by anyone else's rules, and to do anything he wanted. It was a style she wasn't unfamiliar with, but she often found people like him hard to deal with. They worked when they wanted to, played when they didn't, and usually missed their deadlines for shows. Men like him wanted to be treated like children. Apparently, his wife was willing to do that. Sasha wasn't, no matter how handsome or charming he was. If he was serious about his work, to some extent at least, she expected him to act like an adult, or at least pretend to be one. Given all she'd heard, she wasn't at all sure that Liam was prepared to grow up. And in the end, charming or not, his work would have to speak for itself.

She walked slowly across the studio to where he had hung several large, bright paintings. There were three more smaller paintings set up on easels. Liam's work was stunning and powerful, his use of colors was strong, and the size of his larger canvases made the work even more so. She stood looking at his work for a long time, quietly nodding, while he held his breath. Xavier knew her silence was a good sign, but Liam didn't. Watching her concentrate silently on his work, Liam was dying. He was literally holding his breath when she turned to him finally, and said five words. 'It's fantastic. I want it.' Afterward, he admitted to her he nearly fainted with relief. Instead, he let out a war whoop of glee, grabbed her, spun her around, and swept her right off her feet, and was grinning at her when he finally set her down.

'Oh my God, I can't believe it... I love you! Oh my God! I thought you were going to tell me you hated it, and it was utter shit.'

'It's not shit.' She smiled at him, excited for him, and grateful to Xavier for finding Liam and telling her about him. 'It's brilliant. Your use of color absolutely makes my heart pound and my eyes water. We can't give you a show for almost a year though. We're overbooked as it is. I want you to open in New York, not Paris.' Paris openings were always quieter. She preferred doing openings of important contemporary work in New York. Xavier also knew that was a good sign, and promised himself to tell Liam later. He didn't want to give away all his mother's secrets while she was standing there. He was thrilled he had made the introduction. He too had been convinced that Liam's work was great, and was relieved and thrilled that his mother agreed.

'Oh my God,' Liam said again, sat down on the floor, and nearly cried. He had been working toward this for nearly twenty years, and now it had finally come. He was going to have a show at Suvery Gallery in New York. It was beyond belief. And Sasha herself was sitting in his studio, and loving his work. She was telling him that he would have to work hard to get ready for the show. 'What can I ever do to thank you?' He looked at her like a vision that had just materialized in his studio. He felt like a boy who had seen a virgin with a stigmata.

'Just paint me some good stuff. I brought a contract with me from Paris, just in case. You can show it to a lawyer if you like. There's no rush to get it back.' She never pressured anyone to sign.

'My ass there's no rush. What if you change your mind? Where is it? Just give it to me, I'll sign it.' He was practically flying. As she looked at him, he hardly looked older than her son.

She knew from the bio he had sent her with the slides that he was thirty-nine. Looking at him, she would never have believed it. He had studied with some very important artists, and had had a few minor shows at small galleries. But he looked like a kid. Everything about him seemed loose and free and young. He was tall, lanky, and handsome. He had straight blond hair that hung down his back most of the time. He had tied it in a ponytail to meet her. But his face was smooth and youthful. He had powerful shoulders, long graceful hands, and he bounced around his studio like a teenager in sneakers, blue jeans, and T-shirt, all covered with paint. He towered over her like an anxious child, as he begged her for the contract.

'It's at the hotel,' she told him reassuringly, suddenly sounding like a mother. Now that he was about to become one of her artists, she felt protective of him. 'I'll drop it off before I leave, or send it by messenger. I'm not going to change my mind, Liam. I never do that,' she said gently. Her voice was calm, and it touched her that he was so excited. He said this was one of the defining moments of his life. She didn't think it was, but she was happy it meant so much to him. That was what she loved best about showing emerging artists. She was able to give them a chance. She had always loved that about that side of the business, working with young artists like him. Although Xavier was right, he wasn't that young, but he looked it. Everything about him was boyish. He was only nine years younger than she was, but he acted about fourteen, and looked somewhere in his mid-twenties, not thirty-nine. He seemed no older than Xavier to her, and made her feel maternal toward, him. 'Do you want to show the contract to your wife?' The studio was such a mess it was obvious he didn't live there, and there was no sign of the wife and three children that Xavier had mentioned.

She imagined that they lived somewhere else, although his clothes seemed to be strewn everywhere, covered with paint. Obviously, his work clothes. She could only assume that there was a neater, cleaner place elsewhere where they all lived.

'She's in Vermont,' Liam said apologetically. 'I'll send her a copy after I sign it. She's not going to believe this,' he said, glancing at Xavier, and then his mother.

As Liam poured them each a glass of wine, all three of them looked happy. Sasha only took a sip, and Liam downed half of his in a minute. He was flying. He had been a real find for her. More than ever, it made her wish that Xavier would come into the business with her. Like her, he had a great eye for talent. They had both inherited it from her father. But Xavier wanted to live in London and be an artist, not a dealer in New York or Paris. Maybe they would open a gallery in London one day. For the first time in years, she thought about expanding. But Xavier was still too young to take on that responsibility. Maybe one day. He had just turned twenty-five, although she had come into the business only a year later, at twenty-six, under the tutelage of her father. 'Can I take you both out to dinner?' Liam asked them hopefully. 'I want to celebrate.' He looked like he was about to explode with excitement, and he damn near did.

106

'I'd love to, but...' Xavier said mischievously, and Sasha knew what that meant. God forbid dinner with an artist and his mother should interfere with his love life. He was definitely not ready for the business. At his age, she had been married, working at the Met, and had two children. Xavier was a long way from there.

Sasha hesitated for a moment. She had hoped to have dinner with Xavier that night, and didn't know he had other plans. But that was typical of her son. She turned to Liam. 'Why don't I take you out to dinner, Liam. I'm your dealer now, you don't need to invite me. We can get to know each other,' she said kindly. He saw a warmth in her he hadn't seen at first. There was a quiet shyness and stability he liked. Everything about Sasha seemed reliable and solid, and he liked her. At first, he had been terrified of her. But beneath the cool, professional exterior, he sensed that she was warm. Her reputation daunted him, but her persona didn't.

She wondered if he owned a suit. Most of her young artists didn't. And Liam looked no different. In fact he looked a lot worse than some, although he was good looking. He was very handsome, a very striking-looking man.

'I'd love it. I can sign the contract over dinner,' he said with a grin that had dazzled many.

'You should read it first,' she scolded him. 'You have to make sure you're comfortable with it. Don't just sign it without at least reading it, or even showing it to an attorney.'

'I would sell myself into slavery for you, or give you my left nut if you wanted it,' he said bluntly, as Sasha blinked. But she was used to that kind of statement from her artists.

'Actually, that won't be necessary,' Sasha said primly. 'As I recall, testicles are not in our contract. You can keep them both. I'm sure your wife will be relieved.' He smiled at her and didn't answer. And as she looked at him, she was reminded of a beautiful young boy. He was lovely to look at, and despite the boyish appearance and mannerisms, he was an extremely talented man.

'Where would you like to have dinner?' She had been thinking of Harry's Bar with Xavier, but her son was a different breed entirely, he had the right clothes to wear, and knew how to behave. She doubted that Liam had either manners or better clothes than the ones he had on. He was, after all, a starving artist, although if she had anything to do with it, he wouldn't be for long. She thought he was going to be a sensation in New York, and eventually, in Paris. Liam was a real find, that rare commodity of someone with gigantic talent who actually produced great work.

'I'd like to get dressed up and take you out

to thank you,' he said humbly, and it touched her heart.

'How dressed up?' She looked him over with a motherly air. He brought out the mother in her. Everything about him made one feel he was a boy and not a man. All she wanted suddenly was to protect and help him. She was excited about working with him, and launching him on a major career. He was a major discovery for her. It was an important moment not only for him, but for Sasha as well.

'I have a suit and two good shirts. One of them is clean. I think I used the other one to wax my car.' He looked at her sheepishly and she laughed. There was something impish and irresistible about him. He reminded her of Xavier when he was about fourteen, and struggling to become a man. Xavier had become one. Liam hadn't yet.

'Then let's go to Harry's Bar,' she said simply. She loved having dinner there. It was her favorite restaurant in London.

'Holy shit. I can't believe this is happening to me. Can you?' He turned to Xavier with a grin, who smiled happily at his friend. This had turned out even better than he'd hoped. He was thrilled for Liam, and grateful to his mother for giving him a chance.

'Yes, I can,' Xavier said simply.

'Man, I owe you big time.' And with that, Liam slapped him a high five. They looked like two boys in a clubhouse to Sasha, and she just hoped he behaved at Harry's Bar that night. You couldn't always tell with artists, which was why she rarely took them there. But she decided to take a chance on Liam. There was something innocent and enchanting about him, and if he got out of line, or loud and boisterous, she would tell him to behave. Her artists were like children to her, sometimes even the old ones. She felt like their surrogate mother, which was a lot of work, but it was part of what she loved about her job. The artists were her little chicks, and she the mother hen. And although she wasn't that much older than he, Liam looked like he needed a mother, like Peter Pan.

'Let's have dinner at eight. I'll have my driver pick you up at seven-thirty, and you can pick me up at the hotel. I'll be downstairs,' she said as she and Xavier left.

'Don't forget to bring the contract,' he reminded her as they started down the stairs.

It had been a productive afternoon for both of them, and Liam was excited about dinner. He wanted to talk to her about the show, and the amount of work she wanted. He was willing to work like a galley slave for the next year to produce the best work he'd ever done. He wasn't going to let her down. This was his big chance, and Liam knew it. He had worked all his life for this moment.

110

And however badly he allowed himself to behave in his private life, or on his evenings out with Xavier, Liam had always been serious about his work. He had known from his childhood that he had been born to paint. It had set him apart and isolated him even as a child, and later as a teenager and young man. He had always known he was different, and didn't really mind. His mother had always encouraged him, and told him he had to follow his dreams. The rest of his family hadn't been nearly as enthused, and even his own father had treated him like a freak. It had created a chasm between them forever. It was as though only his mother was able to see his special genius. The others, his father, brothers, and even their friends, had just thought he was weird, and his early paintings meant nothing to them. His father called them junk, and his brothers referred to them as scribbles. They shut him out from everything they did, and in his isolation, he had sought solace in painting. Like all people who had suffered early on, Liam was much deeper than he looked. Sasha didn't know that yet, but she sensed it. All of the artists she knew had had some private grief or hell to live through. In the end, it made their lives more painful perhaps, but strengthened their work and commitment to art. Losing her own mother as a child gave her greater compassion for them, and made her more in tune with their sufferings. She understood, better even than she knew sometimes. It was as though there were an unspoken harmony between them.

'I thought you'd like his work,' Xavier said in the car, looking pleased. 'He's got a lot of talent,' he said proudly of his friend.

'Yes, he does.' She felt totally confident, and thrilled that Xavier had found him. She was very proud of her son for his discerning eye.

'He's a nice guy, too,' Xavier reassured her. 'He's kind and decent and honest. He loves his wife and kids. Even if he acts a little crazy sometimes, he's a good man. He's wild, but harmless.'

'It's too bad she's in Vermont. I would have liked to meet her. Who people are married to can tell you a lot about them,' Sasha said quietly, and for a moment Xavier didn't comment.

'She's terrific. They've been married forever. She's been in Vermont for a while.'

'What does that mean?' Sasha looked at her son with a question in her eyes. 'Are they still married, or did she leave him?'

'I think the answer is yes to both. They're still married, and I think they're taking a break or something. He doesn't talk about it. She goes home to Vermont, to visit her parents, every summer. And this year she didn't come back in September. He said she

112

wanted to stay there for a few months. She's been gone since July. He's a great guy, but I don't think he's easy to live with. She put him through school working as a maid in summer and winter resorts. She worked as a secretary here. She pretty much supports him and the kids, and she puts up with all his crazy artist bullshit. I don't think he'd ever divorce her, but I don't think it's been easy for her with all five of them to support. I hope she comes back. She's a good woman, and I know he loves her.'

'Maybe we can make a difference for him now,' Sasha said. It was an old familiar story. Most of her artists drove their spouses insane, and painted while others supported their talent. Theirs wasn't the first marriage that had been strained, or even sacrificed, for the sake of art. She'd heard it all before. 'I could give him a small advance if it would make a difference. I'll see what he says at dinner. Maybe that would help him out with her.'

'It would probably mean a lot. The timing is pretty good for him. His oldest boy is going to college next year. He'll need the money.'

'Hopefully, we'll make him a lot of it. But it doesn't happen overnight.' Although they both knew that sometimes it did. After what Xavier had just told her, she hoped that it would happen that way for him. His family surely deserved it as much as he did. Particularly with a boy going to college. Liam didn't look old enough to have a child in his late teens. He seemed like a teenager himself.

Xavier hugged his mother then, and promised to have breakfast with her the next morning. They agreed to meet at ten, as she knew she'd have business calls to make in the morning. She was planning to leave for the airport at noon, and she wanted to spend her last few hours in London with him.

'Behave yourself tonight,' she said with a mock serious tone, issuing a motherly warning, and he laughed as he walked away. At least this time Liam wouldn't be with him, Sasha thought to herself. But now that she had met Liam, she was less worried about his influence on Xavier. And she suspected Xavier was right. Liam seemed juvenile, and immature perhaps, but harmless.

'See you in the morning!' Xavier waved, got into his car, and a moment later he drove away, pleased with himself. They had done good work that afternoon. Liam was off and running. His fledgling career had just taken a dramatic upward turn.

Chapter 5

Sasha's car and driver picked Liam up at precisely seven-thirty, and came to pick Sasha up at Claridge's at seven forty-five. As promised, she was waiting downstairs, and slipped into the car next to Liam when they arrived. He was wearing a decent-looking black suit, and a red shirt he had painted himself that had once been white. He had forgotten that was what he had done with his other good shirt, the one he had not used to wax his car. He painted it one night when he was drunk, and thought it was funny. Now, as he had discovered that night, it was the only shirt he had. He hoped Sasha liked it. She didn't, but didn't comment. He was an artist. So was her son, and if he had worn something like it to Harry's Bar, she would have killed him. But Liam was not her son.

Without appearing to, she glanced at his shoes, which were almost respectable, but not quite. They were serious, grown-up black shoes, meant to have laces, and for some obscure reason, he had thrown the laces out. He realized while he dressed that he had probably used them for something, maybe to wrap a package he had sent somewhere, but he could no longer remember what. He thought the shoes looked better without laces anyway, and he preferred them that way. He was clean shaven, freshly showered, smelled delicious, and had impeccably clean hair, tied with a plain black ribbon he had wound around the rubber band on his long blond ponytail. He looked handsome and immaculate, and except for the shirt and absence of laces in his shoes, he would have looked respectable, but he was an artist after all. Liam didn't follow the rules, and never had. He saw no reason to follow anyone else's rules but his own, which was partly why his wife had stayed in Vermont, and hadn't seen him since July. In spite of the painted red shirt and ponytail, there was something distinctly handsome and aristocratic about him. He was a beautiful man, and a man of contrasts. In another lifetime or profession, he could have been an actor or a model, a lawyer or a banker, but the shirt he had painted red said that he was not only an artist but a rebellious child. It said, 'Look at me. I can do anything I want. And there isn't a damn thing you can do about it.'

'Do I look all right?' he asked Sasha nervously, and she nodded. She didn't want to hurt his feelings, and the shirt was, after all, a work of art. She didn't notice the lack of shoelaces, until they were standing in

Harry's Bar. And as he hopped onto a stool at the bar, she saw that he wasn't wearing socks either. The headwaiter knew her well, and without saying a word, he handed Liam a long black tie, which actually looked fine with his shirt, once he put it on. She helped him tie it, as she had for Xavier when he was a child. Liam said he hadn't worn a tie in years and had forgotten how to tie one. He looked completely unconcerned. The fact that everyone else in the room was exquisitely dressed, the men in beautifully tailored suits and shirts custom made in Paris, the women in cocktail dresses by important designers, didn't bother him at all. One thing Liam didn't lack was confidence, except where Sasha was concerned. He wanted to impress her, and was not at all sure how. She looked so capable and confident, so quietly poised as she chatted with him, that he suddenly felt like the innocent he was. She treated him like a child. She told him he looked fine when he asked, and she walked into the restaurant proudly beside him, and acted as though every man in the place should have looked like that. It made Liam almost giddy to walk beside her, and he felt like Picasso when he sat down.

He had already asked her about the contract twice in the car. To spare his nerves and her own, she handed it to him at the table. He signed it without looking at it, despite her warnings to do otherwise, and then he beamed at her. He was a Suvery artist now. It was all he had wanted and dreamed of for the past ten years of his life. It had finally happened, and he was going to savor every moment of it. He knew this was a night he would never forget, nor would Sasha. She suspected that one day they would laugh about this evening, when he had walked into Harry's Bar in a shirt he had painted himself. Despite his youth and zany looks, there was an aura of greatness about him.

After he drank a martini at the bar, she ordered champagne for them, and toasted him, and then he toasted her. She drank two glasses. Then, without batting an eye, Liam finished the rest. By then, he had told her that he was the black sheep of his family. His father was a banker and lived in San Francisco, his two brothers were a doctor and a lawyer, and they had both married debutantes. Liam said he had always been different right from the start. His brothers had tormented him by telling him he was adopted, which he wasn't. But right from the beginning, he'd been different. He hated all the things they loved, hated sports, didn't do well in school, while they were brilliant students. They were both captains of the varsity teams they played on, in football, basketball, and hockey. Instead, he had sat alone in his room, painting. And they teased him cruelly, by throwing away his paintings. Liam told Sasha that his father had let him know early on that he was a severe disappointment and an embarrassment to them. For a brief nightmarish year, to punish him for bad grades, he had been sent to military school. He had snuck into the cafeteria one night, and painted caricatures of all the teachers on the wall, some of them pornographic, which had been his clever plan to get expelled, which, he told Sasha with a broad grin, had been very effective. And once he got home, the torture at the hands of his family continued. Finally, not knowing what else to do with him, they ignored him completely. They acted as though he didn't exist, forgot to call him to dinner at night, and didn't bother to speak to him when he was in the same room with them. He became a nonperson in his own family, and eventually a total outcast. The worse they treated him, the worse he got, and the more he misbehaved. Since he didn't fit in, or comply with their rules and plans for him, they completely shut him out. More than once, he had heard his father say he had two sons, instead of three. Liam didn't conform to the way his family did things, so they shunned him. And eventually, he acted out his outcast role in school as well. He was called on to paint scenery for the drama club, or if they needed posters or signs. But the rest of the time, no one paid any attention to him, in school or at home. The other students referred to him as 'the wacky artist,' which had been a deep insult at first, and then he decided that he liked it, and played it to the hilt. Sometimes, as a teenager, he wondered if he was insane.

'I figured out that if I let myself be just what they said I was, a wacky artist, I could do anything I wanted, so I did. I did whatever I felt like.' And eventually, since he never bothered to study, he got expelled from one school after another. He had dropped out of school finally in his senior year, and never bothered to graduate, until his wife forced him to get his diploma once they were married. But school had meant nothing to him. It was just a place where he was tortured for being different. According to Liam, no one except his mother had ever recognized or cared that he had talent. Art was not an acceptable occupation in his family. Only sports and academics mattered, and he didn't qualify in either, or even attempt to. Sasha wondered if he had had an undetected learning disability to be so resistant to school. Many of her artists did, and it had been a source of deep unhappiness for them, compensated for by their artistic talent. But she didn't know Liam well enough to ask him, so she didn't, and just listened to his story with compassion and interest.

He insisted that he had known he wanted to be an artist from the moment he came out of the womb. Once on Christmas morning, before everyone got up, he had painted a mural in their living room, and after that he painted the grand piano and the couch. The shirt was obviously just a more recent version of the same form of art. He had been seven on that fateful morning, and couldn't understand why no one liked or appreciated what he'd done. His father had spanked him, and in a somewhat disconnected but emotional recital, he explained that after that, his mother had gotten very sick. She died the following summer, and from then on, his life was a nightmare. His only protector, and the only person who loved and accepted him, had vanished. Some nights, they didn't even bother to feed him. It was as though he had died with her. And art became his only comfort, and outlet, his only remaining bond with her, since she loved all that he did. He told Sasha that for years and sometimes even now, he felt as though he was painting for his mother. There were tears in his eyes when he said it. Everyone else in his family acted as though he was crazy, and still did. He said he hadn't seen his father and brothers in years.

He had met his wife, Beth, during a ski trip to Vermont, after he left home at eighteen and was painting in New York. He had married her at nineteen, when he was painting and starving in Greenwich Village. She had worked like a dog, according to Liam, and supported him ever since, much to her family's chagrin. They were as conservative as his family and didn't like him either. They hated him for his lack of responsibility and inability to support their daughter. He and Beth had three children, two boys who were seventeen and eleven, and a little girl who was five. They were the light of his life, and so was Beth, until she went back to Vermont, to her family, the previous July.

'Do you think she'll come back?' Sasha asked with a look of concern. There was something so gentle and vulnerable about him that it made her want to put her arms around him and fix everything for him. But she knew from experience with other artists that the messes they created in their lives were often damn near impossible to fix. His relationship with his family sounded as though it was beyond salvation, and probably not even worth trying. But it tugged at her heart when she listened to him talk about the lonely childhood he'd had and then about his wife and kids. He seemed lost without them, and Sasha sensed much left unsaid. Liam looked at her honestly in answer to her question about Beth returning, hesitated for a moment, and then shook his head.

'Probably not.' He sounded convinced. He believed now that Beth was gone forever.

'Maybe when she knows things are looking up for you financially, that might make a difference.' For some reason she couldn't fathom, for Liam's sake, she wanted Beth to come back. Sasha wasn't as sure Liam did. He looked sad about their separation but seemed to accept it as inevitable. They had been married for twenty years, and it obviously hadn't been easy. Mostly for her. He looked like a man who had committed a crime, felt deep remorse, but knew he couldn't change it.

'That wasn't the problem. The finances, I mean.' He seemed to be clear about that, and Sasha couldn't help wondering what the problem had been. They were eating their pasta by then, with a very good French Bordeaux.

'What was?' Maybe the kids had put too much strain on them. Sasha wondered if it was that. Or simply the inevitable grind of time.

'I slept with her sister in June.' He looked sad and sounded hoarse as he said it, and in spite of her best efforts not to, Sasha looked shocked. If nothing else, it was incredibly stupid, to betray a woman who had held down countless jobs to support him and their three children for twenty years. And Xavier had said she was a nice woman. Maybe Liam wasn't such a nice guy. His confession was certainly an indication of that.

'Why did you do that?' she asked him as one would a child.

'We got incredibly drunk while Beth and the kids were away for the weekend. I told her when she got back. I figured Becky would. They're twins.'

'Identical?' Sasha found the story fascinating but pathetic, and she got sucked into the drama with him, as he told it. Just as she had with the stories about his parents and brothers. She wasn't even sure why yet, or if he deserved it, but she liked him. And wanted to help him. But she was horrified by his betrayal of his wife. To Sasha, it spoke of a lack of moral fiber that upset her a great deal. But there was also a childlike innocence about him that made one want to forgive him, no matter how serious the crime.

'They're not identical, but close enough. Becky has been after my ass for years. The next morning, I couldn't believe I did it, but I did.' He looked as though he were going to cry as he said it. And when he told Beth, he had.

'Are you an alcoholic?' Sasha asked him somewhat sternly. He was certainly doing a good job on the wine, but he didn't seem drunk to her.

'No. Just stupid. Beth and I have been fighting a lot for the last year. She wanted

124

me to go out and get a job. She was sick of working and starving for art. And her parents kept telling her to leave me and come home. Her father is a carpenter, and her mother is a teacher. They think my art is shit. I was beginning to think so, too. Until today.' He smiled at Sasha gratefully. He was hard to resist. Even after hearing his confession of adultery, it was hard to be angry at him. He was right. It was just plain stupid. And in spite of it, there was something innocent and likable about him. She couldn't explain it rationally, she felt drawn to him as a person, and even as a man.

'What does Becky do?' she asked, sounding suspicious.

'She's a bartender in a ski resort. She makes a hell of a lot of money, and screws a hell of a lot of guys. She's always wanted me. And maybe I wanted her, too. I don't know. Twenty years is a long time with one woman. I was a virgin when I married Beth, and I never cheated on her till now.' But even he knew it was wrong. 'There's no decent excuse,' he said to Sasha honestly. 'It was a rotten thing to do.'

'Don't you think eventually she'll forgive you?' For his sake, Sasha was hoping she would. He was a decent, ingenuous guy, who had only made one mistake, although admittedly a big one, in twenty years. And supporting all five of them single-handedly

125

couldn't have been fun for Beth.

'I don't think she'll ever forgive me. She's been jealous of Becky all her life. Becky always gets the guys. And Beth got me, three kids, and a lot of work. I've never made a decent living. Beth supported us all these years, and believed in me the whole time. Until I slept with Becky. I called her and the kids at Christmas, and she said she's filing for divorce. I can't blame her. She's had it with me. At least I'll be able to send her some money now. She deserves it after all these years.' He was a decent guy, just somewhat disconnected from reality, maybe even because he was artistic. She had heard much worse stories before his. But the way his marriage had ended saddened her for both of them. It was a terrible waste, and a shame. Everyone was paying the price for his mistake.

'How long has it been since you saw your kids?'

'Not since she left. I couldn't afford to fly back. And her parents would probably kill me. Her father is pretty pissed.'

'She told him what happened?'

'No. Becky did. She hates me too. She wanted me to leave Beth and marry her. She said she's always been in love with me. Some weird shit happens sometimes with twins. Or at least it did with them. Beth says that Becky has resented her all her life. She's

126

a gorgeous woman, and no guy has ever wanted to marry her. She got pregnant at fifteen and her parents made her give the baby up for adoption. I think it screwed up her head. She tried to find him when he turned eighteen, about six years ago, and she found out he had died about two years before in a head-on collision. She's a mess. I think she blames herself. Maybe she hates Beth because she has three terrific kids. I don't know. It's pretty complicated stuff.'

'It sounds like it. Sounds like you walked into a minefield with her last June.'

'I know I did. Beth says Becky set me up. She's been waiting twenty years to do it. Three bottles of cheap white wine, and I blew twenty years of marriage with the most decent woman in the world.'

'Why don't you fly to Vermont and talk to her? I can give you an advance, Liam. I was going to anyway.' He looked like he needed it, even before she knew he hadn't seen his children in six months.

'It's too late,' Liam said simply. 'She got back with her high school sweetheart. She says they're getting married as soon as our divorce comes through. His wife died last year and left him with four kids. He has some money, he runs a ski resort, and he's willing to support Beth and my kids. Sounds like a better deal to me than being married to a wacky artist. She seems to think so too.'

He seemed unhappy, but was philosophical about it.

'Are you a wacky artist, Liam?' Sasha asked gently. In some ways, he seemed like it, in others he didn't. Most of all, he seemed immature, but kind. It was incredible to think that a man as good looking as he was had only slept with one woman in his life, other than a one-night stand with his wife's twin. There was a sordid side to it, but he seemed like a nice guy, and Xavier said he was. She trusted him. And all of Sasha's instincts told her Liam was a good person. Foolish and immature perhaps, but at the core, a good man.

'Sometimes I am a wacky artist,' he answered. 'Sometimes I just want to be a kid. How much harm is there in that?'

'I guess that depends on who gets hurt. Beth did, in this case. And your kids. And it sounds like you did too. But Becky is hardly without blame here.'

'She doesn't give a damn about anyone but herself. She never did.'

'Apparently.' Sasha fell silent, thinking about it, and then realized Liam was watching her.

'What about you? Xavier thinks the sun rises and sets on you. He's crazy about you. That's rare for a kid his age to feel that way about his mother. And talking to you, I think he's right. He is lucky to have such a loving mother.' Liam had had one too, but lost her too soon.

'I'm crazy about him, too. He's a terrific kid. So is his sister. I'm a very lucky woman.' Sasha smiled at Liam.

'Maybe not so lucky. I know your husband died last year,' he said, sounding sympathetic.

'Yes, he did,' she said calmly, but her eyes filled with tears, which embarrassed her. Her sorrows were not Liam's problem, and she didn't want to burden him with them, or share her grief. 'He died fifteen months ago. We were married for twenty-five years.' And he had been the only man in her life too. They had that in common, as well as losing their mothers when they were children, and all the inevitable emotional fallout of that which had impacted both of them severely.

'Being a widow must be hard for you,' he said, looking sympathetic, as they finished their pasta, and he gazed at her with gentle eyes.

'It is. It's better than it was in the beginning, but it's very hard some days.' He nodded, as though he understood. He had lost Beth through his own stupidity, and one fatal mistake. She had lost Arthur to fate. 'But you go on. You have no other choice. My work helps.'

'You can't curl up with your paintings at night. Have you gone out with anyone?' It wasn't his business, but she decided to answer him anyway. She didn't want him to know how vulnerable and lonely she was. If she was going to represent him, she had to appear strong to him, or so she thought.

'No, I haven't. What about you?' She was curious about him. As he was about her. After all he'd told her about his family and marriage, there was a connection between them, beyond what she had expected, and almost surely beyond what she wanted. For the first time with one of her artists, she realized she was attracted to him, and there was absolutely no way she would allow herself to indulge it. They could open up to each other over dinner. They were two lonely people who had suffered major losses in their childhoods, and had lost their childhoods as a result, and had lost people they loved in their adult lives too, but she would never allow the bond between them to go further than that. She had no intention of acting on her attraction to him. She was far too self-disciplined and sensible for that. Nor would she allow him to indulge his feelings for her, if he had any, which seemed unlikely to her.

'I went out with a couple of people,' Liam admitted. 'Xavier introduced me to them.' He smiled at his friend's mother, who was now his dealer. The connection between them seemed funny, even to him. 'I just couldn't go there. They were just kids. And what was the point? I was still too upset over

Beth. It was last summer, right after she left. I haven't been out with anyone since. I guess now that I know she's getting married, it's different. But I haven't seen anyone I want. Most of the women who are willing to hang out with artists are pretty wacky themselves.' He smiled as he said it, and looked suddenly more grown up. 'What about you? What do you want?'

'Nothing. I don't want to be one of those pathetic women who are desperate to find a husband. And I think dating at my age is disgusting. It seems so humiliating and awful.'

'Not if you find the right guy,' he said gently, and she shook her head.

'I already did. He died. That's it for me.'

'That's so stupid,' he said, looking angry. 'You're too young to give up like that. And too beautiful. How old are you?' He figured her for forty-five at most, because he knew Xavier's age. Maybe two years younger, if she had married at eighteen.

'I'm forty-eight. That's old enough to quit. I had twenty-five great years.'

'And you could live another fifty. Do you want to spend them alone?' He looked horrified by the idea. She didn't. She had accepted what she believed was her inevitable solitude long since.

'No. I wanted to spend the rest of my life with him. And I would have, if he'd lived. I don't have that choice now. And the other options don't appeal to me. I don't think they ever will. It seems more dignified to give that up than to run around looking for just anyone to fit the bill.'

'He must have been a great guy, if you loved him that much.' Liam was even more impressed after talking to her over dinner. She was an amazing woman, and he genuinely liked and respected her.

'He was wonderful,' she said sadly. 'We were crazy about each other. It was just very, very bad luck that he died.'

'It sounds like it. But he died, Sasha. You didn't. If you had died, and he didn't, he probably would have found someone else too. We all need someone to love. Life's just too damn hard to be alone.' The last six months without Beth and the kids had been hell for him.

'I'm not so sure it's much easier if you wind up with the wrong person. Like Becky. I got it right the first time. I don't think I could ever be that lucky again. Why take the chance?' she said wistfully.

'Because you might get lucky again. You're a good person. You deserve it. It wouldn't be the same. It would be different. But different isn't always such a bad thing.'

'I can't imagine myself dating,' she said honestly, as the waitress set three small bowls of candy down in front of them, and a plate of cookies. 'Just the little I've seen of it looks terrifying to me.'

'Yeah, it does to me too.' He laughed then, at the absurdity of their situation. 'I do the same thing you do. I get lost in my work. I haven't stopped painting since she left.'

'It works for me.' Sasha smiled, and as long as there were talented artists like Liam, what she did would keep working. 'It's hard now that the kids are gone. At least in Paris, I'm close to Xavier, and I go to New York a lot. But it gets to me at night,' she confessed, and he nodded.

'It gets to me then too. And I miss the kids like crazy. I figure they're better off without me right now, and they have Beth's future husband. She says he's a great guy, and a good father. Probably better than I am. They're a lot better off with Beth than with me. He's more respectable than I am, and more traditional. Beth says that's good for them. There's nothing wacky about him.' He sounded humble and defeated as he said it. He had lost not only his wife, but his kids.

'You're their father, Liam. You can't abandon them. You should go to see them soon.'

'Yeah,' he said vaguely, 'I will.' But he didn't sound convinced, which disturbed her.

She had called the restaurant earlier and asked them not to present a bill. She didn't want to embarrass Liam. And after they ate the candy and had coffee, they walked outside and got back in her car. She told the driver to take her back to the hotel, and then drop Liam off at his place. But once they got back to the hotel, he told her he could take a cab from there. He asked her if she wanted to have a drink, and she really didn't. They had had enough champagne and wine. She rarely drank.

'I'll walk you to your room, and then I'll leave,' he said reassuringly. She had enjoyed his company all evening, and it was nice having someone take her home. She could feel the familiar loneliness creeping up on her, and he could feel it too. Nights were agony for lonely people, which they both were. And then she smiled as she looked down at his shoes as they walked up the stairs, and she noticed the absence of socks again. She couldn't resist teasing him about it, now that she knew him a little better. 'I couldn't find any,' he said, looking unembarrassed. 'Besides, I'm an artist. I don't have to wear socks.' He said it with a defiant look and she laughed.

'Who made that rule?' she asked him.

'I did,' he said proudly. 'I'm a wacky artist. I can do anything I want.' When he said it, he looked about five years old, and she could see a lifetime of mischief in his eyes. He was severely allergic to all forms of authority and control, as he perceived it.

'No, you can't do whatever you want. We

all have to follow rules.' She felt like a schoolteacher as she said it, and he laughed at her.

'Is there a rule about socks?'

'Absolutely.' As she said it, she was thinking about sending him a box of socks and shirts. He obviously needed them, and maybe shoelaces too. She wondered if he'd wear them. Probably not. He obviously loved being unconventional and making his own rules. And then she wondered if he didn't wear underwear either, and blushed at the thought.

'What were you thinking?' He had seen the look on her face.

'Nothing.' She looked embarrassed.

'Yes, you were. You were wondering if I wear underwear, weren't you?' He had guessed, and she blushed again.

'No, I wasn't.' She giggled as she lied.

'Yes, you were. Well, I do. Or at least I am. I managed to find those.'

'That's reassuring,' she said grandly, and he laughed at her again.

'Was that in the contract I signed? That I have to wear underwear and socks? Because if it is, then I'm going to tear it up. No one can tell me what to wear, or what to do.' It was classic teenage rebellion. Liam Allison had major control issues, or so it seemed. He had been swimming upstream all his life, fighting convention, and breaking rules.

135

'Actually, I think it is in the contract, now that you mention it.' She was teasing him right back, and enjoying it quite a lot. They had reached her door by then.

'No, it's not,' he said, looking stubborn and petulant. Like a naughty child.

'Yes, it is,' she said firmly. 'It says that hereafter you have to wear underwear and socks at all times.'

'You can't make me!' he said loudly.

'Yes, I can,' she said, looking prim but firm, and then he grinned as he looked at her, and much to her surprise he bent down and kissed her and silenced her. She had the key in her hand, and dropped it and her handbag in her amazement at being kissed. After they did, she stood looking up at him. 'Why did you do that, Liam?' she said softly, horrified by the fact that she had liked kissing him. A lot, in fact. Too much. Way, way too much. He picked up the key then, and gently pushed open the door to her room. He stood looking at her, and without saying a word, she walked into the room and he followed. Within seconds, two feet into the room, he was kissing her again, and pushed the door closed with his foot. She was overwhelmed by the conflicting sensations she felt.

She wanted to stop him. She meant to. She had every intention of stopping him, but she couldn't. The worst of it was that she didn't want to stop, and neither did he. He just went on kissing her until he picked her up in his arms, and put her gently on the bed. There was one light on in the room, and he reached over and turned it off. He said nothing to her. He kissed her and undressed her, and a moment later they were in bed together, naked, and making love, before she knew how it had happened. She wanted to stop him, but she couldn't. She didn't want to stop him. She wanted to do exactly what they were doing, and so did he. They were two starving people who had found each other and couldn't let go. The pull between them was too powerful to resist. And although very different in lifestyles and appearances, they both sensed that they were kindred spirits, and soul mates of some kind. They needed each other in their respective loneliness, and clung to each other until they lay exhausted and breathless in each other's arms. She lay looking at him in the darkness, stunned at what they'd done, and he smiled at her with the gentleness of a very loving man.

'I think I'm in love with you,' he said softly, and she felt tears sting her eyes as he said it. She thought she would never hear those words again, and now he was saying them to her, and she didn't even know him, nor he her. Yet in her heart, she sensed that she knew him. She could sense the loneliness of his childhood and his vulnerability as a man.

'That's impossible. You don't know me,'

she said softly, as the tears rolled slowly down her cheeks. They were tears for Arthur, and for Liam, and finally for herself.

'It is possible, and I do know you. And I want to know you better.' He had told her a lot about himself that night, and wanted to learn more about her.

'This is crazy, Liam.' She propped herself up on one elbow, and looked down at him, as he gently brushed the tears off her cheek in the moonlight. Everything he did seemed tender, loving, and kind.

'Maybe it is crazy,' he admitted. 'But maybe it's what we both need. I know I do. And I think you do, too.'

'What, sex?' She sounded insulted. She wasn't going to be his one-night stand like Becky. Besides, this was ridiculous. She was his art dealer, not his girlfriend. They had been total strangers until today, and still were. What was happening to her? She felt totally adrift in an unfamiliar sea, swept toward him by a current that was much stronger than she was, and that she couldn't resist.

'This isn't about sex, Sasha. You know that, too. Or not just about sex. Although that was pretty good.' In fact, it had been terrific. Remarkably so, considering they were virtually strangers. It had been incredible for both of them.

'It can't be about love. We don't even

know each other.'

'I hope we will,' he said gently. Above all he appeared to be a kind person, and an incredibly attractive man. Too much so for his own good, and hers. She was viscerally drawn to him, and realized now she had been from the moment they met. She had tried to ignore it, but couldn't.

'This is impossible,' she said again. 'I'm your art dealer, and I'm nine years older than you are.'

'So what? Do you have rules about that, too?'

He looked unimpressed by the difference in their age, which seemed unimportant to him.

'Yes, I do have rules about that. I don't sleep with my artists. I never have, and I don't intend to start now,' she said firmly, as though to remind herself.

'I think you just did. Besides, you were married then. The rules are different now.'

'So I'm going to start sleeping with my artists? I don't think so, Liam.' She was suddenly furious with herself, and before she could say more, he kissed her again, and ran his hands gently across her body. Every inch of her tingled when he touched her. She felt as though she was losing her mind over him. This time, she didn't even try to stop him. She wanted him even more than the first time, and afterward she lay in his arms and

139

cried. This time they were tears of relief. He pulled her closer to him and put his arms around her and held her tight until she stopped. She felt as though a dam in her had broken, and she was flooded with emotions.

'I love you, Sasha... I don't even know you, but I love you. And I know I'm going to love you more in time. Just give me the chance.' He pleaded with her. He wanted her more than he had ever wanted anyone, even Beth.

'This can never happen again.' Her words were muffled in his chest, and he smiled.

'Next time I promise I'll wear socks,' he said, never loosening his grip on her.

'I mean it, Liam,' she said softly, as she drifted off to sleep in his arms.

'I know you do, Sasha ... I know you do... I love you anyway.' And as he kissed her hair scattered across the pillow, he smiled, holding her, and fell asleep. It was the first good night either of them had had in months.

Chapter 6

Daylight streaming into Sasha's room at Claridge's awakened her and Liam at nine the next morning. He woke first, and lay holding her. And then, as though she sensed him watching her, she stirred. She could feel his arms around her, as he lay behind her, and for a minute, she didn't know who it was. And then she remembered. She closed her eyes and groaned.

'Good morning, Sleeping Beauty,' he said softly, and pulled her closer to him. She rolled over slowly and looked at him. They were nearly nose to nose, and he looked as beautiful to her in the morning as he had the night before. Her heart sank as their eyes met. She couldn't believe what she'd done. Just seeing him there, naked and handsome, with his long blond hair on his shoulders, his body warm next to hers, she knew she had lost her mind.

'This didn't happen,' she said firmly. But she couldn't bring herself to get up, or pull away from him. Everything about him made her want him even more.

'Yes, it did.' He laughed as he said it, looking enormously pleased with himself, and she thought she had never seen a man as beautiful as he was.

'We can't do this, Liam. It's impossible.' And it would never be any different. He would always be nine years younger than she was, which bothered her, no matter how little it bothered him, and he was an artist she represented. Even if she refused to represent him, he would still be too young, in her opinion. The age difference was more a matter of his state of mind and boyishness than the dates on their passports. And she couldn't refuse to represent him just because she'd been a fool. And an old fool at that. She felt like one now. She'd been starved for love, companionship, and affection, even sex. But that was no excuse for what she'd done. She was furious with herself, and even slightly with him. But not furious enough to get out of bed. Now, or the night before.

'It's not impossible, unless you want it to be. You said that last night, right before we made love the second time.'

'I was nuts. I plead temporary insanity,' she said, rolling over onto her back and looking up at the ceiling, to avoid looking at him. It felt so good to just lie there next to him, and feel like a woman again. But it was forbidden fruit she knew she couldn't allow herself to eat again. 'Do you have any idea how crazy this is?' she asked, turning her face to look at him. His eyes were green and enormous, his face nearly perfect, but just imperfect enough to make him look like a man. He looked like an actor in a sexy movie. He needed a young starlet to costar in it with him, not a woman her age. She knew it, even if he didn't, or didn't want to. She knew it for both of them.

'It isn't crazy, Sasha. You're a woman, I'm a man. We like each other, we're both lonely. We have the same interests, we both live for art. What's so wrong with that?'

'Everything. I look, and feel, old enough to be your mother. You're a friend of my son's. I represent you. How's that for a start? And besides, you're still in love with your wife.' She hadn't doubted it for a minute the night before, as he told her the story of Beth and her evil twin.

'You do not look old enough to be my mother. You're a spectacular-looking woman, and you're only nine years older than I am. So fucking what? And I am not in love with my wife, anymore. Besides, she's no longer my wife. We're getting divorced. You and I are both free, unattached, lonely as hell, and over twenty-one. That sounds possible to me. What's your problem?' He looked mildly annoyed.

'I'm still in love with my husband,' she said sadly, but she didn't cry this time. Liam waited for a moment before he answered, and he touched her face gently with one finger when he did.

'Sasha, he's gone. You're alive, he's not.' She had proved that amply to both of them the night before. 'You have a right to be happy with someone. Me, or someone else. You can't hide yourself away anymore. It's not right.'

'Yes, I can.' She rolled over and turned her back to him, and still did not get out of bed. He couldn't see if she was crying, but he put

143

his arms around her anyway, and pulled her close.

'Sasha, I know this sounds crazy. I hardly know you, but I think I love you. I feel like I've been waiting for you all my life.'

'That's insane,' she muttered, still turned away from him. But something of what he said rang true, even to her, although it made no sense. 'We drank too much. It wasn't love, it was wine.' She tried to dismiss what had happened, but convinced neither him nor herself.

'Well, whatever it is, I want more of it. Why can't you just let this happen and see where it goes?' He was pleading with her.

'And then what?' She turned to face him again. She looked genuinely tortured by what they'd done. 'Where could this possibly go? You need someone your own age. I'm older than you are, I'm your art dealer. I'm conservative, you're not. We'd be the laughingstock of Paris.' Particularly if he showed up at one of the functions she went to, with no socks and a painted shirt. She was a respectable person, with a serious life, and Liam wasn't. He was exactly what he said he was, a wacky artist, and he was Xavier's friend. Her kids would be totally upset if they knew, just as she was now.

'I don't want someone my age, Sasha. I want you.' And then he thought about it for a minute, and looked at her again. 'Do I embarrass you?'

'You could,' she said honestly, 'but I'm not going to give you the opportunity to do that. I'd look like a sex-starved old fool if I went out with you, Liam. This could never work.'

'Yes, it could. And you're half right at least. You are sex starved, but you're not a fool, young or old.'

'Yes, I am,' she said, looking miserable, and he kissed her then to silence her and cheer her up. She was beyond cheering, but not impervious to his touch, far from it. In spite of all her resolve and determination not to let this happen, or continue, she responded instantly to his touch. It was more powerful than she was. She had never experienced anything like it in her life, not even with Arthur, whom she genuinely had loved for more than half her life. But as Liam had pointed out, he was gone. And Liam wasn't. Within seconds, their bodies were entwined. And she moaned softly with pleasure as he began making love to her again.

It was quarter to ten on the bedside alarm clock when they finally lay breathless and sated in each other's arms.

'Oh my God,' she said when she saw the time. 'Xavier will be here any minute. I'm having breakfast with him.' Liam laughed.

'Well, I'd better get my ass out of Dodge.' He unwound his long, lean limbs from hers, got up, and stood looking down at her. 'I've never wanted any woman as much in my life. When can I come back?'

'Never,' she said sternly. 'I'm leaving for the airport after breakfast. Liam, I mean it. This has to stop.' But the one she needed to tell was herself. She had never felt so confused and out of control in her life. She felt like she was on a roller-coaster ride to hell. She could imagine only the worst happening, and she couldn't let it. She had to get control of herself. 'I won't let this happen again.'

'Then you are a fool,' he said sadly. 'I don't believe you are. I'll call you tonight.'

'Liam, don't. I want to represent you. You're a fantastic artist, and you could have an important future. Let's just do that. Don't jeopardize it now.'

'Are you telling me you won't represent me if we're lovers? Because if you are, screw the gallery and the contract. You mean more to me than that.' They were powerful words, and he meant them.

'You're insane,' she said, sitting up in bed, staring at him.

'Possibly. My family thinks I am.' He was pulling on his jeans and T-shirt as he said it. He didn't have time to shower. He knew he had to get out before Xavier arrived, or she'd never forgive him. 'You decide, Sasha,' he said, looking down at her, as she stood next to the bed where they had made love three times. The three best times in her life. But she couldn't make this decision based on sex. She truly felt as though she had lost her mind. And she knew she had to find it again, and fast.

'Don't call me,' she said, trying to sound as though she meant it. She wanted to mean it, and knew she had to. Whatever this had been, it had to end, even before it began. 'I'll get in touch with you about your work.'

'We can do both,' he said reasonably, and she shook her head, as he pulled her toward him for one last kiss. She was standing naked before him, shocked by how comfortable she was with him. After talking over dinner, and making love with him, she felt as though she had known him all her life. She was totally at ease with him.

'No, we can't do both,' she said, sounding desperate. 'I won't be your dealer and your lover.' She also didn't want to be the older woman in his life. She'd never done that before and didn't want to start now.

He kissed her, and left without saying another word. She stood staring at the door for a long moment, fearing what could happen, and determined to put walls up between them. From that moment on, she told herself, she was his art dealer and nothing more. She rushed into the shower, and the phone was ringing when she got out. She was afraid it was Liam, but it was

Xavier. He was just leaving his apartment, and said he would be there in five minutes.

'That's fine, darling,' she said calmly, as her hands shook. 'I'm running a little late myself. I'll meet you in the lobby in fifteen minutes.'

'Did you make all your calls?' Xavier sounded like he was in good spirits. He must have had fun the night before. She shuddered thinking of what he would think of his mother if he knew what she had done. She felt utterly debauched.

'What calls?' she asked, sounding distracted. 'Oh ... yes ... those ... of course... I'm just running a little late. See you in a few minutes.' She hung up and sat down on the bed, shaking. What she had done was insane. But the insanity was going to stop. She was a sensible person, and Liam was nothing more than a badly behaved overgrown boy, and had made a lifetime career of not growing up. She reminded herself, to frighten herself further, that he had committed adultery with his wife's twin. It was hardly a recommendation for his morality and good judgment. And no matter how beautiful he was, he acted like an irresponsible kid, and prided himself on it. So had she, she told herself. She had to be the grown-up here. Liam was incapable of it.

She threw what she had brought to London into a bag, dressed hastily, brushed her hair and put on makeup. And fifteen minutes later, she was in the lobby when her son walked in, looking handsome and young. His stride and confidence and the way he dressed reminded her instantly of Liam. They were contemporaries in lifestyle, attitude, and behavior. Two wild young boys.

'You look happy,' Xavier said, looking pleased. 'I never see you with your hair down. It looks nice, Mom.' She realized with horror that she had forgotten to put it up. She had been in such a rush, she hadn't even noticed it in the mirror. It was a clear sign, to her and to Xavier, that something was different. She had let her hair down in some very major ways, and it was time now to put it back up, and keep it that way.

'Oh, thank you. I was just in a rush.'

'You should wear it that way more often. How was dinner with Liam?'

'Fine ... fun ... no ... actually, it wasn't ... he's a bit ridiculous, isn't he? He showed up without socks or shoelaces, in a shirt he painted himself.' Maybe if she ridiculed him to Xavier, she would see how foolish it was herself. But she felt like a traitor as she said it.

'He's a nice guy. Hell, Mom, some of your other artists look a lot worse,' Xavier said with a shrug, as she reminded herself that she had never slept with any of them. But Liam was different. None of them had ever made her feel the way he did, just looking at him from across the room. She had felt the pull between them the moment they met, and had told herself she was imagining it. She had tried to deny it, but couldn't. As it turned out, it was a lot more than imagination. Worse yet, it felt real.

They had breakfast in the lobby. She drank tea, and stared at the scones on her plate. She couldn't eat them. She wasn't hungry. Xavier wolfed down his own – and hers. He was starving.

They talked about nothing in particular for an hour and he waved as she left for the airport, while she wondered if he would see Liam that day, and what he might say. She would kill him if he intimated anything to her son. But she trusted him not to do that. He wasn't mean or spiteful, just irresponsible and young for his age. Very young. He seemed far more Xavier's age than hers or his own. She forced herself not to think about him on the way to the airport, and took some papers out of her briefcase.

She couldn't concentrate on a single word she read. She sat staring at his contract with his signature on it, hastily signed at Harry's Bar, and for a moment thought of tearing it up. But she couldn't do that to him. He had given her back both copies, and she reminded herself to send him his copy from Paris. He had left her with his cell phone

150

number, but nothing in the world could have induced her to call him. She hadn't given him hers. Nor her home number. All he had was the gallery number in Paris, and she prayed he wouldn't call to talk to her. If he did, she would refer him to someone else. Anyone. Just not her. She didn't want to hear his voice again, at least not for a long time. His voice had a deep, sexy rumble with a gentleness that stirred her. She had noticed it right from the first. Now she loved his voice, and damn near everything else about him, except the way he behaved. The last thing she needed at her age was to be involved with a self-proclaimed wacky artist who acted like a juvenile delinquent. What she had said to him that morning was true. If she became openly involved with him romantically, she'd be the laughing-stock of Paris, and even New York. She had a reputation to protect. Liam didn't. He cared about neither his own nor hers. He had nothing to lose by being involved with Sasha. She had everything to lose, even if only the respect of her children, colleagues, and friends. She was acutely aware of it, as she boarded the plane at Heathrow. It had been an outrageous incident, a one-time-only, totally insane out-of-body experience, and there was absolutely no way she would ever let it happen again. Ever. As the plane took off for Paris, she promised herself to

151

get and stay sane.

It was four o'clock when she walked into her office in Paris. Despite the sun in London, it was raining in Paris when she arrived. She had trouble finding a cab at the airport, and she was soaked when she got to her office. It was sobering after the heady experience she'd had in London, and it had brought her to her senses.

'My God, you look awful,' Bernard, her gallery manager, said as he passed her in the hall. 'Or very wet, in any case. You should go home and change before you get sick, Sasha.'

'I will in a minute. I have to make some calls. And by the way.' She smiled at Bernard, and he noticed that in spite of the wet hair and drenched clothes, she looked better than she had in months. For the first time in over a year, she looked relaxed and happy. Obviously, her visit with her son had gone well. 'We have a new artist. A friend of Xavier's in London. He signed the contract, we have to send him his copy. A young American. His work is gorgeous.'

'Good. I look forward to seeing it.' She enjoyed the contemporary side more than he did. Like her father, Bernard was more traditional, but he had great respect for Sasha's eye for new work and emerging artists. She had an unfailing sense for what would sell.

'I told him we'd open with a show in New York.' He nodded, and they went to their respective offices. When she walked into hers, she was surprised. There was an enormous bouquet of red roses sitting on her desk, and she was relieved to see that her secretary hadn't opened the card. The very fact that they were red roses had looked personal to her, so she had left the envelope sealed, much to Sasha's relief, when she saw who they were from. She didn't want her office thinking she had a secret lover. She didn't. She had made a mistake, it had been corrected, and would stay that way.

The card said, 'It's possible. I love you, Liam.' She tore it up in tiny pieces and threw them into the wastebasket, feeling embarrassed. The roses must have cost him a fortune, and she knew he couldn't afford them. She was touched, and tempted to call him, but she forced herself not to. She had made a vow of silence and she intended to keep it, no matter what it cost her.

Instead of calling him to thank him for the flowers, she wrote him a polite note that could have been written by his grandmother, or art dealer. There was nothing personal about it. She handed it to her secretary with his copy of the contract, and his phone number and address. She told her to open a file on Liam Allison, he was one of their new artists.

'The flowers are lovely,' Eugénie said to her. What Sasha had told her explained the flowers. They were sent by a new artist, a handsome gesture for a starving artist. Maybe this one wasn't starving. Roses in January were expensive. For a minute, Eugénie had wondered if Sasha had a boyfriend, but she didn't. Just a new emerging artist. But at least Sasha looked happier than she had in a long time. She had looked morbidly depressed ever since Arthur's death. And there seemed to be a new spring in her step now. She looked relaxed after her trip to London.

Sasha went back to her part of the house at six that night, relieved that Liam hadn't tried to call her. She made herself a cup of tea and some soup. She took a hot bath, and tried not to think of him, which was far from easy. The night before at the same time she had been having dinner with him at Harry's Bar. She fought even harder not to remember what had come later when they went back to the hotel.

She was startled out of her reverie when the phone rang at midnight. It was Tatianna. She had found a job that morning. She was going to be working in the art department of a fashion magazine, coordinating photographs, and doing whatever else they gave her to do. She was happy and excited, and then, after sharing her news, finally turned her attention to her mother.

'How was London?'

'It was fun.' She forced her mind away from Liam. 'I saw Xavier, and lots of artists.'

'How was Xavier's friend?'

'What friend?' Sasha sounded panicked in answer to the question.

'I thought he wanted you to meet one of his friends, to see his work.'

'Oh, that friend,' Sasha said, sounding relieved. 'He was fine. We signed him.'

'Wow, he must be good. Lucky break for him.'

'He's very good. We're going to give him a show in New York next year.' She forced herself to sound serious and professional as she said it.

'I'll bet that made him happy.' Artists begged her all the time to introduce them to her mother. It always annoyed her. She didn't want to be used as a conduit to Sasha. Xavier was much more relaxed about it. 'When are you coming to New York?'

'Not for a few weeks. I have a lot of work to do here. You can always come over for a weekend, if you want to.' Sasha loved seeing her children, and spending time with them.

'I hate it when it rains there. I talked to a friend who got back today. She said the weather was disgusting.'

'It's not lovely,' Sasha admitted to her. 'It was sunny in London.'

'It's supposed to snow here tomorrow. I think I might go skiing this weekend.'

'Be careful on the roads. When do you start the new job?' Sasha yawned, it was late for her, and only six o'clock at night in New York.

'Tomorrow.' Tatianna sounded ecstatic, and for a moment Sasha envied her. Her life was just beginning. Sasha felt as though hers was ending. All her best years were behind her. The children had grown up. Arthur was gone. She had nothing to look forward to, except work, and one day grandchildren, which didn't interest her particularly. She felt like a very old woman after she said good-bye to her daughter and lay on her bed. As she did, she couldn't help thinking about Liam. It had been nice of him to send her roses. And foolish. 'It's possible,' he had said on the card she tore up. She knew it wasn't.

She slept fitfully that night, thinking of him, and was at her desk at nine the next morning. It was only eight o'clock in London. She wondered what Liam was doing, and if he would try to call her. It was Saturday, and she didn't need to be at work, but she had nothing else to do. She had turned down several invitations to dinner parties and luncheons for that weekend. The weather was terrible, and it was too depressing just sitting in her house. She'd rather be working. He called her at four o'clock that afternoon, and she didn't take it. She asked the young woman working in the gallery to tell him she was out, and to call Bernard on Monday. Bernard, very sensibly, did not work on weekends. He had a wife, three children, and a house in Normandy where he took them on the weekends. When Arthur had been alive, she hadn't worked on weekends either. Now it was all she had to fill her days and distract her. Ever since Arthur's death, the weekends were brutal.

They closed the gallery at six, and she went back to her house at seven. She had brought a stack of art magazines home with her, and turned on the lights. It was dinnertime, and she wasn't hungry. She reminded herself yet again, as she made a cup of tea, that there was no point thinking about Liam. It would get her nowhere, except miserable and crazy. The doorbell rang as she poured the tea. It rang endlessly, which told her that the guardian was out. She ran across the courtyard to the big bronze outer door, with no idea who it could be. No one ever rang their doorbell at night.

She looked through the peephole and could see no one there, and then hit the buzzer to open one side of the big bronze door. Maybe someone had left something outside. As she pulled the door open and looked around, she saw Liam standing in front of her, drenched, in the pouring rain. He was carrying a small bag, and wearing a

157

sweatshirt and jeans. He was wearing a pair of old cowboy boots, and his long blond hair was plastered to his head in the rain. She stood staring at him and said not a word as he looked down at her, and then she stepped aside so he could come into the courtyard at least, and stand sheltered from the rain.

'You told me not to call you from London,' he said, smiling at her. 'So I didn't. I called you from Paris. I didn't call till I got here. I figured you'd be home by now.'

'What are you doing here, Liam?' She looked upset more than angry. And somewhere deep inside of her, she was frightened. With very little effort from either of them, this could get out of hand.

'I came to see you.' He looked more than ever like a giant child. 'I haven't been able to think of anything but you since yesterday. So I figured I might as well come to see you. I missed you.' She had missed him, too, but he was a risk she just couldn't afford.

'The roses were beautiful,' she said politely.

'Were? Did you throw them away?' He looked instantly disappointed.

'Of course not. They're in my office.' They were still standing under the sheltered part of the courtyard. 'I told my secretary they were from a new artist.'

'Why do you owe her an explanation? You're a free woman.'

'No one is free, Liam. Or at least I'm not.

158

I have a business, children, employees, clients, responsibilities, obligations, a reputation. I can't go around acting like a love-starved schoolgirl.' She said it as much to herself as to him.

'Why not? It might do you good for a change to let your hair down.' It was the same thing her son had said, literally, when he saw her with her hair loose in London. But for some reason, Liam unhinged her. And that was not what she wanted. She wasn't going to throw her life away and make a fool of herself, falling for this crazy overgrown boy. 'Can I take you to dinner somewhere?' As he asked her, she suddenly thought of her infuriating dinner with Gonzague de St. Mallory at Alain Ducasse the month before, when he had expected her to sleep with him to sell a painting. How insulting that had been. This wasn't. Foolish perhaps, but sincere, and not insulting. Gonzague was a lot less of a man, or even a gentleman, than this self-declared and proud-to-be-wacky artist.

'Why don't you come in, and I'll cook you something? The weather is too miserable to go out.' She led the way back to her house, the door was still standing open. 'Where are you staying?' she asked nervously. If he had said with her, she wouldn't have let him in her front door.

'At an artists' hostel in the Marais, near the

159

Place des Vosges. I stayed there last summer.' She nodded, and led the way into her living room. The house was eighteenth century, as was the furniture. The art was all contemporary and modern. It was an artful mixture that few could have accomplished. The end result was elegant, cheerful, and cozy. There was a huge fireplace in the room, which she had had rebuilt in white marble. There was only one lamp lit in the room, a tall silver torchère she had bought years before in Venice. There were tall candlesticks with candles in them all over the room. She never bothered to light them. It was too much trouble. They walked through the living room, past the dining room, and straight into the kitchen, which was a big cozy room with French provincial furniture, an enormous marble table, and paintings by emerging artists on every wall. The predominant colors were yellow and orange, which conveyed an illusion of sunshine. There was a huge white Venetian chandelier over the table, and with the flick of a switch, she lit it. The room was warm and inviting, and when Arthur had been alive, they had always sat there for hours. They used it more than the living room. The chairs were covered in soft brown leather. 'Wow, Sasha, this is gorgeous. Who did it?'

'I did.' She smiled at him. 'It's a bit eclectic. The rest of the house is more formal.' As was the gallery, and the wing of the house where her father had lived. The antiques and paintings he had collected were exquisite. But Sasha liked her part of the house better. So did Liam. He loved it and felt instantly at home.

She put some soup on the stove for him, and offered him an omelette, which he accepted gratefully, and admitted he was starving. He hadn't eaten since lunchtime.

'I can make pasta, if you have some,' he offered. She hesitated, and then nodded. She didn't want him lingering. She was going to feed him, scold him for showing up on her doorstep, and send him off to his artists' hostel in the Marais. What he did after that was his business. She was not going to make it hers, now or ever.

They both got busy cooking, and half an hour later, they were sitting next to each other at the kitchen table, talking, arguing about two of the artists she represented. He thought one of them was excellent and promising, and worthy of the opportunities she'd given him; he said the other had no merit and no talent whatsoever and was an embarrassment to her. According to Liam, his style was imitative, superficial, phony, and pretentious. 'I can't stand him. He's a total asshole.' Liam had strong opinions on most subjects.

'Yes, he is,' Sasha conceded. She didn't like him, either. 'But his work sells like

hotcakes, and museums love him.'
'They just kiss his ass, because his wife has money.' And then he looked at her sheepishly and chuckled. 'I guess people could say that about me one day, if you and I wind up together.' The way he said it made her tremble. 'Don't worry, we won't. You'll never have that problem.' She looked sad as she said it. 'There's another good reason for us not to "wind up together," as you put it.'

'I want you to notice something,' he said, as he pulled up one soaked leg of his blue jeans, and pulled off his cowboy boot with some effort. She couldn't see anything remarkable. He was wearing white cotton athletic socks, and he pointed at the one she was staring at. 'You see that. Socks. I wore them for you. I bought them at the airport.' You couldn't see them in his cowboy boots, but like a child who had done something to please his mother, he wanted her to know he had done it, and to get credit for it.

'You're a good boy, Liam,' she said, teasing him, but touched nonetheless. It was obvious that he wanted to please her, and win her approval. But he needed a lot more than socks to be a grown-up, and he just wasn't. Everything about him shrieked of boyhood and wacky artist. And as he had told her so proudly before, no one was ever going to control him. His father had tried, and his brothers, and Liam had defied them. Sasha didn't want to. She wanted him to control himself and be an adult. Even coming to Paris had been a lovely gesture, but it was still wild and impulsive, and did not respect what she'd asked him, to stay away from her, and forget the moment of insanity they had indulged in London.

'What were you going to do tonight, before I got here?' he asked her with interest as they finished their dinner. Both their contributions to the meal had been delicious. They were both good cooks.

'Nothing. Read. Go to bed. I don't go out much.'

'Why not?' He frowned as he looked at her.

'Obvious reasons. Sad. Alone. It depresses me to go to parties by myself. I feel like the fifth wheel all the time, or the only solo act on Noah's ark. My friends feel sorry for me, which is just too depressing. I only go out when I have to, with clients.'

'You need to get out more,' he said matter-of-factly, as though she had hired him as a consultant on her social life. 'You need more fun in your life. You can't just sit here in an empty house, reading and listening to the rain outside. Christ, if I did that, I'd be suicidal.' She didn't tell him that sometimes she was, that more than once she had considered it, since Arthur died, and the only thing that had stopped her was knowing she couldn't do that to her children. Otherwise, she would have. Instinctively, he sensed it. Given the way she was living, and the solitude she had imposed on herself, he didn't blame her. All she had in her life now was the gallery, and occasional visits with her children. 'Tomorrow I'm taking you to the movies. Do they have samurai films in Paris?' he asked with interest, as he helped her clear the table. She laughed at the question.

'I have no idea. I've never seen one.' If nothing else, he amused her. He made her laugh sometimes as she hadn't in years, or maybe ever.

'You have to. They're terrific. Very good for the soul. You don't even need to read the subtitles, just listen to the noises. They chop each other up in little bits, and make a lot of really great noises. It's a deep psychological experience. Xavier loves them.'

'He never told me,' she said, smiling at him.

'He's probably embarrassed. He considers himself a serious intellectual. There's nothing intellectual about samurai movies. I hate the movies he goes to, they always put me to sleep.'

'Me too.' She laughed openly. 'He loves all those terrible Polish and Czechoslovakian movies that go on forever. I won't go with him.'

'Good, then you can come to the movies

164

with me. I'll even take you to a chick flick. How long has it been since you've been to a movie?' She thought about it for a minute, and realized it was the same answer to that as to everything else in her life.

'Not since Arthur died.' He nodded and didn't comment, and glanced at her freezer. She had a modern American refrigerator and freezer, which was rare in Paris. Arthur had insisted on it when she remodeled the house. They had big, beautiful American bathrooms, too, a major luxury in France.

'Do you have ice cream? I'm addicted to it.' There were worse things to be addicted to, she realized. Like him, for instance. He hadn't even bothered to drink wine with dinner, although she'd offered.

'Actually...' She opened the freezer and stared inside. There was nothing in it but ice. She never ate desserts or ice cream. All she had in the refrigerator was what the house-keeper left her for dinner. Some salad, a few vegetables, homemade soup, and now and then some cold cuts, cheese, or chicken. She didn't eat much. Liam ate like the healthy young man he was. She turned to him in some embarrassment. 'No ice cream. I'm really sorry.' She couldn't even remember the last time she'd bought some, or eaten any.

'That's a major problem.' He looked seriously concerned.

'I'll know for next time,' she said, as

though there would be one, which she was determined there wouldn't, and then she had an idea. She hadn't been there in years, not since the children were small. She had a new child in her life now. She had Liam. 'Put your jacket on. We're going out,' she said with a look of sudden inspiration, as she stood smiling at him.

'Where to?' he asked, as she put her raincoat on, and picked up her handbag. She was still wearing the serious black pantsuit she had worn to the office. A moment later, they were outside. She led him to the garage, and got behind the wheel of her tiny Renault. He nearly had to be a contortionist to get in it with her. His legs were too long for her small car, but for Sasha it was perfect.

She drove to the Île St. Louis and found a parking place for her little car, and then tucked her hand into his arm, as they walked under an umbrella. They stopped in front of an ancient brown storefront marked Berthillon, and she looked proudly at him. 'This is the best ice cream in Paris.' She explained the system to him of how many 'balls' in what kind of cone, or cup, and what toppings. He had pear, apricot, and lemon in a sugar cone, and they bought three huge containers of chocolate, vanilla, and coffee. She had a single ball of coconut, and they chatted happily on the way back to the car. She gave him a brief scenic tour,

166

driving home, although he said he knew Paris, but not the parts she was familiar with, and on the spur of the moment, they stopped for coffee at the Café de Flore. It was one of the oldest cafés in Paris. They walked past the Deux Magots as they went to retrieve the car, and it was ten o'clock when they walked into the house again. He decided to try the other flavors of the ice cream they'd bought. This time they sat in the living room, and he lit the candles. It had turned into a delightful evening after all. The kind of evening one couldn't have alone. Going to Berthillon alone would have depressed her, driving around Paris would have been pointless. And coffee alone at the Café de Flore would have seemed pathetic. But with Liam, it all worked, and they had fun. It was the conversation and the political arguments that made it work, the discussions about art, the exchange of opinions, the laughter at his stories and jokes, his irrepressible exuberance and enthusiasm about life that made it fun, for both of them. He may have been boyish, but he was smart, and entertaining to be with. She was beginning to wonder if they could be friends. It was one in the morning when they stopped talking and she yawned.

He asked if he could use her phone then, to call the artists' hostel. He had meant to call them from the airport but hadn't. He came back minutes later, looking sheepish. 'That was stupid,' he said, looking embarrassed. He hadn't even kissed her that night, and she was grateful for it. If he had, she would have told him to leave. She had promised herself that, before things got out of hand again.

'What happened?' She was snuffing the candles out. He was going to be leaving in a minute. The evening had gone well, and had been easy. If she could just get over her insatiable attraction to him, everything would be perfect.

'I didn't call them soon enough. They're full. I can probably find a hotel somewhere,' he said, looking at her with unspoken questions, and she suddenly looked worried.

'Are you asking me if you can stay here?' she asked him pointedly, wondering if it had been a manipulation or if the artists' hostel in the Marais really was full. But he did look genuinely embarrassed. He just wasn't organized, and never had been. He had told her that Beth had done everything for him ever since he was nineteen, until she left. And at first he couldn't manage without her, but was learning.

'I wasn't going to,' Liam said honestly. 'I didn't want to put you on the spot. I can sleep at the airport if I have to, or the train station. I've done it before, it's no big deal.'

'That's silly,' she said practically, and then

168

took a deep breath.

'You can sleep in Xavier's room. But Liam, I won't sleep with you. I don't want to turn my life into a mess, nor yours. If we go on doing what we did yesterday, it will only be confusing.' He didn't recall either of them being confused the night before, but he said nothing and nodded.

'I'll be good. I promise.' He knew this would have been hard for her, too. She had lived here with her husband and children. The house was not a clean slate for her, unlike the hotel room in London. He didn't want to upset her, or frighten her, and he knew he would if he made a move on her here.

He followed her respectfully as she led him to Xavier's room, on the floor above her own. His room was directly above hers, a good-looking young man's room, with simple decor, in navy blue, and a painting she had given him years before for Christmas, of a woman and a young boy. He had loved it at the time, and it still hung there as a reminder of her son's childhood. The room had *oeil de boeuf* round windows that looked out onto the garden. Liam liked knowing he was near her, as she kissed him goodnight on both cheeks, and he managed to resist her. He was in no hurry. What he felt for her could wait, if it had to. He lay in bed that night, thinking of her, as she did about him. A thousand times he wanted to run down the stairs to her, but he didn't. He didn't see her again until they met in the kitchen the next morning.

She made him eggs and bacon, and they discussed what they were going to do. Since he had stayed politely in Xavier's room, without arguing about it, or crossing her boundaries, she was no longer anxious for him to leave. The weather was gray but better, and they decided to walk along the Seine. They looked at the Bateaux Mouches, and she pointed out new things to him. He purchased an art book and gave it to her. They bought crêpes from a street vendor, wandered past the pet stores, and laughed at the chickens. Liam wanted to go inside, and talked about a dog he'd had as a child and loved. It had died the same year as his mother. The rest of the time he made her laugh, told her jokes and funny stories. She asked him about his children, and she talked about her own. It was one of those perfect afternoons of ease and comfort, shared confidences and friendship, and love that was unspoken but powerfully felt by both of them, no matter how much she was resisting. He gave her what she had missed for the past fifteen months, companionship, and someone of her own to talk to. He filled her loneliness like foam that expanded and filled it to the brim.

They were standing in the last of the pet shops on the quais when he spotted a cocker spaniel. The man in the pet shop told them it was the runt of the litter, and Sasha said it had the saddest eyes she'd ever seen.

'You should get a dog,' Liam said confidently. 'It would keep you company.' He had thought of the same thing, but it was too complicated for him in England.

'I travel too much. I'd either have to leave it here, or forever be dragging it on and off planes, which doesn't seem fair.'

'You do it. Why couldn't a dog?'

'I haven't had one since the kids were little. It's too much work,' she said practically. 'It would pee all over the gallery and Bernard would kill me, and so would Karen in New York.'

'You can't let other people make those decisions.' But she did. She was doing the same thing about him. She was too afraid of what other people would think if she got involved with him. And he wasn't house-broken either.

They took the puppy out of the cage, and she came to life instantly while Liam played with her. Sasha stood back and watched, as the puppy licked his face and he let her. She was black and white, with a pretty head, black legs, and four white feet. He told her the dog he had had as a boy had been a cocker spaniel, too.

171

'Maybe you should buy her and take her home with you,' she said, encouraging him. He was obviously enamored with her, and looked sad when he put the little dog back in her cage. She whined and barked as they left. Liam looked back at her, blew her a kiss, and waved.

'I couldn't get her back into England,' he explained to Sasha. 'The Brits are so damn complicated. They've relaxed the quarantine rules a little, but you have to have enough papers to get her qualified for outer space. Besides' – he grinned at Sasha boyishly – 'I'm not responsible enough to have a dog. I forget everything when I'm painting. I'd need a wife to get another dog.'

'There's a hell of an admission.' It confirmed all she feared about him, but this time it didn't seem frightening. It was just a simple statement of fact. Liam was well aware of who and what he was. And so was she. He was a charming irresponsible boy.

They went to Berthillon again, and that night she drove him back to the airport. He sat looking at her for a long moment before he even attempted to get out of her ridiculously small car.

'I had a wonderful time with you this weekend,' he said quietly. They hadn't made love. They hadn't done anything insane. They had just hung out together, eaten ice cream, talked, gone for long walks, bought an art book, sat in cafés, and played with a dog. It was everything she'd missed, and different from anything she'd ever had. She and Arthur had had a totally adult life, a life of responsible equal partners doing serious things. There was something wonderful and playful and young about Liam. He was part man, part boy, would-be lover, if she let him, and, in some ways because of his youthful ways, almost like an adopted son.

'I had a good time too,' Sasha said, smiling at him. 'Thank you for surprising me. If you'd asked me, I'd never have let you come.'

'That's why I didn't ask,' he said, as he leaned over and kissed her. She was grateful that he had respected her wishes until then. As he kissed her, she felt everything she had felt for him in London, and had managed to resist all weekend. It would have been impossible for her to do so if he had kissed her before the end. And even more impossible for him. They sat kissing each other for a long time, and then they sat looking at each other. It was impossible to have anything more between them. She wished it could be different, but knew it couldn't. She didn't say it to him this time. There was no need. He knew what she thought. 'I want to come back and see you,' he said before he got out. 'Will you let me, Sasha?'

'I don't know. We'll see. I have to think about it. We may be tempting fate if we try to do this again, or kidding ourselves that we could limit it to this. You're awfully hard to resist.' He kissed her again then and proved it. She could hardly breathe when he stopped kissing her, and she wanted him desperately. She wanted nothing more than to drive him home with her. But she didn't. She knew she couldn't. She got out of the car, and then laughed as she watched him unwind his legs and do the same.

'You're my dealer, for chrissake. With all the money you're going to make off me, can't you at least afford a decent car? I'm going to herniate a disk getting in and out of this thing. Maybe I should give you an advance.' She laughed at him, and followed him into the airport. He was wearing the cowboy boots, his jeans, a fisherman's sweater he had bought in Ireland, and a baseball cap his son had sent him from the States. He looked tall and masculine and young. Everything about him was appealing, even and especially the childlike quality that frightened her so much.

She followed him in silence to the gate. He was the last one to board. Part of her wanted him to miss the plane and stay with her. Another part of her wanted him to leave and never come back to see her again. The two parts were constantly at war.

'I'll miss you,' he said quietly.

'So will I.' She was being honest. She was

always honest with him. She found she could tell him whatever she thought.

He kissed her then, long and hard, as they began closing the door to the plane.

'Go ... you'll miss it...' she whispered. He ran, and turned one last time, with a broad grin, waved, and then boarded the plane. She had no idea when she'd see him again.

As he took his seat, he was thinking of her, and the remarkable blend of contrasts she was. Hard and soft, vulnerable and strong. She was serious and sad at times, when she spoke of her parents or her late husband, and then suddenly funny and happy and even youthful at other times when she talked about her artists, or her children, or her views on life. She was simple in what she expected of life, and unpretentious. Complicated in her rigid ideas about how she felt she should behave in society, and wanted to be perceived. A grande dame and painfully ladylike one minute, and whimsical and mischievous the next. He knew from Xavier that she was a terrific mother, and could sense himself that she was a great friend. Responsible, conscientious, capable, brilliant in her field, and at the same time a small, lonely woman who needed a man to hold her and love her. And no matter how prepared she was to fight him on it, Liam wanted to be that man. However long it took.

Chapter 7

Sasha was quiet and pensive in her office the next day. She sat for a long time at her desk, staring at a piece of paper, lost in thought, without seeing it. She was thinking about Liam, the fun she'd had with him over the weekend, and the sheer stupidity of allowing herself to be with him at all. If she continued doing this, there was absolutely no doubt in her mind, someone would get hurt. And more than likely it would be her. Or maybe him. But she had far more at stake.

She was staring out the window, thinking of it, when Eugénie walked into the room.

'Sasha,' she said hesitantly, 'a package came for you. I'm not sure where you want me to put it.' Sasha assumed it was paintings coming from one of her artists. The ones in Europe sent their work to the Paris gallery, and from there the gallery sent them to New York, if they were assigned to shows there.

'Just put it with all the work that came in last week,' Sasha said, looking distracted. 'We're shipping all of it to New York on February first. Just look at the packing list, and make sure it's not something we want to show here.'

'I don't think you'll want to ship this,' Eugénie said, looking awkward. Sasha frightened her once in a while, particularly lately. And she wasn't at all sure how she was going to react to this delivery.

'For heaven's sake, Eugénie, stop being so mysterious. What is it?'

'Shall I bring it in?'

'Not if you have to uncrate it. I don't want a mess in my office. Just do it in the shipping room. I'll go down to see it later.' Eugénie stood there looking confused, as Sasha got more and more annoyed with her. 'Okay, just bring it in. We can clean the mess up later.' It was obvious that Eugénie felt she should bring it straight to Sasha, who was beginning to suspect that some kind of major problem was about to land in her lap.

Her secretary disappeared rapidly, and backed into the room moments later, carrying something. She seemed to be cradling it in her arms, and then turned to face Sasha, who stared at her with a look of amazement. It was the cocker spaniel puppy she and Liam had played with in the pet shop on the *quai* the day before. The little dog looked terrified, and Eugénie looked just as panicked as the dog. She had no idea how Sasha would react. Much to her relief, her employer just stood there looking stunned, with a smile spreading slowly across her face.

'Oh my God ... what am I going to do with

that?' Sasha looked overwhelmed.

'The man from the pet store said you would know who it's from,' Eugénie said hesitantly.

'Yes, I do. It's from Liam Allison, our newest artist.' There was no point hiding that from her. Sooner or later, that much at least would come out. Hopefully, why he had given her the gift would not. Eugénie approached her then and handed her the dog, who licked Sasha's face as energetically as she had licked Liam's the day before. 'Oh good Lord ... I can't believe this.' She held her for a moment, and then gently set her down. She had been on her feet for less than a minute, when she squatted next to Sasha and peed on the rug. But the damage was small. 'He's insane,' Sasha said, smiling even more, and Eugénie was relieved to see that she didn't seem upset about the rug.

'She's very sweet,' Eugénie smiled at her as the puppy sniffed at the furniture and ran around the room. Every few seconds she would then dash back to Sasha. She was still running around when Sasha focused on her black legs and four white feet. 'Does she have a name?'

Sasha hesitated for a moment and then grinned broadly. 'I think she does. I'm going to call her Socks.' She had four white paws that looked like socks, which were such an issue to Liam. 'Did they bring food for her?'

She had no idea what to give her.

'The man said he brought everything you need, including a traveling bag for when you take her to New York. She even has a pink sweater, and a collar and leash to match.' Liam had thought of everything. She knew how strapped for money he was, and with the hope of what he'd make at Suvery, he had really stretched himself. The dog couldn't have been cheap, and the accessories and supplies had cost him a lot too. She loved his generosity and kindness. Sending her the puppy was a loving gesture and she knew it had been well meant. For all his wild ways, he was a good-hearted person. The moment Eugénie left the room, Sasha picked up the phone. She got him in his studio, on his cell phone.

'I can't believe you did this. You are totally insane. And you spent a fortune, Liam. What am I going to do with a dog?'

'You need someone to keep you company. Or at least while I'm in London. Is she all right?' He ignored the comment about what he'd spent. That was none of her business. He had wanted to spoil her. She deserved that and more, in his eyes.

'She's wonderful. Liam, that's the sweetest thing anyone's ever done.'

'I'm glad.' He sounded pleased. He had been a little worried she would be furious, and was immensely relieved that she wasn't.

She was still in shock. What are you going to call her?'

'Socks,' Sasha said, sounding delighted, and Liam laughed out loud.

'That's perfect. Now I won't have to wear mine. She can just wear hers.' He remembered the four matched snow-white paws.

'You are a totally silly person. And this is probably the craziest thing anyone in my life has ever done.'

'Good. You need a little confusion in your life. You need some nice surprises, and a little less control.' As he said it, Socks looked up at her new mistress with interest, squatted, and peed on the rug again. It was obvious to Sasha that she no longer had any control at all. Neither over him, herself, and surely not over the dog. The puppy was only eight weeks old, and wouldn't be housebroken for months. She was going to have to roll up her rugs at home.

'She was a wonderful surprise, Liam. I'm still a little stunned.' She wasn't even sure how to react, or why he had done it. But she appreciated the gesture nonetheless.

'I was wondering if I could come and see her this weekend. Now don't get nervous. I'm not coming to see you. Just the dog.'

Sasha hesitated, and there was a long moment of silence at her end. He hadn't sent the puppy to pressure her, it had been an outpouring of love for her. Now that he'd been to Paris to visit her, he realized how lonely her life really was. The silence and solitude in her house had made him sad for her. He thought the little dog might help. And if she let him, he wanted to help, too. 'I don't know,' Sasha said honestly. 'Liam, I'm scared. It's just too crazy if we get involved. I think we'd both regret it in the end.' Particularly she would, if he found a woman closer to his age, after she fell head over heels in love with him. She could easily imagine him with a twenty-five or thirty-year-old, rather than a woman her age. An affair between them, from her point of view, could only come to a bad end.

'It doesn't have to be that way. Sasha, stop being so obsessed about my age.'

'It's not just that. It's everything. I represent you. If this goes sour it could screw up our whole working relationship. You're not divorced. You could go back to Beth any day. I'm nine years older than you are, you should be with a woman half my age. You want to be a wacky artist, and my life is so conservative and boring, it would drive you insane.' These days it even bored her. Besides, she couldn't take him anywhere without feeling foolish, and she had no idea how he would behave, but she didn't say that to him. 'There is absolutely no part of this that makes sense.'

'Does love always have to make sense?' he

asked, sounding disappointed. She ticked off her list of concerns like deal points in a contract she was refusing to sign. But that was how her life worked, and how she saw it.

'It should make sense. Relationships are hard enough without taking two people who are as radically different as we are, and trying to make it work. I just don't think we can. And besides, this isn't love, it's physical attraction. It's some kind of insane chemistry that makes me lose my mind whenever you're around.'

'You didn't lose your mind this weekend,' he reminded her. 'I wish you had. But you didn't. I thought we were very well behaved,' he said proudly.

'And just how long do you think that would last?'

'Not long, I hope.' He laughed, and she loved the sound of it. She was smiling as she listened to him, and watched the dog. 'I had to take cold showers all night when I got back to London.'

'That's my point. If we hang out together, one or both of us is going to lose our minds and do something we'll both regret later on.' The attraction she felt to him was like putting a match to dynamite. They had proven that on Friday, after dinner at Harry's Bar.

'So now what do we do?' he asked, sounding discouraged. He wasn't convincing her.

Sasha was every bit as stubborn as he was.

'I become your very respectable art dealer. And you behave like a good boy.'

'I hate it when people tell me what to do. I'm not a child.' He sounded annoyed.

'Sometimes one has no other choice but to do the right thing,' she said sensibly. 'It's much more fun to do whatever you want. But when you do, people get hurt.' She had the good taste not to remind him of his dalliance with his sister-in-law, which had cost him his marriage.

'I want to see you, Sasha,' he said insistently. 'I want to come to Paris this weekend.' And then as an afterthought, 'I think I should see the dog. I'm her father after all.'

'No, you're not,' Sasha said stubbornly. 'She's a fatherless child, and she'll just have to grow up that way, like it or not. You can be her godfather, if you like.'

'All right, all right. She's my god-dog. But I'm coming to Paris this weekend to see you both.'

'I won't let you in,' she said firmly.

'Why not? What else do you have to do, sit in a dark house by yourself and work yourself to death? For God's sake, Sasha, let yourself live for once. You deserve it. So do I.'

'No, you don't, and neither do I, if we're going to make fools of ourselves, or of me. You're just indulging yourself, and I won't let you do that at my expense.' She meant it. The stakes were just too high for her. Only Liam had nothing to lose, except his heart.

'That's not fair,' he said, sounding hurt.

'Yes, it is. It's honest. I'm nearly ten years older than you, and you want to behave any way you want. You don't want to be respectable and conservative. You have no intention of adapting to my life. You want to play at this, have some fun, and play wacky artist. If you do that in my life, Liam, you're going to turn my whole world upside down, and I won't let you do it.'

'I behaved perfectly at Harry's Bar,' he said, sounding miffed, and then added grudgingly, 'except for the shirt and socks. If I knew it was so important to you, I'd have bought a new shirt and some socks, if that's what matters to you, for chrissake.' He was beginning to shout.

'It's not about the shirt and socks. It's about who you are and the way you want to live. You keep telling me no one can control you, no one can tell you what to do. You want to be a free spirit, Liam, and you have every right to do that. You just can't do that in my life. You and I both know that when the spirit moves you, you want to do whatever comes into your head. You think it's funny. Well, I don't. And like it or not, I'm too goddamn old for you. You're my son's best friend, for God's sake. He's twenty-five years old. I'm

184

forty-eight.' His behavior and the rules he set for himself were far more appropriate in her son's world than hers, and Liam liked it that way. In the name of art and independence, he had resisted growing up all his life.

'I'm thirty-nine,' Liam said plaintively. 'I'm closer to your age than his.'

'But you don't want to act like it. That's the problem. You want to pretend you're twenty-five. If I wanted another child, I'd adopt one. That's not the relationship I want with you.' She had raised her voice, too, in answer to his.

'What relationship do you want with me? I thought we worked things out just fine last Friday. And we didn't do badly this weekend, either. I don't want to just go to bed with you. I like talking to you, too.'

'So do I. But you're a luxury I can't afford.'

'You are surely and without a doubt the most stubborn woman I know. I'll be there on Friday, whether you like it or not. We can argue about it this weekend.'

'I don't want to see you,' she said, feeling panicked. Her feelings for him made her feel out of control.

'Well, I want to see you. One more time at least, to discuss this face-to-face. I can't talk about things like this on the phone.'

'There's nothing to discuss. This is impossible, Liam. We have to accept that. We

185

have no other choice.'

'You're the one who's making it impossible. It's only impossible if you want it to be.' He sounded frustrated beyond words.

'Then let's just say I do.'

'This is the dumbest thing I ever heard.'

'Doing the right thing feels that way sometimes. But in this case, that's what we're going to do.' She didn't say that if he had done the right thing with Becky, he would still have his wife and kids with him. Instead, he had indulged himself. And he was trying to do that again, with her.

'I'll call you tomorrow,' he said, sounding depressed. If anything, she had gotten firmer in her resolve not to get involved with him, despite the dog, which was a lovely gift, but still didn't convince her that he was the man for her.

'Don't call me, unless it's about gallery business. I don't want to discuss this with you again. We just go around and around, and drive each other crazy.' But he drove her even more so when she was near him. She had never been as physically attracted to any man in her life. It was hard for her to understand and even harder still to resist.

'I'll call you this week,' he said, but didn't, which Sasha felt was a relief. It pained her to do it, but she believed she had finally persuaded him to let it go. No matter how much she wanted to be with him again, she knew she couldn't.

The one consolation in her life that week was the joy of the puppy Liam had sent her. Socks was adorable, and despite frequent accidents on her carpets, Sasha was enchanted with her. It had been the best gift he could give her. The next best gift was leaving her alone, which he did.

The weather was awful in Paris again that weekend, gray wintry days that seemed relentless. Foggy mornings, rainy nights, and depressing afternoons with bitter winds that chilled you to the bone. She worked late on Friday, went to bed early, and was at her desk at the gallery by nine the next morning, with the dog. Everyone was in love with Socks, even Bernard.

Sasha worked in the gallery all day Saturday, and she was sitting alone in her house with the puppy on Saturday night. Liam hadn't called her since Monday, and in some ways, she was relieved. In others, she was sad. She was crazy about him, but in every way that mattered, he was forbidden fruit. A fruit she was determined not to touch or eat, whatever it cost her. He was a sacrifice she had to make.

It was nine o'clock on Saturday night when her doorbell rang. It wasn't the outer door, but the one to her house. Sasha assumed it was the guardian, since she hadn't heard the bell ring on the big bronze outer

187

door. She was carrying the puppy and wearing her nightgown when she opened it. She expected to look into the ancient face of Madame Barboutier, and instead found herself looking up at Liam. He had shown up after all.

'What are you doing here?' she asked, unhappy to see him. Her heart was pounding and her knees felt weak. But there was no sign of it on her face, and she offered him no warm welcome. She had told him not to come.

'I came to see my god-dog.' Sasha was holding her, and he looked down at Socks and smiled. 'She looks good.' So did he. Sasha didn't. She looked tired and upset, and she was. She had been suffering over him all week. Keeping up her resolve about him had been anything but easy. And now there he was, on her doorstep, looking more beautiful than ever. He was everything she wanted, and couldn't allow herself to have. She was putting up all the resistance she could.

'I asked you not to come here,' she said coldly, on the verge of tears.

'I want to talk to you, Sasha,' he said, looking serious. She could see in his eyes that he was unhappy, too. 'Why don't we just do this for a while, and see what happens? Maybe it won't be a big deal after all.'

'And if it is? Then what? My kids go nuts. My artists think I'm a fruitcake. And we

188

become the talk of Paris and New York.' She didn't paint a pretty picture, but what she described could easily happen and be true. And he knew it, too.

'Do you ever think about anything but disaster or what other people think?' he asked, standing there, still holding his bag. 'What if it actually turned out okay? What if people don't give a damn what we do? What if your artists could care less, and your kids want you to be happy, even if that means being with a younger guy? This could turn out to be no big deal.'

'Until you find some girl your age, or younger, and fall in love with her. I don't want to go through that, either.'

'What if I die, or you do? What if we're struck by lightning one night when we're making love? What about cholera, diphtheria, measles? What if we get nuked in a world war?'

'I'd rather get nuked than make a fool of myself with you. I just don't want to go there, Liam. I'd rather be alone.'

'Don't be so silly. I've been in love twice in my life, once with Beth, which lasted for twenty years, and now with you. I've never told anyone I loved them, except the two of you.'

'You just want me because you can't have me,' Sasha said miserably. She was shivering in the cold and so was the dog.

'Can I at least come in for a minute? I've been driving for hours. They canceled my flight, so I took the Chunnel.' She stepped aside, wishing she had the courage not to let him in, but she didn't. As it had been since she had met him, she didn't have the strength to resist, as he walked slowly into her living room. All the lights were out and the room was cold. She was planning to go to bed with the dog. 'All right, I give up. Let me spend the night. I won't touch you. I'll leave tomorrow before you get up. I'm too tired to drive back tonight.' She looked at him for a long moment, and then nodded. He could sleep in Xavier's room again. She was going to lock her bedroom door. More to keep herself in than him out.

'Do you want something to eat?' she asked politely, setting the dog down.

'Do you have any ice cream?'

'I think so. We bought a lot last week, and I didn't eat it.'

'You should. It would do you good.' He thought she was too thin. She looked like she had lost more weight that week – he hoped it was from her agony over him.

He followed her into the kitchen, with Socks right behind them. She peed on the kitchen floor, and Liam cleaned it up, while Sasha served him chocolate and coffee ice cream in a giant bowl.

'Do you want anything else?' He shook his

190

head, sat down at the kitchen table, and said nothing. There was nothing much left for either of them to say. They had said it all. She had never been through anything as upsetting as this, other than her husband's death sixteen months before. Sasha sat quietly while he ate. And when he was finished, she stood up. 'I'm going to bed. You can sit in the living room if you want. You know where Xavier's room is.'

'Thanks, I'm tired, too. I'll go upstairs.' He followed her up, and she left him on the landing. She could hear him go up the flight to the top floor a moment later, and close Xavier's bedroom door.

She went to run a bath, and had the puppy with her. She didn't bother to lock her door. She knew she didn't need to. He had finally understood, and in the morning he'd be gone. The whole miserable episode of temptation, indulgence, and torture would be over. She could hardly wait for him to leave.

She was standing in her bathroom, brushing her teeth, in her nightgown, when she looked up and saw Liam in the mirror. She hadn't heard him come in. The puppy got excited the minute she saw him, and Sasha looked pained.

'I understand, Sasha. I just want to spend the night with you. One last time. I just want to hold you. I promise I won't do anything you don't want.' The problem was she did want. That had been the problem right from the first. She started to shake her head, and met his eyes in the mirror. There were tears in his eyes and hers too. Without a sound, she dropped her toothbrush, turned to face him, and held out her arms. She wanted to spend one last night with him too. She just wanted to hold him and feel him close to her, before they released each other for good. This moment would never come again, and they both knew it. She nodded silently, as tears rolled down her cheeks. 'It's okay, baby ... it's okay ... everything is going to be all right ... I promise...' he murmured.

'No, it isn't.' They both knew it, but just being there with him felt good. A moment later, they snuggled into her big bed in the chilly room. The puppy was sleeping in her own bed in Sasha's bathroom. Liam turned out the light, and they just held each other and said nothing. She was wearing her nightgown, and Liam was wearing jockey shorts, a T-shirt, and socks. He had bought another pair just for her.

'I love you,' he whispered as he held her.

'Me, too,' she said sadly. 'I wish things were different.' She wished she were younger, and a different person, so she could feel more comfortable about being with him. She didn't love him as she had Arthur. But she was so powerfully attracted to him, and already felt attached to him. This was different from anything she had ever experienced. Perhaps more than love, it was passion. But whatever it was, it felt dangerous to her, and was agony to resist.

'This is all we need for now,' he whispered back, grateful to be holding her, and in her bed with her. It was more than he had dared hope for, when he drove to Paris from London. He had been afraid she wouldn't even open the door, and he was grateful that she had. 'How am I going to live without you, Sasha?' She didn't answer his question, but she was thinking the same thing. They had managed until now. They'd have to manage again after this. All they had was tonight. He was dying to make love to her, but he didn't want to do anything to spoil it. He held her close until she fell asleep.

She felt him stir beside her in the morning, and she was instantly awake. She knew he was going to leave as soon as he got up. She lay beside him, waiting for him to leave her bed. He didn't move for a long time, in the pearl gray early-morning light in the room.

'Are you awake?' he whispered, and she nodded. 'Do you want me to go now?' With every ounce of her she didn't, but she had to let him go.

'In a minute,' she whispered. She reached toward him and held him close to her. She could hardly breathe it was so intoxicating to be with him. And as she held him, she could feel him aroused. Their bodies were glued to each other, and then suddenly they were kissing. The rest happened without either of them willing it after that, and he was terrified when they stopped. He knew that this time she would never forgive him, and he would never see her again. He had broken his promise to her, and couldn't stop himself from wanting her too much. 'I love you,' she said softly. And then she pulled away just enough to look at him. Their faces were next to each other on the pillow, and he had never seen anyone as beautiful in his life, whatever her age. 'What are we going to do?'

'You tell me,' he whispered back, and held his breath.

'I don't know ... I don't want to lose you ... I've already lost too much.' She just couldn't bring herself to let him go. At least not yet.

'Can I stay for a while?' She nodded, and he held her, and a little while later they made love again. They spent the whole day in bed, alternately sleeping, holding each other, and making love. Eventually, he brought food up for the puppy, and two bowls of ice cream for them.

'Have I gone insane?' she asked him, as she ate chocolate ice cream, lying in bed with him. This was all she wanted. Being there with him, with ice cream dribbling down her chin. He gently wiped it off.

'I've never been saner in my life. I can't speak for you.'

'This feels like a dream.'

'If it is, it's a very good dream.' He smiled at her and kissed her.

They stayed in bed together all day Sunday. They shared a bath in her bathtub and went downstairs long enough to eat dinner, and then hurried back to bed, like children running from their parents. There was no one to run from. Nowhere to hide. Sometime during the weekend, Sasha stepped over the line into his arms. She had no idea what they would do now. All she knew was that she wanted to be with him, for however long it lasted.

They cooked together, ate dinner laughing and talking easily, played with the dog, did the dishes, and then rushed back to bed and made love again.

'I'm too old for this,' she said afterward, barely able to catch her breath.

'So am I.' He laughed. 'You're wearing me out.' And then she looked at him, worried.

'When are you going back?'

'How about never?' He was teasing her, but they both liked the idea. 'What if I spend the week here?' It would be a good experiment to see how they did in real life. Sasha hadn't expected him to make the offer, but she liked the idea.

195

'I could tell everyone at the gallery that you came to meet them, and you're staying with me as a guest.' He knew she felt she had to explain things, but however she did that worked for him.

'Sounds fine to me. Or you could just tell them I'm your boyfriend, and we'll be in bed all week.' She looked nervous when he said it, and he kissed her. 'Don't worry, I'm not going to say anything to embarrass you.'

'You better not,' she warned him.

'I promise.'

They lay in bed together and held each other close that night. Sasha was excited at the prospect of spending a week with him. The day before she had promised herself she would give him up, and in the course of a single weekend, she had decided to risk her life with him. She had no other choice now, whether this was possible or not. They would soon find out.

Chapter 8

Sasha looked even more respectable than usual when she, Liam, and Socks walked across the courtyard to her offices on Monday morning. The gallery was closed on Monday, but the offices were open, and it was a good chance for all of them to catch up on deskwork. Sasha was wearing black slacks and a black sweater. And Liam looked like Liam. He was wearing cowboy boots, a leather jacket, white T-shirt, jeans, and a baseball cap. They were planning to go out to buy him more T-shirts and some underwear that afternoon. He hadn't brought enough to last the week, since he only planned to be there for the weekend.

Sasha introduced him to all her employees. He was easy and pleasant, and everyone seemed to enjoy meeting him. He had sent them slides of his work the week before. Bernard said they were anxious to show it. They talked about his solo show in New York at the end of the year. In the meantime, both branches of the gallery were going to show his work, in Paris and New York. It was an incredible opportunity for him. And Eugénie nearly fainted when she saw him. She told Sasha afterward that she had never seen a man as beautiful in her life. Nor had Sasha. That was part of the problem that was doing her in.

That night, as they talked about the gallery, he lay sprawled out on her bed like a young lion, after they made love.

'So what did you think?' she asked him. She was interested in his opinion, from an artist's point of view. She had a rare opportunity for insider information from him, as an artist evaluating the gallery. It was an interesting perspective for a dealer, and she respected his opinion, although her own as well. Her instincts had always been extremely good about the gallery and her artists.

'What did I think?' He looked blank. He was still catching his breath from what they'd just done, and surprised she was thinking of work. 'Well, let's see ... better than last night ... not as good as this morning ... maybe I was tired ... I thought the best ever was on Sunday afternoon in the bathtub...' He went on cataloging and comparing their sexual exploits, as Sasha giggled.

'Liam! Stop it! I meant about the gallery and the employees.'

'Oh, that. Very nice. I liked everyone.' He was much more interested in making love to her than talking about work.

'Be serious for a minute,' she chided him. She loved sharing her work with him. She had loved that with Arthur, too.

'Serious? If we make love any more often, I'm going to collapse in your arms, and you'll have to revive me. I'm older than I look.'

'So am I,' she said, with a look of regret.

'I've never done this so often in my life. I'm beginning to feel like a sex toy,' he said, looking worried. 'Come to think of it, maybe I am. Is that all I am to you?' He was serious for a moment.

'Don't be silly,' Sasha said, lying back on

her pillow. But she had to admit, she was having fun with him. A lot of it.

'I feel like the sex slave of the Faubourg St. Honoré. Maybe I should call the SAMU to rescue me.' The SAMU were the paramedics, the French equivalent of 911.

'I think you're becoming an addiction,' Sasha admitted, but she was having too much fun now to worry. She had put her fears on the back burner for the week, and was enjoying having him around every day.

'Maybe we should go to a twelve-step group. Love Slaves Anonymous. But hell, why spoil our fun?' He looked amused.

'Exactly,' she said, as she leaned over to kiss him. Neither of them could believe it, but they made love again before they went to sleep, and again before she went to work the next day. She felt girlish and giddy and tried not to act it, when she walked in.

Liam arrived shortly after, and enjoyed seeing the gallery once it was open. Sasha was pleased to discover that Bernard had invited Liam to lunch. They all seemed to like him, which was at least something. She'd been worried about how he would fit in, but so far he did.

Liam spent the rest of the week wandering around Paris, looking up artist friends in the Marais, and Sasha did her best to lighten her workload so she could spend time with him whenever possible. Although sometimes she had to meet with clients who were expecting to see her and buy important paintings. Liam walked in on one of those meetings, toward the end of the week. He was wearing a T-shirt, leather motorcycle jacket, baseball cap, jeans, and his cowboy boots. And, unbeknownst to anyone but Sasha, socks and underwear. He was determined to be proper and civilized that week. She introduced him to the clients she was meeting with as soon as he walked in, looking for her. He hadn't hesitated to interrupt her, which upset her. And she was looking stern and somewhat irritated, as he leaned down and kissed her on the mouth. Sasha was furious with him. Her clients were in their seventies, the wife was an Italian princess, and the husband the head of an important French bank. Her clients didn't get more conservative than them. Sasha had worn a Chanel suit with a skirt for the meeting, and pearls. She looked as respectable as they did. Liam looked like James Dean with long blond hair, which was definitely not their thing. She introduced him as one of their artists, and was somewhat unnerved when he sat down, uninvited, to have tea with them, and then changed his mind and poured himself a drink. He made himself totally at home, which didn't go unnoticed by her clients either. The princess looked shocked, and the banker was obviously annoyed. All Sasha could do was hope they thought him an eccentric artist, although his kissing her on the mouth certainly tipped their hand, and would have been hard to explain. What's more, they wanted Sasha's full attention. They had just bought two paintings for half a million dollars each. Liam looked singularly unimpressed by the paintings standing on two easels, and commented that they were very pretty, but not exciting. Sasha wanted to kill him. As soon as they left, she turned on him with a vengeance.

'What in God's name were you thinking, to say something like that? This is how I earn my living. Those two people just bought two paintings for a million dollars, in cash, and I don't care if you think what they bought is exciting or not, and neither do they. You could at least have pretended you liked them,' she said, fuming. 'And how dare you walk into a meeting? This is my business, not my bedroom. Have you lost your mind?' He had just done exactly what she feared he would. He had embarrassed her with important clients, and he didn't look the least bit apologetic. It was the control thing. No one was going to tell him what to do or how to behave. Boundaries and rules didn't exist for him.

'I never lie about art,' he said, looking nonplussed, as he stretched out on the couch in her office. 'I have too much integrity to do that. And I was being polite. I told them they weren't exciting. Actually, I thought they looked like shit. They're from a terrible period in the artist's lifetime, and he did much better work before that.'

'I'm perfectly aware of that, Liam, but those two paintings are what they wanted, so I located them. It took me eight months to get them from a dealer in Holland, and you damn near screwed up the sale. Besides which, you can't just stroll through here and pour yourself a drink while I'm meeting with clients. You have to show some respect.'

'So do you,' he said, looking annoyed. 'You think you run the world here. I'm every bit as good as they are. You can't just sweep me under the rug because someone with a fat checkbook walks in the door.'

'Oh yes, I can. They're my bread and butter, and my children's. And if you're going to be here, when I dance to their tune, so do you.'

'Like hell. I'm not your little minion, Sasha. I don't work here. If I'm the man in your life, you have to treat me with respect.'

'Then don't push your luck and show off. You looked like a Hell's Angel, strolling in here and pouring yourself a drink, while they were having tea.'

'That is total bullshit and you know it. All you have to tell them is that I'm one of your artists. That's all they need to know. I'm not going to parade around here in a suit and drink tea because you're selling two rotten paintings that you shouldn't be selling anyway. If that's what they wanted, then educate them, find them something better, and charge them more. But those two paintings were shit, and you know it. And as far as how I look, I'm wearing underwear and socks. That should be enough for you. I'm not going to walk around like a monkey on a leash, in a costume for you.'

'No one's asking you to do that. I'm just asking you to be polite to my clients, look decent, and be discreet. You can wait to have a drink till they leave. And you have no business walking into my meetings. I don't care how independent you are, I'm not going to tolerate that from you.'

'Who do you think you are?' he shouted at her. 'You're not my mother. I can do anything I want. You can't tell me what to do. I love you, but you're not going to control me, Sasha. I'm not one of your employees, or your children. In fact, I'm not even sure what I am to you.' He was working himself into a rage, as she spoke quietly. She was not going to get into a war with him. If she did, she knew no one would win. But she was not going to allow him to behave any way he wanted either. The wacky artist was in full swing.

'You *kissed* me, Liam. On the *mouth*,' she

said as he glared at her from across the room. 'In front of *clients*. That's completely inappropriate and you know it.'

'Don't tell me what's appropriate!' he shot back at her. 'I love you. I didn't stick my tongue down your throat, for chrissake. I gave you a peck on the mouth. What am I, just a boy toy you're having fun with? And that you want to keep in the closet?' he asked, looking insulted. She had hurt his feelings by criticizing him, and she knew it. But he had to learn to behave. This wasn't going to be easy, just as she had feared. She loved being with him privately, but he made her nervous when he strolled around the gallery, doing and saying whatever came into his head. Sometimes he just didn't think. And he was obviously allergic to any kind of rules.

'You're too old to be a boy toy,' she said demurely. He started to say something to her, looking heated, and then burst out laughing.

'You're right. I guess I am. But I feel like that sometimes. You're so uptight when you meet with clients, and so sniffy. Why don't you just relax? They might like it better too.'

'They're not that kind of clients. People who buy emerging artists are different, Liam. These kind of clients expect you to be stuffy and uptight. If I weren't, they'd be buying from someone else who is. Believe me. I've been in this business for twenty-three years.

And I watched my father do it from the time I was a little kid. I know what I'm doing. There are certain rules about this.'

'You and your rules,' he grumbled, but he got over it quickly. Quicker than she did. He had upset her terribly walking in on her client meeting. As far as Sasha was concerned, it didn't bode well for the future. It had unnerved her. In spite of that, she took him to dinner at Le Voltaire that night. It had become his favorite restaurant too. He didn't have to get dressed up to go there. He could wear his jeans, leather jacket, and cowboy boots, even though some of the most stylish and sophisticated people in Paris went there. He was in a much better mood after a great bottle of wine. But she was still uneasy after their brief but heated quarrel that afternoon. He had felt disrespected, and she had been outraged at his cavalier behavior while she was conducting business. He was going to have to learn the ground rules very soon. Something had to give, and he was it. If not, they were going to run aground very quickly. It took her the rest of the evening to calm down, and by the next day she did.

For the rest of the week, everything went smoothly between them. Bernard commented to Sasha that Liam seemed to be staying in Paris for a long time, but she didn't think he suspected why. She told him that Liam couldn't afford to stay in a hotel, and was

205

using Xavier's room, which made sense to him. But if he stayed with her often, and for long enough, she knew that sooner or later their secret would come out.

They had an easy, fun weekend. They went to the movies, had lunch at the Brasserie Lipp on Sunday, and coffee afterward at the Deux Magots. She tried to take him to the bar at the Ritz for a drink, but they wouldn't let him in wearing jeans, unless he was staying at the hotel, which Liam said was dumb. It was, but they had rules, too. Liam had very few. His were about being decent and kind and affectionate, not about behaving properly. And he was always loving to her. There was no doubt in her mind that she loved him, but she was nonetheless worried that he would do something alarming to expose their situation, and she wasn't ready for that to happen yet. Letting him stay with her in Paris for a week and hang around her office was a major step for her. And she was not going to go further than that. Now or maybe ever.

They were lying in bed on Sunday night, when Liam asked her casually what she was doing the next day. It was her first clue that he wasn't planning to leave on schedule. She didn't mind, as she loved being with him, but she was also aware that his continuing presence was going to become harder to explain, at the gallery, if nowhere else. They were the only ones who knew he was staying with her. He suggested they have dinner the following night with some of his friends in the Marais.

'Does that mean you'd like to stay?'

He nodded and smiled sheepishly at her. 'Yes, if it's okay with you.'

She hesitated for a fraction of a second, weighing the risk, and then smiled at him. She loved his being there with her. And she'd come up with some explanation. 'Yes, it is.'

But she was hesitant about meeting his artist friends, since some of them might know her and then she remembered that she was busy anyway. He looked instantly disappointed and a little hurt. She kissed him and explained that she was going to a black tie dinner, given by important clients. They had bought a Monet from her that summer, and she had accepted the invitation weeks before. Taking him with her to a formal dinner at a client's house was an experiment she was not prepared to venture yet, which he said he understood, but he looked annoyed nonetheless. All she had said to him was that she was not allowed to bring a guest.

'Then tell them you can't come,' he said, looking petulant, which she purposely ignored.

'I can't do that, Liam. They're the most important clients I have.' She was sincere about that.

'And what am I?'

'The man I love. But don't bring this to a showdown. You're talking about my work.'

'Would you have taken Arthur?' he asked bluntly. They both knew she would have. But everything about that situation was different. Arthur could have gone anywhere, and did. Liam couldn't. He didn't want to play the game. And Arthur acted like an adult. Liam didn't.

'That's not fair,' she said, looking unhappy. 'We were married. He was as proper and conservative as my clients. He was a banker, for God's sake.'

'And I'm a young punk.' He had added anger to the petulance by then.

'No,' she said calmly, 'you're a wacky artist, remember? That's what you told me. And you don't want to be "controlled." If you want to wear a dinner jacket, be proper, and act like a banker, you can come anywhere with me you want.' It was a major concession to him. But he didn't want concessions. He wanted freedom to behave any way he wanted, wherever he went, with or without her.

'They should accept me as I am. And so should you,' he said angrily.

'I do. They won't. If you want to go places like that with me, then you have to play their game. So do I. Those are the rules of the road. I can't take you with me this time, because it's too short notice. But if you're serious about this, we'll buy you a dinner jacket, and you can come with me next time, to something else. If you're willing to play by their rules. That's the deal.'

'Fuck them,' he said, suddenly very angry. 'Who the hell do they think they are? I'm twice the man they are. I heard this shit from my father when I was growing up. I'm not going to play that game for anyone, Sasha, not even for you.'

'You don't have to,' Sasha said calmly. 'You don't have to go to any of the stuffy things I do. But if you want to, you have to follow the rules. That's just the way it is.'

'And who makes those rules? Some pompous old asshole in a monkey suit? Why should I behave like him, and dress like him? Why can't I be me?'

'Because those pompous old assholes have all the money and power and make the rules. He who has the gold, rules. And if you want to go out in that world, then you have to be civilized, and play by their rules.'

'If you were proud of me and loved me, you'd take me anyway.' He was a child in full revolt, as she felt her heart sink. She had been afraid it would come to this, and it hadn't taken long. This was the second argument they'd had in less than a week. It confirmed her worst fears that this wasn't going to work. There were many things she loved

209

about him, his kindness, his warm, open affection toward her, his sense of humor, his intelligence, his talent, how fabulous he was in bed. But his temper tantrums and immaturity were definitely not on that list.

'I am proud of you, and I do love you. But I'm not going to take you into that world, if you're going to make a fool of me, or yourself. If you want to behave any way you want, you will make a fool of both of us.'

'What's more important to you, Sasha? Them or me?'

'You both are. I love you. But I live in that world. That's who I am. I told you that the first time we met. This is the problem we are always going to have, unless you want to give up being a wacky artist and walk into my world like a man. If you want to continue playing wacky artist, or wild young man who can't be tamed or controlled, then you have to let me go into that world by myself. It's as simple as that. That choice is up to you.'

'I'm who I am. And I'm not going to change that or kiss anyone's ass, for you or for them.'

'You have the right to make that decision. But you don't have the right to force them to accept you, if you won't play by their rules, or mine.'

'This is really about you, isn't it? And not about them. You want me to pretend I'm Arthur. Well, I'm not. I'm me.'

'This has nothing to do with Arthur,' she said to him through clenched teeth. 'Look, why don't you have dinner with your friends tomorrow? I'll go to my stuffy dinner, I'll leave early, and join you wherever you are in the Marais.'

'What, and go slumming? Lady Bountiful will leave the mansion and meet her peasant boyfriend in the slums? If I'm not good enough for you to take me with you, then I'm going back to London tomorrow.' He had originally been planning to leave then anyway. His offer to stay on had come as a surprise to her.

'That's up to you,' she said quietly. 'I'm doing the best I can, Liam. Sometimes this is going to be a stretch for both of us. We knew that from the first.'

'Yeah, we did. I just didn't realize that the one we'd be stretching is me. Just how much humiliation do you expect me to take? You tell me how to behave in your gallery, what not to do to offend the clients. I have to tiptoe around, not kiss you, and not pour a drink. And if I want to go out with you anywhere that matters, I have to dress like Little Lord Fauntleroy and act like Malcolm Forbes. Well, I'm an artist, Sasha. I'm not a trained monkey or a banker, and I won't let you cut off my balls.'

'I'm not trying to cut off your balls. We live in different worlds. This was bound to happen. We are going to have to have a lot of understanding and flexibility with each other if this is going to work.' Neither of them knew yet if it even could, and it was beginning to look like it couldn't, if he was going to insist on doing his wacky artist routine and going everywhere with her. The two just didn't mesh. She had warned him of it before. And now they had hit a wall.

'I told you, I'm not going to let you cut off my balls. I'm going back to London tomorrow. When you get your priorities straight, give me a call.'

Listening to him, she wanted to scream.

'This isn't about priorities, Liam,' she said, sounding desperate not to lose her temper with him. It was frustrating trying to reason with him, like an angry child. 'It's about playing by the rules, and living in different worlds. Like entering a club. If you want to come into this club, you have to follow their rules.'

'I'm never going to do that, Sasha. Never. If I wanted to do that, I'd still be living in California with my father, and taking shit from him. I'm not taking shit from anyone anymore, and sure as hell not from you. If you want me in your life, then take me, but don't tell me how to behave by whose rules. If you love me, there are no rules, or shouldn't be.'

'There are always rules,' she said sadly. 'I have to play by those same rules. I can't behave any way I want. I can't show up in blue jeans tomorrow, or wearing cowboy boots and a baseball cap. I have to show up looking like they do, with my hair combed and an evening gown. I have to be just as proper as they are, and fundamentally I am, because I believe in their rules. It keeps things civilized.'

'I don't want to be civilized, dammit! I want to be me. I want to be respected and accepted for who I am, however I want to behave, not for who I pretend to be, because I'm willing to kiss their asses. I'm not going to kiss anyone's ass ever again.' Their argument was obviously bringing up things from his childhood, because even she could see that his anger at her was out of measure. He was beside himself as he ranted. And nothing she said made sense to him or induced him to calm down. On the contrary, it seemed to make it worse. She felt utterly hopeless as she listened. He was out in the stratosphere somewhere, on his own.

'I'm not asking you to kiss anyone's ass, Liam. Least of all mine. You can behave any way you want. But if that's what you want, then you have to play on your side of the fence, and stay in your own world, or in our private world, which is fine with me too. But if you want to cross over to the other side of the fence, and go there with me, then you have to play by their rules.'

213

'Fuck their rules. And come to think of it, Sasha, fuck you. If you're not proud of me, if you're embarrassed because I'm younger than you are, if you don't respect me for who I am, then I don't want to be with you. And I don't want to be here. I'm going home tomorrow. You can call me when you make up your mind.'

'About what? What am I supposed to make my mind up about? What do you want from me?' She was feeling dazed. Some of what he was saying was so unreasonable, it just wasn't making sense. And none of it was news. He had known who she was, and what she stood for, right from the first. Those had been among her primary concerns about him, other than his age. His age was the least of it. His lack of boundaries and immature behavior was far worse. He was behaving like a five-year-old.

'Either you take me into that world with you, just as I am, and don't try to leave me at home like some hooker you've hired for the night, or I'm out of here for good. I'm not going to be left at home, like some piece of garbage. And I'm not going to be told how to behave.' He stormed at her, as she fought back tears. She wanted him to be better than this. She wanted it to work, and it never would like this.

'Then figure it out for yourself,' she said, suddenly as angry as he was. 'Stop acting like such a baby, saying you won't take a bath or put your suit on, and you can throw your dinner on the floor anytime you want to. If you want to come downstairs and eat with the grown-ups, then be one. That's all it takes, for chrissake. You can't play wacky artist forever, unless you want to hang out with other children who are as badly behaved as you are. If you want to do that, then don't whine because I can't take you out. I'd like to, for chrissake, I'd like that very much, but I'm not going to embarrass myself while you show off and try to prove how outrageous you can be. If you love me so much, Liam, then grow up and learn to behave. I'm not taking a badly behaved spoiled child out with me. *You* think about it, and *you* make up your mind. I already did. I'm here with you. Now you live up to your end of the deal, or forever hold your peace. It takes more than just love and being good in bed to get on in the world. At some point, like it or not, we all have to grow up. Maybe it's right about that time for you. You figure it out. Go back to London if you want to, and when you decide to grow up, give me a call.'

They never said another word to each other that night. For the first time since he had been there, they each stayed on their side of the bed, with a vast chasm between them. Liam was deeply wounded by what he viewed as her disloyalty, and everything she'd said. And she was furious at the tantrum he had thrown. He was acting like a very badly behaved child. They each got up in the morning silently. He showered, shaved, and dressed. And before she left for the office, he packed his bag and stood looking at her in the front hall.

'I love you, Sasha. But I'm not going to let you control me, or tell me what to do. I respect myself too much for that.'

'I love and respect you too. I really do,' she said honestly, 'both as an artist and a man.' Although she was a little unsure about how respect-worthy he was as a father, she didn't know him well enough to judge that yet, and she had never seen him with his kids. But there were so many things she liked about him, and she was falling more in love with him each day. But not enough to give up her whole life for him. She was too old for that. And she liked her life, just as it was. 'This isn't about control. It's about mutual respect. If you respect me, then come into my world, play by their rules, and act like a gentleman. If you don't want to do that, which is your right, then don't complain if I visit people in my world alone. You can't have both. You can't do your "I'll do whatever I want" routine in the polite world, Liam. You're too old for that. Even children can't behave that way.'

'I'm never going to be anyone different than I am. And if you love me, you have to accept that, and be willing to take me anywhere, just as I am.'

'I can't. I can't do that to myself, or my kids, or the reputation I've built for all these years. I can't let you make a fool of me in public, Liam.' And she knew he would. She had heard too many of his exploits from Xavier, although she had never seen him act out herself. The scene of him walking in on her meeting at the gallery was enough for her. And a tantrum like today. She had serious concerns. 'It's bad enough that I'm almost ten years older than you. I know that's not a lot, but it feels like it to me, given your behavior and ideas. That's hard enough, and will raise enough eyebrows as it is. Don't ask me to usher you into all the loftiest places, and then reserve the right to play outrageous wacky artist, just so you can prove a point. That's not loving or respectful of me, and who I am. You knew who I was, and how I live. You said you could do this, and do it right. I believed you. Now you don't want to deliver. You want to do whatever you want in my world, and you can't. Neither can I. No one can. We all have to behave and toe the line. I hope you come to your senses, because I love you, and I want to be with you. And what you're doing is not fair to me.' The fact that it was even a conversation or an argument was frightening her. Who was this man? And why was total freedom so vital to him, at her expense?

'I'm the one who's getting screwed here, and being disrespected,' he said, almost pouting. 'You want to call all the shots.'

'The only shot I'm calling is that I'm asking you to grow up. Either be civilized, or let me do what I have to do, while you play with your friends. You can be as outrageous as you want, but if that's what you want, then don't expect me to take you out and show you off. If you want to be outrageous, then stay home with me and do it privately, not in public.'

'I'm not going to be your dirty little secret, Sasha. If that's what you want, then find another man. Either take me out and show me off, just as I am, or all bets are off.'

'Then I guess they are, for now anyway. Think about it, Liam. I hope you come to your senses when you go back to London. If this starts to make sense to you, then give me a call.' He looked at her, nodded, never stopped to kiss her, picked up his bag, brushed past her, and slammed out the door.

After he left, she sat down and thought about everything that had happened. She loved him, but not enough to turn her life upside down for him, and give up who she was. It was too late in the day for her to do that for anyone. Not even Liam. She knew she was in love with him. But maybe not enough.

Chapter 9

The days after Liam left seemed to drag at first. In the short time he was there, she had grown used to being with him, talking to him, eating with him, making love with him. Even Bernard commented when he left, and asked if he was still around. Sasha said he had gone back to London.

'He's a sweet boy, but it must have been hard on you to have him around for that long.'

He had stayed with her for ten days, and she had loved everything about it, until the last few days when they began to argue. It also struck her that Bernard called him a 'boy.' That was the essence of the problem she was having with Liam. He was a boy, not a man, and acted like one. At times he was age appropriate, at others he was an unruly teenager. She expected more of him at nearly forty. He really was Peter Pan. She thought Bernard was being sarcastic with his comments at first, and curious about their relationship. And then she realized he was sincere in what he'd said about her house-guest. He thought Sasha had been an incredibly good sport to let him stay there for so long. Apparently, their secret was still safe. It would never have occurred to Bernard that Sasha was involved with Liam. And in any case, it looked like the relationship was over. She sat and waited for the phone to ring at night, once Liam went back to London. It never did. He never called, nor did she. They had come to an impasse over his ridiculous demands and childish behavior. She hadn't expected their affair to last forever, but she had expected it to last longer than it had. There was no point calling him, since he had made his terms clear to her. Either she would take him out in public in the circles that she moved in, no matter how proper, and no matter how he behaved, or the deal was off.

The conditions he had set were impossible for her, whether or not she loved him. She had no compromise to offer him, other than what she had said to him before he left Paris. At the end of the month, she stopped waiting for the phone to ring. She knew he was gone. And as he sat waiting to hear from her in London, he knew the same. It had taken weeks, instead of years, but they had parted ways. She had been right from the day they met. It was impossible. She reminded herself that it was better to face it sooner than later. But as she waited for the call that never came, she was sad anyway. As childish as he was at times, there was an appealing side of him, and she truly missed him.

It took two months for Sasha to make her peace with it, and even then she was still sad about his disappearance from her life. But there was no one to tell. No one had ever known about them, so there was no one to turn to for advice or comfort. She couldn't mourn him with others, or speak to anyone about him. She just had to accept the fact that he was gone. She knew it would never have worked anyway. He was too immature, too difficult, too unreasonable, too determined not to grow up. He had proven all that to her when he had a tantrum and vanished.

Sasha went to New York in February and March, and both times ran into a blizzard. Tatianna loved her new job. And the gallery was doing well. She was planning to visit Xavier in London in April, and she braced herself, knowing that Liam would be somewhere near. She just hoped she didn't run into him with Xavier. And she couldn't say anything to Xavier about avoiding him, or it would expose their secret.

Shortly before Sasha left for London in April, Eugénie told her they'd had an e-mail from Liam. He had finished several new pieces of work, and thought Sasha should come to see them. He had volunteered to send transparencies, but wanted his dealer to see the work in the flesh. He said in the e-mail that it was the best work he'd ever done.

'Oh,' Eugénie remembered, as she reported on the e-mail to Sasha at the end of a long day, 'he said to send you his best, and hopes you're okay.' Sasha was in fact okay. After more than two months of silence from him, she was a lot better than she had been in February, but she was still annoyed at him. And it sounded stupid to her to send her his 'best.' His best what? She had already seen his best and his worst. Although she had believed herself to be in love with him for about a minute, he had put her off forever with the way he'd behaved. He had pulled an incredibly childish move on her. She was tired of self-indulgent artists, who were not so young, but pretended to be, and still behaved like teenagers well into middle age. At thirty-nine, in her opinion, he was far too old to act the way he had when he left Paris. Still, she was hurt that she had never heard from him again. She had far too much pride to call him.

She told Eugénie she was going to a dinner party that night, and it reminded her again of her blowout with Liam while she was getting dressed. She was leaving for London the next day to see Xavier. She didn't know what she was going to do about Liam and seeing his new work. She represented him, but she was in no hurry to see him again. He had created a very awkward situation for her, in fact for both of them.

She was glad that she hadn't introduced him to her world. His absence now would have been embarrassing to explain.

The dinner party she was going to that night was being given by the American ambassador to Paris. He had invited several important artists and dealers, an American writer who was visiting Paris, and someone had told her there was a famous actor coming, too. It sounded like a motley crew to her, and she wasn't in the mood. For reasons known only to herself and Liam, she had been testy and short-tempered with everyone for the past two months, although lately she had been in a slightly better mood.

She wore a black lace dress to the dinner party at the ambassador's residence, her hair in a bun as always, and a new pair of very sexy shoes, although most of the time, she wondered why she bothered. She hadn't gone out with anyone, nor did she want to, since she and Liam had had their brief, ill-fated fling. She had known right from the beginning that their affair was doomed. She felt stupid for having allowed him to convince her to try it. But in private moments, she admitted to herself that she had wanted it as much as he said he did, and in her heart of hearts she had hoped it would work. It was too bad it didn't. He was a talented artist, but a totally immature man. It was no surprise to her now that Beth had left him, and taken their kids. Being married to him for twenty years must have been a nightmare for her.

She forced him from her head, as she had for two months, as she walked into the ambassador's residence that night. With the exception of a rock star and two actors, Sasha knew everyone there. In its own way, Paris was a very small town. The whole world was these days.

At the dinner table, Sasha was seated next to one of the actors, who was completely self-involved, and had nothing to say to her. He was far more interested in the woman on his right, who was married to a Hollywood producer. He was busy charming her, and had been for an hour when Sasha turned her attention politely to the man on her left. She knew she had seen him somewhere, and then remembered who he was. He had once been considered the wizard of Wall Street, and had since retired. Arthur had introduced her to him at a party in the Hamptons once. And much to her surprise, he remembered her.

'It must have been about ten years ago,' she said, looking impressed. He was about Arthur's age, who would have been fifty-nine by now. He had been gone for a year and a half.

'I was very impressed when we met. I've been in your gallery several times.' He smiled at her, and she noticed that he was a good-looking older man. She no longer remembered if he was widowed or divorced, and by now he could have remarried, if that was the case.

'The gallery in New York?' she asked, to keep the conversational ball rolling. She had no particular interest in him, but he was easy to talk to, far easier than the actor on her right, who had virtually ignored her. There was nothing she could do for him.

'I was speaking of the gallery here,' her dinner partner explained. 'I live here now.' His name was Phillip Henshaw, and she couldn't help wondering what had brought him to Paris. He had retired young, just as Arthur had hoped to. 'Both my daughters married Frenchmen and moved here. When my wife died, I decided I needed a break from New York. I've been here for five years, and I love it.' Sasha noticed then that he had a soft southern drawl, and a moment later he explained that he had been born in Louisiana. He and the ambassador had gone to the University of Virginia together. The wife of the ambassador was from Georgia. Phillip went on to explain to Sasha that he had a house in Provence, and a flat in London. He managed to get to each of those places about once a month.

'I'm going to London tomorrow, to see my son, and some artists.' She smiled easily at him.

'So am I, going to London, I mean.' He returned the smile, and then a little while later said he had been sorry to hear about Arthur. 'It's not easy, finding yourself alone at our age, particularly if you've been happily married.' He touched her heart with what he said.

'That's why I moved back to Paris. It was just too depressing to stay in New York after Arthur died,' she confessed.

'Do you still have your house in the Hamptons?' He remembered that as well.

She nodded, and then sighed. 'I never go there anymore. All those familiar places we used to love are just too hard.' They talked about New York for a while, and discovered they knew many people in common. The good thing about talking about her old life with him was that it kept her mind off Liam. He had distracted her constantly for the past two months. She was angry and disappointed by how things had worked out, and frustrated by the way their affair had ended, in silence. Worse yet, now she had to get over it, and act impartially as his dealer. Getting involved with him had been even more foolish than she had feared. But she wasn't devastated, as she had been over Arthur. She was just disappointed and sad, and finally philosophical about it.

She was surprised, as she left the ambassador's residence, when Phillip Henshaw asked her if she would like to have dinner with him the following night in London. She told herself that maybe she could sell him some art for his houses.

'That would be very nice,' Sasha responded. He suggested Mark's Club, which she and Arthur had always liked. It was another establishment owned by the same man who had started Annabel's and Harry's Bar. Phillip offered her a ride home then, and she thanked him, but said she had come with a car and driver. She didn't like driving herself at night, when she was dressed up and went to parties. He walked her to her car, and told her he'd pick her up at Claridge's the following night at seven. She thought about him on the way home. There was nothing exciting about him, but at least he was intelligent, polite, and pleasant. And it might be nice to have dinner with a friend in London. She didn't know what Xavier's plans were, but she was planning to spend the afternoon with him, and if he was free, she could have dinner with him the following evening. She still had to figure out what to do about seeing Liam. Maybe nothing. Maybe she could have Bernard fly to London to meet with Liam, although the gallery manager would think it strange that Sasha hadn't seen him, particularly since Liam had stayed with her when he came to Paris. It was going to be awkward to explain it. Everything about their situation had become awkward, thanks to Liam.

She caught a nine o'clock flight at Le Bourget the next morning, and with the hour's time difference and the short flight, she was in London at exactly the same time she had left Paris, nine A.M. She was settled into her usual suite at Claridge's by ten-thirty. She called Xavier, agreed to meet him for lunch, and then set off to see two of her artists.

She arrived promptly at one to have lunch with her son, at the restaurant he had suggested, and as she walked out into the garden where he was waiting for her, she was shocked to see he had brought Liam. It was small comfort to see that he looked as uncomfortable as she did. Apparently, she learned later, Liam had been in Xavier's studio all morning, and her son couldn't think of a plausible excuse not to bring him, since Sasha was his dealer. He liked Liam, although Xavier was sorry to miss some time alone with his mother. He loved talking to her.

'Hello, Liam,' she said cautiously, as he stood up to greet her. Being obliged to have lunch with him felt like a nightmare to Sasha. It was the first time she'd seen him since he stormed out of her house in Paris. As usual, he was wearing one of his eccentric but sexy outfits. A T-shirt, a leather jacket, baseball cap, and this time paint-splattered pants and high-top red sneakers. But despite her irritation with him, she had to admit, as always, he looked incredibly handsome. And his blond ponytail was two months longer.

'How've you been, Sasha?' he finally turned to her and asked, sounding awkward. Until then, Xavier had been carrying the bulk of the conversation, and he was surprised to notice some sort of strain between them. He had gotten the impression before that they were on good terms and very friendly. Although he suddenly realized that Liam hadn't mentioned her lately.

'Have you two had some sort of artistic difference of opinion?' Xavier finally asked with a look of amusement. He knew them both well, and that they had strong opinions. The atmosphere between them was tangibly stressed. You could cut it with the proverbial knife.

'Yes,' Liam said, looking angry and unhappy.

'Not at all,' Sasha said politely at exactly the same moment.

'Well, which is it, yes or no?' Xavier asked them. He was laughing, as Liam squirmed in his seat, and his mother looked icy.

'She wouldn't take me to a party in Paris, when I was staying with her. I thought that was pretty rude, since I was her houseguest.' That was one way to explain it, Sasha observed. The last thing she wanted was for Xavier to get caught in the middle, particularly since he only knew half the story and she didn't intend to fill him in on the rest. She was pleased to see that Liam had obviously not shared his story of their brief affair with him, since Xavier appeared to know nothing about what had happened. He was completely in the dark.

'What were you wearing when she wouldn't take you to the party?' Xavier asked comfortably, as dealer and artist, previously lovers, glared at each other. It was obvious that Liam was still furious with her.

'I don't know ... the usual stuff ... what difference does it make?' Liam growled at him, while Sasha watched them both in silence.

'A big difference, at the kind of parties she goes to. If you want my guess, that's why she didn't take you.' Xavier spoke as though his mother weren't present. Sasha said nothing. 'She won't take me either. The people she knows are incredibly stuffy and pretty boring. Sorry, Mom.' He glanced over at Sasha apologetically, and she nodded. She had said the same thing to Liam right from the beginning.

'That was what I told him,' Sasha interjected. 'I told him he couldn't do his wacky artist thing with those kinds of people. And he told me I couldn't control him.'

'You probably can't,' Xavier said sensibly, and then looked at Liam. 'What's with the wacky artist thing? If you want to do that, why would you want to go to those parties? Personally, I'd pay her money not to take me. I hate them.'

'So do I. I just don't want to be left home like a four-year-old, or be told how to behave when I get there.'

'What difference does it make if she takes you? You're one of her artists, Liam. Not her husband. My father didn't love going to them either. He said most of her important clients bored him to tears. He got out of going to those parties every chance he got.' Sasha smiled at the comment and Liam looked pensive. 'You sound like a jealous lover,' Xavier chided, still not understanding what had happened, for which Sasha was profoundly grateful.

'Or a spoiled brat,' Sasha added. 'I told him you can't behave like a goofball if you go to those parties. He informed me that he'd behave any way he wanted. End of story.' End of romance. But thank God Xavier didn't know that. From what Liam was saying, Sasha was amazed her son didn't suspect it. It had never occurred to him for a single second that his friend might have slept with his mother. She turned to Liam then, and reminded him of what she'd said two months earlier. 'Anytime you want to dress and act like a grown-up, you're welcome to come to anything with me. In the meantime...' Her voice drifted off, and Liam rolled his eyes.

'You sound like my father.' He looked angry at her again, which surprised Xavier. His mother was right. Liam was being childish and bratty, and he didn't always side with his mother, but this time he felt he had to.

'You were a kid then,' Xavier reminded him. 'You're an adult now. You just turned forty. Hell, that's fucking ancient...' And then he glanced at Sasha. 'Sorry, Mother.'

'Not at all. It's not fucking ancient, but it's old enough not to have a tantrum about a party.'

'My father and brothers never took me anywhere. My father called me a freak, and my brothers said I was a weirdo. I was always an outcast. That's why I left San Francisco. I just got tired of it. I'm never going to let anyone treat me that way again.'

'You probably were a weirdo,' Xavier said with a look of amusement. Watching Liam, and the look in his eyes, Sasha felt suddenly more sympathetic. She had obviously tapped into some serious wounds from his childhood. And he had had no mother to protect or defend him from his father and brothers' insensitivity and cruelty. Looking at him, she suddenly wanted to put her arms around him, but she couldn't. 'You still are a weirdo sometimes,' Xavier said, and Liam smiled. 'Hell, what do you expect? You're an artist. I'm weird, too. It's a sign of greatness and talent. I like being a weirdo, so do you. And you couldn't get me to one of those parties if you paid me.'

'I just felt left out, I guess. It was like the old days when I was a kid. I guess it hit a nerve. I was being told I couldn't go somewhere unless I acted like someone I wasn't. Maybe it was old tapes in my head that made me crazy, and not your mother.' Liam glanced at Sasha anxiously, and wanted to apologize to her, but he couldn't. Their eyes met and held for a long moment. And miraculously, Xavier missed it.

'Shit, man, you were only a houseguest. She probably couldn't take you to the party anyway.'

'No, I couldn't,' Sasha added. 'The argument was more about theory, and freedom of behavior.'

'And control,' Liam added. 'When people insult me like that, it just makes me crazy. I was always left out as a kid, like I wasn't related to them or something, or good enough to be one of them. They were always trying to control me and make me behave the way they wanted, and I just couldn't.' It went even deeper than that, Sasha realized. It was about having lost the protection and unconditional love of his mother at seven. That's who she had been dealing with that night, a seven-year-old boy who had lost his mother. It suddenly explained a lot of things to her, and the immature behavior she'd seen in Paris. Her heart went out to him as she sat there listening to him.

'All right, are we all on the same page now?' Xavier turned to Liam. 'You obviously had some kind of psychotic break, or déjà vu or something. My mother goes to parties given by the most boring people on the planet, that no one in their right mind wants to go to. And you're a wacky artist, and shouldn't go to places like that, with people like she knows. My mother's fine, the people she hangs out with aren't. People like us need to hang out with each other. Not people like she knows or sells to, or it'll stifle our talent. Just hang out with me, and forget her fancy bullshit. Believe me, you'd hate it. Now, can we all relax and have lunch? I'm going to the bathroom. You two kiss and make up so she sells your paintings and isn't pissed at you, and when I come back, we'll all have a nice time, like we did last time. Right, children?' They both smiled at him. Xavier had broken the deadlock they couldn't for two months, even if he didn't know the whole story. 'Thank you.' He got up and left them, and disappeared into the men's room, while Liam looked at her. He still loved her, and thanks to Xavier he was no longer angry at her. Now that he thought about it, it hadn't really been about her. It had been ancient history that had more to

234

do with his father and brothers than with Sasha. She had hit a hot spot for him, and pushed all his buttons. So much so that he had been unable to listen to reason, until Xavier translated it for both of them two months later.

'I'm sorry, Sasha,' Liam said softly. 'I missed you so damn much. You're the most stubborn woman on the planet. You never called me.'

'You never called me, either. And I missed you, too. I'm so sorry. I never really understood what it meant to you or why. Now I do. I didn't mean to hurt you.' She reached out and touched his hand as she said it.

'You didn't. They did. I got you confused with them for a minute.' A long minute. It had been more than two months since he left Paris. 'Let's get together for a drink before you leave London.' She nodded, just as Xavier came back to the table.

'Everybody happy again?'

'Very.' Sasha beamed at him. 'You're an excellent mediator. I should use your services more often.' She saw when she turned to look at him that Liam was smiling at her.

They ordered lunch, and both men talked about their work, while Sasha listened. She was never happier than when talking to artists, particularly these two. After lunch, they went to Liam's studio and looked at his recent paintings. They were even better than his last ones. She beamed at him when she saw them.

'My God, Liam, they're fantastic.' She could tell that he'd been digging deep into his soul to come up with what she saw on canvas.

'You do good work when you're pissed off,' Xavier commented with amusement.

'Sometimes,' Liam said, looking sad, and Sasha saw it. She squeezed his hand as she brushed past him. 'I was only pissed off in the beginning. After that, I was miserable. Actually, that's when I do my best work. I hate that that's true, but it always is,' he said, looking exhausted, as he stared at his canvasses. He had had a lonely two months without her.

'That's true for me too,' Xavier admitted.

'I wish I could say I'd been as productive,' Sasha added. The last two months had been painful for her without him. She wished she could spend time alone with him now, but she had to see another artist. She was glad she had seen Liam's work though. And maybe now it would be better for both of them, if she was only his dealer. Their brief affair had obviously been a disaster. But thanks to Xavier, at least the war between them was over.

'What are you both doing tonight?' Liam asked, as Sasha left them. She was obviously in a hurry.

'I'm busy,' Sasha said quickly, and Xavier said he had a date.

'One of your boring parties?' Liam asked her with a look of amusement.

'No, a quiet dinner with a potential client.' Although she didn't owe him any explanations.

The war was over, but so was their romance. With luck, they'd be friends now.

'What about tomorrow?' Liam wanted to see her again before she left for Paris, and it was more comfortable for both of them now with Xavier present.

'I'm free,' Xavier chimed in.

'Me too,' Sasha said, although she had wanted time alone with her son. It would be different if Liam joined them.

He suggested dinner at his favorite pub, Xavier agreed readily, and Sasha more reluctantly, but after all he had said at lunch, she didn't want to be rude to Liam. She could have breakfast alone with Xavier the next morning, before she went back to Paris.

Sasha agreed to pick them both up the following night with her car and driver, although being in a noisy pub was not how she liked to spend her evenings. She was doing it for both of them, and maybe a little more for Liam. She felt loving and protective of him when she left.

She was busy for the rest of the afternoon, did some errands on New Bond Street before she went back to the hotel, and had just enough time to change before Phillip picked her up for dinner. She was brushing her hair and sweeping it into the bun she always wore, when Liam called her.

'I'm glad we met today,' Liam said sadly. 'Xavier did us both a big favor. Or me anyway. I'm really sorry I got so crazy in Paris.'

'That's okay,' Sasha said, holding her hair up with one hand, and the phone with the other. 'Those things happen. I really felt badly about it today when you explained it.' He had told her about his father before, but somehow she hadn't made the connection. What Liam needed more than anything was a mother. But she didn't really want to be one to him. She had her own children. Maybe he needed mothering more than romance. But with the difference in their ages, it made her feel even older. Maybe as his dealer, and not his lover, she could give him more of what he needed from her.

Most of her artists needed mothers, and expected her to be one. Part of her role with them was nurturing them. She didn't mind doing that, at least with Liam. Maybe it would help him. Not that there was anything in it for her now, except her commission on his paintings. She was still attracted to him, and she still felt the same electrical charge when she looked at him, but what she felt for him now was different. Her feelings for him had gone underground, and in some ways seemed deeper. She loved him, but she was able to look at him now without wanting to tear his clothes off. She had sublimated what she felt for the past two months, and what she felt for him now more than anything was compassion. It was better, and healthier for her, than the insanity she had felt for him earlier that winter when they first met. Although she missed what they had shared. It was as though her feelings for him had matured and been transformed somehow since the last time she'd seen him. She was content to be his dealer and friend, and nothing else.

'Are you happy?' he asked her, and she smiled at the question.

'If you're asking me if there's someone else now, there isn't. It's taken me a while to get over what happened. I was pretty disappointed when you left Paris.' It had been particularly hard for her to lose him after losing Arthur. 'I got past it. Things happen. I never thought it could work between us. I was just sorry to find out that I'd been right and it couldn't.'

'It could have, if I hadn't lost my marbles.' Liam sounded embarrassed.

'You didn't. Maybe you were right. It was pretty rude leaving you behind, and treating you like a secret. I just didn't know how else to do it.'

'I didn't either. It doesn't seem like such a big deal now, but it did then.'

'It did to me too. I'm glad Xavier defused it.'

'He's a great kid, Sasha.'

'I know. I'm very lucky.' She looked at her watch then. Philip was arriving in ten minutes, and she still had to do her hair and put on makeup. 'I hate to do this, but I have to run. I'm being picked up in ten minutes.'

'Why is it that I think you're having dinner with a date and not a client?' It was both, but it was no longer Liam's business, and it never would be again.

'Maybe you're feeling paranoid,' she teased him. 'Go paint something. I'll see you tomorrow.'

'Have a nice time tonight,' he said, and for a minute, she felt the old stirring, but now she could resist him. Enough time had passed, and she had gotten sane.

'Thanks, Liam.'

She rushed around her room for ten minutes after that, trying not to think of him. And when Phillip called from the lobby, she was ready. Much to her surprise, they had a perfect evening. It was everything a first date should be. Polite, courteous, interesting, intelligent, and amusing. He was a nice man and good company. He'd had an interesting career, loved to travel, and had friends in many places. He played tennis and golf, read

240

voraciously, had a serious interest in art, and was obviously deeply attached to his children and grandchildren. Sasha felt no great chemistry for him, but she enjoyed the evening. She found it was a relief to feel none of the things she had felt for Liam. What she experienced in Phillip's company was easy and peaceful. She didn't even care if she sold him a painting.

They had dinner at Mark's Club, and afterward he took her to Annabel's. She was home in good order, shortly after midnight. He said he was going to Holland the next day to see about a sailboat he had ordered, and he would call her as soon as he got back to Paris. It was a delight to be with someone so intelligent and pleasant. There was none of the excitement or torture she had been through with Liam.

She slept peacefully that night, saw an artist the next day, visited two galleries, and went shopping. She got back to the hotel in time to change into jeans to meet Xavier and Liam. She felt as though she were going out with her two boys. The pub Liam had chosen was as noisy and crowded as she feared it would be. They could hardly hear each other as they shouted across the table during dinner. Afterward, they went to the bar, where Xavier flirted with assorted women, and Liam tried to have an intelligent conversation with Sasha. She couldn't wait for the evening to

241

end, and instead it seemed to go on forever. It was odd for her being there with Liam. The women crowding around them, and lusting after him openly, were all in their early twenties. As she looked at them, and at him, she knew she didn't want to be there. Ten minutes later, she told them both that she had a splitting headache. She left them there, happy and drinking. Neither of them was drunk when she left, but she suspected they would be eventually. It was a far different evening than the night before with Phillip. As polite and civilized as that was, this was loud, disorderly, and chaotic. And as she rode back to the hotel alone, she realized that the evening and where they spent it made her feel sad and ancient. She didn't know why, but it had depressed her to see Liam. This was the price she had to pay for her foolishness in getting involved with him. Now, each time she saw him, she would have to remember what had happened, and why it ended. Because Liam was not an option for her. It could never have worked.

She was relieved to get back to the hotel, and take her clothes off. She put on her nightgown and lay on the bed, enjoying the silence, and thinking about him. It was weird to think now that he had once been hers, and now he was available to all those young, excited, and faceless women. She believed, as she always had, that he should be with women closer to his age, and younger than she was. The one thing she didn't know, and maybe never would, was who she belonged with. Maybe no one. She felt out of place and lonely everywhere now, in Liam's world, and her own.

She turned the lights off at eleven o'clock, and was sound asleep when the phone rang. For a minute, she had no idea where she was, and then she remembered. The voice on the phone was deep and familiar.

'I'm downstairs in the lobby' was what he said for openers.

'Who is this?'

'It's Liam.'

'I was sleeping.'

'How's your headache?'

'I think it's better.' She didn't want to tell him she'd never had one.

'I need to talk to you.' He sounded anxious.

'I'll call you tomorrow.' She didn't want to see him. It would just make her sadder. She had left him where he belonged that night, in the pub, with all those excruciatingly young women.

'I don't want to wait till then. Please, Sasha ... let me come up and see you.'

'I don't think that's a good idea.' She was wide awake now. 'We've got everything where it belongs. We're friends again. Let's not screw it up by discussing what went wrong and why it did. You're happy. I'm happy. We don't need to go over it again.'

'I don't want to go over anything. I just want to see you.'

'I look the same as I did two hours ago, in a nightgown instead of blue jeans.'

'Please ... I know you're leaving in the morning.' He sounded sad.

'I'll call you from Paris.' She was firm.

'I don't want to talk to you in Paris. You're here now. I want to see you.'

'Are you drunk?' she asked, sounding worried.

'No. But I will be if you don't see me.' He laughed.

She sighed, thinking about it. There wasn't a single good reason to see him. And several bad ones. She was still attracted to him, and she didn't want anything crazy to happen.

'Shit ... all right ... come on up, but if you do anything stupid, I'll call security and have them throw you out.'

'I won't do anything stupid. I promise.'

She got out of bed, put on a dressing gown, and walked into the living room of her suite. He was there before she had finished tying the belt on her bathrobe. He knocked once. She opened the door and looked at him. He looked tall and lean and beautiful, and the same stirrings were there, but this time she didn't heed them. She stepped back from the door and waved him in, looking sleepy.

'I'm sorry ... I don't know why, Sash ... but I had to see you.'

'Well, now you see me.' She smiled at him, and sat down in a chair, as he walked over, kneeled down, and put his arms around her.

'I'm sorry I was so stupid before. I thought you were demeaning me, and it drove me crazy. I wanted to go with you that night, and I wanted you to be proud of me. I just didn't know how to say it.'

'I didn't handle it well either. Sometimes that happens. The crazier you got, the more I dug my heels in. I told you it was impossible. It never could have worked between us.'

'It's still possible, if you want it to be. I've been doing a lot of thinking.'

'Don't start that again. I don't want to argue with you. And I'm not going to do anything stupid.' She crossed her arms over her chest as she said it, which took a considerable amount of effort. What she really wanted was to put her arms around him, but she wasn't going to let that happen. She still had feelings for him. And he'd been drinking. A lethal combination, as they had proven too many times.

'How was your date last night?'

'Charming, intelligent, respectable, and unbelievably boring,' she said, without thinking, and then stared at him. 'I can't believe I just said that. I had a perfectly nice time, with a perfectly decent person. I don't know why I said that.' She was upset by what she'd just said. The words had just slipped out.

'Probably because it's true. Sasha, I love you.' He said it with a look of desperation. 'And I don't give a damn if we keep us a secret. I realize now that it would have to be. It would make a mess if it weren't. I don't care if we never go to parties together. I just want to be with you, and share what we had before I blew it all to shit in Paris.'

'You didn't blow it all to shit,' she said kindly, 'we both did. This was never meant to be. I told you, Liam. It's impossible. How stupid are we both going to be? We got lucky. We hurt each other, but we didn't do an incredible amount of damage. Next time we could, and end it very badly. Let's just quit while we're ahead. I'll be the art dealer, and you be the artist.' As she said it, he stood in front of her, leaned down, and kissed her. And hating herself for it, she responded. 'Okay, so I love you. It doesn't change anything. I'm not going to do this. It's impossible. *Impossible.* How many times and how many ways do I have to say it?' He kissed her again, and this time when he stopped, she was breathless. 'Liam ... don't ... please ... we'll just drive each other crazy again...' He couldn't stop kissing her, and she couldn't stop kissing him.

'I'm already crazy,' he said miserably. 'I have been ever since I was stupid enough to

246

walk out on you in Paris.'

'You weren't stupid ... and I don't want you to be my secret. You were right. You deserve better. And I can't give it to you. I'm not ready to tell the world I have a boy-friend or a lover or whatever you are who's ten years younger. It makes me feel like a dirty old lady.'

'Nine,' he said between kisses.

'Nine what?' He was confusing her with what he was doing. Her head was spinning.

'It's nine years, not ten. Don't exaggerate.'

'All right, nine. I'm still not ready to tell people. And you deserve better than being a secret.'

'I'd rather be your secret than your nothing.'

'I'm your dealer.'

'I want you to be my woman.' And all she wanted as he kissed her was to be his woman. But as soon as she would be again, everything would get crazy and confusing, just as it had in Paris. 'And I want to be your very own wacky artist.' She laughed at him then.

'Well, you're that in any case, even if all I am is your dealer.'

'Sasha, give it a chance again ... please, for both our sakes. I really love you.'

'I love you, too. I just don't want us to drive each other crazy. And we would. You know it. I would do something that would freak you out. I'd insult you without meaning to. And you'd show up at a board meeting wearing a loincloth and sneakers.'

'A loincloth?' He backed up and looked at her. 'A loincloth? I don't even own one.'

'Then buy one,' she said, smiling. 'Every wacky artist should have one. You could wear it to parties I take you to.'

'What about a toga? I could show up at a board meeting or a black-tie dinner wearing my bed-sheets.' He grinned.

'That's too easy,' she said to him between kisses. She was in his arms by then, and he was carrying her into the bedroom. He deposited her on the bed where they had made love for the first time. He stopped and looked at her then, and she lay on the bed and looked at him.

'I won't make you do this if you don't want to,' he said softly.

'I should hope not,' she said, with a look of amusement. 'Oh God, Liam ... what are we doing?' She loved him, but she was frightened.

'We're starting where we left off, only better,' he said, sounding convinced.

'How do you know it will be better? Maybe it will be worse.'

'I know because I love you more than I did two months ago. I know because I want it to work. I want to prove to you that it is possible, and that you were wrong when you said it wasn't. I want you to be wrong.'

'So do I,' she whispered as she held her arms out to him. He untied her bathrobe then, and she took off his clothes. She wanted to believe it was possible. She wanted it to work with him. She wanted to be everything he wanted, and she wanted him to be her dreams. And as he made love to her, they both found everything they had missed and longed for for the past two months.

Afterward she looked up and smiled at him, and this time she had to laugh.

'I can't believe we're doing this again. What a couple of lunatics we are, Liam.' In spite of herself, she looked pleased.

'You're a lunatic.' He grinned at her. 'I'm only a wacky artist,' he said, looking proud, and feeling as though he had come home again.

Chapter 10

The next morning they made love again before he left. They took a shower together and laughed about what they were doing again. There was a sense of humor about their relationship now, a kind of wonderment, an ease and sense of goodwill about it that they hadn't had before it ended in Paris. She wanted more than anything to believe it was possible. But with the difference in their lifestyle and age, she was still afraid it wasn't. It all depended on how tolerant they could be of each other. In her opinion, therein lay the key to their success: an ability for each of them to let the other be who they were. She had no idea if either of them was capable of that. This time it was going to take skill, luck, and magic for it to work.

He kissed her before he walked out the door. Standing in the doorway in her bathrobe, she watched him saunter down the hall. She was terrified that it was still impossible, but she was unable to resist him. He turned and smiled at her, and as their eyes met, everything inside her melted. She loved him more than ever before, this time for who he was.

She was smiling broadly when she met Xavier in the lobby for breakfast half an hour later. Liam had promised to meet her in Paris that weekend, and she had another idea as well. She had been planning a trip to Italy, to see new artists in May. She wanted him to come with her, and was going to mention it to him that weekend.

'You look like the proverbial cat that swallowed the canary,' Xavier commented with a grin. 'What's up, Mom?' He was wondering about the date she'd had the night she came to London, and he asked her about it. 'Someone special?'

'Nope. Nice, but boring.' She liked Phillip Henshaw, although she had no chemistry with him. But now that Liam was back, Phillip had flown right out the window, and didn't even know it. She knew what she was doing with Liam was insane, but she felt compelled to try it again. She reminded herself that doing the same thing again and again, and expecting a different result, was the definition of insanity. But there was absolutely no way she could resist him, and she didn't want to. She was so happy he was back in her life. She could hardly wait for the weekend. They had talked about her coming to London to see him on weekends too, but she was afraid she'd run into Xavier. She was definitely not ready to tell her children. First, they both wanted to see if this could work. She was betting on it, and so was he.

Her driver took her to the airport, and when she got back to Paris, she was all smiles. Bernard and Eugénie saw it the minute she walked into the gallery.

'Well, you're in a good mood,' Bernard commented drily. And when she got home that night, she was happy to see Socks. She was happy to see everyone now that Liam was back. Something was so different and so much better with him in her life.

She had a busy week at the gallery, and when Liam arrived on Friday night, she was waiting for him. She had made a cassoulet, which he said he loved, pasta, salad, and even bought fancy pastries for him at Fauchon. They ate in the dining room, put the music on, and lit all the candles. It felt like a honeymoon to both of them. And on Saturday she invited him to join her in Italy for three weeks in May. He was ecstatic. Everything was better than it ever had been for both of them.

He drove to Paris every weekend for the rest of April. They went to Deauville for one of them. They stayed in a funny old hotel and walked on the beach and gambled. Miraculously, no one in her life seemed to know what was going on. He arrived late on Fridays, lay low on Saturdays, and on Sundays they walked around, or drove into the country. They went to mass at Sacré Coeur, visited Notre Dame, and walked in the Luxembourg Gardens. They never ran into anyone she knew, and she turned down all invitations on weekends. Not because she was hiding him, but because she wanted to savor every moment she could spend with him. And once or twice, they dined with his artist friends in the Marais, who nearly fainted when they found out who she was. Most of them were half her age, which made her uncomfortable, but she knew being with them was something she had to tolerate for his sake. They told them they were friends. She knew he needed to see his friends. She saw hers, and the clients she entertained during the week, while he worked in London. They both knew it would be too complicated if he spent the weeks in Paris, and there would be no way they could keep their secret, with her gallery right in the same house. They had agreed this time to keep their affair quiet, until they felt more secure with each other again.

They left for Italy on the first of May. They began their trip in Venice just for the fun of it, and spent four glorious days like a honeymoon at the Danieli. He had flown in from London, and she from Paris, and they met there. They did all the tourist things, rode in a gondola under the Ponte dei Sospiri, which the gondolier said would bind them to each other forever. They had sumptuous dinners, shopped, visited churches and museums, and sat in cafés. They were the happiest days they'd ever shared.

From Venice, they rented a car and drove to Florence, where she was meeting with four artists. They did the same things in Florence they had done in Venice, and had lunches and dinners with the artists in between. She liked two of them very much, and thought their work was right for the gallery. She was uncertain about the third, and said she needed to think about it. They were unusual sculptures and possibly too big for her space. And the fourth artist was charming, but she disliked his work immediately. She told him kindly that she couldn't do him justice, and their gallery wasn't worthy of his work. She liked letting people down gently. There was no point hurting their feelings, or crushing them with unkind rejection. As Liam watched and listened, he liked how she did things. She was a good person and a nice woman, and he loved sharing what she did.

They went to Bologna and Arezzo, spent a week in Umbria, driving through the country and staying in small inns. A few days in Rome. A visit to an artist on the Adriatic Coast, near Bari, and they spent the last days of the trip in Naples, visiting an artist whom Sasha had warned him was utterly insane, but she was also very charming, had six children, cooked them a fabulous dinner, and Sasha adored her work, as did Liam. She did enormous paintings in vibrant colors, which would be a nightmare to ship. But by the time Liam and Sasha left her, they were all in love with each other, including the artist's Chinese lover of twenty years who was the father of her six kids. They were beautiful children. And it was a fabulous trip, for both of them.

They spent their last weekend in Capri, in a small romantic hotel. They were both sad at the prospect of going back to real life, and their own worlds. She loved waking up with him in the morning, going to sleep in his arms at night, discovering things together, meeting people, and sometimes just walking around while they shared pieces of their history, or laughed. They had both had difficult, somewhat lonely childhoods. He because he had been a talented artistic misfit in a supremely conservative and unimaginative family, and she because her father had been a cold taskmaster much of the time, although he loved her very much. It was only once she was an adult that he had come to respect her, and her opinions. Liam's family never had, and he still paid a high price for the ridicule and rejection he had suffered at their hands. They had both been shortchanged by not having their mothers present as they grew up. Liam remembered his as a warm, wonderful woman who adored him, and in whose eyes he could do no wrong. He was still looking for the unconditional love he had gotten from her and no one else, and sometimes Sasha felt that he expected her to mother him now. That kind of unconditional love was a lot to expect from anyone who had entered his life later on. Love between adults and lovers was always somewhat conditional, and often fell short of expectations, particularly when not all needs were reciprocally met. She had similar memories of her own mother, and she sometimes wondered if people always believed that those who had died had loved unconditionally. Perhaps they hadn't, or wouldn't have later on. But her memories of her mother were as sweet and gentle as his recollections of his. She wondered sometimes what it would be like if her mother were alive now, although she would have been very elderly, eighty-eight years old. Sasha had turned forty-nine on their trip. Liam had woken her up that morning singing happy birthday to her, and she groaned thinking of it. He had given her a simple gold bracelet he had bought for her in Florence. She never took it off once he put it on her wrist, and knew she never would.

The age difference between them still bothered her at times. There was no avoiding it. They seemed to have more in common than she once thought, the loss of their mothers, their passion for art, the things they enjoyed doing when they were relaxed and had more time. Galleries, museums, churches, shops. When removed from daily stresses, they were both fairly easygoing, loved traveling together, and were curious about life. They were drawn to different kinds of people. She gravitated toward venerable elders, perhaps because of her much older father and the people she'd been exposed to with him all her life. She was impressed by reputations and education, as well as talent. Liam was instantly attracted to all things different, unusual, new, and young. She liked innovation and eccentricity in art, but not in people. When they sat in a café, she watched older people. Liam always gravitated toward youth and within minutes had met every young person in the place. He was most comfortable with people in their twenties and thirties, she preferred people her own age, or older, which created a gap of many decades between the people they wanted to meet and spend time with. It was a difference between them that they both had to learn to respect and tolerate, which was not always easy to do. It bored her to hang out with traveling students, and even young artists. She felt she had nothing to say to them, and wasn't interested in their juvenile ideas. Liam felt there was much to learn from the young, and he identified with them to an unusual degree, for a man his age. Watching him with them, Sasha felt like he was one of them. Liam seemed to feel that way too. And he also said that talking to the people who interested her put him to sleep. It was definitely a stumbling block between them. But traveling on their own, isolated from their familiar lives, they were both somewhat more willing to investigate and explore new worlds.

'What are you doing with someone as old as I am?' she asked him one day, as they left a beautiful fourteenth-century church, and stopped to buy gelati by the side of the road. He looked like a big kid as he ate his, as it dripped everywhere, and she was holding hers in a lace handkerchief she had bought at Hermes. She felt like his mother, or worse, his grandmother, sometimes. 'You're going to get tired of being with an older woman one day.'

It was one of her worst fears, and she always noticed him checking out young women. But so far to the best of her knowledge, he had never acted on it. He just liked to look. She kept a close eye on him, and was more jealous than she was willing to admit. No matter how fit and attractive she was, young bodies were undeniably more appealing than hers.

'I like looking at young women sometimes, all women in fact,' he admitted readily, 'but I love talking to you and being with you. You turn me on more than any woman I've ever known. I don't give a damn how old you are.'

She smiled at him, tossing the last of the gelato away. He was still licking the stick, and then wiped his hands on his jeans, which made an even bigger mess. She sat looking at him with a rueful grin. It was his childlike style that made her feel old sometimes, not her age.

'I love you, Sash. You're a beautiful woman. And yeah, okay, so you're not twenty-two. Who cares? Twenty-two-year-olds don't get it, don't interest me, and don't understand me. You do.' She didn't tell him that at times she wasn't sure she did either, but she knew what he meant and what he expected of her: tolerance, nurturing, and understanding above all else. He was very needy sometimes, and self-centered, as children are, and he liked the way she nurtured him. Sometimes, when she treated him like a child, it worked best. At other times, he wanted respect, and made a lot of sense when he expressed himself. They seemed equal at times, and not at others. In truth, they were not equal. She was older, more successful, more powerful in the art world than he was, she was respected and important, she had more money. But he was just as talented and smart. He could hold his own, even in her world, if she let him. So far they had not ventured into her world together. And when they did, he would still be viewed as a young artist, and she was one of the most respected art dealers in the world. It was a huge difference between them. People paid more attention to her than to him, which she knew would annoy him. Liam liked being the center of attention, which he always was with young girls. People her age expected more of him than great paintings, good looks, and blond hair. They expected him to be a serious person, and at times he wasn't. But with him, she wasn't always serious either, and she liked that about the time they spent together. She loved being playful with him. Sometimes they laughed so hard at each other's stories, or their own, that tears ran down their cheeks. No one had ever made her laugh like Liam. Or made love to her the way he did.

There were a lot of benefits to the combination they offered each other, and also some risks.

When they were in Rome, they went to visit an art dealer she liked and had done business with, a man in his late sixties whose ideas she respected. When they saw him, Liam had been having an off day. He acted like a bored schoolboy while they sat in his office. Liam had been sitting there pouting, swinging his foot, and kicking the desk, until Sasha turned to him quietly and asked him to stop. He was so furious over the reprimand that he had stormed out. Her colleague had raised an eyebrow and didn't comment. And she had been forced to decline lunch as a result.

Afterward, they had had a huge argument about it, and how badly behaved she thought he had been. It was the only unpleasant moment on the trip. Later, Liam had apologized for it, after they made love that night. He said he had been bored and tired, didn't like the way the man looked at Sasha, and it made him jealous. His confession touched Sasha, but it was too late to convince the Roman art dealer that the man she had brought with her was an intelligent, civilized adult. And it didn't bode well for the future yet again. There were lots of meetings like that in her life, and sometimes Liam just wasn't up to it. In fact, he rarely was. When he was bored or felt left out or unimportant, he almost always acted out, more often than not, like a child. Sometimes it was hard to believe that he was forty years old. At times, he seemed half his age, and looked it, which was part of his appeal, but also his greatest downside in Sasha's life. They still had a lot to work out. But all in all, their trip to Italy was a huge success.

Sasha called her children several times while she and Liam traveled. They both had her itinerary, as they always did, but rarely called her. It was almost always Sasha who called them, because she was harder to find, and she often turned off her cell phone. She and Liam were registered in hotels as Liam Allison and Sasha Boardman, which Liam said sounded like a law firm, Allison and Boardman, or tax accountants. And once in a while the hotels got it wrong and registered them as a single person, Allison Boardman, which they didn't mind. Tatianna was amused by it when she called her mother in Florence, and laughed, saying that she had asked for Sasha Boardman and they said all they had was an Allison Boardman, which was obviously the right person but the wrong first name. It meant nothing to her. If it had happened to Xavier, he might have wondered. But Tatianna made no association between her mother and Liam, except that she knew Sasha represented him. So it never occurred to her that he was there. Sasha laughed along with her at the stupidity of operators in hotels, even good ones, to screw up her name.

She wasn't aware of it at the time, but the same thing had happened to Bernard, when he called her from the gallery in Paris. He had corrected the error of the first name, and they had insisted, and then corrected it themselves to Mr Allison and Mrs Boardman, which had stunned him, but he said nothing to Sasha about it until she got home.

It was her first day back, and she was working her way through the mountain of correspondence, files, and slides from aspiring artists that had accumulated on her desk during her three-week absence. It was overwhelming, but the price she had to pay for her trip.

Bernard had stopped in her office for a minute, sat down across the desk from her, and looked at her cautiously, wondering if it was the wrong time to broach it, or if he even should. But he was always concerned about her, like an older brother. He had been trained by her father, just as she was, and had worked for the gallery for more than twenty years. He had started there before she moved back to New York and opened the gallery there. He was ten years older than Sasha, but in an odd way, she had always felt as though they had grown up together, and they had, in the art world.

He sat looking at her across the desk for a long minute, as she glanced at some slides. She had told him all about the artists she'd visited, and the one she particularly liked in Naples. Sasha was enamored with her work, and the artist herself.

'Am I correct in believing that you had an art consultant with you?' He asked gently, and then quickly added, 'You don't have to answer me if you don't want to, Sasha. It's none of my business.' She stopped and looked at him thoughtfully, and then nodded.

'How did you know?'

'The hotel in Rome had you registered as Allison Boardman, and when I corrected them, they explained it was Mr Allison and Mrs Boardman.'

'The same thing happened when Tatianna called me in Florence, more or less. Fortunately they didn't tell her the last part, about the Mr and Mrs.'

'Is everything all right?' He looked concerned. He always worried about her, and always had. Ever since Arthur's death, there was no one to take care of her. She took care of everyone else, even him. She was an extraordinary employer and friend, just as her father had been before her. Bernard had deep loyalties to them both, and trusted no one else, except his wife.

'I think everything's fine,' Sasha said calmly, and smiled at him. 'It's not what I expected to be doing with my life. And it's a little unusual to say the least.' She was still embarrassed by the difference in their age, and wondered if she always would be.

'I wondered, when he stayed with you for ten days. That's a lot of hospitality to offer anyone, even a good artist. Was that when it started?' He was curious as much as concerned.

'No, that's why he came. It started in January in London, when I went to see his work with Xavier. The same day, in fact. It has started and stopped several times since. I'm not sure what to do about it, to be honest. We're very different, and he's nine years younger than I am, which is awkward. And ... what can I say ... he's an artist ... you know what that's like.' They both did. He laughed as she said it.

'So was Picasso.' Bernard smiled at her. 'People put up with him. Liam's a nice boy.' He liked him, and respected his work, although he preferred more traditional painters.

'That's the problem,' Sasha said honestly, relieved to have someone to talk to about it. Bernard was a sensible man, and her friend. 'He's young for his age. Sometimes he's a boy, and sometimes he's a man.' She sounded philosophical about it. But they both knew that with a life as complicated as hers, she needed a man, not a child, as her partner.

'We're all children sometimes. My wife still treats me like I'm twelve years old, and I'm fifty-nine. Actually, to be honest, I like it. It makes me feel comfortable and safe, and loved.' He said it honestly as Sasha watched him with pensive eyes.

'I think Liam feels the same way. His mother died when he was seven. I like taking care of the men in my life, of everyone in fact, but I don't want to be a mother to him all the time, and I might have to be. I also don't want to look like his mother, and sometimes I'm afraid I do that too.'

'No, you don't. Nine years isn't much of a difference, Sasha.' He wasn't opposed to the match, and it wasn't his business to be. He was just concerned for her, and he wanted her to be happy. He knew how lonely she had been since Arthur died, and his heart ached for her. There was nothing any of them could do to help her. Maybe Liam could.

'That's true. But it feels like a big age difference with Liam. He hangs out with twenty- and thirty-year-old artists, and I feel a hundred years old when I'm with them.'

'That's a problem,' Bernard admitted, and then sighed. 'You don't have to make any big decisions. At least I hope not.' He didn't want her running off and marrying him on an impulse, but he knew Sasha wouldn't do that. She was a wise, sensible, very cautious woman, although the affair with Liam was certainly unusual for her, and showed a side of her he had never suspected.

'Don't worry. I won't do anything hasty. I'm not planning to do anything at all, just enjoy our time together, for as long as it lasts.' She still believed it wouldn't last long, and had no great hopes for the future. Bernard was relieved to hear it. He thought an affair with Liam was fine. A lifetime was something else.

'Do the children know?'

'No, they don't. Tatianna would probably kill me, and I'm not sure how Xavier would feel. He and Liam are good friends. That's hard to predict. I'm in no rush to tell them, and I won't if I don't have to. Who knows where it will go. Our time together has been very erratic. We stopped seeing each other from February to April. We just got back together before this trip, and it was lovely. We'll see what comes next.' She sounded extremely philosophical about it, and not stressed.

'Keep me posted,' Bernard said as he stood up. He was glad he had asked her. It all seemed discreet and sensibly handled to him.

That was all he had wanted to know. And she seemed happy with Liam. 'Let me know if there's anything I can do to help.' That was enough for him for now.

'You just did. Just keep it quiet. I'm not planning to tell anyone, at least not until we see how this works for a while.' Bernard agreed. It had helped her to talk to him. She'd been worried that the people in her life would be horrified and fall out of their chairs in shock and disapproval. Bernard seemed perfectly comfortable with it, which made Sasha feel more at ease. She had no intention of telling Eugénie for the moment, or anyone else at the office or elsewhere. Although Eugénie took his calls, when he called the gallery, which was rare. Most of the time he called on her cell phone. And she was not planning to tell her children for a long time. She and Liam had agreed on that, and thought it was a wise decision. Telling her kids could complicate things, and they had enough to adjust to and deal with as it was. But so far so good. This time.

Liam came to Paris for the next two weekends. The weather was beautiful, they had a great time together, and they were both in good spirits. They spent all of their time together when he was there, and saw none of their friends. There was too much they wanted to do together, and they had little enough time as it was. They didn't want to share it with anyone, his friends or hers. And during the week, he had been hard at work preparing for his December show in New York. She was anxious for the world to see his work. He could hardly wait, and the work in his studio in London was going well.

They were walking in the Bois de Boulogne with Socks when she asked him about his children in Vermont, as she often did. She always encouraged him to talk about them. She knew he missed them a lot. It had been a year since he'd seen them. The divorce was in progress, and would be final around Christmas. Beth had told him she was getting married as soon as it came through. He said he had made his peace with it, and Sasha was convinced he had. They had both moved on. But the children still needed him, in her opinion, as he did them. Maybe more than he thought, or was willing to acknowledge. In Sasha's opinion, he seemed all too amenable to letting Beth handle them, and staying out of the way.

'Why don't you go over and see them this summer, Liam?' she encouraged him, as he threw a stick for Socks, who retrieved it. He had taught her a few tricks as well, and she had turned out to be a lovely dog. Sasha was crazy about her, even more so because she had been a gift from him. 'I have to spend time with my kids in August.' They all had time then, and she loved spending every minute with them that she could, particularly when she and her two children could go away on vacations, which was becoming rarer and rarer as they got older and had ever-busier lives. She knew that one of these days they would have serious significant others, and it wouldn't be possible at all. These were her very last chances to do it, and each year seemed like the last one. 'Maybe we could go away somewhere this summer after we both spend time with our kids.' She was always organizing him, which annoyed him at times and amused him at others. He knew it was just what she did. For everyone. She was a classic mother hen, which he also loved about her, especially when she mothered him.

'I don't even know if they want to see me,' Liam said honestly. He said often that they were angry at him for staying away for so long, which was what Sasha had feared. He called them infrequently, and when he did, the conversations were difficult. They blamed him openly for the demise of the marriage. Beth had told them enough to upset them, without the gory details, but none of them had forgiven him. It made calling them hard, and the distance had taken its toll as well. Sasha was afraid that if he waited too long to see them, the damage would never be undone, or not for years. She had warned him of that, too. After only one year, there was still time. His children were young. His oldest son was eighteen and leaving for college in September, his middle child, also a son, was twelve now, and his daughter had just turned six. They were young enough for him to rebuild a relationship with them, but only if he made an effort. And she knew he loved them. There were often tears in his eyes when he spoke of them, and he said he missed them. But he was beginning to feel they were Beth's children now, more than his. She saw them every day. He didn't.

'Why don't you ask them?' Sasha suggested. 'Do you think Beth would let you take them somewhere?' She thought of offering him the house in Southampton, but she didn't want to interfere, and she didn't know if Tatianna planned to use it. She suspected she would. Both her children loved that house, and the memories they had there of their childhood. She had tender memories there, too. Of them, and Arthur.

'I'm not sure how she will feel about letting me take the kids. She's not too fond of me these days.' As Sasha knew from what he'd told her, the support he had sent her for the past year had been skimpy. Beth was being helped by her future husband, which embarrassed Liam and complicated matters further. Sasha had given him an advance, but Liam had to live, and buy paints and canvas. He couldn't afford to send her much. They both hoped it would improve after his show. But in the meantime, his financial situation was still tough. And as a result, so was Beth's.

She'd been dealing with that with him for twenty years, and she was sick of it. Liam didn't blame her. She was going to be much better off with her new husband. He was happy for her. And he was happy with Sasha. The only thing missing in his life now were his kids.

'Why don't you call her and the children?' Sasha prodded, and he promised to do that during the week. After he did, he called Sasha, and reported on his conversation with Beth. He sounded pleased, and thanked Sasha for pushing him to do it.

'She doesn't want me taking them away. I can't afford to anyway. But she said I can come to visit, and take them for a few days if I want to. Her parents have a cabin on a lake near where she lives, and she said I could use that. The kids love it. The boys love to fish there.' It sounded like the perfect solution to both of them. Beth wanted him to come that month. They had other plans for the rest of the summer, and were planning to visit her future in-laws in California, and take a trip to the Grand Canyon.

'That sounds great,' Sasha said, sounding delighted. 'I was going to talk to you about that anyway. I have to be in New York later in June, and I was thinking about staying for a few weeks. I was going to ask you if you want to come with me. As long as we're relatively discreet, you can stay at the apartment with me.' Tatianna was so busy with her own life, she hardly saw her mother when she was in town, never showed up unannounced at the apartment, and never stayed there now that she had her own place in Tribeca. Liam's presence would be easy to hide.

'I probably shouldn't take the time off right now, with a show coming up, but God, Sasha, I'd love it.' It sounded great to both of them. They had missed each other more than ever after their trip in Italy in May. She missed living with him. And there was lots for them to do in New York. 'When are you going?'

'In about ten days. I was going to ask you about it this weekend.'

'Count me in. I'll come.' He was thrilled.

'If you can spare the time, we could spend part of the month there,' Sasha suggested. They both loved the sound of it. Their trip to Italy had been a huge success, and hopefully this would be too, although a little different since Sasha had to work. 'We could spend the Fourth of July in New York and then come back to Europe.'

She was planning to work at the Paris gallery in July, and then leave on vacation with the kids in August. They were going to St. Tropez, which her children loved, and she had chartered a boat to entice them. Both of them were planning to bring friends, which was fine with her. The only part of it she didn't like was that she hated leaving Liam for three weeks. She had some vague plan to see if she could invite him on the boat for a weekend, as a 'visiting artist,' but she wasn't sure yet if she could pull it off. Tatianna had a keen nose, and Xavier knew him. At her most devious, she thought of asking Xavier to invite him, but she didn't want to tempt fate. There was a distinct possibility, and it was more than likely, that she wouldn't see Liam for three weeks. But at least they'd have the rest of June in New York.

They were both excited when they talked about it that weekend. He had lots of artist friends in New York, in Chelsea, Tribeca, and SoHo. And there were places and events where she wanted to take him. There hadn't been so much as a hint of his wild and wacky artist side since they'd gotten back together, and she was feeling confident about going out with him, particularly in New York, where her life was so much less stuffy and formal than it was in Paris. He was going to fit in perfectly in New York. And they were both looking forward to it.

'Maybe,' she said wistfully, as they lay in bed on Sunday morning, 'we could spend a few days at the house in the Hamptons. It's a beautiful place, and I used to love it.' In the twenty months since Arthur's death it had been too painful for her. Maybe now it would be different.

'I like the Hamptons,' Liam said casually, and then went back to talking about going to the lake with his children. Sometimes he didn't listen. Sometimes he was just a boy. And sometimes he needed everything to be about him and only him. She knew it wasn't personal, or a sign that he didn't love her. She understood it now. It was just the way he was. No one had ever listened to him as a boy. And now he had Sasha to hang on his every word. He loved that about her. 'I wish you could come to Vermont with me,' he said, as he rolled over in bed and looked at her nose to nose. Their lovemaking just before that had been as sweet as ever. It seemed to get better over time, although she found that hard to believe since it had been fabulous since the beginning.

'You need to be alone with your children, to get reacquainted with them,' she said sensibly. He knew she was right. He was a little scared to see them. He knew that both of his sons were angry at him for staying away for so long. At six, Charlotte was just excited to see Daddy. He had talked to them a few days before on the phone. He hadn't even called them in months. Sometimes it just slipped his mind. Beth had always made excuses for him, and covered for him in his paternal lapses, but she wasn't willing to do that anymore. He also suffered from comparison to her fiancé, who was present and attentive to them. As a result, Liam had taken a hit for his year of absence. He had some serious repair work to do with them now, and he knew it. He was anxious to take it on. And thrilled to be spending the rest of June in New York with Sasha.

'Will you go to a Yankees game with me, Sasha?' he asked, lying on his back and looking up at the ceiling with a grin. He looked like a kid who could hardly wait to go to camp.

'I'll do anything you want, within reason. I have to work, too. But I think we can manage to do both, work and play. And I want you to see the space where you're going to have your show.'

'Mmmmm...' he said, smiling at her. 'You make me feel like a king.'

'That's a good thing.' She smiled at him, nestling next to him. Sometimes he made her feel like a queen. And sometimes he made her feel like the Queen Mother.

Chapter 11

Liam flew to Paris on a Friday night, and they flew to New York together from Paris on Sunday morning. She had treated him to the ticket, and they settled into first-class seats side by side. He looked like a kid at a birthday party, and took advantage of everything they offered. Caviar, champagne, he ate his lunch and most of hers, reclined the seat into a bed, covered himself with the duvet, and took a nap. He even changed into the pajamas, and for a moment, wearing the plastic bag on his head like a hat, he showed distinct signs of slipping into his previous unruly behavior. He watched two movies, ate a snack, used everything in the toiletry kit, and invited Sasha to join the mile-high club in the bathroom.

'I think we may have to sedate you for the next flight.' She grinned at him, after declining his offer to join the mile-high club. 'We did that to Xavier once, because he always got airsick as a little kid. He had an adverse reaction to the medicine, and took off like a jet engine out of control. I've never seen a kid so hyper. After that, we just let him throw up on the flight till he outgrew it.' But she had never seen anyone enjoy a flight so much, or appreciate it as vocally, as Liam. He didn't stop thanking her from takeoff to landing.

'I always thought it was normal to sit with my knees wrapped around my ears, and my neighbors' elbows in my chest. This is a hell of a lot better,' he said, looking ecstatic, as he laid the seat back again and stretched his legs out.

He was still in great spirits when they went

through customs in New York, and joked with everyone in sight. As usual, he made friends with all the flight attendants, most of whom Sasha knew and who knew her from previous flights. He called the customs inspector by his first name, and had an animated conversation about baseball with their skycap, while she located her car and driver. 'Exuberant' didn't begin to describe it. But mostly he was just happy and grateful and excited to be there. And in spite of his acting like a spinning top, Sasha loved being with him.

He calmed down finally when they got to her apartment. He was impressed by how elegant it was. He appreciated the quality of the antiques and was somewhat taken aback by her paintings. There was a Monet, two Degas, and a Renoir, a series of priceless Da Vinci drawings, and countless others he hadn't even seen yet. In many ways, her apartment in New York was far more formal than her wing of the house in Paris, which she had kept simpler and more modern when she redid it. New York showed the evidence of a lifetime of collecting important artists, most of which had been purchased by her father and given to her as gifts.

'Wow, Sash ... this is heavy stuff...' He stood in awe before a somber El Greco she had never liked, and kept in a hallway. She finally dragged him away long enough to show him her bedroom. She had a moment of hesitation herself, because she had never shared it with any man but Arthur. But it was time now. She was ready to open her doors and her life to Liam.

She asked him to put his things in the guest room, just in case one of her children turned up at some point, and she didn't want to shock the maid who came to clean daily, and had during most of her marriage. Liam didn't seem put off by her asking him to do that. He dropped his bag in the room down the hall and then wandered into her bedroom with a dish of ice cream. He looked perfectly at home as he sprawled out in Arthur's favorite chair, flipped on the TV, and caught up on the baseball game in progress. And then he looked up at Sasha with the boyish grin that turned her knees to mush, and burst out laughing.

'Boy, is this cool, Sash. I feel like I died and went to heaven.' He had grown up with money too, though perhaps not quite this much, but his family was prominent and solid. The only difference was that they had always treated him like a misfit and an outcast because he was artistic and different from them. He felt completely at ease and welcome in her apartment, and lately in her life. It made all the difference in the world to him, and now to Sasha. They were both in high spirits and enjoying the relationship they shared.

She suggested they go to a nearby restaurant that night. She checked in with Tatianna before they left, and as she had suspected, Tatianna was busy with friends, had a thousand plans that week, and told her mother she'd stop in to see her at the gallery when she had a free moment, more than likely on her lunch break. Sasha felt completely secure when she settled into bed with Liam that night. The housekeeper wasn't coming in till noon, and by then she and Liam would be long gone, she at the gallery, and he to visit his friends in SoHo. Their secret was safe here. And for all anyone would know, if discovered, Liam was nothing more exotic than a houseguest.

Liam won her heart forever when he put an arm around her that night in bed and pulled her closer to him. Despite his own excitement to be there, he had seen her face earlier that day when they entered the room. He had a feeling that being there with him was hard for her, and brought back memories of the past.

'Are you okay?' he whispered, lying close to her. She knew instantly that he understood, and she nodded.

'Yes, sweetheart, I am ... thank you for asking.'

'I don't want to do anything that would offend you here. If you want, I'll sleep in the other room.' She looked up and smiled at him.

'I'd miss you too much. You're fine here,' she said, and kissed him. It was a gentle kiss and not one that suggested she wanted anything more from him than the understanding he'd just given her. He kissed her just as gently and held her close to him, as they did nothing more than cuddle that night.

She took him to the gallery the next day, and he was impressed by the space and the way they had used it. He liked the artist's work that they were showing, and squinted, imagining his own work in the same place. It was perfect for him, and now he had a better idea of how many pieces he'd need, how many horizontals and verticals. It was inspiring to him just being there. She introduced him to all her employees. Marcie, her assistant, nearly fainted when he sauntered in, and rolled her eyes in awe at Sasha behind his back.

'Oh my God, he looks like a movie star,' she said breathlessly, as Sasha laughed. She hated to admit it, but sometimes he did. She liked it better when they were home in old worn clothes, with uncombed hair, looking a mess. Sometimes it was daunting being out with him, and it made her feel her age.

'He's a nice guy, and a good artist,' Sasha said casually. 'I'm glad we happened to be in New York at the same time. I think he's on his way to Vermont to see his kids.' Marcie nodded, impressed by him. Not only was he a hunk and talented, but he was even a good father. She had already idealized him after knowing him for five minutes. Sasha knew him better and was a little less dazzled by him than Marcie. She just loved him, clay feet and all. And like anyone else, he had them. So did she.

He spent the morning at the gallery with her, meeting everyone, and looking around. He looked in the racks, went upstairs to see the classical work, and then left for SoHo to meet his friends. He whispered to Sasha that he would see her at the apartment later, and she nodded.

Providentially, five minutes after he left, Tatianna walked in. She was on her way to pick up something from a photographer, and stopped in to see her mother. She looked happy and pretty as she always did and, as Sasha looked at her with new eyes now, extremely young. She was exactly the age of the women Liam always chatted with and admired. She had just turned twenty-four. Looking at her with a fresh perspective, Sasha felt ancient. She knew she was going to have to get over feeling that way if she and Liam were going to make it work. She had never thought about her age before, and now she was obsessed with it. Everyone else looked young to her. And she felt old.

'Hi, Mom. How long are you here for?' Tatianna asked as she grabbed a piece of chocolate from a dish and kissed her mother.

'A month, I think.' As always, Sasha was thrilled to see her daughter.

'That's a long time.' Tatianna was surprised to hear it. In recent months, her mother never stayed in New York long. The apartment she'd shared with Arthur depressed her, and she always said she felt his absence more acutely here.

'We're opening a show this month, I have to curate it, and I figured I'd stick around for a while. How's everything with you?'

'Great. I just got a raise, my editor hates me, and I want her job.' Tatianna was on top of the world. She smiled as she looked at her mother, happy to see her.

'That all sounds normal.' Her mother laughed.

'See you soon, I gotta go now. I'm late. I just wanted to say hi.' She had a cab waiting outside, and blew out as fast as she blew in, taking a handful of chocolates with her, in lieu of lunch. Sasha kissed her quickly, and she was gone.

Sasha had a busy day in the gallery, working on the new show. She curated their shows herself, and loved to do it. She had to tear herself away to meet Liam at the apartment at six o'clock. He was eating ice cream and pizza in the kitchen when she walked in, and kissed her on the mouth.

'Mmmmm ... delicious. What is it? Rocky Road?'

'Fudge Brownie,' he corrected her. 'I always forget how good the ice cream is in the States. In England, it tastes like shit.'

'It's worse in France.' She smiled at him. 'Gelato is good...' She sat down at the kitchen table and looked at him, it was nice to see him there at the end of a long day. He seemed right at home.

'Gelato is for sissies,' he corrected. 'This is the real thing. Have a piece of pizza, I'm taking you out.' She didn't want to tell him she was tired after a long day, and jet-lagged. He looked vibrant and full of life. He'd had a great day with his friends.

'Where are you taking me? Do I need to change?' All she wanted was to fall into a hot bath and relax before going to bed. She was exhausted after hauling paintings and curating all day.

'Yeah. Put on blue jeans,' he said, as he rinsed the bowl and put it in the dishwasher. He was good about those things when he was with her. His own place was a total mess. He'd been living in his studio since Beth and the children left, and camped out in a sleeping bag on a cot. This was grand luxury for him. 'I got tickets to a Yankees game,' he said victoriously. 'I bought them from a friend.' He glanced at his watch. 'We have to leave in ten minutes. The game starts at seven-thirty, and there might be traffic.' He had lived in New York years before, for about a year, and always forgot how much he loved it till he came back again. He loved the electricity and excitement, and the Yankees best of all.

Sasha tried to look enthusiastic for his sake, and went to change. Once in a while, she wondered what she was doing with a man his age, who acted half his age. He needed someone like Tatianna, and instead he had wound up with her. She didn't bother with the pizza, but washed her face and combed her hair instead, and put on jeans and a white T-shirt and sandals. She pulled a shawl off a shelf, and ten minutes later was back in the kitchen. He was ready to go, wearing a Yankees cap he had brought with him from London.

'Ready?' He smiled down at her ecstatically. He chatted with her elevator man on the way downstairs, and told him they were going to the game. They were playing the Boston Red Sox. And he said it was going to be a great game. The Yankees were on a winning streak, and he told the elevator man they were going to cream them.

By the time they were in Yankee Stadium, Sasha was feeling better. The jet lag seemed to have receded again, he bought her a hot dog and a beer, and told her about both teams and the best players. He was a total fanatic about baseball, which Sasha thought was cute. It was a far cry from the stuffy dinner parties she didn't take him to in Paris. And actually, she liked this better. It was all new to her. She had never been to a baseball game in her life.

While they waited for the game to start, she told him she had seen Tatianna briefly that day, and he said he was looking forward to meeting her. Sasha couldn't help wondering how they'd get along. She hoped they would. It would make a difference in their relationship, she knew, if eventually her kids accepted him. She knew Xavier would, since they were friends, although she had no idea how he'd feel about Liam being involved with his mother. She worried about her daughter. Tatianna was unpredictable as to whom she liked, and whom she didn't. It was never an easy call, and she had stronger and far more critical opinions than her more easygoing brother.

Liam explained everything that happened at the game to her, and the Yankees won, six to nothing. He was ecstatic, and chatted animatedly with her all the way back in the cab. They went to bed right afterward, and again, didn't make love, and Sasha slept like a log. He was leaving for Vermont the next morning, to see his kids, and told her he'd be back in four days and would call her from

Vermont. She dropped him off at Grand Central Station, and went to the gallery after that. She felt silly, but she missed him as soon as he left. He had promised to be back by the weekend. She was thinking of taking him to the Hamptons, depending on how she felt. It had taken a little adjusting to get used to having him in the bed she had shared with Arthur at the apartment, and Liam had been sensitive about it. She was sure he would be in Southampton too. She just didn't know how she would feel. Their bedroom in Southampton was where she had seen Arthur for the last time. It was a sacred place to her, and she wasn't sure Liam belonged there. Yet. Or maybe ever. She needed to feel her way along on that one, and was in no rush to decide.

She was busier than she expected all week, went to several cocktail parties, had lunch with Alana, who was now happily married and spending every penny she could of her new husband's money, and saw Tatianna for dinner. Other than that, Liam had called her regularly to report on how he was doing with the kids. It had been difficult with his oldest son at first. Tom blamed Liam entirely for the divorce. Beth had finally told him the ugly details of the incident with Becky, and Liam was livid about it when he called Sasha. She told him to calm down and try to work it out with his son. It was better by the end of the week. They had spent a tearful night talking about it, and both father and son felt better in the morning. His twelve-year-old, George, had been happy to see him, but had developed a nervous twitch in the course of the year, and was on medication, which Liam thought he didn't need and wouldn't give him. He had called Beth about it, and she had threatened to pick them up at the cabin if Liam didn't give George his medication, so finally he did. And Charlotte was adorable and easy, thrilled to see her daddy, and the only mishap was that she fell off her bike and sprained her wrist. But other than that, everything had been fine. A typical weekend with kids, particularly kids he hadn't seen in a year. None of it surprised Sasha, although some of it shocked Liam. He had been in denial about the fallout of his absence during the entire time. Seeing them again woke him up.

'It's hard to walk into their lives after a year, and pick up where you left off,' he said to Sasha late one night when he called her. 'Everything is changed, they're all different,' he had complained. But they were still his kids, and she had given him all the advice she could whenever he called her. He was grateful for her support, and looked exhausted but happy when he arrived back at her apartment late Friday night. He had just gotten off the train. And he looked delighted to see her. He had his baseball cap on backward, his jeans were torn at the knees, and he hadn't shaved all week. Other than the beard stubble, he looked like a boy coming home from camp.

She ran a bath for him, made him something to eat, handed him a bowl of ice cream, and he lay in bed and looked at her like an angel who had just come down from heaven.

'It was hard, Sash,' he admitted to her, as he ate the ice cream.

'I knew it would be,' she said calmly, happy that he was back.

'I didn't. I guess I told myself it would be like the old days when I saw them. It's not. It's different. They've changed. We felt like strangers at first. They were all really pissed at me.' The only surprising thing was that he hadn't known that. He'd been in denial, and expected time to stand still. But from what he said, after four days together, he had opened the door to healing and a better relationship with them. It had been a wonderful trip, and they were great kids.

'You have to come back and see them more often. It's not fair if you don't.' If she had to, she'd give him a ticket. She knew how important it was, even if he didn't. But she thought he understood it better now that he had seen them. They loved and needed him in their life. He was their father. Even if their new soon-to-be stepfather could provide better for them, they loved and needed Liam, and he had seen that. He had hated leaving them at the end of the four days.

She rubbed his back when she got into bed, and gave him a massage, and afterward he made love to her. It was the first time he had made love to her in that bed. But it was no longer hers and Arthur's. It felt like hers and Liam's now. He fell asleep almost the moment they stopped making love, and he looked like a big beautiful boy in her bed, as she lay beside him, stroked his hair, and kissed him in the moonlight.

Chapter 12

When Liam woke on Saturday morning after he'd been to Vermont, Sasha suggested to him that they go to Southampton for the weekend. She had been thinking about it all week, and hadn't mentioned it to him, because she wanted to be sure she felt she could do it. But as she made breakfast for him, she thought it was a good idea, and Liam was thrilled. It was a hot sunny day and he couldn't think of anything he'd rather do than go to the beach.

They left the apartment in New York shortly after eleven, and by one-thirty they were there. She had been quiet on the ride out. Liam drove, and he looked relaxed as they chatted from time to time, mostly about his kids and the time he'd spent with them in Vermont. He was still slightly concerned about his oldest son, Tom, having discovered that since the last time he'd seen him a year before, he had turned into a very angry young man. He was going to the University of Pennsylvania in the fall, on a scholarship, and with his future stepfather's help with the dorm. Tom had pointed out to Liam several times that his mother's fiancé had done more for him in the last six months than Liam ever had. Liam had explained to Tom that he was a starving artist, and Tom said he didn't give a damn, and called Liam a flake and a lousy father. Tom had also confronted him about his one-night stand with his mother's twin. Liam was still furious that Beth had told him.

'That isn't fair,' Sasha said, frowning. 'Your ex-wife shouldn't have told him.' It made Liam look terrible in his children's eyes, and she felt sorry for him, although it had been a stupid thing for him to do. But people made mistakes, and regretted them. It was obvious that Liam did. Sasha felt that his betrayal of their marriage should have remained between him and Beth.

'She didn't hold much back.' Beth had

told Tom all about their father's sins, his one adultery, and financial irresponsibility for twenty years.

'How was she when you saw her?' Sasha asked, wondering about her.

'I didn't. She was out when I picked them up. Their grandmother was there, and she didn't say two words to me. Becky was at the house with Beth's new guy when I dropped them off. I hope she doesn't pull the same stunt with him. He's probably a lot smarter than I was.' He sighed then, and looked at her. 'He seems like a nice guy. And the kids really like him.' She could tell, listening to him, that Liam felt left out. But at least he had gone to see them and opened up communications with them again, even if it had been hard with Tom at first. Liam had told her the night before that Tom had finally calmed down and warmed up. But he wanted to vent his anger first, and it was obvious that he had. She still thought Beth had been wrong to be so open with them about their father's fatal mistake. No matter what the end result, the incident itself should have remained known only to the adults. In her opinion, children didn't need to know their parents' sins, and she said as much to Liam.

'I think she's still pretty bitter about what I did. She sounds like it. She and Becky have always been jealous of each other.' He hadn't said a word to his ex-sister-in-law when he dropped the children off. Just nodded and drove off. Becky had said nothing.

By then, Sasha and Liam had reached the house in Southampton. It was a big rambling white Victorian that had reminded them of New England when she and Arthur bought it twenty years before. It looked like houses they had seen in Martha's Vineyard and Nantucket, and it had a wide covered porch all around it. She and Arthur had always loved sitting there on warm nights, and sometimes even all bundled up in winter, sipping hot chocolate. She tried to force the memories from her head as she opened the door for Liam. She usually walked in through the kitchen, but this time she decided to go in through the front door, so it would be different.

'It's a beautiful old house, Sasha,' Liam said, as he looked around. They had kept it rustic and simple, but it looked comfortable and inviting. There was nothing pretentious about it. There seemed to be no important art, just pretty things, big inviting leather chairs, and two canvas-covered couches. And then he saw the painting by Andrew Wyeth over the mantel. It was stark and bleak and beautiful, and one of his most famous paintings. It looked just like the beach outside, on a winter day. There were little tufts of snow on the ground, and you could sense a stiff breeze in the air on the canvas. It was without a doubt the work of a great master.

'Wow!' Liam said, as he stood staring at it in awe. He had admired Wyeth all his life. 'I'd give my ass to own a Wyeth.' He whistled and then smiled, as she laughed.

'My father gave it to us for a wedding present.' There were a lot of things like that in the house, mementoes, treasures, things the children had made, early American furniture they had bought together on trips through New England early in their marriage, or when Tatianna was in college and they drove up to see her. There was a beautiful old battered refectory table in the dining room that Sasha had bought in France. Everywhere he looked, Liam saw things that he knew instinctively that she treasured. The house had deep meaning for her, and he realized easily that it had meant a lot to her to bring him there. Even more than her New York apartment. Much more. This house was far more personal, and more important to her.

'I think I'd move here if I had a house like this,' Liam said admiringly as he sprawled out on the couch, took off his baseball cap, and looked around.

'We used to spend the summers here when the children were small. They still love it, although neither of them comes out here very

293

often. I think it makes all of us sad. It was Arthur's great love, and at one time mine.'

'And now?' he asked, looking at her tenderly. This was yet another side of her that he was glad to know. She had as many facets as a diamond, and shone as brightly, although he could see that her eyes were sad.

'I've only been out here once since he died. But I didn't stay. I couldn't. This morning I knew I wanted to come here with you.' He was touched and flattered, as he stood up and walked over to put an arm around her. She was letting him into her private world, which he knew was the best gift she could give him. 'I should probably change some things and redecorate. Everything's looking a little tired,' she said, glancing around. It looked worse than she remembered, as she suddenly saw it through Liam's eyes.

'I like it like this. It makes you want to sit down and stay forever.' She smiled at him. That was how she had always felt about it, and in some ways still did. The only thing missing was Arthur, but Liam was here now.

'Are you hungry?' she asked, as she pulled back the curtains and raised the shades. Sun streamed instantly into the room, and they could see the ocean and the beach from where they stood. She had brought a bag of groceries from the city to make lunch and breakfast for him. She thought it would be fun to take him to one of the local restaurants for dinner.

'I'm okay. I could make something for you.' He carried the bag into the kitchen and set it down. It was a huge old country kitchen, with a giant butcher-block table in the middle of the room, and worn counters. The house looked well used, and much loved, because it was.

He made both of them turkey sandwiches, and opened two cans of soda, which he drank out of the can and Sasha poured into a glass. As soon as they'd finished eating, he suggested they walk on the beach. They hadn't been upstairs to her bedroom yet, and he had a feeling that was going to be hard for her, too. The house was full of memories, and one much-loved ghost, her husband. Liam wanted to tread gently here, and he thought the air would do her good.

They walked down the beach for nearly an hour, holding hands most of the time, in comfortable silence. He stopped to pick up shells from time to time, and at the far end of the beach, they sat down, and then stretched out and looked up at the sky. It was a brilliant blue and the sun was bright. The sand was warm beneath them.

'This is my favorite place of all your houses,' he said as he lay there with an arm around her. 'I love it here.' She could see he did. 'I wish my kids could see it one day. They love the beach.' And so did he.

'Maybe they will,' she said quietly, then sat up, and looked down at him with a gentle smile. He always looked so beautiful to her, especially here at the beach, with his blond hair loose and blowing in the breeze. Hers was in a braid, which she often wore at the beach.

'Do you swim here?' he asked with interest.

'It's still pretty cold this time of year. I don't usually brave it until after the Fourth of July, and it's still cold then. It doesn't really warm up till August.' And by then, she'd be in St. Tropez with her children. She wanted Liam to join them for at least one weekend, and had said as much to him, but they hadn't planned it yet.

'Do you have a wet suit at the house?' Liam asked.

'I think Xavier left one here.'

'Maybe I'll go in this afternoon. Want to join me?' She laughed in answer.

'I'm not that crazy. You must be a tourist,' she teased him, and then they walked back to the house.

He found the wet suit in the garage, while she unpacked their things upstairs, and came down looking pale. Every time she saw her bedroom and the huge four-poster bed, she thought of the last time she had seen Arthur, when he told her he loved her, the morning she left for Paris. And the next day he was dead. But she didn't mention it to Liam. It was her private cross to bear, and she didn't want to spoil the weekend for him, or make him feel uneasy in her bed.

He was already wearing the wet suit when she came downstairs. He looked like a very tall, blond seal, and he had tied his long wheat-colored mane into a ponytail. 'I'm going in. Do you want to watch me?' He reminded her again of when Xavier was small and whatever he did, was always shouting 'Watch me, Mom!'

'Okay.' She followed him onto the beach, and sat down while he waded in. At least it was bearable in the wet suit. She knew it wouldn't have been otherwise. He swam for a few minutes and then came out, dripping the chilly water of the Atlantic all around him.

'Shit, it's even cold in the wet suit.' He shivered, and she smiled.

'I told you.' But he looked as though he enjoyed it.

They walked back to the house then, and she took him upstairs. She had unpacked his things and hung them in the closet next to hers. She had had a lock put on Arthur's closet the year before. Everything was still there. She hadn't cleared it out yet, and had no idea when she would, if ever. This was his house, too. Even now. In some ways, it always would be. Liam was a guest here. He

297

was well aware of it as he looked around the room. There was a strong male influence in the decor. There were a lot of paintings of birds and fish, and a large one of a sailing ship over the bed. She hadn't brought any of her contemporary pieces here. Most of those were in Paris. This was a whole other life. Even he could sense Arthur here, although he'd never known him.

Liam took a hot shower after his swim, and they drank wine, sitting on the porch. She had made a reservation at a small fish restaurant. They drove there at seven, both ordered lobster, and drank more wine. As they chatted over dinner, he could see Sasha relax.

They sat on the porch again when they went home, talking softly in the moonlight, and at midnight, they went upstairs. He could tell this was another one of those places that was sacred to her, and he didn't make love to her that night. They just lay in bed and cuddled. And in the morning, she didn't tell him that she dreamed of Arthur that night. It was a peaceful dream. He was walking away from her on the beach, she didn't try to catch up to him. And when he turned to smile and wave at her, he looked happy, and then he disappeared.

She made Liam a huge breakfast of scrambled eggs and waffles. They had a big well-used waffle iron in the kitchen. Liam made coffee. They walked on the beach, lay on the porch, and Liam took a nap in the hammock. By late afternoon, as the sun started to go down, they decided to spend another night. Their time together there had been absolutely perfect, and just what they needed.

They cooked dinner together that night, slept peacefully, cuddled up together, and drove back to the city on Monday afternoon. She didn't even bother to go to her office. And they had dinner with friends of his in SoHo that night.

They met at an Italian restaurant. There were four artists and two sculptors. They talked about galleries and shows, the work they were doing. They were younger than Liam, she guessed most of them to be in their late twenties and early thirties. Liam introduced her only as Sasha. She stopped and listened as one of them mentioned her gallery over dessert. She was a pretty young woman who said she was going to drop some slides off the next day, as Sasha glanced at Liam, and he smiled. He didn't explain who Sasha was, and on the way back uptown in a cab, she asked him if the girl was any good.

'She will be. She's not ready for you yet.' It seemed funny to her to be anonymous among them. Funnier yet that they didn't realize who she was. There was something about it she liked, although she felt a little bit of a fraud, as she listened to them talk openly about rival galleries and then hers. Her name had come up more than once as a legendary figure.

'What are you doing tomorrow?' she asked with a yawn as she got into bed beside him. She missed the beach.

'I'm going to a Yankees game,' he said with a look of delight.

They were leading a very nice life. Beach, friends, artists, baseball games for him, work for her. It seemed magical and easy to both of them, and she was grateful for his presence. Without meaning to, he had changed her life, and added something she'd never had. A youthful side of life that had eluded her when she married young and had babies. Even before that, she had been busy learning from her father, and then later working for him. She had never led the casual, unconventional life that Liam was still enjoying at forty. None of these people had tasted success yet, or the responsibilities and burdens that came with it. They worked hard but made almost nothing. Few if any were married, and no one but she and Liam had children. They seemed to have no responsibilities at all. Liam did, but his were being taken care of by someone else, his ex-wife and her future husband. She would have liked to meet his children. Maybe one day that would happen. And in the meantime, he still seemed like a child to her.

Sasha was busy at the gallery that week, preparing for the opening the following week. She curated all the shows herself, and sometimes even hung the paintings, working late into the night.

By Friday, she was exhausted and ready for another weekend at the beach. This time they left on Friday, just as she and Arthur used to. They got to the house by nine, sat on the porch, and went to bed early. And this time, ever so gingerly, they made love. Everything seemed to go fine. She was getting used to having Liam in her private world. It was a major step for Sasha, even more than for Liam.

On Saturday, as they walked down the beach, she told him she was invited to a party, and asked him if he'd like to come. It was being given by a well-known Hollywood actress. The movie set had recently discovered the Hamptons, and Sasha had met her two years before through friends. She had received the invitation the month before, and Marcie had reminded her of it on Friday, before Sasha left. It sounded like fun. It was supposed to be a big clambake, with entertainment and a band. When she told Liam about it, he looked surprised at the invitation. She had never invited him to a party before, and he knew she'd been reluctant to do so.

'You want me to come?' He was flattered. She had never offered to take him to any other social event before. This was a first.

'Yes' was all she said, without explanation. He didn't question her further.

The party began at seven, and they arrived at eight. The invitation had said informal, but Sasha knew that some of the women might dress up a bit. She wore white slacks, a white silk sweater, and a string of pearls, with her hair in a loose bun. Liam wore jeans, a T-shirt, and a blazer she had brought for him, without telling him why she had, along with a pair of loafers she had found in his closet in the guestroom.

'And you don't have to wear socks,' she teased him. 'It's considered fashionable here if you don't.'

'Then maybe I should. I'd hate to start being fashionable now.' He had taken great pleasure all his life in swimming against the tides.

In the end, he didn't, and they both fit right in. They made a striking couple, and Liam admitted to her in a whisper that it was impressive meeting their movie star hostess and her famous friends. There were at least a dozen faces there that anyone in the world would have recognized at first glance.

'I wish I could tell someone,' he whispered. But the only person he had to tell was her.

'It always impresses me too to meet people like that,' Sasha confessed.

They stayed until nearly one in the morning, danced to the band that had been flown in from L.A., and they both looked happy and tired when they got back to the house. He had been a perfect gentleman all night, and she had felt totally comfortable with him. Several of the women there had been with much younger men, with far greater age differences than hers and Liam's. It was the rage in Hollywood for older women to date younger men. She commented on it to Liam as they got into bed.

'I told you I hate being trendy,' he said, looking unconcerned. He had had a terrific time, and was proud to be out with her. 'Besides, nine years is no big deal.'

'Maybe not to you,' she said with a giggle as she snuggled next to him and he turned off the light. 'I'm not sure my kids would feel that way.' And on bad days, neither did she.

'When am I going to meet Tatianna?' he asked in the darkness.

'Probably at the opening this week. She doesn't always come, but she said she would this time.'

'Do you think she'll like me?'

'Maybe. It's hard to tell. Tatianna is tough to predict. She has strong opinions. She loves some people, and others she hates. It'll go a lot better if she doesn't know you're involved with me.' She had no intention of telling either of her children for the moment. It was none of their business. She and Liam were still taking their relationship out for a spin. They hadn't decided to make a down payment on it yet. But so far they were doing well. Even she had to admit it, although she had doubted it was possible. So far so good.

Chapter 13

Liam was excited about the show at her gallery that week. It was going to give him a sense of what they'd be doing for him in six months. And he liked the artist whose show it was. He was a young man from Minnesota whom Sasha had discovered at the art fair in Chicago the year before. He did powerful, provoking work. She had been at the gallery till two in the morning the night before, hanging his paintings, standing back and looking at them, then moving them around again, until she liked it. She was a perfectionist in all things.

Liam had stuck around till midnight to watch her do it. She was so lost in thought and concentration, she hardly talked to him, and finally he left. He was sound asleep in her bed when she got home.

The next day Sasha was at the gallery all day. She showered and changed her clothes there, and was greeting guests when Liam walked in for the party at six o'clock. She looked beautiful in a white linen suit, in stark contrast to her jet-black hair, dark eyes, and summer tan. Her eyes were a deep sable brown, and sometimes looked almost black. She smiled at him the moment she saw him walk in. She introduced him to the artist, and several more people, and then left him to greet others. He was wearing black slacks, a white shirt, his loafers, no socks, no jacket or tie. But in the uptown arty group, what he had worn seemed appropriate and didn't stand out. The artists wore all manner of dress, her clients wore suits and ties. There were several well-known models there, a famous photographer, who bought her work frequently. Writers, playwrights, art critics, museum people, and others who just came for the free ride and the champagne and hors d'oeuvres. It was a standard New York art opening, only better, because Suvery Gallery was top of the line.

Tatianna walked in at eight o'clock, the crowd was thinning out by then, but there were still plenty of people scattered through the exhibition rooms. She was on her way to dinner somewhere, and came because she had said she'd stop by. Her mother's openings were old hat to her. She was wearing a simple turquoise silk summer dress and sexy high-heeled silver sandals, and she looked striking as she walked in. With her halo of almost white blond hair and big blue eyes, she looked nothing like her mother. Liam saw her stop to talk to Sasha and wondered instantly who she was, and then he saw her kiss her mother, as the two women exchanged a warm hug. He knew then it was her daughter, but nothing about their appearances, nor their style, would have suggested to anyone that they were related. Tatianna was slinky and sexy, and everything about her was standoffish and cool. Sasha was far warmer and more animated, introducing people to each other, smiling, and talking. The essence of Sasha was warm and inviting. To Liam, the core of Tatianna seemed cold. Sasha had told him that Tatianna was shy. She stood apart from everyone for a moment, as her eyes swept the room. He could tell from looking at her that she was used to men admiring her. At twenty-four, striking in her youth and beauty, she was at the height of her game. Her mother was much humbler, and although she was striking too, part of her charm was that she was unaware of her beauty, and always had been. Sasha had tremendous charisma and charm. Liam found Tatianna daunting, just watching her from the distance. He kept his eyes on her as people came to talk to her, and then as though sensing him, she turned her head and her eyes met his. He had the feeling she didn't like him, even from across the room.

He waited a while before going over to talk to her, so she wouldn't suspect anything. He didn't want to appear anxious, or as though he were pursuing her.

He nearly bumped into her as he walked by her, and helped himself to an hors d'oeuvre from a passing tray. She was standing, looking aloof, while three young men crowded around her, and she sipped a glass of champagne. He decided to join the group.

'Hello,' he said pleasantly, 'I'm Liam Allison. Nice show, isn't it?' She looked at him as though he had said something rude. Everything about her body language told him not to enter her space. Sasha was far more nurturing and welcomed people in. She was the consummate mother.

'Yes, it is,' Tatianna said, seeming indifferent to him. 'Are you an artist?' He looked like one, almost everyone there did, and she had met a lot of them in the course of her life. She wasn't easy to impress.

'Yes, I am. I'm having a show here in December.'

'What kind of work?' He explained his theories to her, and suspected she hadn't listened to a word, which would have been correct. She had heard it all before. She seemed to lack her mother's innocence, vitality, and excitement about life. He liked Sasha a whole lot better. Independent of his relationship with her mother, he would never have pursued this girl. She was far too cool and snooty for him. And he was far too old and arty looking for her. The men she went out with were preppy and traditional, and most of them worked on Wall Street. She thought the men she met in the art scene, even at her mother's gallery, were self-centered jerks. She assumed the same about him. With only a few words of conversation between them, they took an instant dislike to each other. In an effort to warm things up a little, if only for Sasha's sake, he mentioned that he knew her brother. She nodded, and seemed not to care. She realized then that she'd heard his name before, but Xavier always had crazy, badly behaved friends. Tatianna didn't.

A few minutes later, Sasha arrived to join them. She had seen them circling each other, and was worried. Tatianna looked annoyed, never a good sign. Liam looked curious about her, and Sasha was afraid he would give it away if he asked her too many questions, or was too friendly. Tatianna seemed to suspect nothing. She just didn't want to get to know him, and there was no reason why she should, that she knew of.

'Have you two met?' Sasha asked, appearing casual, as she put an arm around her daughter and stood apart from Liam, looking like an art dealer and a mother, and nothing more. And surely not his woman.

'Yes, we have,' Liam said with a warm smile at Sasha, which her eyes returned.

'Liam is one of our artists and a friend of Xavier's from London. That's how I met him. He scouted him for us. He's having a show in December. What are you up to tonight?' Sasha asked Tatianna. She looked beautiful, undeniably, but Sasha hated it when you could see her body through her dress, which one could. But she looked no different from the other young women at the party. These days they all dressed like that at her age. It always made Sasha nervous, but she said nothing. Tatianna was old enough to wear what she wanted, and do as she chose.

'I'm having dinner at Pastis, with friends,' Tatianna said vaguely, and glanced at her watch. It was a small diamond one her father had given her on his last Christmas.

'It was nice of you to come uptown for this, sweetheart,' Sasha said with a warm smile. She knew Tatianna did almost nothing on the Upper East Side, except for work. Like most people her age, her entire social life was downtown.

'I said I would.' Tatianna smiled at her

mother. You could tell that the two women were close, although very different. Tatianna respected her a great deal, even if she didn't like meeting her artists. She was impressed by what her mother did, and proud of her for expanding the empire her grandfather had built. Tatianna still remembered him. He had always scared her when they lived in Paris. Xavier had liked him better.

'We're having dinner at La Goulue,' Sasha said casually. It was one of her favorite places, and Tatianna wasn't surprised. It was close to the gallery, the food was good, and it was full of life, and trendy people. She had already taken Liam there, and he liked it a lot.

Tatianna left a few minutes later, and after she did, Sasha came back to talk to Liam.

'So did you two hit it off?' She looked slightly worried. They had looked like two dogs circling each other right up until Tatianna left.

'She's beautiful,' Liam said honestly. No one could have denied that. 'A little scary, though. I don't think she likes me.'

'Don't be put off by her. That's just her style. Men approach her constantly, she wears a lot of armor.' And fangs, Liam thought, but he would never have said it to her mother. He had taken a visceral dislike to her. She seemed like a spoiled brat to him. Xavier was a whole different kind of being.

But even their friendship had done nothing to impress her. Liam was convinced nothing would.

They left for dinner after that. Sasha had invited a number of people she thought he'd enjoy, along with the artist whose show it was. There were fourteen of them for dinner at a long table at La Goulue, where everyone fussed over them, and Sasha. She kept a motherly eye on everyone, and saw to it that every detail was attended to, and everyone had a good time. Her caring manner defined what Liam loved about her. She was warm and nurturing and attentive to everyone. Girls like her daughter were only interested in themselves. Sasha made a real effort to make Liam feel important, comfortable, and welcome, and he loved her for it. It was what he needed most from her.

Nothing in her behavior that night suggested to anyone that there was something going on between them. She gave nothing away, not a look or a touch, or anything she said. She made it clear that he was important to her as an artist, and nothing else, and she was the attentive dealer. She was every bit as kind to the others as she was to him. He complimented her on it when they got back to her apartment, where he felt totally at home now. Tatianna would have been incensed to see him sprawled out, smoking a cigar, in her father's favorite chair in their bedroom. But fortunately, she couldn't see it. To Tatianna, everything that had been her father's was sacred, including her mother. She had frequently said that she was glad Sasha wasn't dating and hoped she never would. Her older brother was far more realistic. All he wanted was for their mother to be happy, whatever and whoever it took.

'Sasha, you are amazing,' Liam said, smiling at her through his smoke rings. She even let him smoke there, and said she liked the smell, which in fact, she did. Arthur had also had a fondness for good Cubans. 'The opening was terrific. You managed to make everyone feel important, even me. Hotchkiss loved it.' Hotchkiss was the artist they'd been showing. 'He felt like he'd died and gone to heaven. He kept telling me how lucky I am to be represented by you, and he doesn't know the half of it.' Liam laughed, and so did she.

'I'm glad you enjoyed it,' she said, looking genuinely pleased. She was a hands-on dealer, particularly with him. But it was her style to be totally involved with both her artists and her clients. She loved what she did, and was brilliant at it.

'Who wouldn't?' he said, admiring her as she put on her nightgown. She was totally at ease with him, and felt as though she had been living with him for years. 'Tatianna scared me,' he confessed, as he finished his cigar, and Sasha got into bed and looked at him.

'Don't be silly. She's just a kid. That's the way she is. She's very cool. She was very attached to her father, and she's very possessive about me. I told you, she's very black and white about things. But her glare is worse than her bite. She probably thought you were just another horny artist, lusting after her. I wish she didn't wear those dresses, though. It's no wonder men stalk her.'

'She's knock-out looking,' he conceded, but he wasn't nearly as blithe about her as her mother. Sasha obviously knew her better. 'She's so different from Xavier. He would talk to a homeless person and make him feel like a king. I felt like dirt under her feet.' It was a slight exaggeration, but not by much, and Sasha was sorry to hear it.

'She's a little spoiled, from all the attention she gets. She looked pretty tonight.'

'She is pretty.' But her icy style turned him off. Sasha was a brightly burning candle, lit from within. Tatianna was an iceberg, or looked that way to him.

'She's a lot like my father. He was scary, too, although I think you would have liked him.' She also knew her father would have had no interest whatsoever in his work. Emerging artists had never been his thing, right to the end, although he liked the profits her pet passion had brought them. But he had never understood or cared for the work.

'What are we doing tomorrow?' Liam asked, as he got into bed with her. He had a certain look in his eye, and designs on her body, to which she was not opposed. They had made her bed their own.

'I thought we'd go out to the Hamptons,' Sasha said as he folded her into his arms.

'Sounds good to me,' he said, and then kissed her in the dark.

'It does to me, too,' she whispered as she kissed him back, and then forgot everything but him.

She went to the gallery the next day, was pleased with the reviews for the show, and they left for Southampton after dinner. They bought groceries on the way and got there at ten o'clock. They sat on the porch, talking for a while, while Liam ate ice cream, and they chatted about nothing in particular. They went to bed early, made love again, got up and went for a walk on the beach the next morning. They were settling into an easy, comfortable way of life. And that afternoon, sitting on the beach, he talked about moving his studio to Paris, maybe in the fall. It would be easier than commuting from London every weekend, which was tiring, and expensive for him. And he wanted to be close to her during the week.

They both knew that sooner or later, people would find out about them. Bernard already had. But Liam was not trying to shove his way into her life. He accepted that their lives and lifestyles were different, but what they had shared so far felt great to him. This was definitely possible, for both of them. He thought it was terrific, and Sasha was slowly but surely becoming convinced. Contrary to her fears in the beginning, it was not impossible at all.

They went to a movie in Southampton that night, and were cozily tucked into bed afterward, giggling and talking, when they both heard a sound. It sounded like someone downstairs, and they thought it was an intruder.

'Do you have a panic button on the alarm?' he whispered to her, and she shook her head.

'I have a thing somewhere, but I don't know where it is,' she whispered back. They could definitely hear someone moving around, and then heard a step on the stairs. Liam glanced around her moonlit bedroom, grabbed a poker from the fireplace, and yanked her bedroom door open, as they heard a step right outside. And as he pulled the door toward him, he flipped on the light, and stood in her bedroom doorway, stark naked, with the poker in his hand. He found himself less than a foot from Tatianna, staring at him with a stunned expression. There was a young man just behind her on the landing. She screamed the moment she saw

Liam, and so did he. It was a scene beyond belief. The young man with her took a step toward him, as Sasha leaped out of bed and came to stand right behind Liam. She was also naked, and astounded to see her daughter. Tatianna had said nothing about using the house that weekend. She thought her mother no longer went there at all. Sasha hadn't mentioned her recent trips there, and had no desire to explain Liam's presence in her life.

'My God, Mother, what are you doing?' She burst into tears, and the man with her discreetly headed down the stairs. He had instantly figured out what had happened, and decided to remove himself from the scene, a wise decision. 'Are you *insane?*' And then she turned to Liam, sobbing, 'What the fuck do you think you're doing in my father's bed? What are you both thinking? Don't you have any respect for Daddy?' she screamed at her mother. 'How can you bring him here? How could you? Is this what you do when you're in Paris? You just run around screwing your artists?' Without thinking, for the first time in her life, shaking from head to foot, Sasha slapped her daughter and Tatianna slapped her back, as Liam groaned and set down the poker. He was shaking, too, and ran into the bedroom to put something on. All he was able to find in the chaos of the moment were his jockey shorts, which wasn't a vast improvement, but it was better than standing there with his privates hanging out. He hadn't had time to put on clothes when he thought he was protecting Sasha from a burglar. He would have preferred to face a man with a gun than Tatianna.

'Everyone calm down ... please...' he urged both crying women, to no avail. Tatianna was still screaming at her mother, in a state approaching hysteria. 'Just stop! Let's go downstairs and talk,' he said in the calmest voice he could muster. Neither of them listened, and then Tatianna turned on him again.

'Get out of my parents' house, you bastard! You don't belong here!' He was at a total loss for words, in the face of her fury. He had never been in a situation like this. Thank God Beth hadn't walked in on him with Becky, or it might have been worse, although he couldn't imagine anything much worse than this, being attacked by Sasha's irate daughter, and the horrified look in Sasha's eyes. It was awful.

'Don't speak to him that way,' Sasha was shouting at her. 'He's my guest.'

'He's not your *guest*. He's your *lover*. And you're both disgusting.' She spat the words at her mother turned on her heel, and ran down the stairs, and within seconds they heard the door slam, and the car she'd come in drive away. If she'd been planning a romantic weekend, she had gotten something very different, and so had Liam and Sasha. Sasha sat down on the stairs, put her face in her hands, and sobbed, as Liam put his arms around her. This was not the way she had wanted Tatianna to find out about them. She was devastated, and cried for hours.

'She'll never respect me again, Liam. She thinks I dishonored her father's memory, and I suppose I have,' she said, looking morbidly depressed and badly shaken. 'She called me a whore and a slut. Oh my God ... I can't believe this happened.' Neither could he, and there was very little he could do, except comfort her, to make it better. He thought Tatianna had behaved like a monster, no matter how surprised or upset she was. She had said things to her mother that could never be forgotten or taken back, even if Sasha chose to forgive her, which knowing Sasha, he was sure she would.

'This is none of her business,' he told Sasha firmly, once he got her back to bed, which took hours. He wasn't even sure if he should be in the bed with her, but she needed him, so he decided to stay. 'You haven't done anything wrong. You're a grown woman, your husband has been gone for almost two years. You have a right to a life without him. You were in the privacy of your own home, with a man who loves you. You have nothing to apologize for,' he said, and kissed her gently.

'She owes you an apology, Sasha. What she said to you was inexcusable.' And even if Sasha did, he had no intention of excusing it, or forgiving her, anytime soon. She had called him a piece of shit and a two-bit gigolo, which had cut him to the quick. He would have liked to slap her too, but of course he didn't. For Sasha's sake, if nothing else. There was no point adding fuel to a fire that was already blazing out of control. But they were both smarting from Tatianna's verbal attack on them, and her outrage at finding her mother with Liam, in what had once been her parents' bed.

'It's her house too,' Sasha said miserably. 'She has a right to be here. I just didn't want her to know about us so soon, and not like this.' She felt like a prostitute who'd been caught entertaining a john. Her daughter had made her feel like the lowest of the low. They finally fell asleep when the sun came up, after talking about it for hours, ad nauseam. She cried herself to sleep in his arms, and they both woke up to the sound of the phone at nine-thirty. It was Xavier, calling from London. His sister had called him the night before, and told all. Her version was pretty ugly. She had said that Liam was strutting around the house naked when she walked in, and had obviously been screwing their mother. Xavier had been startled at first, particularly by the picture she painted. But when he calmed down, and thought about it for several hours after that, he wasn't entirely opposed to the match. In fact, not at all. He liked Liam. He was just sorry for everyone that it had come to light in the way it had. It was two-thirty in the afternoon for him when he called them. And his mother cried the moment she heard him on the phone. She was deeply remorseful.

'Darling, I'm so sorry ... I couldn't ... I thought ... it wasn't the way it looked to Tati ... oh God ... what am I going to do?' She was sure her relationship with her daughter was destroyed forever, and she had never felt so ashamed in her life. No affair was worth destroying her family over. She loved Liam, or she thought she did, but her children still came first. And she was terrified Xavier would be angry too.

'First, you have to calm down,' Xavier said sensibly. He had said the same thing to Tatianna, when she called him at six in the morning his time, screaming and crying hysterically, and calling their mother a whore. He had told her to shut up immediately, and she had. They had talked for hours. He had assured her that Liam was a nice guy, a good friend of his, and he had introduced them, although he hadn't expected this to happen. In fact, it had never occurred to him. But he thought their mother had a right to happiness, with whomever she chose. It was not up to them. She had obviously been discreet about it, as he pointed out to Tatianna, since no one seemed to know. Even he hadn't figured it out when he saw them together. And she certainly was no whore. She was a lonely woman with a lover who happened to be a few years younger than she was, which was none of their business.

'How can she do that in Daddy's bed? That's disgusting!' Tatianna had wailed. She had worshiped him and still couldn't believe he was gone. And now to add to her misery, someone had taken his place and was sleeping in his bed.

'Tati, it's her bed too. Where do you expect her to go? We're lucky she lets us use the house. She doesn't have to. Dad left it to her.'

'She could go to a hotel.'

'That would be sordid. She has the right, Tat, and I promise you he's a decent guy. I know him well.'

'Like hell he is. He's a starving artist, and he's after her money. Our money,' she reminded her brother, hoping to pit him against his friend. It didn't work. Xavier knew Liam better.

'I don't think so,' Xavier said thoughtfully. 'I really don't. I think he likes her.' At least he hoped so, which was what he wanted to know when he called his mother. 'Is this serious, Mom?' he asked her honestly, and she hesitated. She didn't know what to say, or what to call it. They loved each other, but they hadn't figured the rest out yet. That's what they were doing now.

'I don't know.' Sasha answered her son honestly. She was always honest with her children. She hadn't lied about Liam. She just hadn't told them. It was a sin of omission, but not commission, which she knew was splitting hairs.

'How long has it been going on?' he asked then, hoping it wasn't a one-night stand, or an irresistible impulse, which would make a liar of him to Tatianna, when he had said his mother didn't do things lightly and this was probably important to her. Which only made Tatianna cry more. She didn't want her mother marrying some ridiculous young artist. That would have been just too embarrassing. And too much for her to swallow. She wanted her mother to mourn her father forever, childish though that was.

'It's been going on for six months. On and off since January,' Sasha said miserably. Liam was listening, lying next to her in bed, and decided to leave her alone to talk to her son. He got up and went downstairs to make coffee.

'Are you going to marry him?' Xavier asked her.

'Good lord ... I don't know ... I keep telling him this is impossible. I think Tatianna proved that last night. I'm not going to do anything that alienates me from either of you. Liam and I haven't figured out where this is going to go, if anywhere. It may not.'

'It won't alienate you from us, Mom. Nothing could do that. We love you. She'll get over it. She was just surprised. We want you to be happy.' He spoke for both of them, which Sasha knew was not the case. Or at least not at the moment.

She groaned ruefully then at the memory of the scene the night before, with she and Liam naked and everyone screaming at each other. Tatianna had described it fairly accurately to her brother. 'It was pretty awful. We thought she was a burglar. Liam went out into the hall with a poker, and no clothes on.'

'So she told me,' he said generously. He was two years older than his sister, which made a difference. And Liam was his friend, so he was not an unknown to him. His mother's affair with him had surprised him too at first, but at least he knew he was a decent person. Tatianna knew nothing about him. 'It's a good thing he didn't just take a swing and hit her in the dark.'

'He turned the lights on, which made it worse, when she saw us.' This time Xavier laughed.

'Well, Mom, you've been outed. But if you're happy, that's all I care about. I'll talk to Tatianna later. I told her to take a Valium and go to bed.'

'Does she take Valium?' Her mother sounded shocked. Neither of her children had ever been on drugs, that she knew of.

'No. But I'm sure someone she knows has some. She sounded like she needed it last night. You should have turned a fire hose on her. She was half out of her mind when she called.' And by then, she'd had a stiff drink, and sounded slightly drunk. She was a total mess, and he told her to get some sleep and call later. 'Can I talk to Liam?' Sasha went to find him in the kitchen. He handed her a cup of coffee, and she handed him the phone. Xavier chuckled as soon as he heard the familiar voice. 'So do I call you Dad now?'

'That's a lot better than what your sister called me. Hey man, I'm sorry. I really am. I didn't mean to create this mess. I wouldn't do that to your mother for anything, or to you.'

'Don't worry about it. Shit happens.' Xavier stepped into his role as head of the family then, defending his mother's interests. 'Do you love her?' he asked soberly. Xavier hoped he did, because he was a good guy, and Xavier wanted to believe he was behaving honorably, and not just on a whim. He didn't want his mother taken advantage of, especially by his friend.

'Yes, I do,' Liam said loud and clear, glancing over at Sasha, who was slumped in a seat at the kitchen table, still looking upset. She felt utterly humiliated.

'Is it too soon to ask your intentions?'

'Probably. We're both still trying to figure that out. It's a little early. It's taken me a lot to convince your mother that this was a good idea. I don't think last night helped a lot. And I'm not even divorced yet.' Then he asked Xavier a question. 'If we ever got there, would you approve?'

Xavier hesitated for a long moment, thinking about it. This was new to him, too. 'I guess so, if you think you can make each other happy. It's not what I expected, but life takes funny turns sometimes. Maybe this could work. I'll let you two figure that out. I'll take care of my sister while you do.'

'I appreciate it a lot,' Liam said with a tremor in his voice. What he appreciated was his friend's blessing on their relationship, more than his help with his irate sister, although that was useful, too, and would mean a lot to Sasha, who still looked distraught. Liam handed her back the phone then and went outside to stand on the porch and look at the beach. It was a foggy day, which seemed appropriate to him.

Xavier tried to calm his mother when she got back on the phone. She was crying softly, and he felt sorry for her. He could easily sense how awful it had been for her. 'Mom, try to relax. I'll talk to Tat. Just try to have a decent weekend. She'll get over it. So will you. He's a good guy. He says he loves you. That's all you need to know.'

'I love him, too,' she sniffed, 'but I'm not willing to lose my children for him.'

'You won't. She'll yell and scream and stomp around for a while. She'll be a diva. That's how she is. You have a right to this, if that's what you want. You have my support. And if you stick with it, and it works, you'll get hers, too. If not, chalk it up to experience and we'll all laugh about it one day.' But no one was laughing yet. Xavier was being incredibly mature and generous, far more so than his sister.

She thanked him profusely, they talked for a few more minutes, and then they hung up and she went out to find Liam on the porch. He was looking out to sea and thinking, and turned as she sat down on the swing next to him.

'I'm sorry, Sasha. I didn't mean to make a mess for you.' He looked genuinely sorry it had happened.

'You didn't make a mess. It just happened. They were bound to find out sooner or later.' Others would, too. This was just not the way she wanted their affair to come to light, to say the least. Neither did he.

They spent the rest of the weekend quietly, and went back to the city Sunday night. She had tried to get through to Tatianna several times on her cell phone, and it was always on voice mail. At her apartment, all Sasha got was the answering machine, and left several loving messages for her. Liam hated to hear her crawling, but he knew how much her daughter meant to her. He thought Tatianna should be spanked, but he said nothing to Sasha. How she handled it now was up to her.

Xavier left his sister several messages, and she called him back in London. But she was intransigent when he tried to reason with her, and furious with him for endorsing Liam.

'You're as nuts as they are. For chrissake, he's about twenty years younger than she is. How crazy is she?'

'She's not crazy, Tat. She's lonely. And he's only about eight or nine years younger than she is,' Xavier said quietly, trying in vain to reason with her.

'He looks like a kid.'

'In some ways, he is. He acts like one, but he isn't. He's an adult. He says he loves her. And I think she loves him. Whether we like it or not, she has a right to be with whoever she wants. And I'd rather it be him than some uptight prick we really hate, or some guy after her money.'

'This is sick, Zav. And he probably is after her money.'

'I don't think so. All he cares about is art. He's a decent guy who was married for twenty years and has three kids.' He didn't tell her that the marriage had broken up because he had slept with his wife's sister. 'You just have to trust her on this one. Maybe they'll get over it. They're not hurting anyone.'

'She'll look like a fool, and so will we, if anyone finds out, or she goes out with him.'

'I've done a lot worse, believe me. And so have you.' He knew all her secrets, and there were a few affairs she wouldn't have wanted to publicize, either. And Sasha was certainly not making her relationship with Liam public. On the contrary, she was keeping it a secret, and hiding out in the Hamptons. But even if people found out, there was nothing disgraceful about Liam.

'She's our mother!' Tatianna raged at him again. She wasn't giving an inch on this one. And when Tatianna dug her heels in, as a rule wild horses couldn't budge her. Not for a while at least.

'That's the point here. Give her a break, Tat. Be decent to her. She needs it. She was miserable when Dad died. I want her to be happy.'

'Not with him.' Tatianna had declared war on both of them, and intended to keep it that way. She wanted to get Liam out of her mother's life, whatever it took. She was determined to save her mother from herself, for her father's sake if nothing else.

They argued about it for nearly an hour and Tatianna never relented. She told Xavier that she wouldn't rest until Liam was gone. From the sound of what she said, Xavier believed her. He thought it was a shame. All he could do now was hope Liam was tougher and more tenacious than his sister. Tatianna was relentless once she set her sights on something. And she had.

Chapter 14

Sasha looked morbidly depressed when she got to the gallery on Monday. Karen, the manager, noticed it, and Marcie asked her gently if everything was all right, when she handed Sasha some more reviews from the show the week before.

'Are you okay?' she asked solicitously, as Sasha looked up at her with tears in her eyes. Tatianna hadn't returned a single call, and that morning at her office they had told Sasha she was out. She didn't want to stalk her, but Tatianna absolutely would not take her calls.

'I had a problem with Tatianna over the weekend,' she told her assistant cryptically. She couldn't have begun to describe the scene of Liam standing in the bedroom doorway naked with a fireplace poker, while Tatianna screamed insults at them both. Every time Sasha thought of it, she cringed, and started to cry again. It had been too awful.

'Is she all right?' Although she'd never had children of her own nor been married, Marcie was the ultimate nurturing mother, which was one of the things Sasha loved about her. She was not only good at what she did, but loving and kind, and wonderful to Sasha.

'I don't know. She won't talk to me. We had a terrible fight. Worse than I can describe.' Marcie knew that hadn't been unusual when Tatianna was younger, but in recent years mother and daughter seemed to get along fine. Until now.

'She'll get over it,' Marcie reassured her. The question now was, would Sasha?

'I'm not sure she will,' Sasha said, as she blew her nose and wiped her eyes on one of her lace hankies. She had acquired the habit from her mother of always carrying a hand-kerchief. It was one of the tender memories of her she cherished. Sasha always had one in her bag. 'It was terrible,' Sasha reiterated while Marcie clucked over her, and came back with a cup of tea, a glass of water, and some cookies, as Sasha looked up and smiled. 'Thank you, Marcie.' Her assistant seemed to hesitate before she left, and then asked Sasha if there was anything she could do to help. She didn't want to pry. 'I wish you could, but you can't,' Sasha answered, and then started to cry harder. Marcie couldn't stop herself then, she came back into the room and gave her employer and friend a hug.

'Whatever it is, it'll blow over, I promise,' Marcie said, nearly in tears herself.

'No, it won't.' Sasha blew her nose again, as the tears continued to roll down her cheeks. 'It's Liam,' she finally confessed, as Marcie stared at her in confusion.

'Liam?' What did he have to do with it? Marcie couldn't figure it out. 'Does she know him?' How did he get into the fight? It was definitely confusing.

'Better than she wanted to the other night. He was staying with me in Southampton.' That still didn't explain it to Marcie, but she looked sympathetic as Sasha tried to fill her in, as best she could.

'And they got in a fight?'

'She called him, and me, every name in the books. Whore, slut, gigolo, bastard. That was just the beginning.'

'My God, what happened?' Marcie looked appropriately shocked.

Sasha looked at her long and hard. She trusted her. She had known her for years, and loved her. She hadn't wanted to share this with anyone yet, if ever, but she needed to now. 'She walked in on us in Southampton. I had no idea she was going to use the house. We were in bed. She walked in. We thought she was an intruder. Liam walked out of the bedroom stark naked with a fireplace poker, and damn near hit her on the head. After that, all hell broke loose.'

'Liam? What was Liam doing in your bedroom?' Marcie looked blank, and Sasha laughed through her tears.

'For heaven's sake, Marcie, what do you think he was doing in my bedroom? Believe me, Tatianna figured it out. Particularly as he was standing there naked, and she had a date with her, and was obviously planning to do the same thing we were, and have been doing for six months, give or take. We've stopped seeing each other once or twice. I'm sure this won't help.'

'You and Liam?' Marcie looked like Sasha had hit her on the head with the poker. 'You and *Liam?*'

'Does it sound as bad as that?' Sasha looked mortified again. The past three days had been the most humiliating of her life. And now Marcie looked shocked, and Sasha was sorry she'd told her.

'Bad? Are you *kidding?* If I could land a guy like him, I'd be a believer forever. He's gorgeous, talented, and nice. What else do you want? What does she want? Maybe she's jealous.'

'She's not jealous. She hates him. She doesn't like artists, she's met so many crazy artists over the years, she thinks they're all flaky, and most of the time she's right. So is he sometimes. But I'm in love with him, and he says he's in love with me. And now Tatianna wants to kill him, and she'll probably never speak to me again.'

'Of course she will. Why have I not been able to figure this out?' Marcie said, feeling stupid. 'How blind and dumb am I?'

'We've been trying to keep it quiet, until we figure it out ourselves. It's actually been working very well now since April, but that's only three months.'

'What are you afraid of?' Marcie asked her gently. Sasha had shared private matters with her before, and she always gave her employer wise counsel.

'Are you kidding? He's twelve years old. I look like his mother, and I don't want to be one, except to my own children.'

'First of all, you don't look like his mother, you don't even look old enough to be Xavier's mother, or Tatianna's, and secondly, all men are babies, and every woman in the world ends up mothering them. If you don't, they run off with someone else who will.'

'Or another twelve-year-old. I don't want to fall in love with a man who is going to run off with a twenty-year-old ten years from now. It could happen.'

'Is he like that?' Marcie looked worried.

'Who knows? I don't think so. He was married for twenty years before he screwed it up pretty stupidly. But he's also irresponsible as hell ... as he puts it, he's a wacky artist.' Although less so lately. 'I never thought I'd fall in love with a man nine years younger than I am, and one of my artists. This is like poetic justice, or God's irony, or some kind of joke or something. I had the most respectable life in the world with Arthur, and now I have fallen in love with an overgrown boy, and my whole life is upside down. And Tatianna may never speak to me again.'

'If she doesn't, I'll spank her for you myself. She'll get over it. The whole scene was probably just a shock. For everyone.' Sasha smiled ruefully as she looked at her friend. It was beyond description.

'We were both standing there naked, Liam holding the poker, while she screamed insults at us, and her date looked like he wanted to crawl under the rug, and who could blame him? I slapped her, she slapped me back. I've never laid a hand on her before, and never will again. It was something right out of a bad movie. Here I am, with my younger lover, in her father's bed, as she put it, and we're both standing there naked. My God, Marcie, how much worse could it get?'

'Not much,' Marcie conceded with a grin. 'But think of it this way. He could be old, fat, bald, ugly, and over the hill, and then think of what he would have looked like standing there naked, holding the poker. If you ask me, you're goddamn lucky it's him. Listen, you've been single for about ten minutes. I've been single all my life, and probably always will be, not because I love it so much, but because there's no one out there. There are either bitter divorced guys paying alimony they resent all women for, screwed-up widowers who think their dead wives were perfect and have forgotten how much they hated them when they were alive, and you can never in a million years measure up to them, there are commitment phobics, drunks, druggies, mean guys, abusers, guys who hate women, guys who are secretly gay, and others who are openly gay and want to wear your dresses, there are boring ones who aren't worth the trouble, guys who smell bad, look bad, are bad, and old guys who can't get it up even with Viagra. I haven't found a guy I could fall in love with in ten years, and I haven't gotten laid in three. I long ago gave up the idea of being in love with the guys I sleep with, or having them be in love with me. Because if I hold on to my principles, which used to be so important to me, then for sure I'm never going to get laid again, and I might not anyway. It sure looks that way. So you're worried about a nine-year age difference with a gorgeous, talented, nice guy you're in love with and who's crazy about you? Tell Tatianna to put a sock in it and get over it. If you don't, I will.'

It was quite a speech, and Sasha knew it was heartfelt. Marcie was a wonderful woman, not beautiful, but nice looking, decently dressed, a dozen pounds over-weight, though nothing one couldn't live with. She was intelligent, well educated, and well paid, and one of the nicest people Sasha had ever known. She also knew that Marcie hadn't had a man in her life in years. There was nothing wrong with her, she just couldn't find one. And no one had bothered or tried to find her. There were a lot of women like that, they both knew, in all walks of life, at every social level, and at every age. People couldn't seem to find each other anymore, which was why computer dating had become so appealing. Sasha had urged Marcie to try it several times, but she was too scared. Sasha wasn't totally convinced she was wrong. Meeting up with strangers on the Internet sounded dangerous to her. What she was saying to Sasha was sensible, and Sasha knew she meant well. She thought Sasha was the luckiest woman in the world to have Liam, and he was the luckiest man to have her. And if Tatianna didn't like it, then too bad for her. Marcie looked incensed when she heard the things Tatianna had said to her mother.

'You really don't think it's shocking that I'm nine years older?' Sasha asked cautiously, still looking sheepish. She was grateful to know that Marcie approved.

'He's not twenty-two, for God's sake. He's legal, he's grown up. He's got kids. You two look the same age. And besides, these days lots of people seem to be doing it. After a certain age, it seems to make sense. You've had a respectable marriage, you've had your kids. You're not looking for the same things now that you were twenty-five years ago. All you need is someone you can have a good time with, who treats you right, and with whom you have something in common, whatever it is. And you two certainly do. You don't have to be together every minute, you don't have to live together if you don't want to. Or you can, if you do. You can have your own lives, your own friends, and get the best out of what you share in between. It sounds great to me. And listen, if you don't want him, I'll take him. He's only three years younger than I am. I'd be happy to suffer the humiliation of going out with him. In fact, I'd be thrilled.' Sasha was no longer crying as she listened to her. She was smiling. Marcie had made her feel that everything was okay, and would be. It made her realize how lucky she was to have him, and how little it was probably going to shock most people. Everything Marcie said made sense. To hell with the nine years. If he was a wacky artist, she could deal with that. Besides, he was behaving perfectly these days.

'What am I going to do about Tatianna?' Sasha asked her, looking serious again.

'Nothing. Just let her cool down. She obviously felt you betrayed her father. You know how crazy she was about him. She thought he walked on water. He was a wonderful man, but let's face it, Sasha, he's gone, sad as that is, and he isn't coming back. I have a feeling that he'd be relieved to know you're happy, if you are. He was one of the nicest men I've ever met. I don't think he'd want you to be alone. Tatianna just has to grow up, and get over it. Give her some space for a while, she will. She can't fight this battle forever.' Although Sasha knew she could be stubborn, and her loyalty to her father could be blind, fierce, and unlimited. It had been in her teens. And now that he was gone, she loved him even more. It was her way of holding on to him. But giving her space was not a bad idea.

'I've left her a million messages. She won't return or take my calls.'

'Then leave her alone. She may be embarrassed about what she said. She should be. How did Liam survive the ordeal?'

'Very graciously,' Sasha said. 'He was very understanding about it. She called Xavier, and he called us on Sunday morning. He was incredibly sweet to both of us. He loves Liam, they're friends, which is how I met him in the first place. He's been trying to calm Tatianna down. Xavier, not Liam. Liam is scared to death of her now, which is going to complicate things even more. It must have been a hell of a shock to him.'

'Make nice on him, he'll be fine.' Half an hour later, after they'd finished talking, he walked into her office, and when Marcie saw him pass her desk, she looked up and smiled. She wanted him to at least feel welcome there. He'd had a tough weekend.

'Hi, Liam,' Marcie said with a friendly wave. He returned the smile, looking grateful.

'Hello, Marcie,' he said, as he walked into Sasha's office and closed the door, with a worried look. 'How did it go today?' he asked as he kissed her.

'Fine.' She didn't tell him about her talk with Marcie. That was girl talk, but it had reassured her a great deal.

'Did you hear from Tatianna?' He had worried about it all day, while he hung out with friends in Tribeca.

'No. I think I'll just let her cool off for a while.'

'Good idea.' He was impressed by how sensible Sasha was being. She looked like she had calmed down a lot since that morning. 'I got baseball tickets for tonight. How does that sound?' He wanted to make her feel better, it was all he could think of to distract her.

'Wonderful.' She looked up at him and smiled. She would rather have gone to a movie, or had a quiet dinner somewhere with him, or even a noisy one at La Goulue, but she knew how much baseball meant to him, and she was happy to do it for him. After talking to Marcie, she was more grateful than ever to be with him, and to have him in her life.

At forty-nine, she knew from other women that there just weren't a lot of men out there for her. The options Marcie had described, or the lack of them, sounded comical, but they were real. Liam was wonderful and the proverbial needle in the haystack, and she was going to hang on to him whether her daughter liked it or not.

Chapter 15

Liam and Sasha spent the Fourth of July weekend in Southampton. It was blazing hot and sunny every day. They cooked, went out to dinner, lay on the beach, swam, and on the Fourth they were invited to a big party that night. It was a barbecue given by people she knew, but not well, and they both agreed it sounded like fun. She had accepted, and at six o'clock that night they went, in jeans and T-shirts and sandals, just as the invitation said. She had bought them both red, white, and blue bandanas, and they tied them around their necks. He smiled when he looked at her as they went out. He said he was the happiest he'd ever been.

'Now we look like twins,' he commented, which was funny. He was as fair as she was dark, he was tall, she was tiny, and she was beginning to forget about their age. Marcie and Xavier had both helped a lot, giving her their approval and support. She hadn't heard from Tatianna since their horrifying encounter in Southampton the week before. Sasha was still letting her cool off.

There were two hundred people at the party, long tables of food, a giant barbecue, line dancers to entertain everyone, and a tent filled with carnival games. Everyone was having a ball, and so were they.

They were sitting next to each other on a log, eating hamburgers and hot dogs, when Sasha realized for the first time that Liam was slightly drunk. Not disgustingly so, but just enough to be slightly out of control. Halfway through dinner, he said he was hot, took off his shirt, and threw it in the fire, with a grin at Sasha. The uncontrollable boy in him began to emerge, and as the night wore on, it got worse. Much worse. She tried to get him to go home with her, but he insisted he was having fun and wanted to stay. By then he was too drunk to notice she wasn't enjoying herself at all. He had started out with rum punch, switched to beer, and then wine with dinner. Afterward someone suggested he try a mojito, and she was horrified to watch him down three of them, without pausing for breath. By then, he was truly smashed. Worse yet, she wasn't. She was cold stone sober, and getting more upset by the minute, which he didn't notice either. He was having too much fun.

The line dancers came back on then, he leaped up to the dance floor and grabbed one of them, the youngest and the prettiest of course, and proceeded to do a sexy dancing act on the dance floor, while the girl he was dancing with got into it and unzipped his jeans. They did nothing more exotic after that, but that was enough for Sasha. She could see the looks of amusement and disapproval all around her, and when he walked back to her afterward, he zipped up his jeans, kissed her hard on the mouth in front of everyone, and grabbed her bottom in both hands, which left nothing to anyone's imagination as to what their relationship was. She had introduced him prior to that as one of her artists visiting from London.

'What's the matter, baby?' he asked her, looking bleary and slurring his words. She was ready to kill him, and all she wanted to do was leave. It hadn't been lost on her that the girl he'd been dancing with looked like she was in her teens, and was probably no more than twenty, younger than her daughter.

'I want to go home, Liam,' she said quietly. She didn't want to lose her temper with him, but she didn't want to stay either. He was out of control, and getting worse by the minute. He ordered a screwdriver then, and she took it away from the waiter when it came.

'What are you doing?' he asked her, trying to grab for it. But sensing what was happening, the waiter just put it back on the tray and disappeared.

'You've had a lot to drink already. I think it's time to go home.'

'You can't tell me what to do,' he said,

lurching as he stood before her. He nearly fell into her arms, and then tried to get amorous again. She gave him a quelling look, but there was obviously no getting him to leave. He was having a ball. 'I'm not your child,' he said, as he put an arm around her shoulders.

'Then don't act like one,' she said in an undertone. He was behaving like a juvenile delinquent, or at the very least, a drunk.

'You can't control me,' he repeated, and she nodded, as people continued to glance at them and then look away. She heard one man comment that Liam was going to have one hell of a hangover tomorrow, while another laughed. She knew them both. They were friends of Arthur's, which didn't help.

'Liam, I'm tired, I want to go home,' she said, pleading with him.

'Then take a nap. You can wait in the car. I want to party. I'm having a hell of a good time.' He lurched forward again and, much to her horror, disappeared into the crowd. She found him again, sitting astride the horse they were using to pull the hayride. The horse was getting skittish, and the handler was asking him to get off, to no avail. He had completely stopped the ride, as people around them watched. It finally took three men from the catering staff and the host to get him off. He had been shouting 'Yippee-kie-yay!!!' while kicking the horse. She wanted to kill him.

Their host helped her get him back to the car. He passed out in the front seat, and she drove him home. She couldn't wake him up when they got there, and she left him to sleep it off in her car. She felt him slip into bed with her at seven o'clock the next morning. When she got up at nine, he was dead to the world. He didn't come downstairs till noon, wearing dark glasses and complaining about how bright the sun was. She said nothing as she sat in the kitchen and read the paper, while he poured himself a much-needed cup of coffee. He came to sit down next to her a few minutes later, and she finally looked up and said good morning. Her tone was like ice.

'That was quite a party last night,' he said, trying to sound casual as she stared at him. 'I guess I had a lot to drink, judging by the size of my hangover today.' He laughed. She didn't.

'Yes, you did' was all she said.

'How bad was it?' he asked cautiously. He didn't remember a great deal about the night before. She did.

'Very bad,' she answered, listing his exploits. Among them, she mentioned his grabbing her behind, which had blown their cover forever among her acquaintances and friends. 'My favorite, of course, was the incident with the horse. You looked absolutely charming, scaring the horse and the children, playing cowboy and shouting "Yippee-kie-yay." I think everyone from here to Chicago heard you.' She was not amused, nor was he. He didn't want to be treated like a child, or scolded by her. He was an adult, and could behave any way he wanted, or so he said. He told Sasha he'd been behaving sensibly for a long time. He needed to let some steam off.

'I told you, Sasha. You can't control me. My family tried to, and I'm not going to let you do that to me. Everyone needs to let their hair down sometimes. So fucking what if I did?' He was being extremely defensive, and felt like shit.

'You embarrassed me,' she said, looking at him. He had started to push the dial toward impossible again, and it had been going so well. She was willing to stand up beside him, and go out into the world with him, even her world, but not if he behaved like this, and claimed rights of total freedom just because he was an artist. If he didn't want to be controlled, then he had to learn to police himself. 'I'm not going to go out with you if you act that way,' she said sadly, even more upset about it because he wasn't in the least remorseful.

'Then don't,' Liam said, sounding belligerent. 'You sound just like my father, and I'm not going to take that shit from you. You can't punish me and leave me home because I have a few drinks at a party.'

346

'You had a few dozen drinks, and you saw to it that everyone in the place who cared to watch knew that we're involved with each other.'

'I'm tired of keeping it a secret.' It had become less and less of a secret during the month they'd been in New York. Bernard knew before that. Marcie knew. Tatianna knew. Xavier knew. And God only knew who else suspected. As long as he behaved, she was willing to come out of the closet with him eventually, but not if he acted like that.

'Then act like a grown-up, and it won't have to be a secret.'

'If you loved me, you wouldn't want to keep this a secret.' He sounded like a wounded child, which was how he felt. He wanted her approval, and for her to be proud of him, not ashamed.

'I do love you, but I'm not going to let you make a spectacle of me. It's tough enough with our difference in age. I need time to get used to that. You seem to need time to grow up.'

'For chrissake, Sasha, nine years is nothing. Give that one up. I am grown up. I'm an artist, and a free spirit. I'm not going to be trained like some circus dog, so you can impress your friends and appease your daughter. Either you love me as I am, or you don't.'

'Is that what this is about? Tatianna? Liam,

she needs time to settle down. This was a huge shock for her. She thinks I betrayed her father. She adored him. This was a tremendous blow for her. And your acting like a savage at parties is not going to help convince anyone that this is a viable relationship, least of all me.' He didn't say a word to her, just strode out of the kitchen and slammed the door. She saw him from the living-room windows, walking down the beach. They were both upset. The night before had been awful. The worst part was, they were both going back to Europe the next day, she to Paris and he to London. They had no time left to bridge the gap and repair the damage if they got into an argument on their last day.

He was still sulking when they drove back to town that night. And when she offered to cook him dinner, he said he wasn't hungry. After all he'd had to drink the night before, she suspected he probably wasn't. She cooked him some pasta anyway, and as they sat at the table together, he finally started to relax.

'I'm sorry I acted like an ass last night. It was stupid. I don't know, I'm not used to all these responsibilities and restrictions. I don't want to have to act a certain way to get your approval and everyone else's. I just want to be me, and have you love me the way I am. Hell, Sasha, sometimes I just want to go have a beer with the doorman. He seems like a nice guy.'

'I'm sure he is. I'm sorry my life feels so restrictive to you.' She looked sad about it. It was the kind of thing she had been worried about from the beginning, with his phobia about being 'controlled.' Any kind of expectations or civilized behavior felt like control to him. But that was what her life was all about. She couldn't do whatever she wanted. And if he was with her, neither could he. He was finding it very hard to live with, just as she had feared. Maybe this wasn't possible after all. 'I don't know what to say, Liam. I don't want to make you unhappy. But you can't go crazy anytime you want.' Fortunately, it had been the only time it happened, but it was a biggie. For both of them. He had been trying to prove a point. Or just lost control, big time.

'What happens when we go back?' he asked, looking worried. He didn't want to lose her because of the way he had behaved the night before. But he didn't want her telling him how to act either. He wanted her unconditional love and acceptance, and said so. But sometimes that was hard to give between adults, particularly if doing so cost too much. And in her opinion, it did. It was a dilemma for both of them, a serious one. In order to prove her love for him, she had to put herself at risk. If it didn't work out between them in the end, people would laugh at her forever, or so she thought. That bothered her a lot. She wanted to stay discreet until they figured it out. The restrictions that put on him were driving him nuts, and injuring his already damaged self-esteem. If they stayed together, he wanted to know he had the freedom to be himself. All she wanted from him was to grow up. It was the one thing he didn't want to do and never had. And underlying all of it was her concern about her daughter's reaction to him. Undeniably, Tatianna and Liam were off to a bad start.

'I'm going to be working in Paris for the rest of July,' she said, in answer to his question about when they went back. 'You can come over whenever you want. I leave with the kids on August first.'

'And then what?' he asked, and she looked blank, she didn't know what he meant.

'What happens when you leave with the kids?'

'I told you. We're going to St. Tropez, and I've chartered a boat. I'll be gone for three weeks. We can go somewhere after that, if you want. I have to be back in New York for a week or so in September. You can come then too, if you like. But you should probably be getting ready for your show.' She sounded like his mother and his dealer, it was the position he put her in sometimes, instead of just the woman he loved, and who loved him.

'What about when you're with the kids? Am I welcome there, too?' he asked, looking both hurt and belligerent again. They had talked about his joining them on the boat for a few days of the trip, especially since Xavier would be there too, and Liam could masquerade as just his friend, or could have, but not now. All of that was before Tatianna had walked in on them naked in Southampton, and all hell broke loose. Now both her children knew who he was, and his role in her life.

'Liam, after what happened with Tatianna, you can't expect to come with us. That's going to take time to calm down.' Sasha still hadn't spoken to her herself. Tatianna was still refusing to take or return her calls, and Sasha had finally sent her a note, hoping to make peace with her. She had heard nothing from her yet. As far as Sasha knew, the war was still on. And Xavier knew nothing different. Sasha had spoken to him several times. He still thought Tatianna would calm down, but she hadn't yet. He said she was being juvenile and stubborn, and had accused her of being a brat. So now she was angry at him too.

'Maybe you need to stand up to her, and tell her the lay of the land,' Liam said, looking annoyed. He was furious with Sasha's daughter, and she didn't blame him. But she didn't want to risk a permanent rift with her daughter over him.

'I need to talk to her first, before I can explain anything to her.'

'And will you do that? Are you willing to stand up for me, or are you just going to let her kick me around, while you kiss her ass?'

'Liam, that's not fair,' Sasha said, with tears stinging her eyes. 'She's my daughter. I'm not willing to lose her over this, even for you. I need to make peace with her first. And we need to see how this works out. If it does, I'll deal with her. But nothing is sure yet.' He knew it himself, but didn't want to admit it to her.

'How long do you expect me to audition for you?' he said, as he stood up and looked down at her, and she looked up at him.

'You're not auditioning. We're trying to see if this can work. There are a lot of differences between us. It's not an obvious fit.'

'I thought it was,' he said, and then walked out of the kitchen. He packed his things in the guest room, while she was packing hers. She wondered if he would sleep with her that night, and was relieved when he did. They didn't make love, they just held each other. Sasha fell asleep, and Liam lay awake most of the night, staring up at the ceiling with a look of grief. It broke his heart that she wasn't willing to stand up for him, or defend him to Tatianna. He had promised her in April that he would keep their affair a secret, for a while anyway. But when he did, he had had no idea how much doing so would hurt him. As he lay in bed that night thinking about all of it, his agony was acute.

Chapter 16

Sasha and Liam flew back to Europe separately, she to Paris, he to London. They got back at roughly the same time, and she called him that night. He sounded distant. They talked for a little while, and he promised to come to Paris that weekend. She wondered if he would. He sounded unhappy with her now. Tatianna had hurt him, and the relationship, badly. She had also hurt her mother. But Sasha was not willing to wage war on her for Liam. Tatianna was her daughter, and had a birthright to the unconditional love he wanted from her. Liam didn't.

He had dinner with Xavier that week, and discussed it with him, but Xavier had had an easier childhood and youth than he had. He had had wonderful parents who he knew loved him. Liam didn't, and had the scars to prove it. They were costing Sasha now, just as whatever she had suffered in her youth inevitably cost him. Their differences in age and lifestyle didn't help either. Sasha was back to wondering again if their love affair was possible. She wanted it to be, but not if she had to ally with him against her daughter. For her, that was too high a price to pay for loving him.

He drove to Paris on Friday night, and they spent a peaceful weekend together. He stayed for the fourteenth of July, and they watched the parade on the Champs Elysées. He thought it was fun but said he missed the Yankees. He also missed his kids. He had wanted to see them again before he left the States, but they were away on a trip with Beth, and he had promised to visit them again in September.

The gallery was always quiet in July, and she was looking forward to her vacation with the children. She said as little as possible about it to Liam, so as not to rub salt in his wounds about not being invited. Tatianna was finally speaking to her again, though barely. Sasha had talked to Xavier, and he had agreed with her that it was probably a better idea if Liam didn't join them on their vacation. More than likely, it would drive Tatianna right over the edge again, and result in a confrontation. Xavier had said as much to Liam, he told his mother. Tatianna wasn't being reasonable, and only time would help the situation. She was obsessed about Liam's existence in Sasha's life being a disrespect to her father.

On their last weekend before the trip, walking in the Bois de Boulogne with the dog, Liam turned to look at Sasha.

'What are you going to do about your vacation?' The question took her by surprise. She thought they had settled it, although neither of them liked the sacrifice they would be making. She wanted him along too, but it was out of the question. As it turned out, he had been waiting for her to change her mind, or Tatianna's. The fact that she hadn't, he interpreted and felt as the ultimate betrayal by Sasha. She was failing to defend him and stand by him. It seemed childish and unreasonable to her. But it was a deal-breaker to him.

'What do you mean? What am I going to do? I thought we agreed that it won't work this year.' If they stayed together, and she hoped they would, there would be other vacations. This one just wasn't going to work. She needed time to work things out with Tatianna.

'You're not going to confront her, are you?' Sasha sighed and looked up at him. His face looked like granite.

'Not now. I will later, if I have to. I hope I don't have to do that. She'll get used to the idea of us in time. Sometimes even adults have a hard time getting used to their parents dating other people.' Sasha attributed it to that and not the horrifying scene at the house in Southampton, which had certainly been an unpleasant way to introduce him to her daughter.

'She'll never accept me, if you don't make her.' He looked stubborn.

'She only started talking to me again last week,' Sasha said sadly. One of them was going to lose here. She didn't want it to be them. 'I can't cram this down her throat, Liam. She needs time.'

'She's acting like a brat,' he said truthfully, but unkindly. Sasha knew it, too. But Tatianna was still her daughter. He said it with a nasty tone in his voice, which annoyed her.

'So are you,' she said softly. He walked away from her then, to play with the dog. On the drive home, he said nothing. He looked petulant and angry, a small boy furious with his mother. A man betrayed by his lover.

She was cooking dinner for them, when he came downstairs with his backpack in his hand and walked into the kitchen.

'What are you doing?' she asked, as fear darted up her spine. She knew before he answered.

'I'm leaving. I'm not going to be treated like a dirty little secret by you, and humiliated by your daughter.'

'Liam, please...' she said, as panic filled her voice. 'Give us a chance. We knew right from the beginning this would take time.

And you're not a secret.' Tatianna knew, which was the problem.

'No, I'm a disgrace. You're ashamed of me.' They both thought of the Fourth of July barbecue when he said it, and Sasha didn't answer.

'I'm not ashamed of you. I love you. But you're asking me to choose between you and one of my children. That's not fair. Don't ask me to do that.' There were tears in her eyes when she said it. He was asking her to do the impossible for him, and dooming them if she didn't.

'That's what it takes sometimes. I need you to love and respect me. You don't.'

'If you loved and respected me, you wouldn't ask me to choose between you and my daughter.' He stood and looked at her and said nothing. And then finally he spoke again, as he picked up the backpack.

'It's over, Sasha. I'm done. We've used up all our tickets. You were right in the beginning. It is impossible. I guess it always was. I thought we could do it. I was wrong, and you were right.' She didn't want to be right. She wanted to be wrong. She wanted that more than ever. It felt as though they had come so close this time. Until he gave her this awful choice.

She started to come toward him, and he put up a hand to stop her. 'Don't! I love you. I'm going back to London. Don't call

357

me. It's over.' And then the final cruelty. 'Give my best to Tatianna. Tell her she won.' Without another word, he walked out of her house. He closed the door quietly this time. She heard the big bronze outer door bang shut shortly after, as she stood alone in her kitchen, staring after him, at the spot where he had been standing only moments before, as tears rolled down her cheeks. She hadn't felt as terrible about anything or anyone since she lost Arthur.

She sat down on the kitchen floor, next to the dog, and stroked her as she sobbed. Socks was all she had left of him now. He was gone, back to his own life, and she knew he meant it this time.

She sat there crying for a long time in the dark kitchen. She didn't bother to turn on the lights. She just sat there, crying, and whispered one word into the darkness. 'Impossible.' By then, Liam was on the road to London, convinced of the same thing.

Chapter 17

The time in St. Tropez would have been fun for her, if her heart hadn't been aching when they got there. Xavier knew instantly when he arrived and met her at the Byblos Hotel, where they were staying, that something terrible had happened. He hadn't seen her look like that since the awful time twenty-two months before, when his father died. Xavier had suspected as much when he ran into Liam in a pub the night before he left, with a beautiful young girl. Liam had been kissing her, and was extremely drunk. Xavier felt his heart drop into his stomach. He knew then it must have ended between Liam and his mother. Except for the single slip that led to his divorce, Liam was no cheater. If he was out with another woman, openly, it was over with Sasha.

'Did you two have a fight?' Xavier asked her quietly, as they had a Pernod on the terrace.

'He wanted me to have a showdown with Tatianna. I told him it was too early. He wanted to come on the vacation. Maybe he's right. But I'm not willing to jeopardize my relationship with her. He wanted too much too soon. I couldn't do it. She's not ready. I think this is about his history with his family. All his life they told him he wasn't good enough, and shut him out. He thought I was saying the same thing. I wasn't. I just wanted some time for Tati to calm down after South-ampton. And this vacation was too soon.' He acted like a child sometimes, and they both knew it. He was, in some ways. A brilliant, talented child who acted out when he felt rejected. The worst part of it was that she knew she loved him. But she loved her daughter more.

'It was stupid of him,' Xavier said, looking annoyed. At twenty-six, he was a lot more mature than Liam. 'I told him the same thing you did. All he had to do was relax, and give it time.'

'I guess he couldn't.' The echoes of his past were still too strong, and maybe always would be. At a certain age, people who loved each other had to accommodate each other's baggage, and if they couldn't, it didn't work. It hadn't for Liam.

Without thinking, Xavier glanced at his mother then. 'I saw him the night before I left London. He was in a pub, drunk out of his mind. It didn't seem like the right time to ask him any questions, but I knew something had happened.' The way he said it told her more than he intended. As she looked into her son's eyes, she asked him a question that would tell her all she needed to know.

'Was he alone?' She could hardly get the words out. She felt a vise squeezing her chest, and Xavier didn't answer for what seemed like a long time, and then shook his head.

'He was with some stupid girl. He probably met her at the pub. It doesn't mean anything, Mom. He was drunk. I'm sure he didn't know her.' Xavier didn't tell her Liam had been kissing her, and she looked about twenty-two years old. But even with what he did say, she felt a knife go right through her heart. It really was over. After that, the rest of the trip was an agony for her. It would have been anyway. It wasn't Xavier's fault. Liam was gone. It was all she could think of.

They spent two weeks in St. Tropez, seeing friends, going to the beach and restaurants at night. They had lunch at Club 55. They had drinks at the Gorilla Bar, and once Tatianna arrived, she and Sasha checked out the shops. Sasha looked agonized from morning till night, and Tatianna didn't seem to notice. Neither of them ever mentioned Liam. And Xavier didn't dare bring him up again. He could see how miserable his mother was from the look in her eyes, even when she tried to be a good sport and pretend otherwise, which she did most of the time. And when she went to her room at night, she cried herself to sleep. She missed him beyond belief. She knew there was absolutely nothing she could do to bring him back. All she could do now was accept it. She couldn't call and invite him to St. Tropez. Tatianna would have walked out. Sasha didn't want to risk it.

They were invited out by friends several times, and Sasha agreed to go when they had children the age of her own, or were clients. But having to sit there and talk to people made her want to crawl out of her skin. She had never felt like that in her life. After Arthur's death, she had remained in seclusion for months. Now she was out in the world, pretending to be fine, which was almost unbearable for her. Nothing she did gave her relief. Day and night she ached for Liam, and knew she couldn't have him. She didn't call, and he never called her. Night after night she imagined him in bars, chasing young women. She felt half-crazed with grief by the time they got on the boat they'd chartered. It was a relief when they pulled up anchor, left St. Tropez, and headed out to sea.

Xavier and Tatianna had both invited friends, at her suggestion. They all enjoyed each other. She didn't need to entertain them. She could lie on deck with her eyes closed, near the bow of the boat, thinking of him, and aching with grief. She stayed on board when the young people went ashore at night. She said she didn't want to spoil their fun. In truth, she just didn't have the strength to talk to anyone. She needed time to grieve.

They went to Portofino, and she went ashore there for a short time. They had dinner at the Splendido, and she agreed to go with them that one time. But in spite of her best efforts, she looked so miserable that night that Tatianna asked her brother what was wrong with her after her mother went back to the boat, claiming a headache.

'Is Mom sick?' Tatianna asked, oblivious to the damage she had caused, or acting as though it had never happened. Xavier wasn't sure which.

'No,' Xavier said unhappily, 'she's miserable. I haven't seen her like this since Dad died.' Tatianna didn't answer, as Xavier looked at her accusingly. 'You made things awfully hard for her, Tat. She didn't deserve it. She and Liam broke up before she came to St. Tropez.' He was sad for both of them, and believed they genuinely loved each other, whatever their age. Liam had looked crazed too the night he saw him. He just expressed it differently than Sasha. He acted out, and she went inward with her grief. Tatianna showed no remorse when he said it.

'She's better off. He was a creep,' Tatianna said, and Xavier wanted to slap her.

'That's a rotten thing to say. Why would you want her to be miserable?' He was furious with his sister. 'I told you, he's a nice guy, and he loves her. And obviously she loves him. What are you going to do now? Sit and keep her company? Hell, no. You have your own life. So do I, and she's alone again.' He was livid, and distraught for his mother.

'She loves Daddy,' Tatianna said stubbornly.

'She did. Now she loves Liam.'

'She was making a fool of herself, and he was probably laughing at her anyway.

363

Besides, it was a shitty thing to do to Dad.'

'She didn't do anything to Dad. He's dead, Tat. He's not coming back. She has a right to have a life, whether you approve or not. The reason they broke up is because she didn't want to upset you, and invite him here. You owe her an apology. Maybe it's not too late for her to fix it. They love each other. They have a right to that. And you don't have a right to interfere.'

'I don't want her to fix it,' Tatianna said, looking devastated.

'After everything she does for us, how can you be so selfish?' He wanted to strangle his sister for her attitude and lack of compassion for their mother, who was obviously suffering the agonies of the damned over Liam, which more than convinced Xavier of how much she loved him.

'Maybe I did her a favor.'

'You should have your ass kicked. He's right, you are a brat.'

'Is that what he said?' She looked furious again when he said it. 'He stood there with his dick hanging out, ready to club me, after screwing our mother,' she said in what she felt was righteous outrage. Xavier just thought she was being a bitch, and said so, which only made her madder.

'You're disgusting. Maybe he should have clubbed you. You deserve it,' Xavier said angrily. Tatianna stomped off in a huff after that, and Sasha noticed the next day that they weren't speaking to each other. She had no idea why. It didn't even occur to her that they had been arguing over her and Liam. Xavier was even nicer to his mother after that, and Tatianna was more pleasant. She was relieved to know that Liam was out of the picture, and considered it a blessing. She never said anything about him to her mother, and Sasha had decided not to bring it up and upset her again. There was no point now. He was gone. And it hurt too much to talk about it.

They had a nice time on the boat, in spite of Sasha's miseries, and they were all sorry when they pulled into port in Monaco. They had a last dinner on board. The young people went to the casino that night, and Sasha went to bed early. The next morning, they all left. Tatianna flew back to New York, Xavier to London with promises to visit his mother in Paris soon, and Sasha caught a flight to Paris, after the young people had left. It had been a long three weeks for her. She had enjoyed her children, but she was relieved to go home, and crawl into bed with Socks. The house in Paris seemed incredibly quiet and lonely when she got back.

She had nothing to look forward to now, except work, which had kept her going before, after Arthur died. But this seemed harder. When Arthur died, she had no choice but to accept it and adjust, however hard. There was no other option. Now, knowing that Liam was alive and well, working in his studio, and probably chasing young women, it was harder still. There was always the remote chance that he might call her, or come back again, except she knew he wouldn't. He was far too stubborn, and she knew how betrayed he felt over her refusing to confront her daughter. It opened too many old wounds of abandonment and betrayal for him, and she knew he wouldn't get over it. She knew him better than that, and she was right.

She had mentioned to Bernard on her first day back to work that if Liam called, she wanted him to handle it for her. She wasn't going to take his calls. She knew he might call the gallery about his upcoming show at some point, and she couldn't face talking to him. It was too painful.

'Is something wrong?' Bernard asked, with a look of concern. She didn't look well, despite her long vacation. Beneath the tan she'd gotten on the boat, he could see that underneath her eyes were dark circles, and she looked strained. He also thought that she'd lost weight, and she had.

'No.' She started to say something, and then decided to be honest. 'It's over.' Her eyes looked grim.

'Oh.' He didn't know what else to say as

366

he looked at her. He could see how unhappy she was. It was in direct proportion to how happy she had been only months before with Liam. 'Are we still doing his show in New York?' Bernard wondered.

'Of course. We're his dealers,' she said, sounding professional, and then walked silently into her office and closed the door. The subject of Liam was as closed as the door.

Eugénie noticed how quiet she was too. When Sasha went to New York in September to curate a show, Marcie was worried about her. Sasha steeled herself not to cry when she told her it had ended with Liam. It had been two months now. She felt as though she had been crawling on her stomach across barbed wire since July. She looked exhausted now that her tan had faded. Marcie thought she looked awful, which was how she felt. Everything reminded her of him, everything seemed empty to her without him. Her bed in Paris was too big. The one in New York was an agony. The doorman asked her how he was. As careful as they had been not to tell anyone, everyone asked for him now. Everybody loved him. And worse yet, so did she. Only Tatianna didn't. She never even acknowledged that she knew he was out of her mother's life. In exchange, Xavier called her often, and she always enjoyed talking to her son.

Xavier had seen Liam several times, but he didn't tell his mother that. He didn't mention him at all. Each time he'd seen him, Liam was with a different woman. He seemed to be making up for lost time, and talked a lot about his divorce. He never mentioned Sasha, which made Xavier suspect that he was still in love with her too. His not mentioning her seemed too odd.

Xavier spent a weekend in Paris with her in October. The weather was beautiful, and they had dinner at Le Voltaire, which they both loved. She looked better by then. She had just gotten back from Amsterdam and had signed two new artists. She didn't mention it to Xavier, but she was steeling herself to go to New York for Liam's show. It was still six weeks off. She knew she had six weeks to get strong enough to see him, and not react at all, no matter how she felt. She had decided to be professional about it. She was his dealer after all. Xavier had seen his recent work, and said it was very good. Bernard had flown to London to see his new pieces too. He was very pleased, and thought Sasha would be too.

The show was on December 1st. Sasha and the children had agreed to meet in New York for Thanksgiving, since she had to be at the New York gallery on the Monday after. She was going to curate the show over the weekend. Thanksgiving in Paris never made any sense. It would be more fun for all of them to celebrate it in New York.

Xavier saw Liam just before he left for New York. He stopped by his studio, and there was a young woman there. Xavier had no idea if she was his new girlfriend or not. She looked about twenty-five, and Xavier just prayed he wouldn't take her to New York. It would kill his mother if he did, and he hoped Liam had the good taste not to do that to her, although they both had the right to pursue their own lives now, in whatever ways worked for them. But Xavier knew how painful it would be for his mother to see Liam with another woman. She wasn't seeing anyone. Xavier had asked her over dinner at Le Voltaire, her eyes had filled with tears, and she just shook her head. He didn't mention it again. He had the frightening feeling she had just given up. At forty-nine, it seemed an incredible waste to him, but she seemed to have withdrawn into herself, except when she was at work. The gallery seemed to be the only thing that could distract her, and he was grateful for that.

'See you in New York!' Liam called out happily, as Xavier left. He was excited about his show. He never mentioned Sasha even once.

Sasha and her children had Thanksgiving at the apartment. She and Xavier went to a movie afterward, while Tatianna went out with friends. It was their third Thanksgiving without Arthur, and the least painful one so far. For the rest of the weekend, Sasha was busy with Liam's show.

The work, as they uncrated it, was absolutely wonderful. Sasha stood back and looked at it, and was proud of him. He had done a fantastic job preparing for the show. It all arrived in perfect condition, and she propped it up against the walls around the gallery, as she decided where to hang it. She was still there late on Sunday night, trying to decide which of two spectacular pieces she wanted to hang in the front, so people saw it the moment they entered. She didn't even hear him come in. The door to the gallery was unlocked. Xavier had come by briefly, and Sasha had forgotten to lock it behind him. She was too busy hanging Liam's paintings. She was staring at the two largest paintings, and heard a familiar voice behind her that made her heart pound. It was Liam, fresh off the plane, in a black turtleneck sweater and jeans, the familiar baseball cap, motorcycle boots, and battered black leather jacket. His long blond ponytail hung straight down his back. He looked more than ever like James Dean. And no longer hers. She told herself that as she turned to speak to him in a deceptively calm voice, and met his eyes squarely. It didn't show to him, but it cost her a lot to do so.

'You did a great job,' she said softly. She was his art dealer now, she reminded herself silently, and nothing else. Their eyes held as they stood watching each other from the distance. He didn't approach to kiss her on the cheek. He stood across the gallery and looked at her, and she looked at him. Times had changed. He looked serious and sad and tired, but as beautiful as ever. 'You've done an incredible amount of work.' It was impressive.

'I've been busy,' he said quietly.

'I suspected you would be,' she said, and then hated herself for the comment. What he did with his spare time now was no longer any of her business. She seemed flustered when she spoke to him again. 'Which one do you like best for the front? I've been standing here for an hour, trying to decide.'

'That one,' he said, pointing to the larger, brighter of the two, without hesitating. 'Don't you think?' He still valued her opinion about his work. Her eye was infallible, and he had the greatest respect for what she did and how well she did it.

'Yes, I do. You're right. I've been standing here like a fool, stumped. But you're right.' She carried the painting to where she wanted to hang it, and he stepped forward to help her. The painting was too big for her to carry alone, but she didn't mind. She often worked late at night, hanging paintings on her own, battling with the painting, the ladder, her tape measure, a level, nails, and her hammer. He smiled as she banged the nail into the wall, and then grabbed the painting, as he lifted it up for her. She was as stubborn and determined as ever. Nothing had changed. He was still smiling when she got down to admire her work. 'Wow! That looks perfect!'

He nodded, looking at it with the critical eye of the artist, but he was pleased too. 'Yes, it does.' He looked around then and was delighted with the way she had curated the show. He had known he would be. As she stood there, looking at him, she was acutely aware that she hadn't seen him in four months and a few days. She tried not to think of it as she walked past him to put her tools away. Just feeling his presence in the same room with her was hard. She still felt the same electric current she always had, but she had to ignore it now, for both their sakes. He seemed to feel nothing at all for her, which was depressing, but she told herself it was probably better this way. This was the only way it could be.

She turned off the lights in the gallery, after he had seen all his work and how she'd hung it, and when they walked outside, she was amazed to see that it was snowing. She had been in the gallery all day and evening, working on his show.

'Where are you staying?' she asked casually, as she set the alarm and locked the door. He followed her out, noticing how tired she looked and how thin she was. Looking at him, and knowing the age of the women he probably went out with, she felt a hundred years old. He thought she looked beautiful, but drawn, and hoped she wasn't sick.

'I'm staying with friends in Tribeca.' He was intentionally vague. He didn't want to get too personal with her. 'I'm going to see my kids in Vermont next week, after the show. Beth is getting married on New Year's Eve.' He didn't know why he told her that, but it was nice seeing her again. Nice but weird, for both of them. It was so odd to have loved someone, as they had, and now not even be friends. Just an artist and a dealer. After this show, she had no idea when she'd see him again.

'How are the kids?' she asked, as they both waited for cabs to come by. The snow was sticking to the ground, there were already several inches piled up, and there were no taxis at all. And then finally there was one.

'The kids are fine,' he answered her, and was going to let her have the cab. They were going in opposite directions, and couldn't drop each other off. Sasha didn't want to take a cab with him anyway. Being that close to him would be too hard. But then she realized that it might be another hour before he found another cab. They had waited nearly twenty minutes for this one.

'Do you want to drop me off, and then go on? You could be standing here for hours,' she offered generously. The snow was falling harder and sticking more. If it hadn't been so cold and wet, it would have been pretty to watch. He hesitated and then nodded. What she had suggested made sense to him. So they both got in.

She gave the driver the address, and they both fell silent.

'I hope we don't have a blizzard, it'll be a mess for people coming to the show,' Sasha mused, as she looked out of the cab.

'I like New York like this,' he said, smiling, as he looked at the snow swirling around them. He looked more than ever like a kid, which wasn't unusual for him. 'How was Thanksgiving?' he asked politely.

'It was okay. Holidays aren't what they used to be. But it was better than last year and the year before,' she said, referring to Arthur. It had been a lot worse in other ways because of him. And by then, they were at her building, the doorman opened her door, and she got out and thanked Liam for the ride. 'See you tomorrow. You'll be a star after this,' she said, smiling at him. And then added, 'You already are. Good luck tomorrow.'

'Thanks, Sasha.' He was grateful to her,

even though things hadn't worked out for them.

The cab drove away, and as it did, Sasha bumped into Tatianna, who was coming by to borrow a dress Sasha had promised to lend her for a party that week. Sasha saw her glance into the cab and recognize who it was. On the way up in the elevator, she said nothing, but as soon as she walked into the apartment with her mother, Tatianna looked annoyed.

'Who was that?' Tatianna asked with a nasty tone in her voice, that immediately set Sasha's teeth on edge. She made a point not to react or take the bait Tatianna threw out to her. They hadn't discussed him since July, five months before.

'You know who it was,' she said calmly. 'His show is tomorrow.'

'Are you back with him?' Tatianna looked at her mother critically, as though she would be a loser in her daughter's eyes if she was, which annoyed Sasha further. Tatianna had done enough damage. She wasn't going to allow her to do more.

'No, I'm not.' But she wished she were. It was too late for that.

'He probably goes out with girls half your age,' Tatianna said meanly, and Sasha snapped.

'That's enough,' her mother said firmly, in a tone that startled Tatianna. 'What he does is none of your business or mine.'

'You're still in love with him, aren't you?' Tatianna accused her, and Sasha faced her square on.

'Yes, I am.'

'That's pathetic.'

'The only thing that's pathetic is that you're mean-spirited enough to say what you just did, carry on this vendetta, and try to dignify it in your father's name. This has nothing to do with him, or you, or even me at this point. Liam is a decent man, Tatianna. It didn't work out between us, and I'm sorry as hell about it. But if you want to rub salt in my wounds, you can leave right now. My life is hard enough, and lonely enough, and miserable enough as it is, without having you make it any worse.' There were tears in Sasha's eyes as Tatianna looked at her, stunned by the power of her mother's re-action. Xavier had told her their mother was in love with him, but Tatianna hadn't wanted to believe him. She thought it was just sex. Now she saw it was much more than that and she hadn't expected Sasha to let her have it with both barrels.

'I'm sorry, Mother,' she said quietly. 'I didn't realize you cared about him that much.' She suddenly understood what she had done and what it had cost her mother. She felt guilty for the first time.

'I do care that much, not that it does me

376

any good at this point,' Sasha said honestly, and wiped her eyes as she took off her coat. For the first time since that fateful night in the Hamptons, Tatianna felt truly sorry for her. She never thought about how lonely her mother was. All she thought about was how much she missed her father, not how alone or unhappy her mother was.

'I just wanted you to be with someone more like Dad,' Tatianna said softly, feeling bad about her comments now, and then she admitted the truth for the first time as tears flooded her eyes. 'That's not true.' She corrected herself, 'I didn't want you to be with anyone, only Dad.'

'I know,' Sasha said through her own tears as she pulled Tatianna into her arms. 'I miss him too, sweetheart, I thought it would kill me when he died. And I didn't expect to fall in love with Liam. It just happened. I didn't want it to, but it did.' She closed her eyes then as they held each other. 'It doesn't matter now. It's over.' Tears rolled down her cheeks as she said it.

'Maybe he'll come back,' Tatianna said, sorry for her and sincerely remorseful. It had taken a long, long time.

'No. It's impossible,' Sasha said quietly, as Tatianna cried in her arms. 'You didn't do it, Tati. If he had really loved me, he'd still be here. It would have fallen apart anyway. It was impossible right from the beginning. You were right.' Sasha smiled sadly at her. 'I'm too old for him. I need a grown-up, whatever that is.'

'Daddy was a grown-up,' Tatianna said, looking as sad as her mother. She felt responsible for what had happened.

'Yes, he was. There aren't many of them around.' She remembered Marcie's speech from the summer, about the losers and jerks that were out there. She believed her. She'd met a few herself in the two years of her widowhood. At least Liam had been sincere and honest and loved her, even if he was immature and childish at times. If nothing else, he was decent and kind. The rest of what she'd seen out there wasn't. She knew there was probably a nice guy out there somewhere, but she no longer had the energy or the heart to find him, or trust him. It was just too hard. She didn't want anyone now. She had two men to mourn – Arthur and Liam.

Tatianna kissed her goodnight shortly after that, and left with the dress she'd borrowed, as Sasha thought about what had happened between them that night. Tatianna had started in on her again about Liam, and this time she had called her on it. It was what Liam had wanted from her in July, and she couldn't do then. It had been the right idea at the wrong time. She owed him that, and had finally done it, but when he wanted it, it had just been too soon.

Unfortunately for her and Liam, it was way too late now. But she was glad she had done it anyway. Tatianna needed to hear it. And she had needed to say it. As her last gift to him, and to herself, she had finally settled the score for him. It no longer mattered now, but it had been long overdue, and had done her good to say it, and tell Tatianna how much she loved him. It was her last gift to him.

Chapter 18

The snow stopped in the morning, the streets were swept, and the night was crystal clear and icy cold as Sasha dressed for Liam's opening. As she always did, she wore something dark and simple. A plain black cocktail dress this time, with no frills or ruffles. She wanted the emphasis on the paintings, not on her.

Marcie had told Liam to be there at five-thirty, to speak to an art critic. They wanted to take a photograph of him with his work. Guests who had received the invitation had been invited for six o'clock.

Sasha left Marcie to handle Liam and the art critic, and when she emerged from her office, punctual for the opening, the critic and photographer had just left. Liam was standing nervously in the gallery wearing a black suit and white shirt, a dark red tie, serious black lace-up shoes, his hair pulled back in a ponytail, and Sasha smiled when she saw that he was wearing black socks. He looked impeccably groomed and dressed, and in spite of herself, her heart gave a little leap. Nothing that she felt for him showed on her face. She was the cool professional art dealer, waiting to steer him through his first major show.

'You look wonderful, Liam,' she said politely, as his eyes took in her figure in the plain black silk dress she'd worn.

'So do you.' He returned the compliment. A waiter offered him a glass of champagne, which he took, and then looked sheepishly at her. 'Don't worry, I'll behave.'

'I had no doubt that you would.' She smiled at him demurely.

'No hayrides tonight, I hope,' he said, referring to the barbecue where he had gotten blind drunk and misbehaved so outrageously.

'No,' she said with a twinkle in her eye. 'I thought maybe we'd do sleigh rides after the show.'

He shook his head and groaned at the vague memory of the Fourth of July. 'Watch out for the horse.'

She smiled, said nothing, and toasted him. 'To the success of your first Suvery show.'

'Thank you, Sasha. To my dealer!' He toasted her as the first guests began to arrive. It was well-organized chaos after that. Hundreds of people wandered through the gallery, to see his work, chatting, talking, laughing, meeting and greeting each other. Introductions, questions, price lists, critics, the curious and collectors mingling to admire his talent. Sasha didn't have a chance to speak to him again all night. She had Marcie standing by to introduce him to people, keep him happy, and make sure he behaved, just in case.

There were no problems, no misadventures, no surprises. The only surprise, and it wasn't to Sasha, was that they sold all but two pieces of his work. He couldn't believe it, he stood staring at Sasha when she told him the good news, and he nearly cried.

'Very impressive, Liam. That hardly ever happens, except with really, really big names. What this means is that they understand and appreciate your work. You should be very proud of yourself.' And then she added, 'I am very proud of you.'

Without saying a word, he hugged her, and then looked embarrassed. He was overwhelmed.

'So, now not only are you a talented artist, but you're going to be a rich one sometime soon. Very soon.' She had already decided to raise his prices after the show. 'I think you should have a show in Paris now. The market there isn't as lively, but once you have a hit in New York, it usually goes very well there too. We'll talk about it before you leave.'

He still couldn't believe it, and looked shell-shocked on the way to La Goulue. Sasha sent him on ahead with Karen and Marcie, while she rounded up the others. Some of the people she'd invited to dinner were his friends, others were clients she wanted to introduce him to, and who had bought his work that night. She had a table for twenty reserved, with Liam at the head, and herself at the opposite end, at the foot. She had surrounded him with his friends. For Sasha, it was awkward being there with him. But she had to do her job now, and do it well, no matter how she felt about him. Several of the artists he'd asked her to invite were women, she had met most of them before, and then, at least, they had only been friends. She had no idea whom he was involved with now, and didn't want to know. The only people her age at the table were clients. The rest of the dinner guests were considerably younger than Liam. Some things didn't change. There was no reason for them to now. He was back in his own familiar world. He no longer needed to make adjustments for her, or even behave himself. But he was very circumspect that night, either because he wanted to be, or in deference to her. This was an important night, and a huge victory for him.

Sasha had an announcement to make at dinner. One of the clients seated at her end of the table had just decided to buy his two remaining paintings. On the opening night, they had sold out his show. Standing at her end of the table, sharing the news with everyone, she toasted Liam again. And this time, he just sat where he was, and looked at her.

He made a garbled toast to her and the client, and said he didn't know what to say, except thank you to everyone, especially Sasha, Karen, Marcie, and the clients who had bought his work. He looked truly undone, and Sasha was touched.

She smiled at him once or twice from her end of the table, but there was no deeper meaning to the looks she gave him. She was just happy for him that the show had been a success. That had been the purpose of their alliance right from the beginning. The rest had just been an added bonus, and never the motivation for her signing him. They had accomplished exactly what she wanted for him: success.

The dinner went on until after midnight, and as she always did, Sasha stayed until the last guest left. She paid the bill, thanked the restaurant, and walked out with Liam into the icy cold crystal-clear December night. It was so cold that when she breathed, it felt like she had needles in her lungs.

'I don't know how to thank you,' Liam said, looking ecstatic. The wines she'd ordered had been excellent, but it was obvious that he hadn't drunk too much. He had been nothing but exemplary all night in every way. He was on his best behavior, and in an odd way, seemed to have grown up.

'You don't have to thank me,' Sasha said simply, 'this is what I'm supposed to do. Introduce emerging artists to the world.' That night Liam had definitely emerged. 'Besides, I make half the money. I should be thanking you.'

'Thank you for believing in me, and giving me a chance. Wait till I tell the kids,' he said, smiling, and then looked down at Sasha again. In her flat winter boots, standing next to Liam, she looked exceptionally small. 'Can I take you for a drink somewhere?' She started to say no, and then nodded. It was probably her last chance. Nothing was going to happen. They were past all that.

They decided to go to the bar at the Carlyle, and chatted in the cab about the show. Liam wanted to know every detail, and what everyone had said. Sasha told him all she knew, everything people had said to her. He lapped it up.

He ordered a brandy when they got to the Carlyle, and she ordered a cup of tea. She had had enough wine at dinner, and the last thing she wanted was to drink too much with him. She didn't want to lose control with him. After this, it would be easier. But this trip was the first time she'd seen him after their torrid affair. She had to find a new way of seeing and dealing with him. Their strictly professional relationship was still new to her.

They chatted for a while about nothing in particular, and then she surprised him and herself by telling him about her conversation the night before with Tatianna. She hadn't intended to tell him, but somehow, before she could stop herself, she did.

'I don't know why I just told you that,' she said, looking embarrassed. 'Maybe I wanted you to know I stood up for you after all. Too late for us, but not too late for you. The stupid thing is that Tatianna backed down as soon as I took a hard line with her.' She looked apologetically at Liam. 'I just wasn't ready to do it in July. Maybe I should have. And I know it's what you needed me to do. But at least I did it now.' She wasn't telling him to impress him, she just wanted him to know that she had finally defended his honor, and her own.

'It's all right, Sasha,' he said gently. 'I understand. You were in a tough spot. We both were. It's funny how those things happen sometimes. Everything collides at once,

385

the past, the present, the future. New people, old people, ghosts from the past. I get confused sometimes between my family and other people. It just hit a lot of buttons for me. She's just a kid, and she's your kid. I should have understood that. I do now. But it took me a long time. Too long,' he said sadly.

'Thank you for being nice about it,' she said with a smile. 'I know it was awful for you. It was hard for me, too, but you're right. She's my kid. And the truth is, as far as you're concerned, she's an adult and didn't act like one. Maybe we all act like children sometimes.'

'I make a point of it,' he said with a rueful grin, and they both laughed. 'In fact, I take pride in it. I've made a lifetime career of being immature.'

'What brought that on?' she asked, looking amused. He was funny sometimes. As she looked at him, she realized again how much she had missed him in the last four months, and always would.

'Old age, I think. I'm turning forty-one.' Listening to him, she groaned.

'Please, don't tell me your sob stories. I'm turning fifty in May. Shit, how did I get this old?' And this stupid, she wanted to add. Suddenly she wished she had confronted Tatianna in July, but the timing wasn't right for her, and wasn't on the cards at the time.

'You're not old, Sasha. You're still young and beautiful. I don't know why everyone gets so cranked up about their age. I do too. I keep wanting to pretend I'm a kid, and I'm not. I'm growing up, much as I hate to admit it. I don't know why we think youth is so wonderful. If I remember mine correctly, it sucked. So did my judgment then. Things are better now.'

'I wish I could say the same.' She sat back against the banquette and looked at him. It was odd. They had gone from lovers to art dealer and artist, and maybe now, in the end, they'd wind up friends. She could talk to him better and more easily than she could to anyone she knew. Except maybe Xavier. But he was her son. There were things she could admit to Liam that she would never say to him. 'Sometimes I think the older I get, the less I know.'

'You know a lot. You're the smartest person I know, about a lot of things. And the best damn art dealer in the world.'

'We make a good team,' she said, and then caught herself, realizing what she'd said, and suddenly embarrassed. She didn't want him to think she was pursuing him. She wasn't. She was making a concerted effort not to, which wasn't easy. 'About art, I mean.'

'We didn't do so badly at other things. Most of the time. We just got out of whack sometimes.' It was a mild understatement, from Sasha's point of view. Out of the eleven months they'd known each other, they'd been separated twice, for a total of six months, which meant that most of the time, they didn't get along.

'You're being generous,' she said, and then finished her tea. They had sat in the bar at the Carlyle for two hours. It was time to go home. They couldn't drag it out any longer, the bar was closing.

The doorman hailed a cab for them, and he dropped her off at her place. She would have loved to ask him up, but she knew she couldn't. She would only want him more, and there was no point. That part of their experience with each other was over, for good this time, and they both knew it. There was no hiding from that now. Age hadn't done them in, life had, and values and life-style, and Tatianna. Destiny. It wasn't meant to be, no matter how attracted they were to each other, and it was obvious they still were.

He looked at her for a moment before she got out. 'Thank you for a fantastic opening.' He hesitated, and touched her hand. 'I'm leaving for Vermont on Friday.' He didn't know how long she'd be in town. 'Can I take you to dinner tomorrow, Sasha? To thank you for tonight, and for old times' sake?' She didn't even know if he had a girlfriend at the moment. She believed he honestly wanted to take her out as a friend.

'I'm not sure that's such a great idea. We always get in trouble when we do that,' she said honestly, and he laughed.

'You can trust me. I'll behave. I promise.'

'The one I don't trust is me.' She was being frank with him, she always was, and had been, right from the first.

'Now there's an appealing thought. "Emerging artist ravished by art dealer, sues for sexual harrassment." I trust you, and if you make a pass at me, I'll yell rape. Why don't we give it a try?' He took the tension out of his invitation, and she nodded. She loved being with him, and talking to him.

'I'll try to control myself,' she said with an impish grin. He was dying to kiss her good-night, but didn't. He didn't want to spoil anything between them now, and he could see that she was scared. So was he.

'I'll pick you up at the gallery at six. I want to come in and admire my work, especially now that it's all sold.' She laughed, got out, and waved as she walked into her building. He waved back as the cab pulled away.

She let herself into the silent apartment, thinking of when he had been there with her. The place felt like it was full of ghosts now. Arthur. Liam. Even the children were gone. The reality of her life now was that she was alone. Probably forever. The one thing she couldn't let herself do, she reminded herself, as she took off her coat, was let herself fall for Liam again, no matter how tempting and charming he was. They had proven it was impossible twice. They didn't need to do it again.

Chapter 19

Liam came to pick her up at the gallery, promptly at six as he had promised. He glanced at his paintings as they left. It was an odd feeling knowing he wouldn't see them again. It was like having put his children up for adoption. He had given birth to them, and now he had to let them go. He felt nostalgic as they rode downtown in the cab. He had made a reservation for them at Da Silvano. They had gone there often in July. It was a popular Italian restaurant downtown, with waiters who sang when they felt like it, and the food was good.

They talked about art, as usual, people they knew, friends of his she'd met, her children and his. He said Tom was doing well in college, and the others were fine, too. Eventually, he talked about Beth. He admitted that it was a weird feeling knowing she was getting remarried. Their divorce was going to be final by Christmas. She still hadn't forgiven him for Becky, and he knew she never would.

'I thought we could at least end up friends. Apparently, we can't even do that. At least you and I seem to have found our way back to friendship, that's something at least.' But they both knew there was always an undercurrent of something else with them. The attraction between them was too strong. Sasha was even worried about it that night, as they sat across the table from each other, eating pasta, and drinking cheap red wine.

They talked about their trip to Italy then. It had been magical for both of them. And then, without thinking, he glanced at her wrist, and saw the bracelet he had bought her. She still had it on. Even after it was over, she had never taken it off. She was embarrassed when she saw him notice it.

'That's silly of me. I get sentimental about things like that.'

'So do I,' he said, and didn't comment further.

'So what are you doing for Christmas, Liam?'

'I don't know. I'm going back to London after I see the kids. I'm just spending the weekend in Vermont. We're staying at a motel, the cabin at the lake isn't heated or insulated for winter.' She nodded, thinking about his children. She had never met them, and wished she had. Maybe she would one day. Maybe he'd bring them to the gallery to see one of his shows. It would be a year before he had the next one, maybe two years. She was going to do his next show in Paris. And after that, in New York again, the following year. As a dealer, she had great plans for him. As a woman, she had none. After all they'd been through, she knew better now. 'What about you? Christmas in Paris?'

'I'm not sure. Tatianna is going away with friends this year. Xavier has a new girlfriend he wants to spend time with. I'm going to be here for a few weeks, I think. I'll probably be back in Paris by Christmas. I was thinking of letting Xavier bring his girlfriend. Time marches on.' She smiled, trying to be brave. But her heart still sank when she thought of Christmas, especially without Arthur, and now him.

They managed to get through the meal without hurting each other's feelings, or bringing up painful memories. They skirted around them carefully, like a minefield, and on the whole the evening was a success. He offered to ride uptown with her in the cab, and she said that was silly. He had to go downtown to Tribeca, which was only a short distance. She had to go all the way uptown to her apartment.

'I don't mind,' he insisted. But any way they did it, it was a bad deal for her. If he was only friendly, she knew she'd feel rejected. And if he reached out to her again as a woman, she knew they'd both regret it.

It was time to let it go.

She gave him a hug and kissed his cheek, thanked him for dinner, and got into the cab alone. Feeling stupid about it, she cried all the way home. She reminded herself that no matter how appealing some things seemed, they just weren't meant to be. And this was one of them. She'd been lucky to have him at all. They were a blessing in each other's lives for a short time. In truth, end to end, they had only spent five months together. It was nothing in the course of a lifetime, and certainly didn't compare to her twenty-five years with Arthur. Her love affair with Liam had been short and sweet, exciting and passionate, full of thunder and lightning. For the long haul, she knew, one needed something simpler, easier, quieter, and more solid. There was nothing easy or quiet about Liam. Or maybe even about her.

She turned the lights on when she got home, put on her nightgown, brushed her teeth, and went to bed. She had just turned off the light when the buzzer rang. It was the doorman downstairs. She couldn't imagine why he was calling, and she got out of bed to answer it. He said she had a guest.

'No, I don't. I'm not expecting anyone,' she said, looking distracted. 'Who is it?' He handed the guest the phone.

'It's me,' he said, sounding foolish. 'May I come up?' It was Liam.

'No!' she nearly shouted into the phone. 'You can't. I'm in bed. What are you doing here?' It was a stupid thing to do, and she was almost mad at him. She did not want to be tempted, although in fact she did. But she wouldn't allow him to do that to her. Not again.

'I want to talk to you,' he said quietly, aware that the doorman was listening. It was a new one he didn't know.

'I don't want to talk to you. Call me in the morning.'

'I'll be right up,' he said with a smile at the doorman, and hung up the phone. He headed for the elevator without hesitating, and it was obvious he knew the way. The doorman didn't stop him as Liam waved his thanks. Two minutes later, he rang her bell. She heard it and didn't answer. She didn't have the heart to have the doorman come up and throw him out, but she could have, and she told him that through the door.

'Go away!'

'I'm not leaving,' he said calmly.

'I won't open the door.'

'Fine. We can talk like this. I'm sure your neighbors will be fascinated,' he said, completely unconcerned, while she leaned against the door, crossed her arms, and closed her eyes.

'Don't do this, Liam. We have nothing to say.'

'Speak for yourself. I have a lot to say.' He started singing then and she knew her neighbors would go nuts and complain. She had no choice but to open the door. She did, and gave him an ominous look.

'If you touch me, I'm calling the police and charging you with rape.'

'Perfect. It will enhance my reputation immeasurably. If you touch me, I'll tell them you raped me.'

'Don't worry. I won't.' He breezed in past her as though he were still staying there, and she followed him in her nightgown. He walked into the kitchen and opened the freezer.

'Perfect. Rocky Road.' He looked delighted and took the container out of the freezer, helped himself to a bowl, and scooped out an enormous portion, after offering some to her. She shook her head, and looked like she was about to hit him. She would have if she'd dared. He looked completely unconcerned as he sat down. He had tossed his coat on a chair in the hall, and was still wearing the heavy sweater and black slacks he'd worn at dinner. And socks. It was cold outside. Even he wore socks in winter. But he was still Liam. Irrepressible and uncontrollable. Her favorite wacky artist.

'Don't eat that. It must have freezer burn. It's been here since you left.'

'I don't mind,' he said, eating the ice

cream, and glancing at her.

'So what do you want to say?' She was still looking fierce, and he smiled.

'I wanted to say that I love you. I thought you should know.'

'I love you, too. That doesn't make any difference. We drove each other nuts. I hurt your feelings. You broke my heart. You walked out. It's impossible. We know that. We don't need to prove it again. We've done that twice. That's more than enough for me.' It had been four months, and she still wasn't over him. If he left again, it would take even longer to get over him. Losing him twice had been bad enough. She wasn't going to try again, no matter how irresistible he was. She was going to listen to her head this time, not her heart. Her heart had gotten her into trouble with him before. Every time.

'Third time's the charm,' he said, as he finished the ice cream, washed out the bowl, and put it in the dishwasher. 'Look how well trained I am. Why waste that on someone else?'

'You just look trained. You're one of those big sloppy dogs that wag their tail, fetch, and play ball. But you're not housebroken, and I know it.'

'Neither are you. We deserve each other,' he said confidently.

'I am too. I am extremely civilized. In every way.' She drew herself up to her full height to look daunting, and failed abysmally. Liam wasn't impressed, or daunted. He was in love with her, not afraid of her.

'Yes, you are civilized, I'll admit. But you're also the most stubborn woman I know.'

'Have you been taking a survey?' she asked, looking suspicious. 'Xavier said he ran into you with some young girl, younger than Tati.'

'There have been a lot of young girls since I was stupid enough to leave you. They bore me to tears. Sasha, I don't know what you did to me when we met, but I can't live without you. I want to come back. I love you. I promise I'll be good this time.'

'You were good last time,' she said, looking at him sadly. 'You were fantastic. I was happy with you. I love you too. But I can't deal with your wacky artist bullshit. Every time I expect you to be respectable, you think I'm trying to control you. Your feelings get hurt if you feel criticized in any way, and you think I'm ostracizing you like your father. I'm not, but I can't always do everything you want. And for you, that means Hiroshima every time it happens. Whenever you get insulted, you walk out.'

'I felt left out,' he explained, as though that made a difference. But the end result was still that he had ended it, and left. And it was now four months later. Too late for her, or so she wanted him to believe.

'I know you felt left out. I've had a shit

time without you. But I didn't want to lose my daughter forever because I sided with you. It was too soon.'

'I understand that now. It took me a while to get it, but I do.' He was sitting at the kitchen table as though waiting to sign a contract with her.

'What do you want from me, Liam?' she asked, looking frightened and frustrated. 'You make me insane.'

'We are insane. Both of us. Insanely in love with each other. Maybe it's a sickness. I don't know. Maybe we should get treatment for it. All I know is that every time I see you, I know I can't live without you. And don't tell me you don't feel the same thing. I know you do. You're just politer than I am, and more adult, or something like that. I wanted to crawl right into that cab with you tonight, but you didn't invite me, so I got my own and came up here to see you. You could at least have invited me to come back here for a drink,' he said, sounding insulted, but he wasn't. He was teasing her, and she knew it. 'I offered to bring you home, and I meant it.'

'And then what? We do something stupid? And what happens after that? We have a great month, or two or three, and then you walk out on me again the next time I hurt your feelings. Liam, I won't do it.'

'Well, I'm not leaving till you say you will. I want to spend Christmas with you. Actually, I want to spend my life with you. I need you. You're the only woman in the world who understands me, and actually cares about me, and takes care of me.'

'I don't want to be your mother, Liam,' she said sternly, 'no matter how old I am.'

'All men want to be mothered. It's the nature of the beast.' Someone else had told her that, and she couldn't remember who. She was trying to think, but it didn't matter. What he was saying was crazy, no matter how beautiful and appealing he was, or how sexy. 'I like that you're older than I am. You make more sense than I do.'

'That's because you don't want to grow up.'

'You can be grown up for both of us. I give you permission.' He looked as though he thought he had solved the problem, but he hadn't, for her at least.

'You have to be a grown-up, too.'

'I hate that part,' he said, snapping his fingers. 'Can't I be a wacky artist till I'm eighty? By then, you can just tell people I'm senile.'

'You can be a wacky artist now, just not all the time.' Although he hadn't been all the time before, either. Just selectively, like at the barbecue, where he had been flat-out outrageous, not just wacky. No one would ever forget it, and certainly not she. 'It doesn't matter what we agree to, Liam. It still won't work. It just won't. It didn't. It really is impossible.'

'That's bullshit. It is possible. You just don't want it to be.'

'Why wouldn't I want it to be possible? Why wouldn't I want to be with you if I love you, which I do? I never stopped loving you. You're the one who walked out. I didn't. You're the one who made it impossible, and proved it. You convinced me. I was thinking it was possible right about then, until you went nuts over Tati, although I'll admit, she was awful to you.'

'She was and I was stupid. I don't know, Sasha. What can I tell you? Other than Beth, you're the only woman I've ever loved. Maybe I'm a slow learner, or dyslexic or something. All I know is I get it now.'

'It's too late,' she said sadly. She didn't want it to be, but it was. For both of them. They couldn't do this again, no matter how tempting.

'It's not,' he insisted.

'It is.' She was as stubborn as he. More so this time.

'I'm going to get drunk in a minute if you don't stop arguing with me. You give me no other choice.'

For a minute, she thought he meant it. 'Do you want a drink?'

'No, I want you.' He got down on bended knee in her kitchen. They still hadn't made it out of the kitchen, and she laughed at him.

'You look ridiculous, stop that. Get up, for God's sake.'

'I won't till you agree to try again. Oh hell, Sasha, what have we got to lose?'

'Our sanity. Mine anyway. I damn near lost it last time.'

'I won't do that again. I promise.'

'You'll do something else worse. I know you will.'

'Then what? So we'll fight for a while, and figure it out. It's a learning process. I'm a slow learner, but God, woman, I love you.'

'You're impossible.'

'Maybe I am. But this relationship isn't.' He walked over then and did what he had wanted to do all evening, and the night before, and hadn't dared. He kissed her, and put his arms around her. He didn't stop until they were both breathless. 'I love you,' he said hoarsely.

'I love you, too,' she whispered. 'Please, Liam ... don't do this to me.' She was absolutely incapable of resisting him, and she knew it. She wanted him too much.

'Please, Sash, give us a chance...' he whispered back. She looked at him long and hard, and then as though someone else had done it for her, totally out of her control, she nodded yes, and then closed her eyes.

With a single gesture, he swept her up in

his arms, walked into her bedroom, and laid her down on the bed they had shared that summer. She lay watching him while he undressed, wondering at the insanity of what they were doing, and profoundly unable to resist him.

'I think I'm possessed,' she said, as she watched him take off his shoes, and then his pants. 'I need an exorcist.'

'I need you,' he said, as he dropped his trousers on the floor and then his shirt. She nearly swooned as she watched him do it, and then he turned off the light. 'All I need is you,' he said as he joined her in bed.

'I love you, Liam ... we better get it right this time,' she warned as he started to make love to her.

'We will, Sash, I promise.'

They made love as though they were addicted to each other. What they shared was beyond reason, beyond promises, beyond words. All they knew, as they lay together, was that they both believed that it was possible again.

Chapter 20

Sasha woke up in the morning, lying next to Liam, and all she could do this time was laugh. 'Tell me I'm dreaming. I must be on drugs ... we are both nuts to try this again.'

'Yes,' he said, rolling over on his back with a broad grin, 'we are and I love it. Think how boring life would be otherwise.'

'Yeah, and maybe even sane. God knows what that would feel like. I can't remember anymore.'

'Sane is boring,' he said, smiling at her.

'Oh God ... don't tell me that...'

'What are we doing today?'

'I don't know about you, Sir Wacky Artist. As for me, I have to work for a living. I have children and artists to support.'

'Not me. I'm sold out,' he said with a look of glee, as he rolled over and kissed her. They were happy again. Life was sweet. 'I'll come back here after Vermont.' He had been planning to fly to London from Boston, but now, in the blink of an eye, all his plans had changed. 'I can fly back to Paris with you if you want. I don't want to intrude on you and Xavier for Christmas. I can go back to London for a few days.'

'No,' she said firmly, 'I want you there. Xavier would love it.' Tatianna wouldn't be there for Christmas anyway. With her father gone now, she found Christmas too depressing with just her mother and brother. But Xavier was ever loyal to her and wouldn't have left her alone. 'Liam,' she said, looking serious, as she sat up in bed. She looked as though she had an announcement to make. 'I'm not going to lose you this time. I don't give a damn what it takes. I don't want to mess this up again. And if you storm out this time, I'm coming with you. I want you to know that. We'll either make this work or kill each other trying. I'll be goddamned if I'm going to lose again.'

'Yes, ma'am.' He saluted, and marched off to the shower. It was so good seeing him there again, with his tall, gorgeous naked body and his long blond hair.

'I mean it!' she shouted after him as he turned on the shower. 'And I'm telling Tatianna today.' She said it as much to herself as to him. She knew Tatianna would be fine with it this time. And this was her life anyway, not theirs.

'I love you,' he shouted back in answer to whatever she'd said. That covered it for him.

She made bacon and eggs and English muffins for both of them. An hour later, he was reading the paper, back in bed, and she was ready to leave for work. He looked like he had never left, and it felt like he hadn't.

'The maid comes at noon,' she reminded him, as she stood smiling at him, with her briefcase in her hand.

'I know. I remember. I'll be up by then. You look very grown up today,' he commented, amused.

'I am.'

'No, you're not. Don't lie to me, Sasha. You're no more grown up than I am. If you were, we wouldn't be doing this.' She was glad they were. Very glad. So was he. Ecstatic in fact. She felt as though she had her life back, what she had back was him. The truth was that she made him grown up, and he made her young. Somewhere in the middle lay the realm of possibility they had been chasing for a year, and seemed to have found. The secret was to keep it. She was ready for the challenge, and so was he. They both knew it wouldn't be easy, but it was worth it to both of them. 'Can you have lunch?' She nodded. 'I'll pick you up at one. I have to do some errands first. I want to do some Christmas shopping for the kids. What do you think they want?'

'I don't even know them, Liam,' she said, laughing at him. He had moved right back in, and lay there in her bed like a king.

'I want to change that soon. Let's go to Vermont together the next time you come to New York.'

'That's a deal.' There was no secret to their relationship now. If they were going to do this, she knew they had to do it for real, no holds barred. She was prepared to do that now, and so was he. It had taken them a year to get in sync, which wasn't as bad as it might have been. Losing him for four months had shown her just how much he meant to her. And he had discovered the same thing. She kissed him before she left, and he leaped out of bed shortly after. He wanted to buy her a Christmas present too. He was going to do it that afternoon. Not just a gold bracelet this time, something better. He had made a lot of money that week, and he could hardly wait to spend some of it on her.

He picked her up at the gallery at one. They went to Gino's for lunch, and then he walked her back to the gallery, before he went to do his errands. He came back in the late afternoon, and hung around with Marcie, while Sasha finished working with a client. She introduced Liam to him before he left, and said that he was their most promising young artist. She kissed Liam's cheek then, and it was obvious that he was far more than that to her. And not a secret anymore. He was beaming when they left the gallery.

'That was nice, what you just did in there.'

'What? Introduced you to the client?' She knew what he meant, and she was happy he liked it. She knew what it meant to him now to be accepted, and sometimes even shown off. He needed that, and if that was what it took to make him happy, she was willing to do it. More than willing. She wanted to, because she loved him, and knew he loved her.

It was amazing to both of them how quickly it all fell back together, as though they'd never been apart. He moved to her apartment from his friend's in Tribeca. Sasha told Tatianna, and she called Xavier in London. She didn't make a fuss this time. She was leery of Liam, but accepted her mother's decision, and was even willing to give him a chance. She realized now how much her mother loved him.

Everything was back on track, better than it had ever been before. It was as though each time they came apart, when they found each other, the mesh that bound them tightened, and they were closer than ever. She felt almost married to him this time, and he commented on it too. She wondered if they ever would, but it didn't seem important. All that mattered was that they were back together. Their relationship had never seemed more possible than it did at that moment, and she felt absolutely certain that this time they would win and it would stick. She had said as much to Marcie that morning, who was happy for her too.

For the next two days, they had lunches and dinners, went shopping, he hung out at the gallery when she was busy, and they fell into their familiar rhythm of making love night and morning, and once in a while in between. Liam was leaving for Vermont the next morning, his presents for his children were packed. And he had a present for Sasha hidden in a drawer in Xavier's room. He had bought her a narrow diamond bangle bracelet this time, similar to the gold one he'd given her before, but this one sparkled and was far more 'grown-up.' He could afford it now. He couldn't have in May. Everything had changed after his show. He had some real money coming in finally, and he was anxious to get back to work again.

His cell phone rang late that night after they'd gone to bed, and at first they didn't hear it. It was in the charger Liam had set up in the bathroom, but it was so persistent, Sasha finally heard it and poked him, and told him what it was. He had already been asleep. He stumbled into the bathroom to get it, wondering who it was. It was Beth. And within seconds, he was wide awake, and staring at Sasha, looking panicked.

'How bad is it?' he asked, and was silent for a long time while she explained. Sasha still didn't know who it was. But it didn't sound good, and his face was pale. There were tears in his eyes when he finally hung up.

'What happened?' Sasha looked worried. Calls at that hour, with those kinds of questions, were never good. She sensed instantly it was one of his children.

'It's Charlotte. That was Beth. They went to see the new house her future husband is building for her, it's not finished yet. Charlotte stepped on a tarp that was covering a hole, and she fell an entire floor into a pile of construction materials lying on cement.'

'Oh my God.' Sasha looked as horrified as he was. His hand shook as he set down the phone, and reached for Sasha's hand. He squeezed it so tight it hurt while he told her the rest.

'She broke her back, and they don't know how bad it is yet. She may be able to walk again, or she could be paralyzed from the neck down. They just don't know. She has a head injury, but it's not as bad as the back. She's conscious now, and in a lot of pain.' He started to cry as Sasha held him. He had to leave immediately. He couldn't wait till morning. She called to rent a car for him, and wanted to go with him, but she thought it would be hard on Beth and the other children to have a stranger there. But she wished she could be there for Liam. She knew he needed her.

They were out of the house in less than ten minutes. He had his bag with him, as they took a cab to the car rental she'd called.

And half an hour later, he was ready to get on the road to Vermont.

'I wish I could go with you,' she said, and meant it, but he agreed with her. It would be awkward to have her there. They were going to be at Charlotte's bedside in the trauma unit, and he knew Beth would be upset if Sasha was with him.

'I'll call you as soon as I know something,' he said, and held her tight for one last moment. He needed all the strength she had to give him. It was one in the morning, and he had a six-hour drive ahead of him, maybe less if the weather was decent, or more if not. Beth had told him it was snowing where they were.

'I'll be thinking of you every minute,' she said, and kissed him through the window. She waved and he drove away. And a minute later, she caught a cab uptown. She had her cell phone with her, and he called her even before she got back to the apartment. He was very emotional, and cried when he talked to her.

'I love you, Sasha ... thank you for being there for me when I need you...'

'I'm right here, darling. I'll be here every minute, praying for all of you.' Poor little Charlotte. It was a miracle she hadn't been killed. Sasha hoped, as he did, that the damage wasn't as bad as they feared. 'Drive safely, sweetheart ... call me when you get there, if you can.'

He called her several times that night, with bulletins he got from Beth about Charlotte. She was in critical condition, but hanging on. They were going to operate that morning when he got there. Sasha felt sick thinking of what they all had to go through. It was a nightmare. She couldn't think of anything worse than a badly injured child. Liam got there at nine in the morning, as Sasha sat, waiting to hear from him. She'd been up all night, with him. She had talked to him every half hour all night. She hadn't left him for a minute. And when he didn't call her, she called him. She was grateful they were back together, so she could at least support him through the ordeal.

She didn't hear from him then till lunchtime, while Charlotte was in surgery. They said she wouldn't be out till evening. And Liam just sat at the other end and sobbed, when he described the condition she was in. Sasha was in tears herself as she sat at the gallery, waiting for news. The results of the surgery sounded promising. It wasn't quite as dire as they had feared, but it was very bad. And when they had a chance to talk about it, Liam said that the man who was about to marry Beth was beside himself with guilt and grief. Charlotte had been with him, looking at where her room was going to be, and he had turned away for a minute to

411

show her something, and that was when she fell. Liam said that Beth was blaming him, but no more than he did himself. It sounded like an excruciating scene for all of them. Tom, Liam's older son, was flying home from college to be with his sister. At least the family was together, or would be. Sasha was only sorry she couldn't join them. She thought of flying up to stay in a hotel near the hospital, so she could support Liam, but he said they were sleeping in Charlotte's room and on cots in the hallway. He wouldn't have been able to see her anyway. So she stayed in New York, and kept her phone in her hand at all times.

She left the gallery at seven, and stayed close to the phone in her apartment. He called her several times that night. The news was a little better in the morning, after another sleepless night for all of them, Sasha as well as Liam. He said Beth was tense, but decent to him. He said she was half out of her mind. They had to cancel the wedding, which was in three weeks. They were putting it off till January, till they knew how Charlotte was. Everyone's life was suddenly upside down, and Charlotte's still hung in the balance. She was nowhere near out of the woods yet.

The days droned on interminably, and by the end of a week, they knew she wouldn't be quadriplegic, but they still weren't sure about her legs. It all depended on how her spinal cord repaired. There was a distinct possibility that she would walk again, but nothing was certain, and if she did, it would take months or even years to get her on her feet again, and she had several surgeries ahead of her. Sasha hated to ask, but was relieved to hear they had good insurance, otherwise it would have been a financial catastrophe for them as well. It was going to take years and cost a fortune to put the little girl back together, and she had a lot of hard times ahead of her, as did Beth, who would be taking care of her. Liam sounded guilty when he talked about it on the phone. But someone had to take care of Charlotte, and he couldn't be there. He lived in London, and would be with Sasha in Paris. He was worried about missing Christmas with her, but that was the least of their concerns. Listening to him, Sasha decided to spend it in New York. If there was any chance he could get away even for a day to spend Christmas with her, it would be a lot easier to get to her there than in Paris, where she had planned to spend it. And they could manage fine at the gallery in Paris without her, they always did, thanks to Bernard.

She called Xavier and told him what had happened, and he felt terrible for Liam, as she did. Xavier knew Charlotte, he had met her many times before Beth left. It broke his heart to think of her paralyzed, and hoped it wouldn't happen. He told his mother to give his best to Liam, and said he'd go to church to pray for his little girl. Sasha had lit a candle for her only that morning, and had gone to mass to pray for her, which wasn't something she did often.

Xavier offered to come to New York to spend Christmas with her, but it was obvious he wanted to stay in London with his new girlfriend, and she had invited him to go skiing with her, so Sasha let him off the hook. There was no question he'd have more fun there. He said he really appreciated it, and promised to spend it with her next year. Hopefully, by then Tatianna and Liam would be with them. But there was too much going on to worry about Christmas this year.

The bulletins from Liam continued for the next two weeks, and they were within days of Christmas by then. Christmas had ceased to exist for all of them at the hospital as they worried about Charlotte, and waited for the prognosis, which was better, but never completely reassuring. It was a relentless strain for all of them. Liam was so tired he was beginning to get testy with her, and he called less often, because he was sitting with Charlotte for eight-hour shifts, to relieve Beth a little. After that, sometimes he fell asleep on the cot in the hallway, before he had time to call. Sasha understood the pressure he was

414

under, or tried to. She was worn out hearing about it from the distance, she could only imagine what it was like for all of them, sitting in the trauma unit day and night, supporting the little girl. Liam said she was in a lot of pain, which agonized him to see. It was a nightmare for all of them. Her heart ached for him every time she talked to Liam. He kept promising to come to New York to see her as soon as he could. She couldn't even imagine when that would be, and never asked. She wanted to lighten his burdens for him, not add to them.

Two days before Christmas, the doctors gave Charlotte and her family the best gift of all. They told them that it would take a long, long time, but she would walk again. Maybe with a halting gait, or a limp, or with braces, but she would walk. Her spinal cord had escaped total destruction, although she would not come out of it totally unscathed. It was going to be a long haul, but it was a better fate for her than they'd all feared. She was going to be in the hospital for at least three months, maybe longer, but they thought she'd make a good recovery in the end, and she wouldn't be mentally impaired. She'd have to be brave to get through her surgeries, but they were optimistic. They took her off the critical list the same day. When Liam called to tell her, Sasha was in tears. And she cried with him. It was still enormously upsetting, but a tremendous relief. It could have been so much worse, and for weeks, had looked as though it would be.

'I want to come down and see you,' he said, sounding exhausted.

'Why don't I drive up? I don't want you to drive in the state you're in.'

'I'm fine,' he said, which didn't sound like an accurate assessment to her. He had been in a state of total exhaustion and near collapse for more than two weeks. She hated to think of him being on the road. But he insisted he wanted to come down the next day, to spend Christmas Eve with her, and then he said he'd have to go back. He was still taking turns doing shifts with Beth and Becky, which sounded awkward to her. But in the crisis, they had no other choice. There was one of them with her at all times, and the grandparents were helping as best they could, and Beth's fiancé. Charlotte had an army of loving supporters, and Sasha and Xavier's prayers. She had mentioned it to Tatianna, too, who was horrified and said to tell Liam how sorry she was. Sasha relayed the message, and he said he was touched and to thank her. Tatianna was spoiled and difficult, but she had a decent heart.

Sasha worried about Liam all the way down on his drive south from Vermont. She called him every hour, and he sounded alert and fine. He had made a point of getting some

416

sleep the night before. She could hardly wait to see him, and was grateful that he was coming to spend the holiday with her, in spite of everything that had happened.

She had put up a tree while he was gone, and decorated it for him. She had a few things under it for him, a funny shirt, a new baseball cap, an art book that had been her father's, and a Cartier watch. She was waiting for him anxiously when he got in at six that night. He had made good time, since for once the roads were clear.

The moment Sasha saw him, she burst into tears. He looked so worn and anguished, and as she held him, he sobbed in her arms. He felt as though he had been drowning for the past two weeks. He had never been through such terrifying emotions in his life. He no longer looked like a boy to her, he had turned into a man, older than his years, overnight. He looked like he'd aged ten years in the past weeks. It pained her just to see him, and there was such strain and sorrow in his eyes. He tried to describe to her what it was like. Just hearing about it made her stomach turn over. It was just awful. But at least now Charlotte was better, and there was hope for her future.

'How's Beth holding up?' Sasha was even worried about her.

'She's been amazing. She never leaves the hospital. George has been staying with friends. And Tom's been taking shifts with

417

us.' The whole family had banded together, even Becky, whom Liam didn't mention much. He still felt awkward about her, and probably always would. Sasha wasn't worried about her, it had been a foolish one-night stand, for which he had paid a tremendous price. Sasha was glad that he had been able to be at the hospital with Charlotte. It was one of those things that a child would never forget, nor would he, or even Sasha.

She cooked a wonderful Christmas dinner for him, ran a bath for him, and then tucked him into bed. He lay looking at her quietly for a long time, and held her hand. He was so exhausted he said very little. He never took his eyes off her, and at midnight they exchanged presents. She brought his to him in bed, and then he got up and went to the guest room to get hers. She was dumbstruck when she saw the diamond bracelet he'd bought her, and put it on her wrist.

'It's so beautiful. You spoiled me.' She kissed him, so grateful to be there with him. And he loved all her gifts, especially the watch, and the book that had been her father's.

He lay in bed, looking at the ceiling, when she came to bed. He made no move to make love to her, nor did she. After all he'd been through, she thought it would be in bad taste. He looked utterly worn out. Sex was the last thing on his mind, and hers. They just wanted to be together, and lay there quietly holding hands.

It was nearly one o'clock in the morning, when he rolled over and looked at her. He had been too tired to go to midnight mass, and she hadn't even suggested it. She was sure God would understand.

'You look so tired, sweetheart. Why don't you go to sleep?' She wanted to cradle him like a child. He needed it so badly, and there was more to come. He was going back to the front lines in the morning. This was his only night of respite, and he had driven nearly seven hours to get there.

'I don't want to sleep. I just want to be with you tonight, and soak up every minute.' It was going to have to last him a long time.

'I'm here. You need the sleep. You'll be too tired to drive tomorrow.' He wanted to be with the children for Christmas by nightfall, or sooner if he could. He was leaving at seven in the morning. All they had left were six hours. 'When things calm down a little, I'll drive up to see you.' It was still too early to intrude on them, but Liam seemed to have no idea how long he'd be there. Sasha was patiently waiting.

'I have to talk to you, Sash,' he said, leaning on one elbow.

'What about?' For a strange moment, she wondered if he was going to propose to her, but it seemed an odd time. Emotions had

419

been running high. She smiled at him, and looked up at him from her pillow. She was so glad he was there, and so was he. But even away from the horror of the hospital, he looked sad. He had been through too much fear and seen too much pain to shake it off with ease. This was going to take a long time for all of them to get over, not just Charlotte. The whole family had been traumatized by her accident.

'I don't even know where to begin,' he said, and closed his eyes. When he opened them again, Sasha was looking straight at him. This sounded important, and she was paying close attention. 'Charlotte is going to need an incredible amount of care, nursing, rehabilitation, therapy of all kinds. She's going to be in the hospital for months, and then we can do some of the rehab at home because she's so young, or she may have to stay at a center. They have one in Burlington.' She understood then what he was worried about. There wasn't even the faintest doubt in her mind. She would do anything she could to help him, and had wanted to tell him sooner but didn't want to intrude or pry.

'The answer is yes,' she said simply, as she leaned over and kissed him, and Liam looked surprised.

'Yes to what?' She had thrown him off balance. It was hard enough to say as it was.

'Yes, if you need an advance. An accident

like this must cost a fortune. I'll do anything to help. The gallery will, and so will I.' Tears came to his eyes.

'I love you. You don't have to do that.'

'I want to.' It was as simple as that.

'We're okay. Our insurance is terrific. Thank God Beth has always been a maniac about insurance. God knows, I wasn't. I always thought it was stupid to pay the premiums we did. Thank God we did. We need it now. I think Beth's parents will do the rest. They've saved a lot of money over the years. And Beth's fiancé wants to help. I don't think he should. He feels responsible for what happened. We'll sort all that out later. We haven't even seen a bill yet. But thank you for the offer.'

'Okay, then what's the question?' Sasha asked, smiling at him, and he took a deep breath.

'There is no question, Sasha. I wanted to tell you something, not ask you for anything. That's why I came down here. To tell you.' There were tears brimming in his eyes.

'Tell me what?'

He closed his eyes for a minute, and then opened them and exhaled the words. He felt like an ax murderer saying them to her. But he had no other choice. 'I'm going back to Beth.' Sasha stared at him for a long minute as though she didn't understand.

'I'm going back to Beth.' He repeated the

words, and she looked as though she'd been shot, as she suddenly sat up in bed.

'As in, to Vermont tomorrow, right?' She couldn't breathe and was clutching at straws. He shook his head.

'As in, to our marriage. She can't do this alone. It's going to be months or years getting Charlotte back on her feet, literally, and she may never totally get there. We just don't know yet.' He was sitting up now too. 'I've never been there for Beth before. I have to do this now. She wants me back, God knows why. I think she's crazy. I was a lousy husband to her for twenty years. I was too busy playing wacky artist and painting to be of any real help to her. But now I have to do this. I can't leave her alone with this, Sash. I just can't. She broke her engagement as soon as this happened. She said she could never forgive him. She asked me to come back.' He sat there looking at Sasha with tears streaming down his cheeks. He loved her. But he also loved his wife. And she needed him, more than she ever had. The very decency that made him who he was, and made Sasha love him, was what was making him leave her now.

'That's not a reason to go back into a marriage. Stay up there for six months if you have to. A year, if that's what it takes. But you don't go back into a marriage just to nurse a sick child. What happens when she gets better? You've got your marriage and Beth for the rest of your life.'

'I didn't leave her, Sasha,' he reminded her. 'She left me, and I deserved it. I would never have left her or the kids.'

'Oh my God. I can't believe this.' They had just gotten back together, and he was in bed with her. But he hadn't laid a hand on her all night. He had just come to be with her one last time, and tell her in person that he was leaving her, this time for good. 'I don't think your mind is clear enough to make this decision right now. Either of you.' She was fighting for her life. But looking at his face, she knew she had already lost. There was no winning this time. It was over. It really was impossible, but for entirely different reasons. And she had no weapons to fight for him. Beth had twenty years of marriage on her side, and three children, one of them critically sick. Sasha didn't have a chance. 'Can't you wait to make this decision, till you're all a little saner and have had some sleep?'

'There's no decision to make here, Sasha. I can't leave Beth alone to deal with this, and I can't leave my kids.' He had grown up and become responsible, and now he no longer wanted her. And she couldn't even argue with him. Because she knew what he was doing was right, for all of them. Except her. She felt as though he had hit her with a wrecking ball, and he had. Liam put his arms around her then, and she cried great wracking sobs, and so did he. 'I'm so sorry, Sasha. I love you. I wanted to do this with you. I wanted to make it work ... but I have to go back. I swear I would have married you if this hadn't happened. I wanted to. But now I can't.' It was a tragedy for both of them. But he loved Beth too, and Sasha knew it. She could see it in his eyes. It was totally absurd, but real, he loved them both. And he owed more to Beth. Sasha had to lose. She was the human sacrifice he felt he had to make for his child.

They lay there crying in each other's arms for hours, mourning each other, and wishing things were different. She wanted to be angry, furious even, she wanted to hate him, but she couldn't. She wasn't angry, she was heartbroken. This was as bad as, or worse, than losing Arthur. Because once Liam went back to her, he really would be dead to her now. This time he truly would never come back, and they both knew it.

'I'll withdraw from the gallery, if you want me to. I don't want to make this any harder on you than it already is.'

'You don't have to do that. That's not fair to you. You can deal with Karen and Bernard.' She knew she couldn't see him, or even talk to him after this. If she did, it would kill her. She had never experienced such pain in her life, or at least not since Arthur died.

They were still lying in each other's arms at six. And at six-thirty he got up. They both looked like they'd been beaten. The worst part was that she knew he was doing the right thing. There was no wacky artist factor in this decision. It was the decision of a kind and noble man, who knew what he owed his family and wife, and was willing to live up to his obligations. For better or worse. All it did was make her love him more.

'What if it doesn't work?' Sasha asked while he got dressed. 'What if, when Charlotte is better, you two can't stand each other? Then what happens?'

'I don't know,' he said honestly, looking at her. They both looked ravaged.

'Something must have been wrong, for you to sleep with Becky. Men don't do things like that unless they're unhappy with their wives.'

'Maybe not. I think we were bored with each other. Beth was tired of being poor. I felt overwhelmed by the kids at times. It was more responsibility than I bargained for, or was ready for. Hell, I married her at nineteen.'

'And that's what you're going back to,' Sasha said somberly. 'Think about it before you do it. You can take care of Charlotte for as long as you need to, without going back to Beth.'

'Sasha, it's done,' he said. It sounded like

a death knell to her. 'I have to. She needs me. She asked me. She can't do this alone. She's not that strong.' Sasha nodded. There were no arguments left. She had tried them all and lost. And she didn't have the heart to try to convince him of what she knew was wrong. He knew he had to go back to Beth, only because he wanted to, not because she asked. He would have thought of it himself. Sasha knew that about him now. Outrageous behavior and all, he was a good and decent man.

She offered to make him breakfast, but he only shook his head. He couldn't eat. They hadn't slept. He left as though he were giving up his life, leaving her. He had wanted so desperately to have a life with her, and it had been taken from them, by the hand of fate, and the fault of neither of them. The hand of God. Destiny. All their dreams had to be destroyed and given up. But it was Beth's turn now, and Charlotte's, and the boys'. He belonged to them. He had made a vow to Beth twenty-two years before, and now he had to live up to it. He felt he had no other choice. Sasha was his dream. And Beth was his life.

He put her gifts to him in the backpack he'd brought, and she looked down at her bracelet and then back up at him. 'I'll never take it off. I'll love you forever, Liam.'

'Don't,' he said as tears rolled down his

cheeks and fell on hers as he kissed her for the last time. 'Forget me. Forget us. Put it away somewhere in your heart, and so will I. You will always be here with me.' He pointed to his heart, and Sasha nodded.

She clung to him as though she would die when he left, and she thought she would. This was the good-bye she had never had a chance to say to Arthur. That night with Liam, they had said it all. He was leaving her, loving her as much as he had for the past year, in fact more than he ever had.

She was whimpering as she walked to the elevator with him, and he pressed the button. She was standing barefoot in her nightgown, with her long dark hair hanging like a child's. The elevator came, he looked at her, got in as her eyes met his, and then the door closed and he was gone. She realized as she walked back into her apartment then, it was Christmas morning.

Chapter 21

Christmas was a blur for her, a nightmare beyond belief. Xavier and Tatianna called to wish her a merry Christmas and check on her, and she assured them she was fine. Although Xavier thought she sounded strange, and called to check on her again that night. He asked if Liam was there and she said he had been, and had just gone back to Vermont. She was in too much pain to share the news with anyone. It was so excruciating, she sat in a chair all day, and hardly moved. She just sat there, staring into space. She was in shock.

The day after Christmas, Sasha was at the gallery at ten o'clock, as she always was, when Marcie walked in and saw her sitting at her desk. Her hair was pulled straight back, she had no makeup on, and her face was an ashy white. She was sorting through some papers on her desk, and there was a rigid quality to the way she sat. As though she were in shock, and when Marcie looked at her and saw her eyes, she was sure Charlotte had died. In fact, Sasha had.

'Oh my God, did something happen to...' Marcie's hand flew to her mouth. She could see that something terrible had happened. Sasha looked like a ghost, as she shook her head and looked away. She had sobbed inconsolably for the last three hours. She knew she would never even hear his voice again. Before he left, they had promised not to call each other. It would be a cruelty to do so, to either of them. She had never done anything so difficult in her life as honor what he'd done. She did it for love of him. She always knew she loved him, but she had

428

never known till then how much. 'Sasha, are you all right?' Looking at her, Marcie was frightened.

Sasha's voice was wooden when she spoke, without meeting Marcie's eyes. 'I'm fine.' She handed her some papers she had just signed. She had begun the rest of her life. It stretched out ahead of her now like a vast wasteland of emptiness and loss. She felt as though every part of her, every fiber, every ounce of her being had died.

Marcie left the room without saying a word, and then mentioned it to Karen, who stopped in Sasha's office to check on her, without appearing to, and came back to Marcie quickly.

'Something terrible must have happened. Did you ask her?'

'She won't talk.'

They both agreed, she looked worse, much worse, than when Arthur died. But it was over two years later, and it was the second major loss she had sustained, which compounded the impact. It had just become two giant losses rolled into one. It brought back everything she had lived through when Arthur died, and in addition now there was the loss of Liam as well. This time forever. There would be no reprieve this time, and she knew it. He was never coming back. In her life anyway, he might as well have died.

Neither woman solved the mystery, and

Sasha said nothing to them all day. She didn't eat. She didn't drink. She didn't move, she just sat there shuffling papers on her desk. She thought of killing herself, but knew she couldn't do that to Xavier and Tatianna. She had been condemned to live, which in her case now seemed far worse than being condemned to death. She had been sentenced to an eternity without him.

Driving to Vermont, he felt the same way. But he didn't call her. He knew he never could again. He had to trust her to the hands of fate, which was where he had put himself. All he could do from now on was know that there was a woman he would never see again, and whom he had once loved with his entire being.

Sasha told Marcie that afternoon that she was leaving for Paris the next morning, and asked her to make the reservations for her. Marcie said she would, and then stopped to talk to Sasha again.

'Are you sure you're okay?' Sasha nodded, and Marcie wondered if something had happened with Liam. Maybe they'd had a fight and broken up again. 'Where's Liam?' was all she asked her. Sasha said he was in Vermont, and he was fine. She knew it would be months or years before she could tell anyone what had happened. The hole he had left in her was filled with too much pain. Marcie left her then and made the reservations. And then she did something she had never done, even when Arthur died. She called Xavier and told him she was worried about her. He said she had sounded strange to him too when he called her on Christmas. 'She looks terrible,' Marcie admitted, hating to worry him, but she didn't know who else to call. Tatianna was away, and Marcie had no idea where she was, and neither did he.

'Maybe I'll fly to Paris to see her this weekend,' he said, thinking about it. He wasn't crazy about the plan, since it was New Year's Eve, but he was worried about her. Something had happened, and whatever it was, she wasn't talking about it, to anyone.

Xavier called her at home that night, and she didn't answer the phone. She was lying in the dark, on her bed, thinking of Liam, wondering what he was doing, how Charlotte was, and what he had said to Beth. She didn't even know if Beth knew about her. Overnight she had become the forgotten woman. She felt invisible, untouchable, unlovable, and completely isolated from the world. She had barely said good-bye to Marcie and Karen when she left. She just said goodnight to them, as she always did, and drifted out to the street. She walked home, and was halfway there before she even noticed it was raining. When she got home, she was soaked to the skin. It didn't matter anymore. Nothing did.

She took the flight to Paris the next day,

spoke to no one on the plane, didn't eat, didn't watch a movie, and slept finally. It was a relatively short flight, and when she got home, she realized she hadn't eaten in days. She didn't care about that either.

When Xavier got to Paris on Saturday, he was shocked when he saw her. She had lost weight, her eyes were glazed, and her skin was almost gray. He managed to get some food into her, and had brought his current girlfriend with him. When he asked his mother about Liam, she was pleasant and vague. All she said was that he was with Beth and his children in Vermont.

A week later, wondering how things were going for him, Xavier called him on his cell phone. He didn't mention the state his mother was in, so as not to worry him. Liam had enough on his plate with Charlotte. Xavier asked him casually when he was coming back to London.

'I'm not,' Liam said quietly. There was a somber tone in his voice that worried Xavier. It was not unlike the flat tone he'd heard recently whenever he called Sasha.

'What do you mean?' Xavier sounded confused. 'Are you going to be stuck in Vermont for a long time?'

'Forever, I guess,' Liam said cryptically. 'I'll have to come back to London at some point to close my studio.' He said that Charlotte was going to be in the hospital for

432

months, and possibly in rehab after that.

'It's damn decent of you to be there with her,' Xavier commended him, and there was a long silence from Liam's end. He knew he had to tell him then. He had no idea what Sasha had said to him, but Xavier seemed to be unaware of what had happened, which surprised him. He knew how close he and his mother were to each other, and he was sure she would have told him. He couldn't imagine why she didn't. It never occurred to him that she was still in shock, and too devastated to tell him.

'I've gone back to Beth,' he said, and at Xavier's end there was nothing but stunned silence. 'I had to. She needs me here. So do the kids. I'll call you when I get back to close up.' Xavier wished him luck, and sat staring into space for a long moment, thinking about what Liam had said. Xavier felt as though he had been shot out of a cannon into a wall. He could barely begin to imagine what his mother must have felt when she heard those same words. It explained everything to him now.

Chapter 22

Sasha moved through her life like a robot for most of January. She went to the gallery, home at night, said little to anyone, and did her work. She had handed over all of Liam's files to Bernard without comment. But as he wasn't working at the moment, while he was taking care of Charlotte, there was nothing to do for him anyway.

They had had two requests for commissions by Liam, which he said he couldn't do for six months. So everything pertaining to Liam Allison was on hold. And so was Sasha's life.

Xavier came back to see her once he knew what had happened, but she refused to talk about it. They went for walks in the park with the dog. He tried to take her out to dinner, but she didn't want to go. She seemed to be doing absolutely nothing these days. Eugénie said she declined every invitation systematically, and she did the same in February in New York. She had shut down everything in her life, except her work.

Xavier had had a long talk with Tatianna about it, and she spent a night in the apartment with her. But nothing seemed to shake

Sasha out of her apathy, as February bled into March and then into April, when she was back in Paris. She flew to New York to curate a show, and Marcie was relieved to see that she looked better. She was thin and pale and seemed tired, but at least the other-worldly look she'd had for months was gone. She looked unhappy, but at least human. It was no secret to anyone who knew and cared about her that she had had a terrible time. They had quietly told each other why, without discussing it with her. It was obviously a topic she was not open to talking about, with any one of them. Sasha had completely sealed herself off from the world. Her body was there, but the spirit was gone.

Liam had come to London in March, closed his studio, and sent everything in it to Vermont. He left Xavier a message, but when he called him back, he discovered that Liam had already left town. He had only been there for two days. Xavier assumed correctly that Liam probably didn't want to see him either. The entire episode, Charlotte's accident, and Liam's decision, had been too traumatic for both of them. They had done their best to bury it and recover on their own. Xavier never even mentioned to his mother that Liam had come to town. It seemed best not to mention him anymore, so no one did.

What Marcie saw in April she would not have called recovery, but at least the hemorrhaging of life's blood from Sasha's soul seemed to have stopped. She seemed to have hit bottom, and was holding there, which was a vast improvement over what they had all observed before. Sasha's downward spiral into despair had been terrifying to watch, but she insisted she was feeling better, and even went out to the house in the Hamptons when she came back to New York in May.

Like everywhere else, it was full of memories of Liam now, but whatever she was thinking about him, she was not sharing with anyone. No one in the gallery had seen or heard from him in months. All they knew from Sasha and occasional e-mails from him was that he was with his family in Vermont, and he said Charlotte was doing better. She was in a rehab center by then, and able to stand up. Sasha was about the same. Her spirit seemed to be standing, but it wasn't walking yet. Her children and employees were anxious to see some sign of life again. Marcie almost stood up and cheered, when she saw her smile in May. She couldn't recall seeing her smile since early December, when she and Liam had gotten back together, briefly, before he left her.

Xavier flew to New York to celebrate her fiftieth birthday with her. All she wanted to do was spend a quiet evening with him and Tatianna. They had insisted on taking her to a restaurant at least, and she had chosen a small Italian restaurant in the village, which she said would be quiet. And in spite of her long months of mourning Liam, she had a nice time with her children.

'I can't believe I'm fifty,' she said, looking rueful. 'How did I ever get this old?'

'You're not old, Mom,' Xavier said gently. They had given her a diamond brooch with two hearts intertwined, from both of them, and she loved it. She was still wearing the diamond bracelet Liam had given her for Christmas. It never left her wrist.

Marcie and Karen had offered to give her a little party, which she declined. The only parties she went to anymore were openings at the gallery. In the past five months, since Liam left, she had simply folded the show. She was like a small, tired animal hibernating in deep winter. Everyone who loved her was waiting for some sign of spring. Whatever it took, she had to get over Liam. And it seemed to be taking forever. It was as though their souls had been intertwined, and without the other half of her, she had curled up and died. Like Siamese twins. In a single year, they had become part of each other. Her life without him now was relentlessly bleak.

On the Memorial Day weekend, she was still in New York, and decided to go out to Southampton. Tatianna was away. And Xavier was in London. She was going back to

Paris the following week. But she was looking forward to spending her last weekend at the beach before she left. It was still chilly, but spring was in the air, and when she left the gallery on Friday night, Marcie thought she looked better. Sasha was under constant scrutiny now, and all her loving observers consulted with each other as to how they thought she was. Her constant insistence that she was fine convinced no one but herself.

As she drove to Southampton that Friday night, the holiday traffic made the trip take forever. And as she sat at a dead stop from time to time, she thought of Liam. It was a luxury she rarely allowed herself anymore. She knew she couldn't afford it. And although the others couldn't see it, she was making efforts to get better. It was a rare indulgence for her to just sit back and think of him. He was still on her mind when she let herself into the house four hours later. By then, it was after eleven, and when she went to bed, it was midnight. She fell asleep, thinking about him, and in the morning, she felt better. It was almost as though allowing herself to bask in the memories for a few hours had relieved some of the pressure.

Navigating the shoals of grief had become familiar to her. She knew from losing Arthur that losing someone was a process, you didn't let go all at once, you let go inch by inch, or millimeter by millimeter. It had taken her a year after Arthur to feel human again. And it had been five months now since Liam. She knew that one of these days she'd get there, and wake up one morning without feeling as though she had a bowling ball on her chest. Little by little, the bowling ball was shrinking. She wondered from time to time how it was for him, or if he'd already forgotten. He had other things now to keep him busy, and she was happy to hear from Marcie that he had reported that Charlotte was so much better. She couldn't help wondering too if he was happy with Beth. There was no way for her to know, and maybe it didn't matter. He was hers now, for better or worse, whichever happened. She knew he would never leave her. He would never have left her the first time. He was the kind of man who stayed forever, once committed. It had been different with them because, however much they loved each other, the commitment had never been made. Just as she had predicted in the beginning, it had been impossible for them, just not for the reasons she'd expected. It had never even remotely dawned on her that he might go back to Beth. Without Charotte's near-fatal accident, she knew he wouldn't have. Fate had intervened.

She forced him from her head again that night at sunset as she walked down the beach. She let her mind drift to other things, like Arthur and her children. Tatianna had

439

had a serious boyfriend since February, one whom Sasha actually approved of. And Xavier was talking about living with the woman he'd been dating since Christmas, which was a huge change for him. It was time. He was twenty-seven.

She felt peaceful and comfortable for the first time in a long time as she sat down in the shelter of the dune grass to watch the sunset. The air was still chilly, but the sun had been warm all day. She lay down on the sand then, thinking about her children, the times they'd shared, the things she'd accomplished, the wonderful moments they'd had together. She had chartered another boat for them that summer. But it was at the beach that she had her private moments. She cherished them as well. They were times to think, and be grateful for her life, which she was starting to be again. She knew that in spite of the losses she'd suffered, she had many blessings, and was grateful for them all.

She was watching the sun go down quickly and wondered if she'd see the green flash as it hit the horizon. She loved watching for it, and as she lay there, she savored the moment. She wanted nothing more than she had right then. She needed nothing, wanted no one. She felt as though she were hanging in space, weightless, without burdens. She felt at ease in her own skin for the first time since December. It was, at last, the beginning of healing, and had been a long time coming.

She saw the green flash and smiled when it happened. It was like an omen of better things to come. There were still spots in front of her eyes from staring into the sun as it was setting, and what she saw then seemed like a vision. She couldn't see him clearly, but she saw his form and outline. She knew she was imagining it, maybe even hallucinating, and then she heard his voice. It was Liam. He was standing in front of her, with his back to the sunset, almost like a movie. She just lay there and stared at him and said nothing.

'Hello, Sasha.' She had no idea why he'd come. The last time she had seen him they had both been crying. This time, she just looked at him and smiled. It had been five months since she'd seen him.

'I was watching the sunset.'

'I saw you from the porch.'

'How's Charlotte?' She didn't want to know how Beth was.

'Much better. She just started walking.'

She didn't invite him to sit down. She just nodded. 'Why did you come here?'

'I'm going back. I just wanted to come and say good-bye.'

'You already did that.' It was a strange, disjointed conversation between two people who had loved and lost each other. They had already said good-bye once, five months

441

before. What was the point of coming back to do it again? 'When are you going back?' It was a meaningless question. When he was going back no longer mattered. He already had, five months before.

'Tomorrow,' he answered, and then finally sat down on the sand beside her. He felt odd standing up and looking at her as she lay there. She seemed smaller than he remembered, and paler, and her hair seemed darker in sharp contrast to the ivory white face. She was more beautiful than he had remembered, and he had thought of her often. She had haunted him, like someone he had killed, and had to live forever after with the floating tormented vision of her face the last time he saw her. 'I just wanted to see you once before I went back.'

'I thought we weren't going to do that.' Her eyes met his and held them. He had forgotten how piercing her eyes were, at the same time gentle and intense. She had kept her part of the bargain. She had never called him. And unlike what he was doing now, she had never shown up in Vermont. Coming back to torture her one last time seemed unfair to her, and she was sorry that he'd come. She would have to climb the hill of healing yet again. And the climb had already been hard enough.

'I didn't call you, because I was afraid you wouldn't see me.'

'You were right. I wouldn't. One good-bye was enough.' And they'd had more than that in the course of the year they shared. 'Why did you come?' She knew there was another reason that he hadn't told her yet. She knew him better by then than he knew himself. But she could see how much he too had changed in the last five months. There was no boyhood left in his handsome face, only manhood. He had had his own journey of pain after he left. He had had three children and a wife to accompany him daily on his travels. She had had no one but herself, and the trip had been harder on her.

'Do you hate me?' he asked her. She should have. But she was beyond that, and had never gotten there anyway. She shook her head. It wasn't his fault.

'No. I love you. I probably always will.' His eyes went to her hand, and he saw both his bracelets still on her wrist.

'So will I.' The sun was down, and it had gotten cold. 'Do you want me to go now?'

She was honest with him. 'Not yet.' This might be her last look. She wanted to savor it before he left.

'I have to drive to New York tonight,' he said, for lack of something better to say. None of the things he had wanted to tell her seemed to make sense now. She had become someone else. Bigger, better, stronger, deeper. Trial by fire. It had purified her in

443

some strange way.

'Why New York?'

'Because I'm going back.' He was being cryptic, and he confused her.

'Back where? Vermont?'

He smiled and shook his head. She had misunderstood. 'No. London.'

'Why there?'

And then he knew he had to tell her. It was why he'd come. He realized when he saw her that he had already caused her too much pain. And even if she still loved him, the doors were closed. He could see it in her face.

'I left Beth. It didn't work. We both knew it in a month, but we tried anyway, for the kids' sake. It doesn't work that way. We left as good friends.' He laughed softly. 'She's happy to be rid of me.' Sasha was watching him intently, trying to absorb what he'd just said. She suddenly wondered if she had imagined him and what she was hearing. Maybe he wasn't even there. Like a vision she had conjured in a dream. A lifelike hallucination.

'What did you just say?'

'I said Beth and I ended it. The divorce is final. I'm going back to London tomorrow. I wanted to see you before I left. If nothing else, I owe you an apology.' He knew that what he had done to her in December was inexcusable. But he had done it for his wife and kids. It was a poor excuse, but at the time it seemed the right thing. Sasha knew it too.

'You don't owe me an apology,' she said gently. 'You did what you had to do.'

'And I damn near killed you.'

'I'm still here.' She sat up slowly. 'I'm tougher than you think.'

'No. You're tougher than you think. I thought of you every day. Constantly.' He stretched out his arm, and she saw the watch.

'So did I,' she confessed. 'Now what do we do?'

Their eyes held, and they didn't reach out to each other. They hadn't touched each other, and maybe never would.

'Impossible or possible? It's up to you,' he asked softly, as the wind chilled them both, and then he moved closer to her. They were almost touching, but not yet. 'What do you think?'

'I never thought you'd come back, Liam,' she said sadly. It was hard to believe he had, or know why he did. He had left her so often, and she had died so many times at his hands.

'I didn't either. I didn't think I could.'

He wanted to kiss her but now the decision was up to her. It had been his last time. This one was hers. He would respect whatever she said.

'Which is it?' He didn't want to press her, but he had to know.

'I don't know.' She sat looking out to sea,

and then she turned to him and smiled. 'Or maybe I do. Maybe it doesn't matter anymore which one it is. Life only gives you so many chances, and then for no reason at all, you get one more. People die, people leave, people come back. Maybe it doesn't matter, if you love each other. I love you, Liam. I always did. More than I knew.'

'More than I knew too. I thought it would kill me when I left you, but I had to do it.'

'I know.' She smiled again and he kissed her, gently, cautiously. It was like touching a summer breeze. He had never forgotten what it was like kissing her and holding her. In the end, he had taken her with him. Beth knew it before he did, and out of kindness sent him back.

He kissed her again and held her, and she whispered something into his chest. He felt it more than heard it, and looked down into her face. 'What did you say?'

'Possible.' It was a whisper, but he heard her this time. 'Possible.' She repeated it. It was all he had wanted to hear, all he'd lived for in the months he was away. He pulled her tightly into his arms then, and she looked up into the face that was a part of her, and had been since the beginning, and she laughed. 'Possible. This time for sure.'

The publishers hope that this book has given you enjoyable reading. Large Print Books are especially designed to be as easy to see and hold as possible. If you wish a complete list of our books please ask at your local library or write directly to:

Magna Large Print Books
Magna House, Long Preston,
Skipton, North Yorkshire.
BD23 4ND

This Large Print Book, for people
who cannot read normal print,
is published under the auspices of

THE ULVERSCROFT FOUNDATION